W9-AAK-977

Austen, Eliot, Charlotte Brontë and the Mentor-Lover

Austen, Eliot, Charlotte Brontë and the Mentor-Lover

Patricia Menon

palgrave
macmillan

#51518565   1-19-05

PR
868
M47M46
2003

c.1

© Patricia Menon 2003

All rights reserved. No reproduction, copy or transmission of this
publication may be made without written permission.

No paragraph of this publication may be reproduced, copied or transmitted
save with written permission or in accordance with the provisions of the
Copyright, Designs and Patents Act 1988, or under the terms of any licence
permitting limited copying issued by the Copyright Licensing Agency, 90
Tottenham Court Road, London W1T 4LP.

Any person who does any unauthorised act in relation to this publication
may be liable to criminal prosecution and civil claims for damages.

The author has asserted her right to be identified as the author of this work
in accordance with the Copyright, Designs and Patents Act 1988.

First published 2003 by

PALGRAVE MACMILLAN
Houndmills, Basingstoke, Hampshire RG21 6XS and
175 Fifth Avenue, New York, N. Y. 10010
Companies and representatives throughout the world

PALGRAVE MACMILLAN is the global academic imprint of the Palgrave
Macmillan division of St. Martin's Press, LLC and of Palgrave Macmillan Ltd.
Macmillan® is a registered trademark in the United States, United Kingdom
and other countries. Palgrave is a registered trademark in the European
Union and other countries.

ISBN 1–4039–0259–3

This book is printed on paper suitable for recycling and made from fully
managed and sustained forest sources.

A catalogue record for this book is available from the British Library.

Library of Congress Cataloging-in-Publication Data

Menon, Patricia.
    Austen, Eliot, Charlotte Bronte, and the mentor-lover / Patricia Menon.
        p. cm.
    Includes bibliographical references (p.) and index.
    ISBN 1-4039-0259-3
    1. English fiction–Women authors–History and criticism. 2. Mentoring in
literature. 3. Women and literature–England–History–19th century.
4. English fiction–19th Century–History and criticism. 5. Brontè, Charlotte,
1816-1855–Characters–Mentors. 6. Eliot, George,
1819-1880–Characters–Mentors. 7. Austen, Jane,
1775-1817–Characters–Mentors. 8. Love stories, English–History and
criticism. 9. Man-woman relationships in literature. 10. Mentoring of
authors–England. I. Title.

PR868.M47M46 2003
823' .8099287–dc21   2003040474

10   9   8   7   6   5   4   3   2
12 11 10 09 08 07 06 05 04

Printed and bound in Great Britain by
Antony Rowe Ltd, Chippenham and Eastbourne

In memory of my father,
Leonard William Mitchell

Contents

Acknowledgements

An earlier version of part of Chapter 2 was first published as follows: Patricia Menon, "The Mentor-Lover in *Mansfield Park*: At Once Both Tragedy and Comedy", *The Cambridge Quarterly*, 29:2, 2000 (146–64). The material appears here by permission of Oxford University Press.

For exemplifying (in the words of George Whalley) the "integrity of perception, judgment and recognition" to which the literary critic aspires, and for his continued help and encouragement, I am indebted to Brian Crick.

Anyone working on a project of this nature owes gratitude to many people for sharing, in unique permutations, their advice, criticism, encouragement and friendship. My thanks go to Cornelia Cook, Jennie Crick, Marion Evans, Patrick Fang, Holly Forsythe, Isobel Grundy, Graham Handley, Paul Hutchinson, Duke Maskell, Catherine Mitchell, John Muggeridge, Leonée Ormond, Brenda Sauchuk and Michael Sauchuk.

Some obligations are very old indeed and I should like to record my gratitude to Dorothy Leader, Frances Mercer, Helen Shackleton and Audrey Cleobury Sunderland.

I wish to thank Niagara College for granting me sabbatical leave and to acknowledge the help of Barry Sharpe, who, as Chairman and Dean, offered both encouragement and practical assistance. I also wish to express my appreciation to members of the English departments at Niagara College and Brock University, and to the library staff of both institutions, especially those who patiently dealt with my many requests for inter-library and extended loans.

I am grateful to those from whom I have received advice and assistance at Palgrave Macmillan, including Eleanor Birne, Charmian Hearne, Julian Honer, Paula Kennedy, Rebecca Mashayekh, Emily Rosser, John M. Smith and the manuscript readers.

In a wider sphere, my gratitude is due to the community of critics and scholars, past and present, whose work I have read with benefit and pleasure. In this connection, I wish to thank the contributors to "Victoria: the electronic forum for Victorian Studies" (http://www.indiana.edu/~victoria/discussion.html#vic) for the generosity with which they share their knowledge.

Finally, for the encouragement and support they have given me, I am grateful to my husband Govind Menon and my mother Jessie Mitchell.

PAT MENON
Fonthill

Prologue: The Mentor-Lover in the Eighteenth Century – Novel, Conduct Book and Archetype

Because the figure of the mentor-lover raises difficult but inescapable questions about the nature of sexual love and its links to the attributes of the mentor – power, judgment and moral authority – it provides a means to investigate, from a particularly revealing perspective, the work of those authors who employ it.

Jane Austen, Charlotte Brontë and George Eliot, writers whose struggles with these questions remain as compelling today as when they wrote, all used the figure extensively, though to varied ends. The reader, attending to the same figure, may follow their explorations of a wide range of interconnected issues stemming from the relationship of love to morality, power and judgment. Among the subjects brought into focus in this way are sexuality, family, selfhood, freedom, conduct, and the nature of male and female roles. To trace the uses they made of the mentor-lover is to follow the developing interests of these three very different women as their work matured, and to identify what distinguishes each from the others. The characteristics they attribute to the figure also provide an opportunity to explore the intriguing correlations between their conceptions of the mentor-lover and their own relationship with their readers, each eliciting a different form of love and electing a different style of instruction.

In the century before Austen, a widespread interest in education directed to living well through attention to conduct and moral principles is apparent from the popularity of conduct books and philosophical works. The close connections between these forms of instruction and the treatment of love within the novel are suggested by the development of Richardson's *Pamela* from a work initially planned to illustrate letter-writing skills and virtuous behaviour, and by the shaping of Rousseau's educational treatise, *Émile*, into an account of an imaginary boy's growth to manhood and love. To these developments Austen, Brontë and Eliot prove variously responsive. Austen, by burlesquing the conduct books, demonstrates, through mockery, her combative scrutiny of their advice. Brontë, alerted by her own experience in the schoolroom and encouraged by her reading of Romantic literature to defend individuality, is sensitive to the interplay between power and eroticism that she sees as intrinsic to instruction. Eliot, reviewer and translator of religious and ethical treatises of her time, and companion of one whose interests spanned diverse fields including literature, journalism, drama and science, draws on the language and imagery of her contemporary concerns to explore the demands of duty.

Probing the nature of love naturally raises related issues, and an examination of the treatment of the mentor-lover is therefore a revealing way to explore and compare the writers' attitudes to such key, and interconnected, matters as sexuality, gender and family. Here, once again, consideration of the universal leads back into the particular. Of the three novelists, Austen feels least threatened by the power of sexual attraction, for though she recognizes that it may induce blindness, she also affirms that it is not necessarily in conflict with judgment, and indeed may prove a stimulus to better choices than may rational consideration. Brontë perceives sexual love as perilous, entailing the risk of self-annihilation which she sees as occurring through the loss of power inherent in the need for another's love. At the same time, however, for her that threat to freedom is as exhilarating and erotic as it is terrifying. Consequently, in her last novel, where power plays a lesser role in the central teacher–student relationship, the erotic element is diminished. Of the three, Eliot appears to be the most concerned with the dangers of sexual love, for, though she wants to believe it may be desirably linked to learning, she is more prone to perceive it as a threat to the selflessness she wishes to inculcate. And since that selflessness, like the conduct-book-heroine's unassertiveness, dictates the accommodation of women's goals to those of the men they love, Eliot, divided against herself, inadvertently brings into doubt the status of her women as complete moral beings.

What appears to be a resemblance between all three, a concern for women and for the freedom open to them within and outside the family, again reveals considerable differences. The connection between love and the family is not a primary concern of Brontë, whose characters are often effectively orphaned, but Austen, like Eliot, is acutely aware of the family's role in shaping conduct, principle, and ability to love. Like Eliot, Austen also recognizes the strength and attraction of family ties, but does not endorse sacrifice to their demands. In fact, Eliot's insistence on self-sacrifice repeatedly places her in conflict with her sense of women's potential since she requires her heroines to renounce freedom in the name of family duty. Brontë gives a superficial impression of a crusader for women's liberty, and indeed is concerned that the middle-class woman's choices are restricted to marriage, service to the family or teaching. On closer examination, however, her obsession with power seems to be less connected with gender than with ego. Austen, on the other hand, by making moral responsibility for oneself and others her primary concern, and by making no distinction between men and women in their duty to make principled decisions, demonstrates her belief that, in the sphere that matters most to her, women must not surrender their autonomy.

Finally, there is the overarching issue of the writer's flexibility: the extent to which each resists generalization and cultural stereotype, instead recognizing complexity and difference, and here Austen is the impressive exception. Writers – like literary critics – can hardly avoid engaging, whether or not they intend to do so, with contemporary issues. It is understandable that Brontë, self-nurtured on romanticism, sees love as endangering individual freedom, and that the mid-Victorian Eliot struggles with the concern that sexual love is incompatible with duty and selflessness – or, indeed, that modern readers discover their own concerns with gendered power struggles in all of these works. It is all the more impressive, therefore, that Austen, although she considers the possibility in her explorations of love's relationship to judgment, does not conclude that the two are inescapably in conflict, challenging a longstanding view of sexual love that was current in the conduct books at the time she wrote.

The primary purpose of this study is to explore the novels themselves rather than the worlds the writers inhabited, to examine the specific rather than the general. But because novelists do not work in isolation, they are inevitably influenced by the circumstances in which they live and the literature they encounter. The ubiquity of the mentor-lover in the poetry and prose of the eighteenth century suggests the value of taking a rapid Cook's Tour of the subject, before concentrating more closely on the specific readings of the works with which this study is primarily concerned. This prologue will touch only on the most relevant elements of that background: the complex relationship between the conduct book and the novel, the widely varied experiments involving the mentor-lover, and the influence of the archetypal figures of Pygmalion and Abelard on the writers of the time.

Evidence of the keen eighteenth-century interest in behaviour and the development of character can be seen most clearly in the conduct books, with their concern over matters of desirable comportment and aspirations, suitable education for middle-class females, and the appropriate links between love and marriage. As William St Clair's examination of the sales of the most popular of these reveals, change and uncertainty seem to have increased public anxiety over such matters, and in particular a flurry of reprinting occurred with every crisis of public confidence over the conflict with France.[1] With her usual acuity, a teenaged Jane Austen lampooned this trend in "Catharine or The Bower", written in 1792. Catherine's guardian aunt laments that her niece, discovered in the arbour with a young man, has not benefited from the conduct books and sermons with which she has been provided,

"... I plainly see that every thing is going to sixes & sevens and all order will soon be at an end throughout the Kingdom. ..." "... the welfare of every Nation depends upon the virtue of it's individuals, and any one who offends in so gross a manner against decorum & propriety is certainly hastening it's ruin."
(*Minor Works* 232–3, ellipses mine, spelling and punctuation as shown).

The top-selling author in the field was Dr John Gregory, but male writers did not monopolize the genre. Of the sixteen most popular conduct books that St Clair studied (505), eleven were written by women, and indeed the female role as guardian of conduct was increasingly recognized not only at the level of authorship but also within the family. Judith Lowder Newton traces the change from Gregory, in 1774, who made few allusions to women's influence on men, to James Fordyce, twenty years later, who saw women's role as being to "promote general reformation" (2–5). Once again Austen registered the shift when, as an adult, she tinkered with a reference in "Catharine", replacing *Seccar's Explanation of the Catechism* with Hannah More's conduct-book-thinly-disguised-as-fiction, *Coelebs in Search of a Wife Comprehending Observations on Domestic Habits and Manners, Religion and Morals*, published in 1809. It was a volume of James Fordyce's *Sermons to Young Women*, however, that she mischievously put in the hands of the tedious Mr Collins, who "never read novels" (68).

By the 1840s, when Brontë and Eliot were young women, writers of conduct books were granting wives and mothers considerable influence in the moral sphere, insisting that they should make conscious use of their considerable influence – though only unselfishly, covertly and in domestic matters (Newton 5). The conduct book was not the only form of writing in which behaviour and the development of character were central. The novel, which fostered (and was fostered by) the emphasis on the individual within society that was an essential part of sensibility and Romanticism,[2] also took these subjects as its own. Critics, even those taking opposite stances on the role of the novel as undermining or supporting middle-class ideals, agree on the central role that the exploration of growth and change in an individual's life played in the development of the genre. Clifford Siskin, with the Foucauldian goal of demonstrating that this interest did not arise because such development is "a truth grounded in human psychology", identifies this emphasis as a "a formal strategy for naturalizing social and literary change" (13, 126). Cates Baldridge, disagreeing with the Foucauldian position, takes the Bakhtinian view of the novel as a chorus of many voices that is by its very nature subversive of "bourgeois ideologies" (8–20). He argues that earlier literary forms often presented character in terms of sudden conversions occurring with a sense of inevitability, whereas the novel deals with "protagonists whose personalities alter and develop, usually in small and discrete steps as a direct result of seemingly nonpredetermined experiences over the course of an extended narrative" (8). That there is such agreement between otherwise opposed critical ideologies on the close ties between the novel and an interest in character and change suggests that these were, indeed, essential characteristics of the developing genre.

Some authors saw in the novel a tool for moral education, or at least professed to do so. Mary Davys, "the relict of a clergyman" (38) and author of *The Reform'd Coquet* (published in 1724), whom Jane Spencer in her account of early women novelists identifies as being "at the beginning of a long line of women writers who create coquettish heroines and the lover-mentors to reform them" (146), contrasted her own "novels" to those that were "offensive to modesty and good manners": "I have with the utmost justice rewarded virtue and punished vice" (38, 39). The perceived need to distinguish the author's own works from those meriting public disapproval was persistent, provoking from the narrator of *Northanger Abbey* an appeal against "that ungenerous and impolitic custom, so common with the novel writers, of degrading, by their contemptuous censure, the very performances to the number of which they are themselves adding" (37). The figure of the mentor-lover must have offered such nervous novelists a particularly appropriate means of providing a moral justification for the novel, although in practice the complexities of fiction were to make it impossible to guarantee readers' responses.

It was Richardson, followed by Rousseau, who made the figure of the mentor-lover central,[3] while anticipating many of the ways in which the figure would be developed in the nineteenth century. Rousseau's unrequited admiration for Richardson was inspired after he read the epistolary *Clarissa*, and both writers made use of instruction as an opportunity for erotic contact. Of the two however, it was Rousseau who (as would Brontë later) combined teaching and eroticism with particular frankness:

> Therefore he gives her lessons in philosophy, physics, mathematics, history – in a word everything. . . . When he can obtain permission to give his lessons on his knees before her, how content Émile is! He believes he sees the heavens opened. . . . On such occasions she does not know exactly what to do with her eyes to avoid those that are pursuing them; and when they meet the lesson does not gain by it.
>
> (*Émile* 426–7)

For Rousseau, mentorship comprised both academic and moral teaching, while for Richardson morality was paramount, as *Pamela*'s evolution from a manual of conduct taught through letter-writing suggests, and Clarissa's uplifting effect on everyone around her confirms. The universal mentor, Grandison, in his relationship to Clementina as her English "tutor" (144, 153, 489) bears only a remote resemblance to Rousseau's instructors, his teaching of language and literature taking place off stage, though his moral influence is always to the fore. In terms of gender, Rousseau's official mentors are generally male, though Julie, initially in love with her tutor, finally becomes mentor to all around her, while Richardson's Grandison is outnumbered two to one by Pamela and Clarissa – clearly in the case of fiction, as with the conduct book, the mentor need not be male.

Despite the two genres' interest in similar subject matter, clarifying the links between conduct-book morality and the novel's growing popularity is far from a straightforward undertaking. It is possible to trace the novel's unsteady movement towards approval, but the match is never perfect. In *Desire and Domestic Fiction*, Nancy Armstrong argues that the two genres eventually allied to transform the English middle classes by defining what came to be thought of as desirable and, indeed, "natural" in women. But as she and others have noted, the alliance was slow to develop, the novel being thought of as a dangerous stimulant to the imaginations of young girls, Gregory, for example, warning of the "terrible conflict of passions" such reading "may afterwards raise in your breasts" (117). Markman Ellis quotes a popular conduct book by Lady Sarah Pennington, first published in 1761, that condemned novels as "Mountains of Dirt and Trash" with only "a few small Diamonds" of morality in them, although a later edition did allow that *The Vicar of Wakefield* was "equally entertaining and instructive." (33). Even Wollstonecraft, who had already published her first novel, *Mary*, before what might be thought of as her own conduct book, *Vindication of the Rights of Woman*,[4] worried that novels were a threat to the imagination of uneducated girls (*Vindication* 196, 227, 224–5), regretting that they "find the reading of history a very dry task and disquisitions addressed to the understanding intolerably tedious, and almost unintelligible" (in this anticipating Austen's Catherine Morland, who preferred novels to history, which she found "dull" by comparison, *NA* 108–10).[5] Wollstonecraft deemed novels acceptable only because "any kind of reading I think better than leaving a blank still a blank. . . ." (306), a very different view from the exuberant defence that would be mounted by the narrator of *Northanger Abbey*:

> some work in which the greatest powers of the mind are displayed, in which the most thoroughgoing knowledge of human nature, the happiest delineation of its varieties, the liveliest effusions of wit and humour, are conveyed to the world in the best chosen language.
>
> (37–8)

The well-used formula for justifying literature, the combination of instruction and delight, was complicated in the case of the novel by the injection of the issue of "realism" into the debate. After a decade crucial to its development, one that had included the publication of *Pamela*, *Clarissa*, *Joseph Andrews*, *Tom Jones*, and *Roderick Random*, Samuel Johnson noted that members of the "present generation", in contrast to earlier readers of romances, were "particularly delighted" to read of "life in its true state." He granted that "these familiar histories" might "convey the knowledge of vice and virtue with more efficacy than axioms and definitions" but insisted that "vice should always disgust", while virtue "not angelical, nor above probability" should invite the reader's emulation, warning that mingling "good and bad qualities" in the "principal personages" risked leading the reader into moral confusion ([The Novel] 35–40). It was becoming increasingly clear that the simple virtue/vice formulation of writers such as Mary Davys would not work in association with the portrayal of "life in its true state", and that to whatever degree the writer attempted to adjust the truth to edifying ends, the novel's complexity would inevitably undermine its ability to impart clear moral instruction, as Richardson had already discovered with his creation of Lovelace, the rake who proved unexpectedly attractive to many readers.

Nancy Armstrong suggests that, by the turn of the century, conduct-book writers were willing to give their blessing to those "polite" novels that promoted (or appeared to promote) the same principles that they did, and thus an alliance was consummated (97). That the novel had come a long way towards achieving respectability was confirmed by Richard (later Archbishop) Whately. Writing of Austen in 1821, he acknowledged that reviewers need no longer offer "an apology for condescending to notice a novel": "we have lived to hear the merits of the best of this class of writings earnestly discussed by some of the ablest scholars and soundest reasoners of the present day" (87). It would, however, be naive to assume that the increasing favour shown towards novels by the nation's mentors ensured that such works would not undermine accepted values. Indeed, as Susan Fraiman shows, the conduct books themselves were not consistent in the precepts they recommended, nor were they without their own subversive characteristics. She identifies these as the anti-romantic (a good husband is hard to find), the female homosocial (female friends may be more important than men) and the Mentorial (girls benefit from a 'male' education) – the last derived from *Mentoria*, a conduct book promoting ungendered education, and given by Jane Austen to her niece Anna (*Unbecoming* 23–31). The terms succinctly convey the ways in which such conventional documents could undermine convention, and, given the lack of consensus that Fraiman demonstrates, the sharing of similar interests between the conduct book and novel speaks as much to the potentially subversive as to the conformist natures of both genres.

Throughout the eighteenth century, the novelists themselves, in prefaces and interpolations, and usually in an attempt to win the public's favour, debated matters of content, technique, purpose and audience. They compared their works favourably to histories, travels, romances, epics, dramas, and biographies. They explored the suitability of the novel to the presentation of tragedy, comedy, burlesque, satire, and ridicule. They considered the problems of imitation or imagination as a basis for plot and character, mulled over the nature of the territory lying between the probable and the possible, discussed unity and length, pondered on national and gender differences, debated ways to present virtue and vice, and – of course – balanced instruction with delight.[6]

Such discussions inevitably contributed to changes in the novel's cultural prestige, a somewhat different matter from its moral status. Sir Walter Scott published anonymously when he turned from writing poetry to the novel, but the disguise was transparent, his new career provoking mock annoyance from Jane Austen for "taking the bread out of other people's mouths" with the publication of *Waverley* (*Letters* 277: 28 September 1814). His prestige, the popularity of his novels and his discussion of the form in his unsigned review of *Emma* (Southam, *CH* I 58–69) presaged a further change in the novel's standing. In a study based in part on the Macmillan archives, Gaye Tuchman and Nina Fortin argue that, in terms of numbers, male novelists began "edging women out" of publishing in the 1840s, a development that Tuchman and Fortin regard as marking the beginning of the general acceptance of the genre into "high culture". This would not be without its benefits for those women writers who shared in the movement to tackle a wider range of material and benefited from the changing readership. When an obituary described Eliza Lynn Linton, a contemporary of George Eliot, as having written "novels simply because the novel was the accredited form of literature in her day",[7] the word "accredited" marked an impressive evolution from disrepute to intellectual respectability.

Just as the links between novel and conduct book are complex, so are those between the mentor-lover and the inculcation of virtue. The figure became so popular in the literature of the latter half of the eighteenth century that literary historians have felt justified in speaking of a convention (Spencer 140–80), but the wide variations in its treatment make disentangling the various lines of influence and resistance impossible. Echoes of the erotic instruction in *Émile* may be heard in the novels of such writers as Mary Hays and Mary Wollstonecraft, in whose fictions mentor-lover relationships figure largely and whose heroines read *La Nouvelle Héloïse*. Yet the uses they made of the figure are underlain by a distrust of Rousseau's combination of eroticism and education and by their hostility to his view of women – he had followed the description of lovemaking from *Émile* quoted earlier with the assessment that "the art of thinking is not foreign to women, but they ought only to skim the sciences of reasoning. . . " (427). Just as the novel (and even the conduct book) might affirm, reflect, question, or shape moral and social assumptions, it was clear that by the turn of the century the mentor-lover within it might similarly embody all of these roles.

If conduct book and novel contributed their shared concerns to a climate conducive to the growth of interest in the mentor-lover, other literary influences offered ways of envisioning the figure – one of these being Pygmalion. He and his initially anonymous statue were the subject of an adaptation from Ovid by Dryden, published in 1700, and the tale subsequently provided a subject for a *scène lyrique* by Rousseau in which the hitherto anonymous statue is first given a name, Galatée. The legend tells of a king disgusted by what he perceives to be widespread female immorality, and the statue he sculpts and then loves, a tale with an apparently idyllic ending when the statue is brought to life by Venus and becomes his wife. Dryden added Pygmalion's admission of "Madness" to Ovid's account, but it was the insanity of sleeping with a marble figure that was thus described – the implications of moulding a lover to one's needs apparently raised no concern either for Ovid or for Dryden. Jonathan Swift, by contrast, though he did not compare himself directly to Pygmalion, acutely identified the possible moral and psychological dangers in his poetic version of his relationship with Vanessa Van Homrigh,[8] to whom he had become an informal tutor:

> Why she likes him, admire not at her,
> She loves herself, and that's the Matter
>
> (*Cadenus and Vanessa*, lines 682–7).

The hazards were as plain to Maria Edgeworth as they had been to Swift. Her novel *Belinda*, published in 1801, reveals the foolishness of a character who, Pygmalion-like, attempts to custom-educate his bride-to-be. This figure was apparently based on a family friend and disciple of Rousseau, Thomas Day (Butler, *Edgeworth* 39) who educated two orphans from whom he might later choose a wife (although in the end he took neither), an poignant illustration of the continuing interactions of philosophy, fiction and life.

Poetry, plays and paintings inspired by the story seem, except for Dryden's adaptation, to have come later to England than to the continent. Not long after Austen's death, however, the tale was in common-enough currency that Hazlitt chose the subtitle *The New Pygmalion* for his painful autobiographical account of his disastrous obsession with a lower-class girl

(Liber Amoris, published in 1823) whom he failed to 'sculpt' to his wishes. As a subject for drama, literature and art, Pygmalion would become more popular during George Eliot's time, in treatments by William Morris, W. S. Gilbert and the painter Edward Burne Jones among others.[9] Though the tale of Pygmalion provided one model around which the ideas of the novelist might play, the letters of Abelard and Héloïse offered a much broader range of inspiration. In *Daniel Deronda*, George Eliot evoked, as an ideal, the love affair of the medieval monk with his brilliant pupil:

> . . . more potent still is frequent companionship, with full sympathy in taste, and admirable qualities on both sides; especially where the one is in the position of teacher, and the other is delightedly conscious of receptive ability which also gives the teacher delight. The situation is famous in history, and has no less charm now than in the days of Abelard.
>
> (280)

The medieval letters,[10] apparently written after the lovers had entered cloistered life, were widely read in the eighteenth century, usually in an English rendering, published in 1713, of a late seventeenth-century French version. The French ghost-writer, not content with the original account of seduction, pregnancy, undesired secret marriage, castration and forced parting, added yet more incidents and characters to increase its scandalous nature. The letters also became available in England in the Latin version, published in 1718, and later in another more accurate – and less popular – English translation published in 1787. Even when stripped of salacious additions, the letters reveal a relationship to which Eliot's word "charm" hardly seems applicable. The brilliant and controversial theological thinker and popular songwriter Abelard, almost forty when he deliberately engineered his employment as tutor to Héloïse, looks back on his planned seduction of a star-struck seventeen-year-old with repulsion, characterizes their love as lust and rejoices in his castration, portraying himself as a grim warning against the dangers of sexual appetite:

> I considered all the usual attractions for a lover and decided she was the one to bring to my bed, confident I should have an easy success; for at that time I had youth and exceptional good looks as well as my great reputation to recommend me, and feared no rebuff from any woman I might choose to honour with my love. Knowing the girl's

knowledge and love of letters I thought she would be all the more ready to consent.

(66)

Consider the magnanimous design of God's mercy for us. . . so that by a wholly justified wound in a single part of my body he might heal two souls.

(147)

Héloïse, on the other hand, recalls her initial hero worship and subsequent devotion, and the sexual longing she still feels, although she has been nun, and subsequently prioress, since their parting more than a decade ago:

the pleasures of lovers which we shared have been too sweet – they can never displease me and can scarcely be banished from my thoughts. . . . Even during the celebration of the Mass. . . . Even in sleep. . . .

(133)

The nature of the relationship is far from the nostalgic fantasy conjured up by Eliot's imagination, but she may have been evoking not the original letters but the best-known version of the story. This was Pope's poem, *Eloïsa to Abelard*, published in 1717, shorn of many of the original narrative details, its central subject the cloistered Eloïsa's undimmed sexual longing:

From lips like those what precept failed to move?
Too soon they taught me 'twas no sin to love:
Back through the pleasing paths of sense I ran
Nor wished an Angel whom I loved a man.

(Lines 65–70)

This distance from the earliest documents, and the fact that Pope was more concerned with the pain of separation and sexual frustration than with the complexities of the teacher–student relationship, made possible an ever-increasing freedom of invention for later writers, untrammelled by inconvenient reminders of the lack of "charm" in the original Paris classroom. The value of a tale that had both a historical base yet remained malleable for the writer's purpose was not lost on Samuel Johnson who noted that "the heart naturally loves truth" while nevertheless rejoicing that the story had been "diligently improved" and including among the poem's virtues that the tale was "known from undisputed history"–with the beneficial consequence that the "imagination ranges at full liberty without straggling into scenes of fable" ("Pope" 395).

The popularity of Pope's *Eloïsa to Abelard* helped to ensure that the schoolroom lovers remained in the public mind throughout the century and it may well have been an encounter with the poem, recently translated into French, that led Rousseau to choose *La Nouvelle Héloïse* as part of the title of his "collection of letters" tracing the consequences of the love of Julie and her tutor. Indeed, the first translation of Rousseau's novel into English was titled simply *Eloïsa*, presumably a further result of the popularity of Pope's poem.[11] So well known was the work that, in 1791, when Elizabeth Inchbald[12] published *A Simple Story*, she did not think it necessary to explain to her readers why the heroine thrust her blushing face out of the window in the presence of her priestly guardian when a jealous suitor unkindly quoted lines from *Eloïsa to Abelard* (24).

Meanwhile, the medieval lovers' bodies, so troublesome to them in life, were not forgotten in death. In 1792, the turmoil of the French Revolution triggered the first of four reinterments of their bones, each time minus more "relics". The last move occurred in 1817 (the year Austen died) to a shared grave-site in the Père-Lachaise Cemetery. Shown on the jacket of this book in an engraving published in 1829, it has remained an attraction for lovers and tourists to this day (McLeod 234–42). The adulation accorded to the couple also serves as a reminder that readers may respond on a very personal level to an author, reacting with an emotion that may resemble love in one of its many forms. And though many modern academics may resist or deny this tug of attraction as a matter of professional principle, such inhibitions do not appear to have constrained earlier novel readers any more than those who avowedly read "for pleasure" today.

Nor, as the courtship between the conduct book and the novel suggests, has a novelist's Abelardian intent to instruct the reader always been felt to be a cause for rejection – although readers of more recent times have felt discomfort in the face of overt attempts at authorial mentorship. The views themselves, however, might be a source of contention, particularly given that any treatment of the mentor-lover is likely to raise issues that challenge readers' values, a possibility increased by the passage of time. And because problems connected with love and judgment are likely to be hard to resolve, exploring the use of the figure is a particularly effective way of detecting authorial loss of control – ambivalence, uncertainty, unquestioned assumptions, unresolved issues, incomplete conclusions – as well as the disjunctions between what writers claim (or imply) that they believe and the evidence derived from their language.

Austen chose, as did Brontë and Eliot after her, to draw on a tradition that was in no way defunct, with such complex elements and history that it embodied questions that still have the power to provoke debate. And by the time Austen (with an eye for conventions as sharp as that of any later literary historian) began the first drafts of her works, the figure of the mentor-lover had already become so well-entrenched in the expectations of readers as to attract her critical attention. The sceptical nature of her interest is suggested by her placement of the relationship at the centre of *Northanger Abbey*, a work burlesquing the literary formulae of the day, and confirmed by the more serious and extended scrutiny she accorded the figure in three of her other novels.

1

"Saturated with the Platonic Idea"? Judgment and Passion in *Northanger Abbey, Pride and Prejudice* and *Emma*

Although Jane Austen was obviously intrigued by the role of the mentor-lover, her interest in it, unlike that of Charlotte Brontë and George Eliot, did not approach the obsessive. There is no evidence to suggest that she herself was involved in such a relationship; the figure is absent from her juvenilia and is of limited importance in two of her published novels. It is also difficult to trace a straightforward development in her treatment of the subject, a result of her commitment (perhaps encouraged by initial problems in achieving publication) to careful revisions. Her work on the revisions overlaps with the commencement of new novels, making her an author in continuing dialogue with herself: redefining, modifying, working with seeming oppositions both within and between novels, demonstrating the inadequacy of the obvious in the face of more particular discriminations. Add to this that two works, one early and one late, were published posthumously, perhaps not fully revised, and it is clearly counterproductive to adhere to a strict chronological treatment. As a consequence, *Northanger Abbey* and *Pride and Prejudice* are here explored in conjunction with *Emma* with which they have more in common, while *Sense and Sensibility* provides an introduction to *Mansfield Park*, the only work among the three darker novels to be centrally concerned with the mentor-lover, its many variations on the theme demanding extensive treatment.

The classic exposition of Jane Austen's interest in the mentor-lover appears in Richard Simpson's 1870 review and is founded on a widely agreed premise:

... we can see clearly enough her habitual exaltation of judgment over passion, of the critical over the poetical and imaginative faculties.

(245)

"Passion" is a word capable of varying implications, sometimes suggesting a combination of strong emotion with sexual feeling, sometimes restricted to one or the other, but here the context suggests Simpson includes both. He also echoes the long-established consensus that constituted qualified praise from some like G. H. Lewes ("exquisite as miniatures", Southam, *CH* I: 149) but blame in the eyes of others such as Charlotte Brontë, who surely also included sexual passion among the "stormy sisterhood":

Can there be a great artist without poetry? ... Miss Austen being, as you say, without "sentiment", without *poetry*, maybe *is* sensible, real (more *real* than *true*), but she cannot be great.

The Passions are unknown to her; she rejects even a speaking acquaintance with that stormy sisterhood.

(Emphases original, Southam, *CH* I:126–8)

It is a view, though less extremely put, that still remains in currency: "Jane Austen's heroines are women of *sense* ... who refuse to be overcome by sexual passion" (Mellor 53, emphasis original). Such judgments are characterized by an assumption of a world structured on an inevitable opposition between judgment and passion, ignoring the possibility that this may misrepresent the complexities of human relationships, that judgment and passion may be different in kind rather than inevitably opposed. It may be that Austen's views are more flexible than those of her readers, a possibility best tested at the point where judgment and passion intersect: her explorations of the mentor-lover. Simpson (as have many after him) concluded that Austen believed that mentorship is the best underpinning for love:

The didactic intention is even interwoven with the very plots and texture of the novel. The true hero, who at last secures the heroine's hand, is often a man sufficiently her elder to have been her guide and mentor in many of the most difficult crises of her youth. Miss Austen seems to be saturated with the Platonic idea that the giving and receiving of knowledge, the active formation of another's character, is the truest and strongest foundation of love. (244)

The exploration that follows offers a reconsideration of this time-honoured view and its relationship to the critical axiom that Austen, assuming their opposition, exalted judgment over passion.

It seems reasonable, while allowing for uncertainties about the extent and completeness of the late revisions, to discuss *Northanger Abbey* first, treating it as essentially an early work. From the point of view of this study, it is of most interest as a benchmark against which the greater complexities of Austen's later treatment of the subject can be measured, providing as a case for later comparison Henry Tilney, a lively young clergyman who meets a girl whose mind is "about as ignorant and uninformed as the female mind at seventeen usually is" (18) and who elicits from her not only love but the conviction that "Henry Tilney must know best" (153). One could hardly hope for a clearer example of the basic prototype of the species, as well as a classic theme on which variations might later be developed, although critical responses to this particular model have varied.

Over a century after Simpson, Julia Prewitt Brown, for example, approvingly compares Henry to a "Virgilian guide who leads the heroine to truth" adding that "Tilney and Knightley are archetypal teacher heroes" (*Novels* 41). But Henry has also come in for a good deal of critical hostility. Judith Wilt condemns as "sinister" the "deliberate manipulation, almost terrorization of the lover-student by the lover-mentor" here, as in *Mansfield Park* and *Emma* (*Ghosts* 144–5). Joseph Litvak, following Wilt in identifying Henry as a "lover mentor", links him with his "ineptly malevolent parent" though portraying him as "the practitioner of a more systematically euphemized, more suavely generalized, and thus more conveniently misrecognizable male sadism" than the General's ("Charming Men . . . " 251–2). Unconvinced that Austen herself repudiates Henry, Diane Hoeveler identifies Henry with Austen, castigating them both: "In valorizing Henry's smug enlightenment attitude, it would appear that Austen shares or at least would like to share Henry's outlook and privileges; it would appear that Austen wants to be one of the boys" ("Vindicating"132). Whether as poster boy or whipping boy for the combination of love with mentorship, it seems we are to take Henry very seriously indeed, an assumption at least worth testing, given the apparently light-hearted tone of the work.

That to some degree Austen is engaged in a literary burlesque, with two targets for her teasing, is generally agreed. The first is Catherine, presented as the victim of Gothic delusions. The second is the reader, playfully depicted as the victim of similar expectations: a perfect heroine will be beset with the dangers of abduction and seduction, and surrounded with all the apparatus of wards, disguises, and rescues. So much is made in the first few pages of the droll process of disabusing the reader of such assumptions (a treatment resembling Henry's tantalizing of Catherine's Gothic hopes) that a second function of these early pages goes almost unnoticed: the careful account of Catherine's situation in order to specify the precise extent of her freedoms and limitations as an essential prerequisite to assessing the contributions of the mentor-lover to her development.

First Austen steps away from the extremes, not only of fortune and beauty, but also of opportunity and threat. Susan Morgan points out that "Austen's literary inheritance was a landscape littered with endangered virgins" (*Sisters* 28) but the "violence of such noblemen and baronets as delight in forcing young ladies away to some remote farm-house" (*NA* 18) will clearly not obtrude upon this tale, and though John Thorpe will take Catherine off in his carriage, no rape will occur or even be imaginable by Catherine or the reader. Austen ensures that Catherine must take moral responsibility for herself: she is free to make faulty judgments and live, unravished, to understand, regret, and make amends for them.

Inexperienced in the ways of any society but that provided by the limited environs of Fullerton and the everyday scramble of family life, Catherine is sufficiently gullible to be imposed on, though increasingly unsuccessfully, by Isabella, Austen's superb evocation of a determined but ultimately clumsy man-hunter familiar to everyone from their youth. Yet here also Catherine is not placed at either extreme. She is not a total fool, and in relation to men she proves clearer sighted than most of her literary predecessors: John Thorpe she quickly, if unwillingly, sees through, and she can even suspect, on their first meeting, that Henry Tilney "indulged himself a little too much with the foibles of others" (29). Her principles and nature are good; her judgment is imperfect without being utterly unreliable. There doesn't seem a great deal for Henry Tilney to do, although he is generally supposed to act, for good or ill depending on the critic, as Catherine's mentor. But does Austen allow him such a role? And if so, what, and how much, does he teach?

It is important, to start with, to see through the veneer of glamour, though not to discount the charm or good nature, of Henry Tilney. Although the reader sees him largely through Catherine's bemused and admiring eyes, Austen supplies evidence that his position is an awkward one. Theoretically a free agent, with the prospect of "a very considerable fortune" and a "present income . . . of independence and comfort" (249–50) as a clergyman, with his own parsonage (complete with dogs, housekeeper and household clutter) twenty miles from Northanger, he is actually uncomfortably tied to his home and father by his warm attachment to his unmarried and motherless sister. Henry is, like William Price, a testament to Austen's pleasure in brotherly love – the genuine nature of his affection is never in doubt and Eleanor reciprocates his affection. Consequently, the single reason for both the tie to the Abbey and the discomfort inherent in Henry's situation is (Austen being always thrifty) one and the same: Henry's father. In General Tilney, Austen creates a contemporary addict of conspicuous consumption with desires encompassing not only the most modern of conveniences and the most showy of china but also an heiress for his son, one from whom to breed more resources and opportunities for display. Indeed, the General is a more menacing figure during the period when he favours Catherine (his son is "directed to gain" her, 247) than in his off-stage actions as villain at the conclusion of the work.

The General's need to control appears in his twin obsession with time and food: food that he both grows and eats amid further shows of ostentation and demands for admiration, and that he and those with him must consume according to his own rigid timetable. Both Eleanor and Henry are denied the right to speak or act for themselves, the General supplying what he deems to be his children's deficiencies. It is he who contributes the openly sexual compliments that are absent from Henry's conversation by "saying everything gallant as they went down stairs, admiring the elasticity of [Catherine's] walk . . . " (103). And it is he who supplants Eleanor in her attempt to invite Catherine to Northanger Abbey (already orchestrated by him) "without leaving his daughter time to speak" (139).

Against her father, Eleanor is powerless even when she desires to protect her friend: "you must have been long enough in this house to see that I am but a nominal mistress of it, that my real power is nothing" (225), and it is his sister's circumstance that holds Henry in an uncomfortable extension of childhood obedience. Even the abbey-struck Catherine is sharp enough to notice from very early on that the General casts a pall of silence over both of his normally talkative offspring – a situation that Austen would re-examine in *Mansfield Park*. But though Henry is thus trapped in silence for his sister's sake, he seems unable to throw off his father's domination on his own behalf. The Henry who meekly gives up two days of Catherine's presence in order to prepare for their visit to Woodston surely acts as much out of habitual subordination as consideration for his sister and guest (211). Or to be more precise, Austen places him in a position in which no challenge has been strong enough yet to test his ability to assert his independence, his affection for his sister having protected him against such a requirement. In this, his situation resembles that of Catherine, whose good nature has both protected her against acting wrongly and simultaneously put her at risk from exploitation by the Thorpes.

Given the situation that Austen has constructed, it seems she has deliberately set up a moral difficulty for Catherine's mentor in which the challenge he faces is greater than hers. It is true that Catherine must learn to refine her judgments of the people she encounters, whereas Henry's judgments are usually more confidently made. But she is in the process of continually making small adjustments as she learns to see Isabella or John Thorpe more clearly, while his greater challenge is yet to be met. Though commonly considered her mentor, he has not yet, albeit for good reason, shown more moral maturity than she. Seen in relation to his uncomfortable subordination to his father's whims, the nature of Henry's mentorship of Catherine becomes less clear-cut, and less important, than either the images of the "Virgilian guide" or the "threatening" psychological manipulator suggest.

While free of his father's presence, it is clear that much of what Henry says is said for the pleasure of the saying. Is he really to be taken seriously, instructing a loveable but not fashionably educated female in the requirements of letter-writing, the re-use of muslin, the need for exercise, the value of history, the rules of the picturesque, the similarities between the dance and marriage, the inferiority of women and the importance of a "nice" choice of language? Or is he simply "not in a sober mood" as his sister says on Beechen Cliff (114), temporarily free of the pressure of his father's presence, pleasantly shaken to the point of exhilaration by the uncritical admiration of a pretty girl?

This overall lightness in the novel is the reason that General Tilney, though his mania for control is germane to Henry's situation, nevertheless seems an awkward irruption from a darker world. It may help to explain the over-reaction of critics who, like Tony Tanner, reach for significance by equating the "atrocity" Catherine imagines, General Tilney's murder of his wife, with the bullying of his children, or conflating the nosiness of the gossips of the neighbourhood with the paranoia of the post-Revolutionary period (Tanner 68–70). But there is another component to this over-reaction: a compulsion to defend Austen from writing about marriage and family, subjects many critics apparently consider trivial. Consequently, though critical fashions change, the desire to discover the "important" content "concealed" in the novels continues, unease about Austen's perceived failure to deal with revolution and war being replaced by other attempts at justification more appropriate to recent concerns. Barbara Seeber, for example, suggests that "Domestic tyranny can extend to murder; while critics of *Northanger Abbey* complacently rule this out, the novel does not" (120). Domestic tyranny certainly can extend to murder, but it may also take psychological as well as physical forms, in either case existing on a continuum from slight to intense, and in order for Austen to depict the General as an oppressive and domineering parent it is not necessary to make him a wife-murderer. Seeber points out "That Eleanor lives in fear is evident in her nervousness", adducing the General's insistence on punctuality at the subsequent meal as justification (125). But the Eleanor whose wit and charm return the minute her father is absent is not living in fear for her life, or with the suspicion that her mother has been murdered.

Overpainting the rest of the novel with a darkness it lacks may be a misconceived way of proving Brontë wrong about Austen's ignorance of the "Passions", but it is also a backhanded admission that the critic fears that, unless a wife-murder or the French revolution can be found subversively inscribed within it, the novel holds only the equivalent of a laundry list. It would be more accurate to recognize that the slightness of *Northanger Abbey* lies in the ease with which Austen leads the young people towards maturity rather than in the subject matter of marriage and family life. To read the novel in these melodramatic ways is to be – like Catherine – seduced by a need for the Gothic excesses that Austen burlesqued. A young man's disparagement of the local tattlers (68–71) may be uttered as convincingly in peacetime as in war and is hardly enough to make the blood run cold, nor is the gullible Catherine irreparably damaged by the embarrassing fantasies about the General to which Henry's teasing has contributed. Indeed she matures as a consequence. In Austen's works there are always distinctions to be recognized, discriminations that such "Gothic" readings obliterate, although in this novel Austen must bear part of the blame by making it hard for the reader to discern the greys in relation to her abrupt shifts from light to dark in her treatment of the General.

Two circumstances suggest that the maintenance of a generally doubting attitude towards Henry's pronouncements is more important than deciding precisely which among them are endorsed by Austen. One, exclusive to *Northanger Abbey*, is that, as most readers sense (and often give as a reason for treating the novel as fundamentally an early work), there is a difference in kind between this and the other novels, even the sparkling *Pride and Prejudice*. The whole procedure of learning and change isn't to be taken seriously here – it is amusing because nothing vitally important is at stake, neither Catherine nor Henry, unlike Elizabeth Bennet and Emma, has anything really profound to learn. The second reason for doubting Henry has a bearing on all Austen's works. The essential lightness of the treatment of the mentor-lover here alerts the reader to the possibility that Austen does not invariably imbue the figure with great seriousness. This further opens the possibility that Austen's purpose may not be to teach Catherine or the reader through the content of Henry's pronouncements as such, but that she might intend to provoke both reader and character into an exercise of judgment, into considering how much or what kind of truth he might, or might not, be speaking at any particular moment, requiring discriminations to be made continually and not be replaced by an easier process of wholesale acceptance or rejection. Indeed, Austen seems often to be teasing the reader, demanding that we make decisions about the judgments not only of Henry Tilney but also of the narrative voice – and by extension pointing to her own elusiveness as the reader's potential mentor.

As one of the least complex of Austen's novels, *Northanger Abbey* provides a convenient place to begin to consider why it is possible for some readers to conclude that her works are essentially moral while others have found them evasive or amoral. For example, F. R. Leavis (15), and more recently Jan Fergus throughout *Jane Austen and the Didactic Novel*, argue for her clear moral intent, while it is as vigorously denied by (to select a wide range of examples) Henry James (*Critical Muse* 173) Denis Donoghue (58) and John Bayley ("a peculiar kind of liberation from morality", 8). And, this being a novel in which Austen has often been assumed to identify with Henry, it also seems an appropriate point to begin to consider the potential of the novelist to be the reader's mentor-lover.

Of the two components of the role, that of the beloved author is currently prone to induce unease in academics rather than in general readers. As Deidre Lynch, editor of and contributor to a provocative collection of essays on "Janeites", argues, this may be because "the worry that Austen has been afflicted by the wrong sort of popularity seems a backhanded acknowledgement of the tenuousness of the boundaries between elite and popular culture, and between the canonical and the non-canonical"(8). Certainly, to cruise e-mail lists and websites on the Internet is to become aware of a divide between those resembling fan clubs and those whose participants prefer to think of themselves as engaged in impersonal scholarly discussion. Claudia Johnson points out the comparative recency of this division among readers and traces the movement of academics away from the "Janeitism" as part of a general movement towards professionalism in criticism (*Janeites* 25–44), a movement, I would add, supported to an increasing degree by a shift towards the discussion of works in a language incomprehensible to the non-academic reader.

Overt instruction in the novel (though many still regarded it as acceptable in George Eliot's time) has long been out of favour with readers of every kind, producing what amounts to an allergic reaction, the dreaded term "didactic" arising with all its authoritarian connotations. Agreement with the writer's views may mitigate this somewhat, although even here particular approval is accorded to the concealment of subversive views beneath the apparently conformist grain of the work. Many current critical practices, however, embody strategies that support the rejection of teaching in any form, even the covert or unintended. They range from denial that the author's intentions are of any interest to the reader (if indeed they can be recovered at all) through repudiation of the author's right to a continuing role in the text, and even, in "loose" or "creative" readings,[1] to a refusal to accord meaning to the text beyond what the reader chooses to assign to it. But even the writings of authors (and critics) determined not to preach cannot help but fall somewhere in a range from covert persuasion to the unintended transmission of values, however muddied these matters might be by ambivalence, confusion and misunderstanding, and however difficult it is to recover these values from the texts in their totality.

Austen's contemporary reviewers often touch on the issue of the instruction to be found in her novels, although so briefly that it seems they feel constrained to do so, but have little to say.[2] Of *Sense and Sensibility* the *British Critic* thought, "Our female friends . . . may learn from [these volumes], if they please, many sober and salutary maxims for the conduct of life" (40). The *Monthly Review* suggested that in *Emma*, "The fair reader may also glean by the way some useful hints against forming romantic schemes, or indulging a spirit of patronage in defiance of sober reason" (70), although of the same novel the *Gentleman's Magazine* concluded reassuringly, if ambiguously, "It is amusing, if not instructive; and has no tendency to deteriorate the heart" (72).

However, in a review of Austen's work occasioned by the posthumous publication of *Northanger Abbey* and *Persuasion*, Richard Whately can be found mulling over the same relationship of realism and fiction that had engaged the interest of Samuel Johnson seventy years before and coming to much the same conclusions as his predecessor. He praises a "new school of fiction" (88), of which he considers Austen the best representative, for dealing with subjects both natural and probable. Fresh from his encounter with Catherine Morland's distaste for History – dull despite its reliance on invention and limited to "men all so good for nothing, and hardly any women at all" (*NA* 108) – he considers the new fiction superior as a means of moral education. He does so on Aristotelian grounds, because it is of a "more philosophical character than history", the details of the latter being likely to consist of "exceptions to general rules of probability, and consequently [to] illustrate no general principles." And, unlike Mrs Morland, who recommended that Catherine read a "very clever essay in *The Mirror*" about "young girls that have been spoiled for home by great acquaintance" (*NA* 241), he concludes that work such as Austen's offers an entertaining replacement for the "moral essays" (92) of the past.

That the novel should instruct gives him no pause; it is on issues of overt versus covert teaching that he struggles to balance "taste" and "utility". In Austen's novels, unlike those of Miss Edgeworth, "the moral lessons . . . are not offensively put forward, but spring incidentally from the circumstance of the story: they are not forced upon the reader, but he is left to collect them (though without any difficulty) for himself". He is relieved she is "evidently a Christian writer, a merit which is much enhanced, both on the score of good taste, and of practical utility, by her religion not being at all obtrusive", judging her restraint to be the result of limiting herself to what "she thought would be generally acceptable and profitable". This is a pragmatism on Austen's part that, despite his praise, clearly gives him some unease: "In fact she is more sparing of it than would be thought desirable by some persons; perhaps even herself"(95). The designation of the reader in terms of the inclusive "He" suggests a recognition of the novel as more than simple amusement or a conduct book restricted to an audience of "our female friends". Claudia Johnson concludes that Whately praises Austen because in declining "to assume the ambition to, as well as the authority to, teach the public" she acted appropriately for a *woman* writer (*Jane Austen* xv). Whately certainly never makes this gendered judgment explicit, nor does it seem to me to be implicit, even at the point when, with embarrassing playfulness, he congratulates Austen on being unusually honest for an "authoress" in showing women to have many of the faults of men (100–1). Rather, Whately's assessment marks a point at which the unobtrusiveness of authorial mentorship is becoming more generally desirable, and he sees her as the touchstone for this development.

Nearly two centuries later, in an age much more hostile to any relation between fiction and moral education, Whately, the admirer of concealed instruction, still lives on, reincarnated in, among others, the alien form of the authors of *The Madwoman in the Attic*: "*Northanger Abbey* supplies one reason for Austen's fascination with coding, concealing or just plain not saying what she means, because this apparently amusing and inoffensive novel finally expresses an indictment of patriarchy that could hardly be considered proper or even permissible in her day" (Gilbert and Gubar 128). Whately, wishing to find a Christian teacher, reassures himself that he can see her, though she is strategically half-hidden. Gilbert and Gubar, in search of a feminist, find her similarly half-concealed.

Not every reader, however, finds Austen the pedagogue lurking in the fictional shadows. It is "Austen criticism" that Eve Sedgwick blames "for its unresting exaction of the spectacle of a Girl Being Taught a Lesson" (147–8) and to make a random dip into a range of Austen criticism with Sedgwick's complaint in mind is to become aware that the occurrence of the motif is indeed very frequent. In fact, after being alerted to the popularity of the formula by Sedgwick, I was surprised to note how often I had been using it myself. To take just one example of many, David Devlin begins *Jane Austen and Education* with the example of Catherine, who, like the other heroines for whom "[e]ducation . . . is a process through which they come to see clearly themselves and their conduct", "must shed her illusions and must come to see the world as it really is"(1, 2). The recurrence of this motif in critical writing is puzzling, given that readers are able to detect in Austen almost any postion from the amoral to the moral, from a refusal to teach to a willingness to be the teacher (overt or covert) of whatever lessons the reader holds dear.

Vincent Quinn points out in response to Sedgwick that the "punitive/pedagogical dynamic" depends on Austen's own rhetoric of improvement (320–1). But if so, how is it that the existence and purport of that rhetoric is so frequently challenged? Mary Poovey argues persuasively that "Austen tries to ensure that her readers will share a common ground by making them participate in constructing the value system that governs the novel. . . . and it is through the value system developed in the overall action of the novel that Austen hopes to counter the relativism that the localized ironies might permit"(*Proper* 205). Howard Babb's analysis of Austen's style, suggests how this effect might be achieved through the foregrounding of "conceptual terms" such as "modesty", "judgment" and "understanding", terms that imply an agreement between author, reader and society on the moral import of the language (11–15). Austen's choice of language thus operates in such a way as to set the reader up to feel that "correct" judgments on principle and conduct are not only possible but required.

But the situation is complicated by Austen's range of tones from light to serious, by the well-known irony, and by the Austen slither between the voices of narrator and character. The reader's judgment is repeatedly tested by language that certainly suggests values are being taught – but with a precision that proves elusive. In this way, since her language demands that principled judgments should be attempted, and indeed cannot be avoided, Austen constantly prods us into trying to complete the "Lesson" that the "Girl" is being taught without herself supplying an unambiguous answer. This leads to the reaction that Sedgwick so deplores in the critics, a compulsive attempt to supply the lesson themselves, as indeed I am doing here with The Lesson the Reader is Being Taught. Admittedly, as every teacher knows, if one asks an open-ended question in the classroom, one must be prepared to receive a disconcertingly wide range of answers – but open-ended questions may sometimes be less a pedagogical technique than the consequence of the questioner's own uncertainty. There's no doubt that Austen knows the right questions, and knows that, in the course of living they must be answered, but to a much lesser extent than Brontë and Eliot, is it clear whether she is always confident she knows what the answers are.

The example of *Northanger Abbey* does suggest that in the inescapable position as the reader's mentor, Austen teaches not by straightforward precept but by instance, exploring the way in which principles work out when applied to particular situations, characters, or times, giving full weight to the ambiguities of experience. When this is combined with the pressure of the language towards judgment, it becomes apparent that what Henry and Austen have in common is that their most productive "teaching" is a matter of encouraging the testing of the statements and actions of others against one's own experience, judgment and principles. What the work does not suggest is that the need to strive for judgment is annulled either by the complexities of life or the way in which truth seems ever to recede from one's grasp.

One thing is clear: judgment and love are not shown to be incompatible. In Catherine's case, once her foolish fantasies are revealed, Henry does not shirk the necessity of rebuking her for her suspicions. Austen would return to the difficulty of combining love with criticism, particularly in *Mansfield Park* (with great insight) and *Emma* (with some uncertainty of touch), but here, in a brief passage as moving for the restraint it shows on Austen's part as much as Henry's, he reassures Catherine of his affection. Instead of "despis[ing] her for ever" because of her suspicions, "the only difference in his behaviour to her, was that he paid her rather more attention than usual." (199).

With considerable economy (this episode has been preceded by his clumsier attempts to deflect Catherine from her worries over James, and will be followed by his perceptive and tactful treatment of Catherine's distress over the jilting), Austen also demonstrates that judgment may grow with love, and that consequently Catherine, by being lovable, is as much an agent for change in her lover as he for her. The change culminates in the son's discovering the strength to break free of his father, a courage significantly described as firmly rooted on foundations of both love and judgment: "He felt himself bound as much in honour as in affection to Miss Morland". The situation is the first that has occurred with a moral element clear enough ("the sanction of reason and the dictate of conscience", 247), to jolt him out of the compliance with his father's wishes. Significantly, it is before Austen uses her authorial power to free his sister from dependence on their father that he takes his stand. And while the lightness of touch in this novel must be allowed for, it is noteworthy that Austen can here unhesitatingly resolve a conflict of loyalty between family and love in favour of marriage, a characteristic to be recalled when reading the works of George Eliot.

One reason why *Northanger Abbey* seems less substantial than the later works is that, in Catherine's case, her principles are already strong and she has little to learn from Henry's overt instruction, even in areas less consequential than the moral. Indeed, Henry might very well have admitted, in Elizabeth Bennet's words, "We all love to instruct, though we can teach only what is not worth knowing" (*P&P* 343). The climax of their educational walk, when "Catherine was so hopeful a scholar, that . . . she voluntarily rejected the whole city of Bath, as unworthy to make part of a landscape," comically sums up just how crude the results of the instructional process are. In the case of important matters such as marriage, she knows as well as he does what is entailed, although she feels no need and has little ability to frame her awareness in witty comparisons to the dance. Austen is clearly no more bent on serious instruction of a specific nature than is Henry or the narrative voice.

That the Austen of *Northanger Abbey* enjoys an audience is clear. Like Henry Tilney, it is a pleasure for her to display her wit and powers of invention, while her attitude often closely resembles his teasing "you women" approach, differing only in that it takes the form of "you readers", intended not to distance but to invoke complicity. And finally there are appeals to a shared and lighthearted amusement: "I leave it to be settled by whomsoever it may concern, whether the tendency of this work be altogether to recommend parental tyranny, or reward filial disobedience" (252). Litvak, finding in Henry and Eleanor Tilney "not one but two seductive teachers . . . whose intricate relation to Catherine mirrors Austen's intricate courtship of the reader" suggests that "Like all good pedagogues, Austen knows the best way to make a boring subject . . . interesting is to make the students develop a crush on the teacher" ("Charming" 261). But "crush", though clever in the context, seems somewhat too strong a word for Austen's relations with her reader here: no word better sums up her manner than 'flirtatious'. Readers who find the teasing approach attractive may, like Catherine, choose to continue to dance and possibly learn to teach themselves. Those who don't are given the impression they are welcome to sit this one out. Austen certainly demonstrates her authorial desire to be appreciated, but if she feels a need either to be loved or taken seriously, she keeps it hidden, an attitude that contributes to the appeal of the novel.

But if lack of seriousness in this regard is part of this appeal, it also contributes to this being a less substantial work than her others. In setting Catherine up with considerably more freedom of choice than that possessed by heroines such as Richardson's Harriet or Burney's Evelina, Austen does increase Catherine's moral responsibilities. But Catherine's nature, like Henry's, is from the beginning so free of potentially serious flaws that the difficulty of choice is all but eliminated – to consider any other Austen heroine is to immediately recognize the difference. Something similar is true of the situation of the reader who is made over by Austen in the first pages into Catherine's image: gullible, naive, but good-natured, and put to no serious test throughout. To think of *Mansfield Park* as the example most unlike *Northanger Abbey* is to recognize that it need not be so in an Austen novel: the reader may be conceived as, and therefore forced to become, less simple-minded, and put through a more testing course.

Northanger Abbey, then, treats the role of the mentor-lover without any great seriousness. Nor does the work support the clear "exaltation of judgment over passion" nor even their opposition. Love and the recognition of good qualities are mutually linked in *Northanger Abbey* but not exclusively dependent: Catherine's admiration of Henry contributes to his growing love for her, but that love does not prevent his recognition and judgment of her inadequacies nor is the combination felt as a problem. In *Pride and Prejudice*, the relationship of passion and judgment would come under scrutiny again, but with an important difference. Austen had tackled only what she could handle with ease in *Northanger Abbey*, whereas in *Pride and Prejudice* she set up a mentor-lover situation that proved more troublesome.

To some extent, *Pride and Prejudice* echoes *Northanger Abbey*, in both novels the lovers having the need and the potential to learn something from each other. But, whereas Henry's intent is conscious if generally inconsequential, it quickly becomes obvious that any learning that occurs between Darcy and Elizabeth is accidental rather than deliberate. What precisely Darcy and Elizabeth teach each other has not been much disputed from the time of the novel's first publication. A contemporary reviewer compared their relationship to that of Beatrice and Benedick and stressed Elizabeth's condemnation of herself for her prejudice as well as her "teach[ing of] the man of Family-Pride to know himself" (Southam, *CH* [1]: 46). Critics have subsequently redistributed the faults of pride and prejudice between Darcy and Elizabeth in various permutations, but otherwise have hardly dissented from this early analysis. Juliet McMaster, for example, characterizing their mutual instruction as successful though unintentional, also compares their conflicts to the "merry war" of Beatrice and Benedick (*JA and Love* 48, 49) and Joseph Boone also evokes *Much Ado* (92).

But the odd thing about *Pride and Prejudice* is that there is a disparity between these time-honoured and pleasurable perceptions and the consequences of a more rigorous examination, a discrepancy noted, for example, by Marvin Mudrick (118–19) and Nina Auerbach *(Communities* 38–55). The early Darcy is an ill-mannered boor willing to put up with the flattery of Miss Bingley but not the vulgar hostility of Mrs Bennet (although they share a propensity to utter audible insults), a man who must be converted into a perfect gentleman before the close of the work. This transformation is to be achieved without having the reader question what the patriarch of Pemberley is doing, spending so much time away from his estates, his admiring retainers and his vulnerable sister, in a second-rate rented house with a bunch of bores and toadies, especially given that Bingley's pleasant personality, even his tempting malleability, couldn't be rated much of an attraction. In part, these difficulties appear to result from Austen's need to resolve the contradictory demands made by the traditional plot (poor-but-good girl attracts and redeems spoiled social superior) and an intense personal need for the fundamental moral equality of her lovers: Pamela must no longer be more virtuous than Mr B.

Her problem, therefore is to persuade the reader that Elizabeth has always misjudged Darcy and that her prejudice has contributed materially to her error over Wickham, thus creating a situation of equal fault and equal improvement desirable for a condition of mutual mentoring. Consequently, Darcy has to be shown to be only superficially a de Bourgh figure at the beginning, and to have hidden qualities that Elizabeth has failed to appreciate. To recognize the extent of the difficulties with which

Austen struggles is to demonstrate how important moral equality is to Austen's conception of desirable marriage.

That Darcy's fundamental character and surface manner have always been at odds Austen does indeed attempt to show, slipping the card of the old family retainer from her authorial sleeve to testify to the deceptiveness of his pompous mien (247–9). But the difficulty of reconciling "good principles" (369) with selfish rudeness is never resolved, or even tackled, even though the renovation of his character could have been accomplished in the interim before the Pemberley meeting. Instead we are asked to see that the good Darcy has existed all along. That Austen feels uncomfortable with his portrayal as one who is initially so inferior to Elizabeth is the only explanation for her extensive efforts to reconstruct him retroactively.

To be fair, two of Elizabeth's objections to Darcy, his meddling in her sister's situation and his treatment of Wickham, are plausibly dealt with by being neutralized. Austen achieves the right mix of self-interest, self-confidence and self-justification in Darcy's dealings with Jane and Bingley, from the letter to the closing scenes at Longbourn and final explanations. In this, Darcy remains both credible and (perhaps) even excusable. And Austen handles her heroine's second objection to him brilliantly through Elizabeth's willingness to embrace Wickham's tale of Darcy's perfidy. The combination of self-deception inaugurated by dislike of Darcy and enhanced by Wickham's superficial attractions is accurately analysed by Elizabeth herself after reading Darcy's letter, culminating in her recognition: "Till this moment I never knew myself":

> "I, who have prided myself on my discernment! . . . who have often disdained the generous candour of my sister. . . . Pleased with the preference of one, and offended by the neglect of the other, on the very beginning of our acquaintance, I have courted prepossession and ignorance, and driven reason away. . . ."
>
> (208)

But while Elizabeth's self-criticism is warranted, it is also at this point that Austen begins to exert a pressure on the reader's judgment that can only be driven by her need to make the couple moral equals. For, although this reads convincingly as Elizabeth's recognition and repudiation of her father in her, Elizabeth's self-condemnation is extravagant – Jane's "generous candour" is clearly less desirable than Elizabeth's "discernment".

A further tactic is to focus on the proposal as Darcy's real error, downplaying the prior offences of which this was only the culmination. It is noteworthy that what both refer to here is his behaviour on that particular night, not what preceded it:

> "... my behaviour to you at the time, had merited the severest reproof. It was unpardonable. I cannot think of it without abhorrence".
> "We will not quarrel for the greater share of blame annexed that evening," said Elizabeth.
>
> (367)

> "You taught me a lesson, hard indeed at first, but most advantageous. By you, I was properly humbled. I came to you without a doubt of my reception. You shewed me how insufficient were all my pretensions to please a woman worthy of being pleased."
>
> (369)

We are invited to share in collective amnesia about what preceded that evening and follow Elizabeth's counsel: "You must learn some of my philosophy. Think only of the past as its remembrance gives you pleasure" (368–9).

The initial proposal scene (189–93) itself plays a part in Austen's sleight-of-hand renovation of Darcy, since Elizabeth spends much more time and effort in laying out her (refutable) objections to his treatment of Bingley and Wickham – three pages – than she does to her (irrefutable) objections to his unpleasant behaviour – one paragraph. This enables Austen to use Darcy's letter to shift the issues to those in which Elizabeth has been in error and produces such complete self-condemnation from her that she blames herself for being prejudiced without reminding the reader that she was fully justified or that the issue of Darcy's manner has slipped out of view.

Finally, Austen plays the Beatrice card (it would be played again by Charlotte Brontë, in a variant form, in *Jane Eyre*) counting on the pleasure felt by readers in courtship as conflict. But, although Elizabeth's wit casts a misleading glamour over their encounters – the illusion of a Beatrice-and-Benedick-like "merry war" – it ought to be evident to the reader that Darcy is no Benedick, never "merry", and has undergone no real transformation of character, manners or wit before his first proposal is made. In fact, what may seem "very delightful" in any of the passages between Elizabeth and Darcy rarely holds up to a scrutiny of his side, as an open-minded reading of any of their exchanges will confirm. So why do so many readers accept Austen's "revision" and are so easily persuaded to forget Darcy's ill manners, converting them into a tactic in a witty competition? That Elizabeth's charm is enough for both doesn't seem to be an adequate justification.

The explanation lies in Austen's relish in making explicit the physical attraction between Darcy and Elizabeth – his sexual response to Elizabeth effectively concealing his deficiencies of character and giving a superficial impression that he engages in a "merry war". His repeated smiles, generally in response to one of Elizabeth's sallies, are one way Austen effectively captures the softening effect of Elizabeth's combination of wit and physical appeal on the self-sufficiency, even the hostility, of the unwilling lover. The contrast with the pomposity of his speeches is striking, as random references suggest: "Darcy only smiled," "Mr. Darcy smiled," "he replied, with a smile," "He smiled," "said he, smiling," "said he, smilingly," "Darcy smiled".

There is no doubt he is soon sexually attracted to Elizabeth, and this sways the reader in his favour. There is the stamp of reality in his inconvenient but irresistible urge to reveal his interest to his friends, even to Miss Bingley, whose resentment will inevitably lead to vulgar teasing. But most striking is the fact that it is Elizabeth's personality that arouses his sexual interest and redefines his response to her physical appearance. His often-repeated attraction to her physical charms is inextricable from his fascination with her playfulness, wit and intelligence, a response significantly unlike Mr Bennet's one-dimensional physical attraction to the woman he married.

Clearly, Darcy's attraction is not a consequence of worldly judgment but rather the opposite. In fact, it does Darcy no disservice in the reader's eyes, being both a tribute to Elizabeth and part of the smokescreen concealing his deficiencies of character, that he recognizes her unsuitability and overestimates his self-control:

> Darcy had never been so bewitched by any woman as he was by her. He really believed, that were it not for the inferiority of her connections, he should be in some danger.

(52)

Given the link to "danger", the choice of cliché "bewitched" suggests Darcy's pleasurable excitement in recognizing the threat of sexual attraction to his rational judgment. Subsequently, however, Austen traces a strengthening and broadening of his feelings. By the time of the first proposal, the danger has become a serious reality, and the struggle between pride and feeling makes "bewitched" cruelly frivolous.

The tight-throated "how ardently I admire and love you" – formal despite, or rather because of, the "ardently" – takes its place, to be succeeded by the more diffuse and expanded "my affections" (189, 366) of the successful proposal. It is a mark of the discrepancy between Austen's handling of his love and his character that the shifting language of the lover convinces, while, in regard to his character, trickery is required.

In Darcy's case, his linked responses to Elizabeth's character and her sexual appeal prove a benevolent force, to be trusted despite his prudential judgment, but Austen doesn't encourage easy generalization from this. Elizabeth's attraction to Wickham initially seems to be composed of the same elements: "Elizabeth honoured [Wickham] for such feelings, and thought him handsomer than ever as he expressed them" (80), but hers is a willed response, founded on false perceptions and the creation of her wish for courtship. Austen thus doesn't set judgment aside by endorsing Darcy's love, nor oppose it to feeling; she demonstrates that Darcy's response to Elizabeth is the consequence of an ability to recognize love (however socially imprudent) that Elizabeth, in her wishful response to Wickham, lacks. Even less than in *Northanger Abbey*, does Richard Simpson's conviction of Austen's "habitual exaltation of judgment over passion" stand up to the much more flexible view of passion explored here, although neither does its simple opposite.

For Austen is not blind to the risks inherent in sexual attraction, and neither is her heroine. Through Elizabeth, Austen examines more complex interactions of judgment, feeling and sexuality, exploring their relationship to Elizabeth's refusal to compromise her independence. Paradoxically, Austen lays bare the roots of Elizabeth's admirable qualities in the poisoned soil of the Bennet parents' relationship, revealing her strengths to be as much due to family tensions as to high principles, her determination to stand apart and to make her own judgments being one among various accommodations made by the Bennet children to their parents' marriage. *Pride and Prejudice*, like Austen's other works, is as much about family relationships as it is about negotiating the path to matrimony or, more accurately, about the connection between the two. It is from her parents' situation that Elizabeth learns to distrust sexual attraction and to recognize that there may be difficulties in reconciling love, including love for parents and siblings, with independence of moral judgment.

In the Bennet family, such independence is a quality that is valuable but maintained at painful cost, as Elizabeth's rueful comment to Jane reveals: "There are few people whom I really love, and still fewer of whom I think well" (135). More than most, therefore, she must struggle to recognize that though emotional ties can conflict with judgment they need not, and that though love entails the risk of pain, detachment is not the best answer. Elizabeth must develop a trust in her own nature while daily witnessing a marriage brought about by sexual attraction alone and fractured by incompatibility of values and intelligence. In her self-condemnation as she reassesses her belief in Wickham, her words reveal her view of love (one that Emma would echo) as clearly as her degree of repentance: "Had I been in love, I could not have been more wretchedly blind" (208).

The reflection suggests that some of Elizabeth's resistance to Darcy has been due to a denial of her attraction to him, caused by her distrust of love emanating from her parents' marriage. Darcy blames his conviction that "I believed you to be wishing, expecting my addresses" on his "vanity" (369), but Austen shows that Darcy had been justified in thinking Elizabeth's arch manner resulted from a sexual interest responsive to his. Her disclaimer at the close is truer than she knows, for her "manners" have invited the continuance of Darcy's sexual interest: "I never meant to deceive you, but my spirits might often lead me wrong . . . " (369). Austen powerfully conveys both Elizabeth's heightened interest in Darcy and her false sense that her dislike of him makes it safe for her to dazzle, just as her lack of real interest in Wickham frees her to behave carelessly. Both her deep-seated conviction she is safe from personal involvement and her assertive wit, while contributing to her charm for others, give her the illusion she can put those who endanger her autonomy at a distance.

The pressures to marry – financial security and emancipation from family – only exacerbate her discomfort. The result is the construction of a series of defences, from near-denial – "if I were determined to get a rich husband, or any husband" (22) – to evasion by focusing her concern on Jane's difficulties in love rather than her own. But Elizabeth gives every evidence of having waited not to love but rather to admit her love to herself, the continuance of Darcy's love teaching her to risk acknowledging her own, in Mary Poovey's words "defending herself against emotional vulnerability" (*Proper Lady* 198). But finally, Austen allows Elizabeth to blame her manners and her prejudice for her problems rather than her fear of involvement, suggesting that her creator shares her resistance to some degree.

This conclusion is reinforced by the much greater emotional impact of the mid-novel rejection of Darcy's proposal than the concluding acceptance. It is the lengthy section encompassing the first proposal, Darcy's letter and Elizabeth's response that dominates the work and lingers most vividly in the mind. The tell-tale difference in impact between the first and second proposal is due not only to Austen's characteristic retreat from dialogue into narrative and indirect speech in Elizabeth's final acceptance, "gave him to understand, that her sentiments had undergone so material a change . . . as to make her receive with gratitude and pleasure, his present assurances" (366), but also to the immediate return to the subject of the rejection, not only at much greater length than the second proposal itself, but also in a return to direct speech (367–9), the intensity and immediacy of the rejection reasserting itself at the end of the work.

This suggests that though Austen can reveal the causes and consequences of detachment through her heroine's difficulties, Elizabeth's is a characteristic that she as an author shares – a detachment that renders divisions and misunderstandings a safer and more interesting subject than reconciliations, a weakness supported by an ability to use wit as a means both to charm and to hold others at arm's length. Meanwhile, in her own relation to the reader Austen choses flirtation, keeping her distance while using her appealing performance to disguise her difficulties with Darcy's reform.

In *Pride and Prejudice*, Austen explores the role of sexual attraction with greater honesty and greater ease than she does judgment, open to the possibility that people may be right to love others whom reason would condemn as unsuitable, and to the complexities of the experience of love that such a circumstance engenders. But something of Simpson's formulation does appear in her decision to evade the issue of the relation of manners to character. The attractive but forced symmetry of the lovers coming together through mutual learning and teaching is an appealing testament to her preference for moral equality in her lovers, but it is also a betrayal of her initial interest in the problem of what happens when love and the judgment of the loved one do not fit as easily together as they did in *Northanger Abbey*. This was, however, a problem that she would tackle again.

Despite Austen's interest in the connection between the moral and sexual lives of parents and their children, she had not explored the long-popular subject of love between a young woman and a father surrogate until she wrote *Emma*. Perhaps Fanny's situation in *Mansfield Park*, marriage to a mentor – "brother" who closely resembled his father, challenged Austen to tackle the relationship more directly.

In *Emma*, Austen goes out of her way to draw the reader's attention to the issue of whether a powerful paternal figure ought to enter into marriage with a girl to whom he has acted as mentor. Mr Knightley calls himself a "very old and intimate friend of the family" (9), but, as a consequence of the moral nullity of Emma's father, he has clearly assumed the paternal role with a parent's awareness of her childhood faults and triumphs (37). By insisting on the discrepancy in ages – Emma has lived "nearly twenty-one years in the world" while Mr Knightley is "seven or eight-and-thirty"(5, 9) – Austen forces into prominence two problems deriving from potential characteristics of the father. One is whether moral superiority must inevitably translate into dominance and whether such superiority precludes marital love. The other is whether, given the shared background, the resulting relationship can escape two undesirable alternatives: remaining familial at the cost of sexuality or becoming sexual at the cost of being incestuous.

Given the conclusion of Austen's previous work, *Mansfield Park*, with its concluding retreat into the tight family circle, there is cause to wonder whether Austen is also considering, perhaps even promoting, a similar withdrawal in *Emma*. When Emma declares her inability to call her newly betrothed by his Christian name because, having failed to shock him by using "George" when she was a child, it would now be "impossible" to call him anything but "Mr. Knightley" (462–3), should the reader be amused or disturbed? Are Mr Knightley and Emma drawn to each other *because* of their familial relationship, or has sexual attraction broken the older tie and made each new to the other? When Mr Knightley projects his love backwards in time, "by dint of fancying so many errors, [I] have been in love with you ever since you were thirteen at least" (462), what does Austen intend? Is she, unlike the modern reader made sensitive by *Lolita* and current media concerns, simply untroubled by the remark? Is she daring the reader to object to the possibility of a transition from paternal to sexual love? Or is she using Mr Knightley's stress on their difference in age, by means of a comically retroactive exaggeration, to express wonder that love should be so amenable to radical transformation?

Most of the evidence suggests that Austen intends the last. After the disagreement over Robert Martin, Mr Knightley reminds Emma there is "reason good" for his superiority of judgment: "I was sixteen years old when you were born" (99). Emma's response suggests that she regards this as a tactic to maintain moral dominance:

" . . . no doubt you were much my superior in judgment at that period of our lives; but does not the lapse of one-and-twenty years bring our understandings a good deal nearer?"

"Yes – a good deal *nearer.*"

"But still, not near enough to give me the chance of being right, if we think differently."

"I have still the advantage of you by sixteen years' experience, and by not being a pretty young woman and a spoiled child"

(99, emphasis original)

but while his words support Emma's interpretation, Austen makes use of the context and tone – this is a reconciliation, an old shared joke, and Emma is enjoying the renewal of their amity – to suggest rather that his paternal stance is partly habitual and partly a protective self-deception that has enabled him to declare "I should like to see Emma in love, and in some doubt of a return; it would do her good. But there is nobody hereabouts to attach her . . . " (41).

Austen achieves three ends in their jousting: she demonstrates Emma's desire to challenge Mr Knightley's moral superiority, she exonerates him from any conscious desire to play Pygmalion, and she also begins to chip away at the problem that his paternal relationship to Emma may colour their developing sexual relationship. The last is achieved by engineering a time-lag between the reader's early perception that Mr Knightley is in love and his own later recognition (resulting from Frank Churchill's arrival, 432) that a different relationship is possible, an effect Austen reinforces by introducing Emma to the reader when she is already a self-confident young woman. Though we are told a good deal about their father–daughter past, what we see are two socially (and potentially sexually) compatible adults. Mr Knightley's "Brother and sister! no, indeed" later, at the ball (331), marks his recognition of his completed passage from father to lover, but this discovery has been long anticipated by the reader.

Austen handles Emma's progress with equal confidence through scenes suggesting the lover rather than the daughter: her ability to remember exactly where Mr Knightley stood on the occasion (months before) of Mr Elton's cutting himself (339–40); the handshake of reconciliation as the two play with their baby niece, a scene suggestive of their shared future as parents (98–9); Emma's perception of him as out of place with the older men at the ball (325–6); her regret that he fails to kiss her hand after her visit of apology to Miss Bates (386); and, finally, the realization, with the force of a physical sensation, that "darted through her, with the speed of an arrow, that Mr. Knightley must marry no one but herself!" (408)

This delayed recognition on Emma's part is no mere plot device, however, developing as it does from causes integral to their natures. Mr Knightley's case is less problematic than Emma's: he only needs the stimulus of jealousy to alter his perceptions. However, Austen explores more complex causes for her heroine's slowness, causes that both link back to, and extend, an interest she had displayed in *Pride and Prejudice*, for Emma is averse to marriage. Elizabeth Bennet, however resistant to personal involvement, at least accepted the necessity, even the desirability, of marriage for herself, whereas Emma, financially independent, begins by denying any such desirability.

As so often, Austen provides a family situation that offers interconnected reasons for Emma's condition: the unfamiliarity of marriage as a state, her mother having died when Emma was five; a fear, consequent on that death, of involvement as leading to pain; and perhaps an unconscious absorption of her father's hostility to marriage as threatening change and loss, confirmed by her own experience with Isabella and Mrs Weston. What Austen doesn't offer is any suggestion that sexual love is repellent to Emma in itself but only in so far as it entails emotional commitment. Unobtrusively, in this novel as elsewhere, Austen invites speculation on parents' past lives. Is it a testimony to Emma's mother's determination that Mr Woodhouse fathered any children at all or a sign of the shattering effect of her death that he has come to fear marriage? Austen's permitting him to remember the first line, but only the first line, of "Kitty, a fair but frozen maid" (text given in *E* 489–90) has long puzzled readers. Jill Heydt-Stevenson elucidates the riddle's references to prostitution and venereal disease and John Dussinger sees Mr Woodhouse's reference to the riddle as revelatory of his "dire fears about sexual union as death" (167), suggesting an amnesia that Freud might have identified. It is even possible that Emma's father may simply be repeating lines that he once overheard but never understood. Like Fanny's enquiry about the slave trade, this is a reference more provocative than conclusive and one that raises even more questions about Austen's motives than about those of the speaker.

Austen selects an occasion, during a visit to a home of "sickness and poverty" when Emma boasts to Harriet of her lack of desire to marry, to demonstrate that her resistance to personal involvement is much broader than to marriage alone. Emma's actions are glossed by the narrative voice (there are no hints here that this is self-description concealed in oblique narration) praising her "sympathy" "intelligence", and "goodwill" but Emma's self-assessment is cool: "If we feel for the wretched, enough to do all we can for them, the rest is empty sympathy, only distressing to ourselves" (86–7). This desire to limit emotional involvement is hardly surprising from one who is the sole support of a childish and demanding parent whom she nevertheless loves, a father who requires heroic forbearance in the face of excruciating tedium while simultaneously supplying an excuse for risking no further commitment. Harriet is a suitable friend in the circumstance; more significant as a pet on a leash than for her position somewhere on a lesbian continuum. Marvin Mudrick argues that "Emma is in love with [Harriet]: a love unphysical and inadmissible, even perhaps undefinable in such a society; and therefore safe" (203) and Tiffany Potter argues their relationship is part of a "lesbian subtext" (188).[3] But whether (or to whatever degree) this is so, the relationship is most significantly distinguished by Emma's need for control and distance. Like Frank Churchill, Harriet is only superficially appealing to Emma and therefore offers no real threat to her self-sufficiency.

As Cicely Palser Havely notes, the most common deduction from Emma's characterization of herself as an "imaginist" (335) is that she is "'an aspiring but failed novelist who wishes to rewrite the community around her'" (221), and hers is certainly a nature that draws on the detachment of the novelist who created her: "A mind lively and *at ease*, can do with seeing nothing, and can see nothing that does not answer" (233, emphasis mine). Matchmaking for others provides further personal safety, a preoccupation underlain by the reassuring conviction that love between the sexes is insubstantial enough to permit easy redirection of feeling as required, so that she feels no doubt that Elton can replace Martin with Harriet and that Harriet can be substituted for Emma with Frank (266–7).

And yet Austen makes it clear that there is a level at which Emma does fear serious consequences for herself and that her insistence that "I have never been in love; it is not my way or my nature; and I do not think I ever shall" (84) is, like her matchmaking, whistling in the dark to drive off the demons. Emma fears love because she fears loss of independence and power, in this approaching Charlotte Brontë's women closer than any other Austen heroine. As her explanation to Harriet makes clear, being single, loved, admired and powerful are linked for her in one indistinguishable muddle:

> I believe few married women are half as much mistress of their husband's house, as I am of Hartfield; and never, never could I expect to be so truly beloved and important; so always first and always right in any man's eyes as I am in my father's.
>
> (84)

But if being "beloved" gives control, loving, Emma believes, brings blindness. In a passage in the narrative voice, although one with which Emma might well have agreed, Isabella is characterized as

> wrapt up in her family; a devoted wife, a doating mother, and so tenderly attached to her father and sister that, but for these higher ties, a warmer love might have seemed impossible. She could never see a fault in any of them.
>
> (92)

And much later, Emma reflects

> Harriet Smith might think herself not unworthy of being peculiarly, exclusively, passionately loved by Mr. Knightley. *She* could not. She could not flatter herself with any idea of blindness in his attachment to *her.*
>
> (415, emphasis original)

and has occasion to be grateful she was not "blinded" by Frank Churchill because she was "somehow or other safe from him" (427). Emma has two reasons, therefore, to fear being in love: that as a consequence "her affection must have overpowered her judgment"(419) as she concludes of Jane Fairfax, and that only someone blinded by love to her faults could love her in return. It might seem that Emma is thinking of sexual attraction here, particularly given the "passionately" she attaches to Mr Knightley's supposed love for Harriet, but it is noteworthy that it is not the sexual component Emma singles out as dangerous, but any strong affection including love consequent upon family ties (86), a condition that links her to Elizabeth Bennet. Clearly, Austen could have chosen no more resistant nature than Emma's, fearing emotional involvement, exposure to censure and loss of power, to relate to the most extreme version of the mentor-lover, the father figure.

Emma obsessively notes in the society around her every example that supplies confirmation of her view that love and marriage entail loss of control – of both self and others. From the courtships she observes with such detachment, she deduces that love, for males and females alike, entails real or ritual surrender. The socially acceptable language of love is the language of submission, which, before marriage at least, is the posture required of man, as Elton's charade confirms:

Man's boasted power and freedom, all are flown;
Lord of the earth and sea, he bends a slave,
And woman, lovely woman, reigns alone.

(71)

And Emma's own view of her relationship with Frank is measured by what she believes to be her power over him and the fear she projects on to him: "she was rather inclined to think [his hurrying away] implied a dread of her returning power" (316). But "power and freedom", exactly what Emma desires for herself, are in her view likely to be the prerogative of the man in the long run, for another convention suggests that this talk of male slavery is a mere cover: "a man always imagines a woman to be ready for anybody who asks her" (60).

Furthermore, in Emma's view, the woman most likely to attract is a malleable, silly and beautiful Harriet, who, early on, she could claim to believe was suited even to Mr Knightley (64). The conviction that love blinds contributes to Emma's distress after Harriet's confession of love for him: "Was it a new circumstance for a man of first rate abilities to be captivated by very inferior powers?" (413) The jokes of the narrative voice in *Northanger Abbey* come alive again through Emma, along with reminders of Mr Allen, Mr Bennet and Sir Thomas Bertram. And, despite the fact that Emma's view is repudiated both by Mr Knightley's words: "Men of sense, whatever you chuse to say, do not want silly wives" (64), and even more conclusively by his actions, this is a moment when the reader senses a similarity between the author's view and that of her heroine. "[M]en of sense" are the exception, the remainder being attracted to foolish women whose pre-marital power to captivate is soon replaced by submission.

Emma also finds much to fear in the marriages she sees around her, and here again Austen seems to come close to agreeing with her, in that she creates for Emma, and for the reader, a gallery limited to couples in which one (usually the woman, although Mrs Elton is an odious exception) surrenders to the other. There are no Gardiners or Crofts to offer a contrary model in *Emma*, and no way of shifting the responsibility for depicting the marriages in this way to Emma's biased judgment. Mrs Weston is commended by Mr Knightley for receiving a "very good education" from Emma "on the very material matrimonial point of submitting your own will, and doing as you were bid" (38) a remark in which he appears to differ very little from Emma in her belief that men desire biddable wives. His teasing manner suggests the compliment is an allusion to convention, while Emma's defiance may make her assert more than she fully accepts, but the stereotypes from which these remarks emanate are nevertheless disconcertingly close to what we are shown. If Emma is not to automatically subordinate her judgment to that of her husband, as custom appears to dictate, Austen will have to show the relationship to be exceptional. She will also have to eliminate Emma's fear of loss of autonomy and dislike of criticism, to demonstrate her to be as capable of taking the risks of loving as Mr Knightley, and, finally, to bring them closer together morally.

Austen begins very early to clear up one difficulty: Mr Knightley never has been, and does not become before the work's end, a perfect Grandisonian hero. While there is considerable justification for his anger over her manipulation of Harriet, his own involvement with Robert Martin (he will much later send him to Brunswick Square without consulting Emma, to whom he has recently praised "the beauty of truth and sincerity in all our dealings with each other", 470–1, 446) reveals him working to shape another's life. And though he is irritatingly given to dispensing paternal rebuke and approbation (170) up to the point when Frank Churchill arrives, this subsequently ceases. Jealousy certainly follows, and criticism, but never again his patronising manner.

But what of Emma's sense that Mr Knightley's judgments represent an assertion of his superiority? Does Austen show criticism to be compatible with another form of love than the paternal as she had in the simpler world of *Northanger Abbey*? In the episode at Box Hill she shows that it is. After Emma's rudeness to Miss Bates, Mr Knightley initially takes refuge in the old formula, the only one that appears to give him the right to speak. However, his own acknowledgement of the changed relation from father to "friend" occurs as he remonstrates – regretful but unpatronising:

"Emma, I must once more speak to you as I have been used to do: a privilege rather endured than allowed, perhaps, but I must still use it. I cannot see you acting wrong, without remonstrance. How could you be so unfeeling to Miss Bates? . . . "

(374)

"This is not pleasant to you, Emma – and it is very far from pleasant to me, but I must, I will, – I will tell you truths while I can, satisfied with proving myself your friend by very faithful counsel, and trusting that you will some time or other do me greater justice than you can do now."

(375)

The maturity of Emma's response also marks a difference: unlike her earlier childish reactions to his criticisms, she instantly feels "anger against herself, mortification, and deep concern" and, almost as soon, an adult awareness of Mr Knightley's own pain, followed by self-reproach that her inability to speak has left him without "one word of gratitude, of concurrence, of common kindness!" (375–6). As in *Pride and Prejudice*, the moment in the novel with the greatest emotional impact is one of division between the lovers, although here criticism, self-criticism and regret merge, achieving greater force than in the earlier work.

Most readers are made acutely uncomfortable by the Box Hill incident (a friend says she dreads its approach whenever she reads the novel), but it is nevertheless a scene in which Austen triumphantly asserts that it is possible to intermingle love with judgment, albeit painfully. However, what follows, as Austen characteristically moves to establish moral equality between the lovers, is difficult to assess because, though Austen is able to adjust Emma's position, her treatment of Mr Knightley's becomes more troubling. Because Emma's potential has always been manifest, she can gracefully admit past moral inferiority, and convincingly promise improvement (if not quite the perfection playfully offered in the closing lines). And because her charm and self-confidence mark her as capable of being Mr Knightley's equal in every other way, there is no need to blur the issue of her faults as in Darcy's case. Thus, at Box Hill, the necessary changes in Emma's judgment are achieved, and the issues of moral superiority raised by the work seem settled with Emma's recognition of what she has learned from Mr Knightley and her new self-knowledge. In Mr Knightley's case, it initially seems Box Hill has also demonstrated he has been successful in relinquishing his role as fatherly advisor for that of "friend" without swinging to the opposite extreme, a lover with a love-induced blindness to her faults, a condition already explicitly condemned by Emma and implicitly, in this novel and elsewhere, by Austen herself.

But with his proposal, Mr Knightley loses his nerve and his clarity of vision. At first, in confessing his love, he appears not entirely to abandon his habits of criticism:

I have blamed you, and lectured you, and you have borne it as no other woman in England would have borne it. Bear with the truths I would tell you now, dearest Emma, as well as you have borne with them.

(430)

but the truths he will tell this "sweetest and best of all creatures, fault-less in spite of all her faults" (433) soon prove to be about his love for her. Subsequently, Austen seems compelled to replay the apology on a slightly different tack, apparently fearing she has not convinced the reader to accept his transition from mentor to lover:

> My interference was quite as likely to do harm as good. It was very natural for you to say, what right has he to lecture me? – and I am afraid very natural for you to feel it was done in a disagreeable man-ner. I do not believe I did you any good.
>
> (462)

In both cases he justifiably criticizes himself for his manner (although in the first the emphasis is on Emma's unique ability to have "borne with it", here on naturalness of her objections) and raises important questions about interference and resistance, but above all, about whether one adult has the duty or the right to criticize another. Clearly, however, the first two issues are not intended to be seriously consid-ered, and in passing over them, the reader is persuaded to pass over the other, the duty to criticize, the lesson of Box Hill in this regard being forgotten.

Austen cannot be absolved of cheating here: she relies on an affection-ately ironical presentation of a man in love to permit the reader to suc-cumb, if not to blindness, at least to winking at this rosy view of their past relationship. Placed as this retraction is in the final pages of the work, there is little incentive to stop and consider its implications. Given the reader's desire to achieve closure with the "perfect happiness of the union" (484), and Austen's convincing portrayal of sexual attraction free of any dependence on a power struggle for its vitality, Mr Knightley's retreat from criticism, erasing a potential blot on a picture of "perfect happiness" is made as desirable to the reader as to the characters. Though the genders have been reversed, something of the falsification of *Pride and Prejudice* seems to be repeated here.

But to accept this unproblematic closure is to go against the tenor of the scene at Box Hill and to believe that the rebuke rather than the need for the rebuke is to be the more regretted. By not merely relin-quishing but also repudiating his mentorship, Mr Knightley denies the importance of the difficulties his criticism has raised. Moreover, as part of her move to further level their respective moral positions, Austen implies that Emma has finally learned to know herself. But this desir-able outcome of her recognition of her love for Mr Knightley is obscured by her discovery that in him she has a lover to whom she is, after all, "always first and always right" (84). Thus the problematic issues concerning the relationship of love to moral superiority and criticism disappear into the comedy, and Mr Knightley demonstrates the correctness of Emma's theory of love and blindness after all, abandoning the insights gained on Box Hill that love may coexist, not automatically, but by painful personal effort, with judgment.

What links *Northanger Abbey* with *Emma* is that both Henry Tilney and Mr Knightley embody the truth of this recognition and that Catherine and Emma acknowledge they are right. What links *Pride and Prejudice* and *Emma* is that, though Austen recognizes the oversimplification involved in opposing judgment and love, she also apparently shares her heroines' fears of love-induced blindness and loss of independence, even though she demonstrates that their fears co-exist with a clear-sightedness about those they love. In both these novels she finally encourages the reader to retreat into a retroactive denial of any serious discrepancies between the lovers' moral worth, evading the issue she herself has brought forward. Overall, all three works demonstrate Austen's awareness (very different from that of Brontë and Eliot) that sexual attraction is not necessarily a threat to judgment in itself. But though she demonstrates that it may be a benevolent force, she also makes it clear that it may prove to be the opposite, defying any tidy oversimplifications the critic might wish to make.

Because *Northanger Abbey, Pride and Prejudice* and *Emma* are founded on the attractive supposition that to achieve "perfect happiness" marriage must be based on the prior establishment of moral equality, they either downplay or work towards the elimination of the need for mentorship. Henry Tilney's effervescent good spirits merely spill over into a parody of such a situation, Elizabeth and Darcy's learning and teaching are inadvertent, and Mr Knightley desperately tries to shake off the role of mentor when faced with the recognition that he is in love.

Discussing the history of "Janeitism", Deidre Lynch sees Austen as an unusual challenge to academic professionalism: "The tricky dimension of writing about the history of Austen's reception is, then, how it tugs the writer in two directions, not only toward the public domain but also toward the spaces of intimacy, where Austen, as the confidante who knows and forgives our hidden desires and dislikes, has allowed our love" (15). That Austen elicits from many of her readers a sense that they share an intense personal relationship is undeniable, but may seem inexplicable, given her reservations concerning both love and mentorship, and her use of her wit to deny any desire on her part to be serious, either as mentor or lover. But like Darcy, readers are likely to find evasiveness attractive, and to succumb to the same "blindness" towards Austen that Elizabeth and Emma feared. As a result, when shown we have been tempted into making errors of judgment we are likely to feel amusement rather than annoyance. Indeed, in the face of Austen's appealing playfulness, we are not likely to resent, even to notice, that she has led us to laugh at her characters as Emma did, while encouraging us to see Emma's own sense of superiority as faulty. Uneasy awareness that we have been implicated along with the heroine ought, however, to trouble us, and remind us that Austen's apparently light-hearted mentorship may have a darker underside.

In *Emma* that darkness rarely touches the surface. By contrast, however, in *Sense and Sensibility* it emerges with a savagery that sometimes suggests loss of control, while in *Mansfield Park*, Austen, deliberately eschewing flirtation, makes few concessions to the reader, admitting both the difficulty and complexity of the mentor-lover relationship in ways that have almost invariably proved more troubling to readers than her evasive tactics in the novels of lighter tone.

2

Sense and Sensibility and *Mansfield Park*: "At Once Both Tragedy and Comedy"

Had *Sense and Sensibility* and *Mansfield Park* been the only two of her novels to have survived, perhaps Austen would have evoked affection from fewer readers. *Mansfield Park*, with a hero and heroine who are themselves hard to love, is knotty and elusive in its complexity, while the earlier novel often seems defiantly unsubtle, from the brilliant black farce of Fanny Dashwood's education of her husband in the art of meanness (an unambiguously nasty, if peripheral, example of the mentor-lover) to the unrepressed emotion of Marianne's near-screams of agony at the loss of Willoughby (105). Each of these two "darker" novels is noted for causing discomfort in the course of its reading and dissatisfaction at its end, but there is another resemblance other than Austen's refusal to beguile. Anticipating *Mansfield Park*, the earlier novel is notable for the way in which its structure tends to ensnare readers into the condition of inattentive proofreaders who find not what is there, but rather what they expect – desirable mentor-lover relationships – even though in the earlier novel the promise of such relationships fizzles to nothing while in the later it leads to tragedy.

Austen's obsession with age in *Sense and Sensibility* both suggests the need for, and disappoints expectations of, successful mentorship. Every character of significance has a stated or calculable age, age is often the subject for humour, and discrepancies between chronological age and moral and emotional development are part of an insistent pattern, though the characters prove immune to even the narrative's assertion that improvement has taken place. Many are simply childish in their self-absorption, while others show Austen working out more complex variations on the theme. Marianne, for example, as John Wiltshire

47

points out, appears never to be emotionally weaned from her mother who, in turn, lives vicariously through her (29–30). At the same time, the forty-year old Mrs Dashwood is in effect another sister – "Indeed a man could not very well be in love with either of her daughters, without extending the passion to her" (90) – with judgment less mature than that of her oldest daughter. And Elinor, at nineteen, begins and remains a generation older than everyone else, the only adult in a novel that specializes in making children, and the blind indulgence with which they are treated, the butt of many a dark joke.

Though Elinor's calendar age makes her a rather unconventional candidate to be anyone's mentor, there is a figure who promises to fit the stereotype more closely. Joseph Weisenfarth is not alone in describing Colonel Brandon as such when he includes (among a pattern of Austen's "Pygmalions" and "Galateas") his "shaping of Marianne Dashwood" (*Emma*: point counterpoint" 216–17). The Colonel is an obvious choice by reason of his gravity and age – he is five years younger than Marianne's mother, as the reader is often reminded – and this is how he is usually perceived. But despite Marianne's convalescent resolve to draw on his library for books that will provide her with "a great deal of instruction" (343), he is, in fact, a testament to the power of cliché to shape expectations. As Laura Mooneyham White points out, "Marianne and Brandon do not educate each other. How can they when they do not even have one instance of reported dialogue in all of the novel?" (78).

In any case, Brandon isn't up to being a mentor, for, flannel waistcoat notwithstanding, he has never grown up. It is apparent from his falling in love with Marianne after the tragedy of Eliza, that the "romantic refinements of a young mind"(56), "the same warmth of heart, the same eagerness of fancy and spirits" (205) that appealed to him as a seventeen-year old are the very characteristics he continues to find attractive in Marianne, now the same age. His unwillingness to agree with Elinor that her sister would be the better for being disabused of "the prejudices of a young mind" through "a better acquaintance with the world" (56) is founded in a distrust of experience and of the ability to learn from it. In his view, disillusionment can only lead to moral breakdown and experience of the disasters ensuing from youthful romanticism has done nothing to temper his commitment to it. A romantic himself, the tale Austen gives him to tell is a signal of his condition, a standard from popular fiction (the kind she announced her own emancipation from in *Northanger Abbey*) covering all the angles: an elopement betrayed; a greedy guardian and lascivious husband; a woman deceived, debauched and impregnated; her mandatory end in rescue from the sponging house, repentance and death – with, of course, an echo in her daughter's own fall from innocence. The tale is interlaced with his account of his own naivety, first in his "noble" decision to take service in India leaving the girl he loves unprotected in the hands of a greedy father and brother, and then in the imprudence in his care for Eliza's daughter. The whole is crowned by the culmination of high romance, the step that Eleanor sighs over as a "fancied necessity" (211), a duel with Willoughby. Even the "impossibility" of the romantic's forming a "second attachment", one of the running jokes in the work, is not so much denied as supported by her likeness to Eliza, the first love whom, in effect, the romantic Brandon finally succeeds in marrying (227). Jocelyn Harris suggests that *Sense and Sensibility* is a multiple retelling of *Clarissa*: "The Eliza scenes fail for closely copying their original, the Marianne scenes, which scrutinize and rework *Clarissa*, convince and move" (59). But if the Eliza scenes are seen as criticism of a motif long fallen into cliché rather than failures in themselves, then the reworking of the tale takes on greater import.

If Austen fails to divest readers of their expectations of Brandon's role as mentor, she also fails to convince them (if indeed she tries very hard) of his role as lover. At the close, the narrative voice (sounding suspiciously tongue-in-cheek) asks us to accept that Marianne comes to love the Colonel. Generations of readers have failed to be convinced, in part because the process is couched in ominously sacrificial phrases that engender uneasiness at her conversion. Mrs Dashwood, Edward and Elinor "each felt [Colonel Brandon's] sorrows, and their own obligations, and Marianne, by general consent, was to be the reward of all. With such a confederacy against her, what could she do?"; "that she found her own happiness in forming his, was equally the persuasion and delight of each observing friend" (378–9). It isn't clear whether we are to laugh at Marianne's former convictions or at the transparent machinations of her "friends". Nor is it clear how hollow our laughter is expected to be.

There is no doubt about Marianne's love for Willoughby. It is, however, a love motivated by egotism, directed towards a man who "thought the same" as she (53). It is Austen's demonstration of the vulnerability of egocentrics to manipulation by those who confirm their worth, made possible, as Susan Morgan points out, by Willoughby's familiarity with the code of sensibility, which enables him to know in advance exactly what will please Marianne ("Letter Writing" 107). Although, unlike Willoughby, she is undoubtedly sincere, each lover adjusts to resemble the other in behaviour, endorsing the other's judgments and sharing an immature conviction of knowing everything. The potential dangers of this reciprocal education are clear: a mutual admiration society with the potential to injure the naively self-centred Marianne, while being insufficient to sway Willoughby from his absorption in his own desires. As to her older sister's situation, no reader can long hold on to the hope that Edward will have anything to teach Elinor, nor does he. Glenda Hudson makes an attempt to rescue him from complete moral and emotional idiocy, arguing that "Edward's fraternal love is not metamorphosed into passionate love until Lucy elopes with Robert" (*Sibling Love*, 57). But the novel belies this when Edward admits "I *was* wrong in remaining so much in Sussex", persuading himself that "The danger is my own; I am doing no injury to anybody but myself" (368, emphasis original). If Edward has nothing to teach Elinor, signs of her influence upon him are no more believable than the possibility that she might find lasting satisfaction with a thickhead who requires Lucy's elopement to convince him that his fiancée isn't just a simple good-hearted girl. When, at the novel's conclusion, Elinor criticizes the way he had behaved at Norland, the scolding is cast as love-talk, "as ladies always scold the imprudence which compliments themselves" (368), an indulgent recognition of his naivety that does nothing to reconcile the reader to him, convince us that he is mature enough to merit her "tears of joy" (300), or show him to have learned anything from Elinor. Indeed, his position, if not his personality, makes him an echo of the other idle males including Robert Ferrars, John Dashwood, Mr Palmer, Brandon's brother and Willoughby who are, as Claudia Johnson shows, part of a pattern in the novel of "weak, duplicitous and selfish" men who have little purpose in life but to await, and then spend, the money that they acquire through inheritance or marriage (*Jane Austen* 57–8).

An immature romantic, a manipulative egocentric and an irresponsible naif – the leading males in this novel have little to offer the sisters or receive from them in the way either of love or of mentorship. If we ask where the strongest drive to educate and the most intense love come together in the work, it becomes clear why Brandon and Edward are of so little account. They cannot help but be nullities in the face of Elinor's love for Marianne. Eve Kosofsky Sedgwick, citing the bedroom scene in which Elinor observes Marianne writing to Willoughby, claims it manifests elements of hetero-, homo- and autoerotic love (138–9). However, Elinor's love seems not so much sexual as an emotion of such intensity that it pre-empts the development of an intense loving relationship of any other kind, including the sexual, with the men the sisters marry. Motivating her pressing desire to educate her younger sister aright, it is the strongest emotion in the work, leaving room for very little else. It may be measured by the need that Elinor feels to conceal its strength, the fear that this bond may be threatened by love for others being the most convincing explanation for Elinor's continued unwillingness to ask Marianne about Willoughby, as well as for her decision, which she justifies as due to her promise to Lucy, to keep Edward's situation a secret. Following Elinor's confession of her own misery, it seems her devotion is reciprocated though to a lesser degree – Marianne's is the love of a creature stunned and damaged. Furthermore, as Marianne's mentor, Elinor has apparently been only too successful. All egoism drained, a young woman with a relationship to her husband more characteristic of a George Eliot heroine emerges: "Marianne found her own happiness in forming his" (379). It is a depressing prospect, but it is also an unconvincing one, for, insofar as the novel can be said to end happily, it does so because the sisters are not parted by marriage. The emphasis of the final paragraph is skewed towards the relationship of the sisters, to which all others are presented as adjuncts: "among the merits and happiness of Elinor and Marianne, let it not be ranked as the least considerable, that though sisters, and living almost within sight of each other, they could live without disagreement between themselves, or producing coolness between their husbands" (380).

With the dubious exception of the sisters' relationship, *Sense and Sensibility* treats the possibility of love and mentorship with the dismissive savagery of black humour. By contrast, *Mansfield Park* with its infinite range of greys seems – and is – a very different type of work. Yet in its concerns with sibling affection and its suspicions of love and mentorship, it shows Austen working with similar issues although to very much more subtly conceived ends.

Mansfield Park is the novel that provokes the most disagreement among Austen's readers, both as to its merits and its author's intentions. An examination of the pattern of the mentor-lover relationships within it suggests that in part this is due to the fact that Austen, who elsewhere proved herself aware of the potential for a darker side to such relationships by evading the difficult questions, here risked exploring that darkness more fully. That in neither the earlier *Sense and Sensibility* nor the later *Persuasion* does she make the mentor-lover relationship central suggests the difficulty she found in dealing with its challenges in those novels in which light-footed diversionary tactics could not be employed under the guise of comedy. The problem she faced has its parallel in an episode inside the novel itself when, in the absence of Sir Thomas, Mr Yates infects the susceptible young people of Mansfield Park with the compulsion to put on a play. The project almost stalls over their inability to agree on an appropriate genre: there was "such a need that the play should be at once both tragedy and comedy" (130).

But in *Mansfield Park*, comedy is relegated to the readers' expectations and the edges of the work: it ceases the moment the brisk and distanced summary of the Ward sisters' history modulates, in the course of a discussion of the possibility of fostering Fanny, into the exposure of an unhealthy and contagious mentor-lover relationship. It commences again only in the last chapter with its apparent endorsement of the belief that it really is possible to sort characters into those "not greatly at fault themselves" and "the rest" (461).

However, this shift into a comic closure leads to a related cause of controversy encouraged by Austen's closing designation of characters as sheep or goats. Repeatedly critics reject Fanny for Mary, or Edmund for Henry (or vice versa), or characterize Mansfield, in Trilling's words, "for the author as well as the heroine [as] the Great Good Place" (169). Indeed one of the most striking features of much of the published criticism of the work is that, although there are changes in interpretation and preferences over time, the assumption that characters and places of *Mansfield Park* should be considered symbols of good or evil is remarkably persistent. Like all Austen's novels, however, *Mansfield Park*, at least when shorn of its closing, resists, as I shall argue, all attempts to read it in a schematic way.

Given her desire (even at the cost of evasion) to demonstrate the possibility of achieving equality of love and moral stature by a passage through and beyond mutual mentorship in *Pride and Prejudice*, Austen might have been expected, in her next novel *Mansfield Park*, to push towards the same satisfying resolution. And, as in the case of its predecessor, much in the work suggests this is her purpose. Yet, ironically, the only example in the novel of achieved mutuality in love and mentorship is kept in the wings, hinted at through references to the play *Lover's Vows*. "As you have for a long time instructed me, why should I not now begin to teach you?" appeals Amelia as she manoeuvres her tutor into admitting he reciprocates her love. But this is a relationship that Austen keeps off the stage of the novel and, although rehearsed by Edmund and Mary, is not finally enacted, either in the drama or in their lives. The couple who appear to be the closest approximation to Inchbald's lovers, despite the differences in temperament between the aggressive Amelia and the passive Fanny, are the cousins of the concluding chapter. But theirs is a union requiring a more suspicious examination than is often given, an examination Austen discourages both through the appealing symmetry of their relationship and through belated assertions of its desirability.

Pervading the novel is Austen's development of a complex pattern of fractured mentor-lover relationships: overlapping three-way combinations in which a central figure of each trio cannot find in any one person the satisfaction of both moral and passionate needs and who suffers as a consequence by being divided between two people, one a lover and the other a mentor. Consideration of the intertwined relationships of Edmund, Fanny, Mary, Henry, Maria, Julia, Rushworth and Yates would illustrate many variations on this theme, but the initial pattern may be traced to their elders, for the novel is a cross-generational exploration of the relationship of mentorship and love. In the triangle of Sir Thomas, Lady Bertram and Mrs Norris, lie the origins of the moral, emotional and sexual disjunctions that corrupt the inhabitants of Mansfield Park.

The conditions for tragedy in this relationship are early demonstrated during the discussion of Fanny's "adoption". Sir Thomas Bertram is an Aristotelian figure, neither vicious and depraved nor, despite his pretensions, pre-eminent in virtue and justice. His tragic error has been his marriage to a woman inadequate as both a lover and a mentor, with superficial sexual charms but neither energy nor intelligence. The defence offered by the narrative voice, that she "did not think deeply, but, guided by Sir Thomas, she thought justly on all important points" (449), is less a compliment than a condemnation, for this denies her fallible husband any response that might challenge his moral complacency. Had he sufficient insight, Sir Thomas might well lament, in the words of the stage baron of *Lovers' Vows*, the consequences of choosing a moral nullity for a wife: "I had no instructor but my passions; no governor but my own will" (*LV* in *MP* 500).

But this would not be entirely true, for Sir Thomas has a sister-in-law who, though lacking sexual appeal, has both energy and an intense desire to manage others. Austen demonstrates, in the first discussion of Fanny's future, how the moral vacuum consequent on Sir Thomas's choice of wife enables Mrs Norris, while offering no overt challenge to his self-image as Grandisonian mentor, to seize the wifely role for herself. The conquest is achieved through the guise of submission, shared understanding and repeated flattery, "I perfectly comprehend you, and do justice to the generosity and delicacy of your notions" (6), embodying Austen's caricature of the courtesy book recommendations for the capture and pleasing of a husband in the interest of securing one's own aims. In fact, in her relationship with Sir Thomas, Mrs Norris has taken to heart the defence of conjugal obedience expressed in Hannah More's *Coelebs in Search of a Wife*:

> this scrupled "obedience" is so far from implying degradation, that it is connected with the injunction to the woman to "promote good works" in her husband; [suggesting] a degree of influence that raises her condition, and restores her to all the dignity of equality; it makes her not only the associate but the inspirer of his virtues.
>
> (I:5)[1]

Mrs Norris's particular talent is to corrupt Sir Thomas's better intentions in the interest of gaining and holding power within his household. Because it threatens her plans, she determinedly sweeps away his nervous, but justifiable, concern not to do a "cruelty instead of kindness" to a foster child (6) by playing on his pride of blood: "I could never feel for this little girl the hundredth part of the regard I bear your own dear children, nor consider her, in any respect, so much my own" (7). Indeed, while her own husband is a cypher who conveniently dies after only a shadowy appearance in the novel, she often speaks as if she is actually the baronet's wife: "A niece of our's, Sir Thomas . . ." – and when she corrects herself at such a time, it is more a matter of flattery than abdication of the wifely role: "or, at least of *your's*, would not grow up in this neighbourhood without many advantages" (6, emphasis original). Equally striking is Sir Thomas' responsiveness to this treatment, sometimes giving the momentary impression of speaking as husband to wife: "There will be some difficulty in our way, Mrs. Norris, . . . as to the distinction proper to be made between the girls as they grow up" (10). As his speech (an appropriate term) continues, Austen carefully lays bare the sources of his vulnerability: the blend of justifiable delicacy (Fanny will not have the financial expectations that will make his own daughters more marriageable) with sheer snobbery, concluding in a request that disguises his submission to his mentor as a courtly invitation:

> "It is a point of great delicacy, and you must assist us in our endeavours to choose exactly the right line of conduct."
> Mrs. Norris was quite at his service; and though she perfectly agreed with him as to its being a most difficult thing, encouraged him to hope that between them it would be easily managed.
>
> (11)

The reminder of the existence of another wife ("assist us") is no more than a token; a nullity can have no place "between them".

Austen creates an odd trio who are not only morally but emotionally deficient, so that even the three "parents" together cannot provide the love necessary for the children to thrive. Lady Bertram knows no other love than self-love while Mrs Norris, as substitute mother, considers love to be a combination of indulgence and flattery. As Austen insists, and as the clumsy attempts of Sir Thomas to overcome his emotional woodenness show, good intentions are not enough to counteract this destructive situation, and often he is simply blind to the disastrously incremental effects of the contradictory methods employed in his children's upbringing.

But, most significantly, Austen suggests that Sir Thomas continues to be in the power of sexual impulses of which he is only intermittently aware, and is still prone to be affected by the charms of a young woman, or, negatively, by their absence. Leaving for Antigua, he tactlessly expresses the hope that William will find Fanny not "entirely without improvement – though I fear he must find his sister at sixteen in some respects too much like his sister at ten" (33). Though the meaning of this reproach is initially obscure, it may be understood in the light of his reaction when he returns. For, while readers often give him moral credit for softening towards Fanny soon after his return, Austen suggests that this is in considerable part due to his niece's improved physical charms. His first reaction is his "observing with decided pleasure how much she was grown!" (178). And lest "grown" is thought to be merely a recognition that she is taller, Austen has Edmund assure Fanny, soon after,

"Your uncle thinks you very pretty, dear Fanny – and that is the long and the short of the matter. . . . the truth is, that your uncle never did admire you till now – and now he does. Your complexion is so improved! – and you have gained so much countenance! – and your figure – Nay, Fanny, do not turn away about it – it is but an uncle."
(197–8)

The deftness with which Austen so neatly skewers not only Sir Thomas but the insensitive son who teasingly quotes him, while allowing the reader to feel Fanny's surprise, embarrassment and hurt, is characteristic of the dense texture of the work.

Austen offers a portrait not so much of a man harbouring incestuous lust but rather of one whose perception of any woman is shaped by her sexual appeal, and who, because of his susceptibility, is fearful of the effects of sexual attraction. His being "an advocate for early marriages" (317) implies not only a distrust of Henry's ability to remain faithful, but a more general concern that male sexuality requires the containment of wedlock. He imputes Fanny's resistance to Henry Crawford, accurately, but against all appearances, to an absence in his niece of what "a young, heated fancy imagines to be necessary for happiness" (318) while he finds reassurance in the evidence that Maria plans to marry Rushworth "without the prejudice, the blindness of love" (201), his relief suggesting a distrust of sexual attraction based on his own experience, at some level regretted, with the former Maria Ward.

The evidence for Sir Thomas being a man emotionally improved by his new awareness of Fanny following his return from Antigua is ambiguous at best. Austen makes it clear that his recent awareness of Fanny as a sexual being also prompts his recognition that Henry is sufficiently attracted to her to offer her an advantageous marriage. While the impetus of his own pleasure in her "figure" might not have done more than propel her to an occasional parsonage party, the possibility of Henry's interest leads to the ball, and finally to the exertion of pressure on Fanny to ensure she accepts this financially desirable match.

Seen in this light, the episode of the schoolroom fire and Sir Thomas's half apology for Mrs Norris appear the result of Fanny's new consequence, rather than of avuncular tenderness on her uncle's part. In his altered view of the past, now illumined by Henry's interest, it appears to him that his mentor Mrs Norris has encouraged a "misplaced distinction" and he therefore urges Fanny to understand – adding distance to his apology by his use of the third person – that "Though their caution may prove eventually unnecessary, it was kindly meant" (313). His is a performance of self-deceiving shiftiness that becomes despicable when combined with the alternations of cruelty and "kindness" to which he subjects her. The hurtful accusations

> that you can and will decide for yourself, without any consideration or deference for those who have surely some right to guide you – without even asking their advice
>
> (318)

are so undeserved yet so accurately aimed at Fanny's greatest fears that they seem deliberately chosen to cause the greatest pain to a girl he acknowledges to be "very timid, and exceedingly nervous" (320). The accusations roll on, prudently suspended for tactical reasons to be replaced by the provision of warmth in the schoolroom and the partial (but only partial) shielding from Mrs Norris, acts that make Fanny's unmerited sense of guilt all the greater, while revealing how even genuine (if limited) sympathy and awareness can be perverted. At the very moment when Sir Thomas, unwilling to tell Mrs Norris about Henry's proposal for tactical reasons, appears most clearly to separate himself from his mentor, Austen allows him to reveal that he has actually taken on his sister-in-law's role, pointing up the similarity through commentary:

> Sir Thomas, indeed, was, by this time, not very far from classing Mrs Norris as one of those well-meaning people, who are always doing mistaken and very disagreeable things.
>
> (332)

After a tirade from Mrs Norris against Fanny's "independence" it seems to Sir Thomas, motivated by a Norris-like conviction of rightness, that "nothing could be more unjust, though he had been so lately expressing the same sentiments himself" (324). And Fanny is assured "You cannot suppose me capable of trying to persuade you to marry against your inclinations" (330) even as he plans to transfer the task of overt persuasion to Henry Crawford, and, later, to Edmund.

The best light in which Sir Thomas's scheme for the Portsmouth trip can be seen is another act of "well-meaning zeal", carried out in ignorance of the conditions there and of how oppressive his niece will find them. What cannot be justified is his abandonment of Fanny: it is only after Maria and Julia have run off that he sends for her, and then not for her own good but, as Edmund correctly thinks, "for my mother's sake" (442) and to have an excuse to get Edmund away from London (452). At the end of the penultimate chapter there is no evidence he has unlearned his mentor's lessons in his own treatment of Fanny, although that mentor, having done all the damage of which she is capable, has been reduced to an impotence that makes her, when not "irritated . . . in the blindness of her anger" at Fanny, a parody of her placid sister: "quieted, stupefied, indifferent" (448).

This primary triangle, with Sir Thomas at its apex, is the source of the moral and emotional corruption of the Bertram children in *Mansfield*

Park, and as such is fully worked out in the course of the novel in such a way as to make a very persuasive case for the dangers resulting from the separation of the roles of lover and mentor and upon deficient love and mentorship. In Edmund's case his Aristotelian fall is not due, any more than his father's, to vice and depravity. He has been protected from the worst of the influences shaping his siblings by the long-understood need for him to take up a profession and his solid, quiet temperament leading to his interest in the Church. The inheritance of some characteristics from his father, a seriousness and an acceptance of established principles, has contributed to an easier relationship between them, freeing Edmund to some extent from the fear and resentment that the other children feel. And Austen both names and reveals Edmund's best quality, "the gentleness of an excellent nature" (15) when, at sixteen, he perceives and soothes some measure of his cousin's misery. Sir Thomas's damaged impulses to kindness have clearly survived in Edmund in a stronger and more admirable form, capable of open expression. From the beginning he becomes Fanny's mentor, giving her "a great deal of good advice" and she feels she has "a friend" (17). The echoes of Grandison's inscription of himself to Clementina as *"Tutor, Friend, Brother"* (616) ring warmly here until one remembers what a tangle Richardson's pair got themselves into.

But Austen suggests that Edmund has acquired some of his father's conventionality and emotional blindness, as capable as everyone else of expecting Fanny to adjust with ease to her new life until he is forced into awareness by finding her crying. From the beginning, he establishes a pattern that is to be a constant in their relationship. He attempts to shape her responses for her, simplifies the causes of her misery to fit the orthodox terms he expects, and then, ostensibly for her own good, gently gives a conventional reason to behave as the family desires while falsifying their feelings out of a convenient blindness:

> "You are sorry to leave Mamma, my dear little Fanny," said he, "which shows you to be a very good girl; but you must remember that you are with relations and friends, who all love you, and wish to make you happy."
>
> (15)

That this is no isolated response is clear when Austen provides a later parallel in the less forgivable advice he offers Fanny when she is fifteen and expected to move to the home of the newly widowed Mrs Norris. Fanny, "in distress", tells him of the shocking news: "Well, Fanny, and if the plan were not unpleasant to you, I should call it an excellent one" (25). In a lengthy series of justifications, Edmund shows he is as gullible as his father in thinking that his aunt will take Fanny on. Worse still, he is either capable of deceiving himself about his aunt's character and the benefits to Fanny from the scheme or of lying to his cousin, instead of attempting to protect her from the future she dreads. Some of his father's insensitivity to the depth of another's feelings must play a part, along with a convenient allegiance to the principle of filial respect that excuses him from considering the possibility of challenging a parental decision. Fanny's protests punctuate his advice, but by the end he brings her to concede:

> "I cannot see things as you do; but I ought to believe you to be right rather than myself, and I am very much obliged to you for trying to reconcile me to what must be."
>
> (27)

Austen draws a parallel here to Mrs Norris's flattering treatment of Edmund's father, but Fanny's response is in some ways more dangerous by reason of its differences. Its very sincerity, her belief she should trust to his view rather than her own endanger Edmund's ability to examine his motives critically. His "excellent nature" makes him more subtly vulnerable: a Mrs Norris, though capable of manipulating his father, could not overset his judgment of himself as Fanny can.

In both of these instances, Austen shows Edmund's habitual mode, even when uninfluenced by such special circumstances as the willed blindness induced by having fallen in love. But once he has met Mary, the moral weak spots in Edmund crack open to reveal, not merely a loss of sensitivity to Fanny's welfare and feelings, but a willingness to employ tactics strongly resembling his father's. Alone, unsupported, guilty, Fanny has withstood every pressure to accept Henry Crawford. Edmund, the only person who might sustain her, apprised of the situation by his father, responds manipulatively (and characteristically):

> "So far your conduct has been faultless, and they were quite mistaken who wished you to do otherwise. . . . But (with an affectionate smile), let him succeed at last, Fanny, let him succeed at last. . . ."

> " . . . . I wish he had known you as well as I do, Fanny. Between us, I think we should have won you. . . . I cannot suppose that you have not the *wish* to love him – the natural wish of gratitude. You

must have some feeling of that sort. You must be sorry for your own indifference."

(347, 348, emphasis original)

Hoping, as on previous occasions, for his support, she is thrown what looks like a lifeline, only to find herself pulled deeper into guilt and isolation. Austen's unusual interpolation of a stage direction in the form of his "affectionate smile", draws attention to the theatricality of his performance, the refusal to recognize Fanny's anguish and the artificial insistence on a warm, shared, understanding. Fanny's objections are swept away as they always have been, Edmund "scarcely hearing her to the end" (349). Austen shows that all that is new since their very first conversation is Edmund's unconscious incorporation into the argument of his own concerns about Mary Crawford. It may be too much to expect of Edmund that he recognize that Fanny loves him, but Austen suggests it isn't modesty that blinds him, but insensitivity. The dreadful blundering joviality of "Between us, I think we might have won you" in reference to Henry echoes his earlier heavy-handed account of the nature of his father's admiration, and offers a reminder of his father's blindness to others' feelings.

Austen marks the episode from its beginning to its end with signs of Edmund's treachery. He is clearly aware of the emotional satisfaction attached to the role of mentor and he attempts to use it to further Henry's cause:

> "a most fortunate man he is to attach himself to such a creature – to a woman, who firm as a rock in her own principles, has a gentleness of character so well adapted to recommend them. . . . I know he will make you happy; but you will make him every thing."
>
> "I would not engage in such a charge," cried Fanny in a shrinking accent, "in such an office of high responsibility!"
>
> "As usual believing yourself unequal to anything!"
>
> (351)

It is a well-honed routine, but one to which Fanny no longer responds to with conviction: "Fanny could with difficulty give the smile that was here asked for. Her feelings were all in revolt" (354); her smile, again scripted by Edmund, is as artificial as his had been. Austen signals that the betrayal is complete when Edmund, recognizing further talk is useless "led her directly with the kind authority of a privileged guardian into the house" (355). The identification of father and son is confirmed when they agree on the same tactics, Edmund subsequently showing no more interest in her welfare than his father, making contact only in so far as his need for a confidante arises.

But the resemblances between father and son as mentors also have some disconcerting echoes in their nature as lovers. In Mrs Norris's favour it should be noted that she had been psychologically correct in predicting that Fanny's position would prevent Tom or Edmund falling in love with his cousin. For Edmund, as Mrs Norris predicts, Fanny remains friend, cousin and, after his rejection of Mary, "My Fanny – my only sister – my only comfort now" (444); it is the un-sisterly and un-Fanny-like Mary Crawford with whom he falls in love:

> Active and fearless, and, though rather small, strongly made, she seemed formed for a horsewoman; and to the pure genuine pleasure of the exercise, something was probably added in Edmund's attendance and instructions.
>
> (66–7)

Mary's physical vitality and confidence, her conscious pleasure in her own sexual attractiveness, and a willingness to take the lead (it is she who suggests they "rise to a canter" although Edmund is nominally giving "instructions") make Edmund her very willing pupil (67).

Indeed, in this couple Austen initially presents a wholly engaging depiction of mutual sexual attraction. But she also shows Edmund to be son to Sir Thomas and Lady Bertram, and as such, shaped by their marriage. For this very reason, Mary's active self-assertion, so unlike his mother's manner, both attracts and frightens him. Son, too, of Mrs Norris, he struggles to dissociate Mary from a kind of "liveliness" he has learned to dislike: "there is . . . nothing sharp, or loud, or coarse. She is perfectly feminine, except in the instances we have been speaking of. *There* she cannot be justified." His frequent discussions with Fanny are designed to elicit a reassurance from her that he is right to judge Mary's "lively mind" to be "untinctured by ill humour or roughness" even before he knows her views on marriage or the clergy. But his uncertainty necessitates a pre-emption of criticism, "I am glad you saw it all as I did". As Austen begins the long process of testing the reader's judgment of Miss Crawford in all her complexity, she is careful to offer a reminder that Fanny is no unbiased observer. Even if jealousy played no part, she could not follow Edmund in "a line of admiration" powered by the magnetic force of sexual attraction (64, emphasis original).

Mary, despite her good qualities, is deeply flawed as a result of her upbringing by an unfaithful uncle and an unhappy aunt: unthinkingly

mercenary and cynical in her view of marriage and frighteningly willing to abet her brother's campaigns of emotional plunder. When she
speaks to Fanny of Henry's courtship, her willingness to do so in terms
of power – "your conquest", "your power over Henry" who "glories in
his chains" (360), and "the glory of fixing one who has been shot at by
so many; of having it in one's power to pay off the debts of one's sex"
(363) – reveals not only her acceptance of power as the basis of relations
of men and women, but also her low valuation of love, which to her is
worth only the most hackneyed of clichés. She is obsessed with attacking Edmund's chosen profession, in part for worldly reasons and in part
in reaction against the example of her brother-in-law. Yet, despite all
her defences, conscious and unconscious, she, like Fanny, is attracted to
Edmund by his virtues: "There was a charm, perhaps, in his sincerity,
his steadiness, his integrity, which Miss Crawford might be equal to
feel, though not equal to discuss with herself" (65).

If Edmund is to make headway as Mary's mentor as well as her lover,
it seems more likely that his conduct rather than his speech will con-
vert her. Austen neatly has him both enunciate and illustrate this point
as he defends the clergy:

> "The *manners* I speak of, might rather be called *conduct*, perhaps, the
> result of good principles; the effect, in short, of those doctrines
> which it is their duty to teach and recommend; and it will, I believe,
> be every where found, that as the clergy are, or are not what they
> ought to be, so are the rest of the nation."
> "Certainly," said Fanny with gentle earnestness.
> "There," cried Miss Crawford, "you have quite convinced Miss
> Price already."
>
> (93, emphasis original)

The carefully constructed pronouncements provoke flippancy from his
newest pupil and at their last meeting, when Mary lashes out defensively
under his rebuke: "A pretty good lecture upon my word. Was it part of
your last sermon?" (458), it is his propensity to preach and his choice of
the role of public mentor that she chooses to insult.

In the end, Edmund's conduct and character aren't sufficient to com-
bat the effects of Mary's preconceptions and the influence of her
upbringing and friends, although her wit and liveliness appeal as much
to the reader as to Edmund. Indeed, Austen herself seems to have realized the reader might have difficulty with, in the phrase of Samuel
Johnson, such a "mixed character" and, anxious to preclude confusion,

to have been guilty of putting her own finger unnecessarily on the scales when she has Mary write to Fanny of the possible advantages of Tom's death. Edmund's reactions to Mary in their final meeting are not just a simple victory of right over wrong. Something seems amiss when he repeats a charge he formerly denied in the early stages of his love when he had defended her as "feminine" against his own doubts of her propriety. Repelled by Mary's worldly attempts to hush matters up and designate the elopement "folly" he struggles to express his sense of her failings: "No reluctance, no horror, no feminine – shall I say? no modest loathings!" (454–5). For Edmund, the word "feminine" indicates a belief in a double standard, not only of speech but of moral judgment, although nothing else in Austen's work suggests that she herself believed standards of judgment should differ by gender. This must be Edmund's problem, one more inheritance from his father.

It is at his final meeting with Mary, or at least in his retrospective account of it to Fanny, that Edmund, so appealingly open to Mary's sexual attraction in the course of the novel, appears to revert under stress to something more resembling Sir Thomas's distrust:

> "I had gone a few steps, Fanny, when I heard the door open behind me. 'Mr. Bertram,' said she, with a smile – but it was a smile ill-suited to the conversation that had passed, a saucy playful smile, seeming to invite, in order to subdue me; at least, it appeared so to me. I resisted . . . ."
>
> (459)

As Anne Mellor notes, Mary is "finally depicted as little better than a prostitute, beckoning seductively from a doorway" (58). It's impossible to know whether Edmund's impressions correspond to Mary's intentions; he himself is unsure. More significant is the fact that he interprets the appeal as a sexual one, designed to override his moral judgment, to "invite" and "subdue". His disgust makes him particularly susceptible to the attractions of a docile, sisterly creation of his own who will not, like Mary, attempt to "subdue" him through sexual attraction: "Fanny's friendship was all that he had to cling to" (460). Austen, of course, is already setting us up for another world, the world of comedy in the last chapter in which, to the hero's surprise, he unexpectedly finds love where he least expects it, but this should not obscure her delineation of Edmund's revulsion from an apparent sexual appeal as an inheritance from his father.

No critic denies that either Sir Thomas or Edmund has his faults; the more usual response is to judge those faults as forgivable. Fanny, however, has frequently been seen (with admiration or horror) as being intended by Austen to be perfect.[2] Even the Bakhtinian Baldridge denies the novel the dialogic status it so richly deserves: "the static career of whose immaculate heroine stands at cross purposes with the formal requirements of the genre she inhabits" (62). It is a relief, therefore, to find critics resisting the pressure of the novel's closing to discuss Fanny as a complex human being. Roger Gard, for example, maintains that "Fanny's judgments (those that have a hint of the mean-minded or mealy-mouthed) and her excessive decorum, are typically responses to threats to her precariously held calm" (131–2). John Wiltshire argues that "Jane Austen's representation of Fanny's psychology is so full and intricate that it causes conflict within the novel's ethical, and ultimately conventional, structure" (108), a statement that can equally well be applied to Austen's representation of its mentor-lover relationships. The outward manifestations of Fanny's insecurity have, through time, appealed or repelled depending on both the individual and cultural predilections of the reader. But Austen explores more complex issues: whether, with Fanny's particular combination of inter-related weaknesses and strengths, she can live an independent moral life, whether her relationship with Edmund is advantageous to both, and whether she will share Edmund's ambivalent attitude to sex.

Though the detrimental effects of Fanny's admiration on her mentor are clear, his care for her seems, initially at least, to be wholly beneficial. But, just as the consequences of her grateful devotion enable Edmund to avoid judging himself by calling on her approval, so the relationship has risks for Fanny, for whom his love and his mentorship have always been linked. It isn't surprising, then, to find a seventeen-year-old Fanny hastening to agree with Edmund that Miss Crawford is "very indecorous"(63), both out of a desire to demonstrate she has learned her lessons in propriety as well as out of inklings of rivalry. Nor is it unexpected that she should learn with pain that her role is not to agree with his criticisms but to refute them.

But, as a consequence of Fanny's demure demeanour, what is easier to miss (at least on the evidence of most critical readings) is how quickly after the Crawfords' arrival, Fanny's love for Edmund develops a sexual element. Tony Tanner, for example, considers that the closing of the novel demonstrates Austen's "purposeful – deliberate – intentions to abstain from the whole realm of sexual feelings" (173). Roger Gard believes that Fanny is "neither saintly nor sexy" although, as he points out, some find saintliness erotic (130), a position supported by Hannah More's recommendation in *Coelebs* that modesty is sexually exciting (I:89). But although Sir Thomas and Henry Crawford (undoubtedly both supporters of the conduct-book ethos) are reassured and excited by what they see as a contrast between her unfeigned modesty and her sexual development, Austen goes further than this, showing that Fanny, though unaware others might find her sexually attractive until Edmund teases her about his father, is certainly conscious of her own sexuality. The situation is complicated by Fanny's status. Mrs Norris's belief that the cousins, having been brought up as "brothers and sisters" (6) will not fall in love, while true of Edmund, has been nullified for Fanny by her sense of herself as an outsider, ironically perpetuated by Mrs Norris herself (the issue of whether such love is incestuous is best considered later in this chapter).

Austen's willingness to allow Fanny a sexual life is further impressive testimony to an authorial interest that most critics have denied or ignored. On the second day of Mary's riding lessons, the waiting Fanny is forgotten, and she walks to where she can see the cheerful group admiring the riding of the physically intrepid Mary:

> [Fanny] could not turn her eyes from the meadow, she could not help watching all that passed. . . . Edmund was close to [Mary], he was speaking to her, he was evidently directing her management of the bridle, he had hold of her hand; she saw it, or the imagination supplied what the eye could not reach.
>
> (67)

As she watches, Fanny passes from child to sexually aware woman, from sulkiness to jealousy. That she is capable not just of seeing, not even just of imagining, but of recognizing the possibility she is imagining, that Edmund "had hold of [Mary's] hand" marks her sexual awareness though she is quick to attempt to deny significance to what she sees:

> She must not wonder at all this; what could be more natural than that Edmund should be making himself useful, and proving his good-nature by any one?
>
> (67)

But the statement is concluded with a question mark; Edmund's interest, though "natural", is not simple "good nature", and Miss Crawford is not "anyone", as Fanny now very well knows. There really is no possibility for Fanny to retreat back to childhood from this moment.

And, indeed, the atmosphere of Mansfield, liberated from the oppression of Sir Thomas's presence, is permeated with sexuality released and encouraged by the arrival of the Crawfords, and given expression through the decision to enact *Lovers' Vows*. Mary, much against her will, is unable to maintain the sexual and emotional detachment that has hitherto protected her from more than a mercenary interest in men, while Henry's skilful playing of one sister against the other flourishes on his indifference and their self-centred inability to resist his manipulations. That a good deal of both Edmund's hostility and attraction to the play can be seen in terms of hostility and attraction to the atmosphere of sexual excitement it promotes is clear. But what Austen also suggests is that Fanny's contribution to their shared but faltering resistance is driven by the same mixed motives as her mentor's. This isn't, of course, what Fanny admits to herself: "For her own gratification she could have wished that something might be acted, for she had never seen even half a play, but every thing of higher consequence was against it" (131). But she is alert, with the empathy of a fellow-sufferer "connected only by [her] consciousness" (163) to Julia's "agitations of *jealousy*" (136, emphasis original), while her astonishment at the choice of play when she reads it can only be exacerbated by the recognition that her predicament would be even more "improper for home representation" (137) than that of the play's heroine, Amelia. Like the character, she is in love with her mentor but without Amelia's belief that the emotion is reciprocated or her superior social standing. But it is the expression of love rather than the feelings themselves that Fanny consciously repudiates: "the language of [Amelia], so unfit to be expressed by any woman of modesty" (137).

Austen doesn't simplify Fanny's reaction to acting to virtuous or priggish distaste, instead revealing the mixture of moral qualms, disappointment, jealousy and self-pity she feels when Edmund "consults" her about his taking a role:

> Her heart and her judgment were equally against Edmund's decision; she could not acquit his unsteadiness; and his happiness under it made her wretched. She was full of jealousy and agitation. Miss Crawford came with looks of gaiety which seemed an insult. . . . She alone was sad and insignificant;
>
> (159)

But Austen goes further, offering a much more ambiguous account of Fanny's "innocent" reaction to the highly charged rehearsals, once they begin, when she, unlike Julia, becomes involved in them:

> Fanny believed herself to derive as much innocent enjoyment from the play as any of them; – Henry Crawford acted well, and it was a pleasure to *her* to creep into the theatre, and attend the rehearsal of the first act – in spite of the feelings it excited in some speeches for Maria. – Maria she also thought acted well – too well; – and after the first rehearsal or two, Fanny began to be their only audience, and – sometimes as a prompter, sometimes as spectator – was often very useful. – As far as she could judge, Mr. Crawford was considerably the best actor of all
>
> (165, emphasis original).

From the retrospective position of Henry's reading of *Henry the Eighth*, Fanny's fascination with the rehearsals is passed off (by Fanny or the narrative voice) as a simple attraction to the theatre:

> His acting had first taught Fanny what pleasure a play might give, and his reading brought all his acting before her again; nay, perhaps with greater enjoyment, for it came unexpectedly, and with no such drawback as she had been used to suffer in seeing him on the stage with Miss Bertram.
>
> (337)

But "drawback" seems a mild term in view of the fact that even the sophisticated Mary finds the performance of Maria and Henry ("one of the times when they were trying *not* to embrace") so blatantly erotic that she feels she must protect her brother from even the imperceptive Rushworth's growing suspicions by pretending to admire the "*maternal*" in Maria's performance (169, emphases original). Justified by being "useful", "Fanny believed herself to derive as much innocent enjoyment from the play as any of them", but, in the ferment of strong sexual and emotional excitement that the play engenders, the comparison says nothing more of Fanny's innocence than that the others are far from innocent and she wishes to deceive herself, a self-deception that strongly resembles that of her mentor Edmund. Her discernment of the situation is too sharp for an innocent, but she cannot keep away, drawn to the overtly sexual spectacle.

The climax comes with the arrival (tellingly in Fanny's domain-by-default, the schoolroom) of Mary asking that Fanny read Edmund's part so that Mary can practise Amelia's speeches of love to her stage (and would-be real) mentor-lover, then of Edmund himself with the mirror image of this request. The convergence of real and theatrical roles are painfully appropriate punishment for Fanny's having been tempted into the role of voyeur in the scenes between Maria and Henry. It is a scene in which Austen makes every detail count. Mary's assumption that Fanny can have no sexual interest in Edmund, "But then he is your cousin, which makes all the difference" and her conflation of the two: "You must rehearse it with me, that I may fancy *you* in him, and get on by degrees, You *have* the look of *his* sometimes" (168–9, emphases original) puts Fanny in the discomfiting position of taking the role of the mentor who has moulded her in his likeness, as well as reminding her of her questionable position in loving a cousin. Her awareness is reinforced by Edmund's arrival and his delight in being able to alter his plan from rehearsing with Fanny to using her as prompt for his acting as mentor with Mary, doubly ironic in view of his final return to Fanny. Even Mary's conversion of the schoolroom chairs, "not made for the theatre" but "more fitted for little girls", into furniture supporting declarations of theatrical love and real sexual interest serves as a reminder of the discontinuity between the maturity of Fanny's emotions and the family's consignment of her to the limbo of the ex-schoolroom and being neither "in" nor "out" (48–9). Only a renewed request that she take a role in the play forces her to articulate the strength of the unsuspected power that drew her to the rehearsals, while leaving her unable, or unwilling, to admit to herself the strength of the compulsion: "She was properly punished" (172).

Though Sir Thomas's return provides a brief respite for Fanny, it is followed by the much greater ordeal of being subjected to pressure from all those who claim to know best on Fanny's behalf, to accept an unwelcome suitor. That Austen intended to point a parallel between Sir Thomas the slave-owner and his desire to "sell" Fanny to the highest bidder has become part of the critical argument deriving from the Antiguan visit (Sutherland xxiii–xxv) and Brian Southam provides details of Austen's personal connections with Antiguan estates that make it difficult to argue that Austen was not aware of the implications of choosing such a destination ("Silence" 493–8).

More hotly disputed is the significance of the visit as an indicator of Austen's own assumptions. We never learn Sir Thomas's attitude to the slave *trade* as such, as his reply to Fanny is not reported (the family's "dead silence" and Fanny's diffidence cause the subject to be dropped, 197–8) although, given the date, he is certainly a slave *owner*, and, as

Southam suggests, perhaps his uncharacteristic failure to pursue the conversation denotes his embarrassment. But is Austen on Sir Thomas's side? Edward Said believes she is (*Culture* 80–97), but his reading of the novel in the tradition of Trilling's "Great Good Place" ("*Mansfield Park*" 169), as if Mansfield Park and its owner (and therefore the wealth from the West Indian plantation) are endorsed by Austen, is an oversimplification dependent on giving the closing chapter more weight than the remainder of the novel.[3] On the other hand, sweeping statements of any kind concerning Austen's intentions to condemn slavery and suggest Fanny herself is enslaved seem out of place here. The actions of the navy to which Austen's admired brothers belonged, and into which Anne Elliot so joyfully married, contributed to defence of colonies that had long depended on slavery. And while Austen's references to Sir Thomas's source of wealth implicitly criticize his assumption of a right and duty to think for others, including finding his children homes with a wealthy "bidder", it is too crude a formulation to equate Fanny directly with Sir Thomas's enslaved workers. The echoes from those distant plantations, however, may be heard (though perhaps with more resonance by readers today) in Fanny's recognition that her duty as a dependent is to obey her uncle, and they provide an appropriate backdrop to her inner conflict. As Maaja Stewart points out, the "real issue in the drawing room [is] Fanny's wish to please Sir Thomas" (122). Her resistance to him over Henry's proposal is therefore all the more impressive.

Henry's first urge to make "a small hole in Fanny Price's heart" is initiated by his response (resembling that of Sir Thomas) to "the wonderful improvement" in her looks (229), strengthened by an egotistical desire to overcome her manifest dislike of him (230). It is at this point, with evident intent, that Austen suggests the resemblance between sexual and sibling love, bringing Fanny and William together in a relationship which, were it not identified by the context as fraternal, would surely be difficult for a reader to distinguish from the sexual. Often considered a creator of cool love scenes, Austen ensures that this reunion is all warmth, lit by "the glow of Fanny's cheek, the brightness of her eye. . . ." It is a scene in which Austen explores the complex effects on the watching Henry Crawford, who has "moral taste enough to value" her obvious capacity for "feeling, genuine feeling" while her physical attractions pique his desire to "excite the first ardours of her young, unsophisticated mind" (235).

Austen must know what she is doing here, deliberately evoking a watcher's sexual response to the intensity of this sibling love, a step particularly daring because the narrative voice has just been praising the "fraternal" over the "conjugal tie":

> Fanny had never known so much felicity in her life, as in this unchecked, equal, fearless intercourse with the brother and friend . . . with whom . . . all the evil and good of their earliest years could be gone over again, and every former united pain and pleasure retraced with the fondest recollection. An advantage this, a strengthener of love, in which even the conjugal tie is beneath the fraternal. Children of the same family, the same blood, with the same first associations and habits have some means of enjoyment in their power, which no subsequent connections can supply.
>
> (234–5)

Of course, it is notoriously difficult in an Austen novel to find the exact point at which the narrative voice or the character's thoughts take or give up control, but it seems to me that "An advantage this . . ." has too generalizing a tone to be Fanny's, the question being, rather, whether the narrative voice is endorsed by Austen, which can best be decided by the course of the work as a whole.

This is a part of the novel that has provoked a variety of responses. In a detailed reading, attentive to the complexities of a very knotty passage (one that he finds "profoundly unsettling") Brian Crick suggests that it might be paraphrased as "can the estrangement between a brother and sister who have been especially fond of one another ever be justified by marrying someone from outside the family circle?" (81), tracing the implications of this passage for the relative valuing of familial and marital love through the work to the novel's close, where "the tell-tale signs of irresolution" (104–5) mark Austen's treatment of Fanny's marriage to her surrogate brother. Glenda Hudson, however, has no qualms at all about the appropriateness of "fraternal love" as the basis for marriage, believing Austen intends us to see Mansfield Park as preserved and revivified, concluding that "the incestuous marriage of Fanny and Edmund is healing and curative. . . . a retreat to family life is appropriate and necessary to solidify moral standards" ("Consolidated Communities" 109).

With a view that is radically different from Hudson's, Claudia Johnson discerns in the work Austen's creation of a pattern of incestuous eroticism displayed in references throughout the work, not only in Fanny's interest in William (easily transferred to Edmund) but also the comments of both Sir Thomas and Fanny's own father, the latter making his daughter the "object of a coarse joke" (*MP* 389). Johnson links fraternal and cousinly affection to the erotic interest shown by these father figures, maintaining that Austen builds up "a sustained body of detail that invites us to reconsider conservative political arguments which idealize familial love" (Johnson, *Jane Austen* 117–18).

However, though there are, as I have argued, striking parallels between Edmund and his father, there are also significant differences. To treat the two as one, and then to conflate both with William on one hand and Mr Price on the other neglects Austen's carefully drawn distinctions – we surely do not feel the same distaste for William and Fanny's love that we feel for Mr Price's joke nor Sir Thomas's stiffer admiration. Nor does a wholesale attack on familial love explain the troubling endorsement of the cousins' marriage at the close of the work. I also find it difficult to read the passage on the "conjugal" and "fraternal" ties as ironic to the discredit of the fraternal. It seems to me that Austen does indeed find Fanny's love for William attractive and does rate "fraternal" love so highly that she wishes to bestow its attributes on the "conjugal", in so doing recognizing the element of the sexual that is a component of such a strong emotion.

There are a number of responses the reader may make to this messy problem. It would be easy to simply dismiss this sibling love as "incestuous" and thus automatically objectionable (subsequently either condemning Austen for endorsing it or arguing, as Johnson does, that Austen herself condemns it). But as Sybil Wolfram has demonstrated in her study of kinship, the definitions of incest and arguments usually advanced against it vary from one society to another and each argument can in turn be shown to be illogical (137–96).[4] She points out that the most common popular objection is that the offspring are likely to be defective, a view she counters by arguing from genetics that "inbreeding intensifies characteristics, but good as well as bad" (145). As a justification of Fanny's marriage to Edmund, however, this may prove no defence at all if the intensified characteristics (symbolic rather than genetic) are indeed "bad" and the relationship is based on a retreat from maturity.

The problem of "fraternal" love adds to the reader's difficulty in assessing the intricately linked causes of Fanny's resistance to Henry Crawford and the pressures brought to bear on her by Sir Thomas and Edmund, revealing just how complicated, difficult, and sometimes fortuitous Austen perceives human choice to be. Fanny, with great difficulty given her desperate need to please, withstands the accusations of ingratitude and selfishness, and the implicit threats to deprive her of all she cares about. She asserts by her resistance that her judgment is superior to that of Sir Thomas who has permitted his daughter to marry Rushworth and to that of Edmund who, in his pursuit of Mary, has compromised his principles. That the same principles have proved ineffectual to guide the other young people suggests that it is Fanny's exclusion from Mrs Norris's indulgence that has helped to safeguard her, but the matter is not entirely straightforward, for Fanny's greatest protection has been her hidden love for Edmund, and her high valuation of mutual love. Moral integrity and love together give Fanny strength to overcome her weaknesses, but Austen makes no claim here that the connection between passion and judgment is anything but coincidental, for, while love gives Fanny strength because it supports her principles, it weakens Edmund because it runs counter to his.

When Fanny is recalled to Mansfield Park from Portsmouth, her moods swing violently: initially considering "the greatest blessing to every one of kindred with Mrs. Rushworth would be instant annihilation" (442), she subsequently feels "in the greatest danger of being exquisitely happy, while so many were miserable" (443). Edmund's arrival at Portsmouth and his "violent emotions", "brought back all her own first feelings" (445, 444) – but soon she feels "enjoyment" in seeing the beauties of the Mansfield grounds, followed by "melancholy again" (447). Such mixed and fleeting reactions are both natural and understandable, but, when Edmund comes to unburden himself, declaring he "would infinitely prefer any increase of the pain of parting, for the sake of carrying with me the right of tenderness and esteem" (458), Fanny's resolve hardens. Edmund's self-centred reiteration of his miseries is certainly irritating (and Mary's revelations to Fanny outrageous, if unconvincingly out of character), but what follows is a ruthlessness worthy of Mrs Norris:

> Fanny . . . felt more than justified in adding to his knowledge of [Mary's] real character. . . . He submitted to believe, that Tom's illness had influenced her; only reserving for himself this consoling thought, that considering the many counteractions of opposing habits, she had certainly been *more* attached to him than could have been expected, and for his sake had been more near doing right. Fanny thought exactly the same; and they were also quite agreed in their opinion of the lasting effect, the indelible impression, which such a disappointment must make on his mind. . . . and as to his ever meeting with any other woman who could – it was too impossible to be named but with indignation. Fanny's friendship was all that he had to cling to.
>
> (459–60)

The nature of Fanny's triumph is dubious, her actions suggesting not only a decision to cause pain in order to speed up the cure, but, much worse, also a smug conviction of rightness: "more than justified". Her actions here present a contrast to her earlier refusal to use her knowledge of Henry's behaviour with Maria to discredit him and release herself from Sir Thomas's pressure. Fanny, whose changing language has charted her course from the alternations of the "girlish" and "bookish" to the maturity of Portsmouth, as Kenneth Moler demonstrates (172–9), now regresses to the dangerous role of admirer though now sustained by hypocritical reassurances: "Fanny thought exactly the same, and they were also quite agreed in their opinion". But there is a difference: that "they were quite agreed" becomes "he submitted to believe" and their relationship completes the shift into what it had always had the potential to be: a vehicle for ruthless management methods resembling, though more subtle than, those of Mrs Norris. To say that Mrs Norris and Sir Thomas are finally united in Fanny and Edmund is too crude a formulation to take into account what remains genuinely admirable in the cousins, but enough elements of that earlier "marriage" are present to cause disquiet.

Edmund of the "strong good sense"(21) now appears as the foolish male, a victim of wounded vanity whose self-centred conviction that he will be forever tragically inconsolable will soon be disproved by his recognition that Fanny is "only too good for him" (471). His love and current disillusionment are belittled by the language of this account: "not an agreeable intimation", "it would have been a vast deal pleasanter" (459). The closing paragraph of the penultimate chapter thus provides a transition into the determinedly comic resolution of the last, a chapter denying two conclusions Austen has already demonstrated: that the world is a great deal too complex to be divided into those "not greatly in fault themselves" and "the rest" (461), and that, while the division between mentor and lover is destructive, the coming together of the two roles may be as dangerous in its own way if it involves the mutual reinforcement, rather than the questioning, of the lover's worst qualities.

The difficulty of judging Austen's relationship to the events and to the narrative voice in the final chapter is considerable, partly because the tone, even within the chapter, is uneven, patches of flippancy alternating with passages that are unmistakably serious and appropriate to the tone of the novel as a whole. In fact it seems that Austen, very late in the game, has set herself, unsuccessfully, to satisfy the same apparently conflicting purposes that gave the young people such difficulty when they chose *Lovers' Vows* – to combine both "tragedy and comedy" (130). On the one hand, the narrative voice in the final chapter imitates the "rhyming butler" of the play, comically simplifying the moral complexity of the novel in the same terms : "And if his purpose was not fair, / It probably was base" (*LV* in *MP* 518) with cursory claims to have cleansed the infection, the neat classification of the characters into "fair" sheep and "base" goats, and the perfunctory distribution of the appropriate rewards and punishments. On the other hand, despite the narrative voice's disavowal, there is a good deal of "guilt and misery" (461) in the last chapter that is indeed consonant with what has gone before, although even here the treatment is inconsistent. Tom and Julia are dismissed with conventional tokens of penitence that suggest complete lack of interest on Austen's part, while the accounts of the fates of Mary and Henry Crawford and of Maria and Mrs Norris, though summary, are nevertheless appropriate to the tragic tenor of the work as a whole.

But it is on behalf of the remainder that falsification and special pleading occur. Sir Thomas becomes "poor Sir Thomas"(461), recognizes his past inadequacies as a parent, and is freed from the "hourly evil" of Mrs Norris, who, in an echo of her wifely status, had "seemed a part of himself, that must be borne for ever" (465–6) but is now dismissed as if divorced, ostracized in the company of "their" cast-off daughter. The serious analysis of his failures mixes oddly with the ease with which he is permitted to recognize and repudiate them (along with the adulterous daughter of his own creating). The convincing relapse into cynicism of Mr Bennet after the flurry of Lydia's elopement has no counterpart in consistency here. Furthermore, Sir Thomas's treatment of Fanny is dishonestly trivialized: "He might have made her childhood happier; but it had been an error of judgment *only* which had given him the *appearance* of harshness" (472, emphases mine). The narrative voice allows good intentions to excuse the errors that have led directly to Maria's downfall and a great deal of misery besides: his "liberality had a rich repayment" in the form of both a replacement daughter and a substitute niece (472). But even those good intentions are carelessly recast in a way not supported by the prior text: "He saw how ill he had judged, in expecting to counteract what was wrong in Mrs. Norris, by its reverse in himself" (463), a false claim of deliberate policy indirectly contradicted soon after: "His opinion of [Mrs. Norris] had been sinking from the day of his return from Antigua" (465), by which time, as Austen had demonstrated, his children's characters had been long formed.

Like "poor" Sir Thomas, Fanny is also taken under protection of the narrative voice of the final chapter, as "My Fanny", before the difficult business of describing her equivocal state is glossed over: "sorrow so founded on satisfaction, so tending to ease, and so much in harmony with every dearest sensation, that there are few who might not have been glad to exchange their greatest gaiety for it" (461). Her state is presented not only as emotionally understandable but also as morally unproblematic.

But the final betrayal of Austen's prior revelation of the dangers of Edmund's relationship to Fanny as mentor-lover comes in the nonchalant justification of their marriage:

> With such a regard for her, indeed, as his had long been, a regard founded on the most endearing claims of innocence and helplessness, and completed by every recommendation of growing worth, what could be more natural than the change? Loving, guiding, protecting her, as he had been doing ever since her being ten years old, her mind in so great a degree formed by his care, and her comfort depending on his kindness, an object to him of such close and peculiar interest, dearer by all his own importance with her than any one else at Mansfield. . . .
>
> . . . there was nothing on the side of prudence to stop him or make his progress slow; no doubts of her deserving, no fears from opposition of taste, no need of drawing new hopes of happiness from dissimilarity of temper.
>
> (470, 471)

If Pygmalion does not marry his own creation, the narrative voice implies, his only other choice is a woman with alien and dangerous values. Moreover, the nature of Edmund's "change" towards Fanny is not specified as a change from familial to sexual love but is blurred by the use of the more general "care": "Edmund did cease to care about Miss Crawford, and became as anxious to marry Fanny, as Fanny herself could desire", while flippancy discourages serious reflection on the reader's part: "I purposely abstain from dates on this occasion. . . ." (470). This is a cosy union of mutual admiration all the more distressing because it presents as desirable those aspects of the relationship that Austen has clearly revealed in Edmund's father's situation, as in his own, to be morally and emotionally dangerous. Julia Prewitt Brown goes further, arguing that "At the close of *Mansfield Park*, Fanny is as much married in mind to her surrogate father Sir Thomas as she is in fact to her substitute brother Edmund. . . . Anticipating Freud, Austen implies that for the woman, the classic sex partners are father and daughter"(*Jane Austen's Novels* 99), but striking as this statement is, I think it over-schematizes the more complex pattern of resemblances and differences for which I have argued.

Although to trust the tale but not the teller in regard to *Mansfield Park* is, in most areas, to free the body of the work from the narrative voice of the final chapter, some problems in that chapter stem not so much from the betrayal of earlier insights, but from the culmination of contradictions already established. Fanny completes her transmutation to sister–mother, making up for the emotional and moral deprivations of Edmund's childhood and Edmund becomes her brother–child, a replacement for William and her Portsmouth siblings. The confusion over "fraternal" and "conjugal" love, earlier highlighted by the unironic treatment of Fanny's relationship to William, is thus perpetuated. The potential of "incest" to intensify characteristics, "good as well as bad" here works against the couple, intensifying the worst. Unfortunately, the pressure to bring fraternal and conjugal love together results in the undercutting of the central insight of the work, that to marry your own admiring creation is a terrible moral risk for both of you. And yet, denial of this recognition is what the last chapter demands.

But there is yet another problem that cannot be blamed on the closing chapter. From the beginning Austen has shown what is wrong with the particular situation of Edmund and Fanny and suggested the temptations to which the mentor-lover is in general prone; however, by exploring the dangers of dividing lover from mentor she has set up a logical structure that presses towards uniting the two in one person. As a result, Edmund in the last chapter is so clearly less mature than Fanny that Austen's determination to achieve moral equality for her couples as a prerequisite for marriage, central to her work (although, as noted, not achieved in *Sense and Sensibility*), is undermined. Regrettably, as Julia Prewitt Brown argues, part of Edmund Bertram is annihilated when he marries Fanny ("Civilization" 95).

Although a familiar problem from *Emma* and to a lesser extent from the other novels discussed, the question as to how to explain the flippancy that characterizes parts of the closing chapter[5] cannot be evaded in the predominantly serious *Mansfield Park*. Is it the consequence of Austen's loss of interest once the traditional closure of the marriage plot has been reached? Is it a test of the sentimental reader, with covert warnings about life's uncertainty? Is it a general recognition that the complex questions raised in the novel are not subject to any form of conclusion, and that, therefore, a happy ending is no more true or false than any other? Is it an unsuccessful attempt to yoke a tragedy with a comic finale to placate her readers? As such it would be consistent with the would-be actors' motive in choosing *Lovers' Vows*: "There were . . . so many people to be pleased" (130).

The truth probably consists of some combination of all of the above. As mentor, Austen declines to pose true/false questions, and while this refusal has much to recommend it as a pedagogical device, it brings with it the ancillary "benefit" of blurring her own uncertainties and difficulties. What is clear, however, is that in her relationship to her readers in all but the last chapter of *Mansfield Park*, Austen is less interested in pleasing them than in any other of her novels and even less willing to lead them to the recognition of a definitive ideal, a change that helps to account for the acute discomfort many feel with the work of a writer they expect to be both charming and assured. It is much harder to love the author of *Mansfield Park* than of *Pride and Prejudice* or *Persuasion*, and in this novel Austen relinquishes flirtation to Mary Crawford.

Though the complexities of *Mansfield Park* challenge any too-simple formulation, Austen's treatment of the mentor-lover in her works as a whole suggests that she is principally interested in the mentor-lover relationship as it contributes to, or works against, what she sees as an ideal end: a marriage founded on both moral equality and mutual sexual love, on both judgment and passion. This is true both when passion is ultimately feared or denigrated as it is, for example, in Abelard's presentation of it – attitudes Austen clearly condemns in Sir Thomas, Edmund, or Mr Bennet – and also when a character such as Fanny is tempted to adopt Héloïse's self-denying devotion. Austen's attitude remains steady whether the mentor-lover relationship is marginal as in *Northanger Abbey* and *Sense and Sensibility*, (supposedly) mutual as in *Pride and Prejudice*, perilous as in *Mansfield Park*, or something to be outgrown as in *Emma*. This is an ideal she never abandons, despite her partial recognition that judgment and passion, though not automatically opposed, are also not amenable to being neatly integrated with or balanced against each other, and despite the unsolved difficulties arising from the conflict of this insight with the comic endings of the various novels.

In fact, it is Mr Bennet, speaking out of his recognition of the ideals he has betrayed, who reveals just this problem as he seeks to counsel Elizabeth after Darcy requests her hand for a second time:

> I know that you could be neither happy nor respectable, unless you truly esteemed your husband; unless you looked up to him as a superior. Your lively talents would place you in the greatest danger in an unequal marriage. You could scarcely escape discredit and misery. My child, let me not have the grief of seeing *you* unable to respect your partner in life.
>
> (376, emphasis original)

While there is no difficulty in prefacing either "respect" and "esteem" with a word such as mutual, the difficulty lies in reconciling a desire both to "look up" to a "superior" and to repudiate an "unequal marriage". We applaud Mr Bennet's words without examining too closely their inherent contradiction. That Austen reaches for the goal of mutual love combined with moral equality, however impossible to perfect in life as in art, is what makes her view of the responsibilities and rewards of marriage so attractive; that her closings claim success in the endeavour remains problematic.

In 1814, soon after she had begun *Emma*, Austen wrote to Cassandra, "Do not be angry with me for beginning another letter to you. I have read the Corsair, mended my petticoat, & have nothing else to do" (*Letters* 257: 5 March 1814). Less than three years later, in "Sanditon", Austen began a caricature of a would-be-Byron, Sir Edward Denham, whose account of his favourite reading materials marked him as one whose ideals were totally antipathetic to hers:

> The Novels which I approve . . . are such as exhibit the progress of strong Passion from the first Germ of incipient Susceptibility to the utmost Energies of Reason half-dethroned, – where we see the strong spark of Woman's Captivations elicit such Fire in the Soul of Man as leads him – (though at the risk of some Aberration from the strict line of Primitive Obligations) – to hazard all, dare all, atcheive all, to obtain her. . . . and even when the Event is mainly anti-prosperous to the high-toned Machinations of the prime Character, the potent, pervading Hero of the Story, it leaves us full of Generous Emotions for him; – our Hearts are paralized – . . . .
>
> (*Minor Works* 403–4, punctuation and spelling as shown)

A little over thirty years later, Charlotte Brontë would write of Jane Austen, in language almost as fevered as Sir Edward's, and with only slightly less reliance on capital letters:

> The Passions are perfectly unknown to her; she rejects even a speaking acquaintance with that stormy Sisterhood; even to the Feelings she vouchsafes no more than an occasional graceful but distant recognition; too frequent converse with them would ruffle the smooth elegance of her progress. Her business is not half so much with the human heart as with the human eyes mouth hands and feet; what sees keenly, speaks aptly, moves flexibly, it suits her to study, but what throbs fast and full, though hidden, what the blood rushes through, what is the unseen seat of Life and the sentient target of death – this Miss Austen ignores; she no more, with her mind's eye, beholds the heart of her race than each man, with bodily vision sees the heart in his heaving breast.
>
> (Southam, *CH* 1:128)

But there was another link between the two authors besides Brontë's repugnance for what she perceived to be Austen's ignorance of "The Passions". Sir Edward Denham's future was secured by an irony of fate: he was to be reincarnated repeatedly in Brontë's juvenilia, and, as "the potent, pervading Hero of the Story", would reappear in the person of another Edward – Edward Rochester. As if looking forward in time, Austen, in whose works mentorship was a relationship best left behind in the growth to mutual maturity, provided a criticism of Brontë sharper than any Brontë would make of her. The worlds Brontë created had more in common with the schoolroom of Abelard than Austen's "elegant but confined houses" (Brontë in Southam I:126), schoolrooms where teaching and learning were erotic activities likely to lead to "Aberration from the strict line of Primitive Obligations", where judgment and passion were opposed, and passion was a cause of elation and fear because it threatened annihilation rather than mutual completion.

3

"Slave of a Fixed and Dominant Idea": Charlotte Brontë's Early Writings – Preliminaries or Precursors?

It was Charlotte Brontë who, more than Austen or Eliot, felt the "charm" of recreating a charismatic Abelard within a schoolroom setting. In two novels, the first and last she wrote for publication, the lover–teacher relationship is central, in another the heroine marries her tutor at the conclusion of the work, and in yet another the governess-heroine narrowly escapes marriage to her cousin-instructor but marries her "Master". Variations on the same relationship also occur in her juvenilia, while her pain-filled love letters to the teacher in her own life were rescued from the wastebasket by his wife and pieced together to be scrutinized by posterity.

It is this apparently close relationship between Brontë's early writings (including her correspondence) and the novels published in her lifetime that raises questions about their similarities. Are the resemblances between her immature efforts and her later works central, as Fannie Ratchford approvingly claims ("they show her genius . . . was full-grown and self-conscious in all its fire and passion before she set foot on the continent", xiv)? Or were the early features eventually outgrown, as Christine Alexander, equally approvingly believes ("it was only grudgingly and over a period of years, that childhood romance gave way to the balanced perception of reality that marks her mature work", 246)? The purpose of this chapter is to examine the characteristics of the early works, reserving until the next chapter judgment as to whether a regrettable element of immaturity persists in the later material or is transmuted into insights of a different calibre.

Brontë's works have always aroused strong responses. Immediate praise from her contemporaries was quickly followed by complaints of coarseness, although *Jane Eyre* has always remained popular with a substantial number of novel-readers in the general public. Works such as Sandra Gilbert's and Susan Gubar's *The Madwoman in the Attic* have both insisted on her importance and brought academic and popular readers closer together, in particular by their emphasis on Brontë's assumption that power is the key issue in sexual relationships including marriage. If Brontë's writings do indeed link love with power, then readers must decide whether she is right in judging the connection to be inescapable and also whether they are willing to live with the consequences of that belief.

Brontë began writing in childhood, producing, with her siblings, an astonishing quantity of material. Set in the imaginary world of Angria, several of the stories she set down in her early twenties show her interest in the lover as mentor. Among these, "Passing Events", "Mina Laury", "Henry Hastings" and "Caroline Vernon" were written between 1836 and 1839 during her vacations from teaching at Roe Head School and in the months following her release from that hated position before she went to Brussels (Alexander 256). In these early writings, power is undeniably the force that shapes the nature of love and through Mina Laury, Brontë explores the emotions of a woman consumed by passion for the already-married Zamorna, the Byronic ruler of Angria, accepting treatment that Jane Eyre would later resist:

> She took it as a slave ought to take the caress of a Sultan, & obeying the gentle effort of his hand, slowly sunk on to the sofa by her master's side. . . .
>
> ("Passing Events", *Five* 46)[1]

and being rewarded by his response:

> I give you such true and fond love as a master may give to the fairest and loveliest vassal that ever was bound to him in feudal allegiance.
>
> ("Passing Events", *Five* 48)

It is apparent that Brontë is both attracted to Mina's submission and also desires to stress its paradoxical magnitude, an ambivalence that will be detectable in later works.

I have never in my life contradicted Zamorna – never delayed obedience to his commands – I could not! he was sometimes more to me than a human being – he superseded all things – all affections, all interests, all fears or hopes or principles –

("Mina Laury", *Five* 147)

Strong-minded beyond her sex – active, energetic & accomplished in all other points of view – here she was a weak as a child – she lost her identity – her very way of life was swallowed up in that of another –

("Mina Laury", *Five* 165)

One of Brontë's last Angrian stories, "Caroline Vernon", features an adolescent heroine, Zamorna's ward, whose rebelliousness and naivety combine to reduce her to a situation similar to Mina Laury's – when the heroine places herself in Zamorna's power, he announces: "If I were a bearded Turk, Caroline, I would take you to my harem" (*Five* 353) – and take her he does. The prose is purple but the narrative tone is determinedly ironic, an uneasy mixture which fails to conceal the erotic charge that mastery holds for young Charlotte Brontë, with its most striking component the loss of identity in that of another:

she has a mentor who, not satisfied with instilling into her mind the precepts of wisdom by words, will, if not prevented by others, do his best to enforce his verbal admonitions by practical illustrations that will dissipate the mists on her vision at once and show her, in a light both gross and burning, the mysteries of humanity now hidden, its passions and sins and sufferings, all its passage of strange error, all its afterscenes of agonized atonement. A skillful Preceptor is that same one, accustomed to tuition. Caroline has grown up. . . longing only for the opportunity to do what she feels she could do, and to die for somebody she loves, that is not actually to become a subject for the undertaker, but to give up heart, soul, and sensations to one loved hero, to lose independent existence in the perfect adoption of her lover's being. This is all very fine, isn't it reader. . . .

(*Five*, 364)

This passage is a first draft that Brontë excised from the novelette, but its features live on in the published fiction: the engulfing of one lover by another made explicit in *Jane Eyre*, where Rochester sees in Jane his "likeness" and she, drawing support from the language of established religion, feels herself "absolutely bone of his bone and flesh of his flesh" (576). The motif persists as late as *Villette*, where Paul insists that he and Lucy share affinities of appearance as well as fate (532), a survival suggesting that, for all Brontë's apparent scorn, Caroline Vernon's loss of "independent existence in the perfect adoption of [the] lover's being" remained for Brontë the measure, both exhilarating and threatening, of passionate love. The fascination with domination also extends to the sphere of work, as it would do in the novels. In another of the late Angrian tales, "Elizabeth Hastings", Brontë's own profession provides an appropriate arena for its exercise:

> she was dependent on nobody – responsible to nobody. . . . The little dignified Governess soon gained considerable influence over her scholars. . . . she was as prosperous as any little woman of five feet high and not twenty years old need wish to be. . . .
>
> (*Five* 243)

> "when I've got two thousand pounds I'll give up work & live like a fine lady".
>
> (*Five* 249)

Here, Brontë, brought to the point of nervous breakdown by her hatred for her life as teacher at Miss Wooler's Roe Head School, understandably dreams of independence in a transformed version of the life she knows, but the fantasy reveals her conviction that social recognition and comfortable prosperity demand the exercise of power in the achievement and bestow more power in the aftermath. As a professional, Elizabeth, unlike other heroines of the juvenilia, is able to withstand pressure to become the mistress of a Zamorna-like figure to whom she is attracted. Self-sufficient, protected against loss of selfhood by her financial independence, this precursor of Jane Eyre need not succumb to the fate of becoming a "slave". Other Brontë women would also be characterized by their relationship to professional work or by the conditions that keep them from it. Caroline would imagine that being a governess would offer an escape from her dependency, while, as Judith Lowder Newton points out (91–3), others such as Polly in relation to her father and Graham, or Miss Marchmont to her dead fiancé, would define themselves by their dependence on – and dedication to serving – men (Newton 91–3).

The haphazard but repetitive nature of most of these writings, apparently dashed off and often left unrevised, suggests the tales are the uncontrolled outpourings of a private fantasy feeding on clichés of power and submission, a pattern succinctly summed up by Diane Hoeveler and Lisa Jadwin as "a sadomasochistic Byronic paradigm that emphasizes the destructiveness of overpowering emotions and casts love as a pleasant and inevitable process of destruction" (28). The increasingly ironic tone suggests greater awareness of self-indulgence and consequent self-criticism, but also an inability to abandon the fantasy. The figure of the rake would surface again in Rochester, and the language of mastery and slavery would continue to shape the depiction of relationships in the later works. Love would again be defined as the loss of self, and the problem of reconciling the dangers of this surrender with the attractions of love would persist.

To turn to Brontë's correspondence for more light on her youthful cast of mind is to discover the extent to which the language of her early fiction intermingled with that of her personal relationships. While she was teaching at the Roe Head School, her letters revealed a painful emotional breakdown that manifested itself in religious anguish and a hysterical dependence on her friend Ellen Nussey for reassurance and love. In February of 1837 she had written to Ellen, in terms worthy of the Angrian heroine, Mina Laury, for whom Zamorna was "more to me than a human being":

> Why are we to be divided? Surely, Ellen, it must be because we are in danger of loving each other too well – of losing sight of the *Creator* in idolatry of the *Creature*.
> (*Letters* I:164: 20 [?20 February 1837] emphases original)

"Idolatry" was to remain a remarkably persistent theme. Jane Eyre was to say of her love for Rochester: "I could not, in those days, see God for his creature: of whom I had made an idol" (*JE* 346), and similar phrases survive into *Villette*, where Miss Marchmont confesses, of her dead lover:

> I still think of Frank more than of God; and unless it be counted that in thus loving the creature so much, so long, and so exclusively, I

relationship is male with male, Crimsworth and his self-appointed mentor Hunsden fitting rather awkwardly into the pattern of conflict that Brontë had established in the juvenilia as male–female, a pattern that would also be so much in evidence in the relationships of Jane with Rochester, Lucy with Paul or Shirley with most of the men she encounters. However, here it is William Crimsworth who is cast as the combative first-person heroine:

> "Are you grateful to me?" [Hunsden] asked presently.
>
> In fact I was grateful, or almost so, and I believe I half liked him at the moment, notwithstanding his proviso that what he had done was not out of regard for me: but human nature is perverse; impossible to answer his blunt question in the affirmative, so I disclaimed all tendency to gratitude and advised him if he expected any reward for his championship to look for it in a better world, as he was not likely to meet with it here.
>
> (50)

If these words were given to Jane or Lucy, no reader would find them out of place and Brontë herself, while writing *Shirley*, admitted privately to James Taylor: "In delineating male character I labour under disadvantages: intuition and theory will not always adequately supply the place of observation and experience" (*Letters* II:188: [?1 March 1849]). This explanation, however, does not account for the female relationships in which two women display some of the characteristics of lovers, suggesting the issue is more complex.

Other explanations for Crimsworth's "femininity" are conceivable, including unacknowledged homosexuality or a denial that emotional differences might be dependent on gender.[2] But both of these hypotheses are too tidy an explanation of the confusion that prevails; it seems rather that, for Brontë, gender differences are fluid and changeable, dependent on the characters' control of power. Crimsworth takes on "female" characteristics with Hunsden and "male" with Frances, while Shirley with Caroline, and Lucy with Ginevra act as "male", although they become "female" in other circumstances. The same fluidity can be seen in Brontë's own letters, where she uses the same verbal formulae to Ellen and to Heger when confessing herself dependent upon each.

Of course, to write of "male characteristics" is, in itself, to raise the question of what particular stereotype is encompassed by the phrase, and

have not at least blasphemed the Creator, small is my chance of salvation.

> (101)

That Ellen was a woman and apparently unremarkable in personality is of less significance than that Brontë's early vocabulary for love remained consistent from her juvenilia and personal experience to her last novel. Love is linked to idolatry, and thus to a total, but frightening, submission. The same view of love prevailed when, in March 1839, about the time Brontë was working on "Henry Hastings", Ellen's brother Henry made an unromantic proposal of marriage to Brontë, who explained her refusal to Ellen in language again appropriate to Mina Laury or Caroline Vernon:

> . . . I had not, and never could have, that intense attachment which would make me willing to die for him – and if ever I marry it must be in that light of adoration that I will regard my Husband. . . .
>
> (*Letters* I:187: 12 March 1839)

After unhappy experiences at Roe Head and in two positions as governess, it was clearly a relief to Brontë to cease to teach and to become a pupil at the Heger's school in Brussels. Characteristically, her account to Ellen of this reversal is couched in the familiar vocabulary of submission, accompanied by a proud recounting with manipulative tears worthy of Jane Eyre:

> I was twenty-six years old a week or two since – and at that ripe time of life I am a schoolgirl – a complete schoolgirl and on the whole very happy in that capacity. It felt very strange at first to submit to authority instead of exercising it – to obey orders instead of giving them – but I like that state of things. . . . it is natural to me to submit and very unnatural to command. M. Heger . . . [is] a man of power as to mind but very choleric & irritable as to temperament. . . . When he is very ferocious with me I cry; that sets all things straight.
>
> (*Letters* I:284: [May 1842])

The preoccupations of the juvenilia suggest that Monsieur Heger was a disaster waiting to happen, a man to whom she was predisposed to respond by long-ingrained patterns of fantasy. Though only six years older than she, he was a figure of authority by reason of his position and his disposition, and thus it must have seemed both justifiable and pleasurable to surrender to his ferocity, which alternated appealingly with an intensely personal concern for his students' well-being (Fraser, 190). Even the forbidden nature of the attraction, however humiliating or painful she felt it, was characteristic of the form of love to which she had so long retreated in fantasy. Indeed, Ratchford points persuasively to strong verbal echoes of both the juvenilia and of Brontë's correspondence with Ellen Nussey in her subsequent letters to Heger, detecting notes of "hysteria, as if she had unconsciously dramatized herself and lashed her emotions up to character" (162–3). And to add to the satisfaction of surrender there came a welcome reversal of roles for someone attracted to, but fearful of, submission, when she was asked to teach English to Heger and his brother-in-law.

Brontë's desperate letters to Heger after she had left Brussels a second time, with their emphasis on the word "master" (which echoes so lovingly through *Jane Eyre*), show her struggling to make the teacher–pupil relationship her defence:

> I do not seek to justify myself, I submit to all kinds of reproaches – all I know – is that I cannot – that I will not resign myself to the total loss of my master's friendship. . . .
>
> (*Letters* I:379: 8 January 1845, translation)

> I have not been able to overcome either my regrets nor my impatience – and that, is truly humiliating – not to know how to get the mastery over one's own thoughts, to be the slave of a regret, a memory, the slave of a dominant and fixed idea which has become a tyrant over one's mind. . . .
>
> (*Letters* I:436: 18 November [1845], translation)

Despite the denial, "I do not seek to justify myself", self-justification (or the disclaimer of its necessity) would be a preoccupation for Crimsworth, Jane, Louis and Lucy, a pattern that Janet Gezari traces through Brontë's fiction: "the vindictive acts of others inspire acts of self-vindication that are themselves vindictive" (31). Indeed, much of the later fiction and her comments on it would have the appearance of a justification of Brontë herself and of her conception of love. Most telling of all in these letters to Heger, submission to the teacher is celebrated, but capitulation to her own emotions is condemned as "slavery".

Thus, even before the commencement of her professional career, Brontë had been personally involved in a mentor-lover relationship. She had, in her unpublished writings, already shown a fascination with

authority, whether deriving from the state, from a profession, fro riches, or from the role of the guardian or teacher. In these writings s had linked such authority to love through the exercise of, or submissio to, sexual domination. She had explored the possibility that the pos tion of mentor might not only allow one to exercise power in the sexua sphere, but also to resist it. She had experimented with the potential o the experienced mentor's role to elicit and shape the sexual response o the less sophisticated. Finally, she had demonstrated her conviction that sexual love posed the threat of voluntary self-victimization, while at the same time revealing her fascination with the erotic potential of that struggle for power. Now, after her return from Brussels, and as part of a joint attempt on the part of the sisters to find a means of earning a living outside the classroom, she attempted a full-length novel.

Unpublished until after Brontë's death despite her determined efforts, *The Professor* has never had great success with readers, in part because of the repellent nature of Crimsworth, the narrator and central character. Brontë herself, however, considered "the middle and latter portion of the work. . . . as good as I can write; it contains more pith, more substance, more reality, in my judgement, than much of *Jane Eyre*" (*Letters* I: 574: 14 December 1847). Though she made a determined attempt to break away from the "wild, wonderful and thrilling" (*P*, "Preface" 4) that characterized her Angrian fantasies, the concerns and language of the novel often echo those of her earlier work. The reasons for one such survival, the choice of a male narrator, are unclear. They may simply have been the result of habit although other reasons have been suggested, including Brontë's desires to avoid being stereotyped as a female author, to play both herself and Heger, or to distance herself from the Brussels experience from which the novel derived ("Introduction", *P* xvi). But her choice of a male narrator who is also the hero of his own tale is not merely of interest from a personal point of view, for it was intimately bound up with another survival from Angria, a concern with the relationship between power and gender.

This is not, however, an issue neatly to be resolved into the cliché of male domination, for same-gender relationships sometimes take on sexual characteristics in Brontë's novels as a result of her association of power with erotic love – there would, for example, be sexual feeling (of varying intensity) in all-female relationships such as those of Shirley and Caroline or Lucy and Ginevra. In Brontë's first novel, the same-gender whether Brontë herself subscribes to the same stereotype as her readers, contemporary or modern. Is it only the reader who finds Crimsworth "female" because he exhibits "shyness", "a sulky tenderness, and the disposition to coquet" as an early reviewer wrote (quoted in Knies 94)? Is it the reader who finds Hunsden "male" because he is socially and financially the more powerful of the two friends, repudiates sentimentality and makes the initial moves to control Crimsworth? Does Brontë disregard or even reject any such distinctions, or only some? *The Professor* raises such issues, but offers no clear resolutions although it does suggest that, even if Brontë recognizes that the exercise of power is considered a stereotypically male prerogative, males and females of her creation will not necessarily conform to such expectations. It is a position that does not neatly align her with those feminists who see in her a champion, conscious or otherwise, of women as inevitable victims of the "patriarchy".

The novel also makes clear that it is power, whatever the gender of those who hold it, that is the crucial element in human relationships. Wealth is one source, with the consequent ability to give, and thus to control. Like Rochester and Shirley, Hunsden enjoys such power, but he will not bestow any favour without profiting from it. Giving Crimsworth his mother's portrait, Hunsden ruminates on the "stupid pleasure" obtained from witnessing a "fool's ecstasy", and while this causes Crimsworth "pungent pain", he feels that it simultaneously frees him from any debt to Hunsden: "you have paid yourself in taunts" (209–10). Whether or not Hunsden is to be understood as attempting elaborate and covert tact, or whether Brontë herself is sparing Crimsworth the embarrassment of acknowledging subordination consequent upon acceptance of a favour, the episode clarifies her view of the link between teasing and obligation. The expression of hostility, mock or otherwise, offers desirable protection from loss of power through indebtedness. This convoluted ritual, designed to nullify the threat of domination, and often engaged in by both donor and recipient, is repeated to the point of obsession in the later novels, although it is Jane Eyre, of all Brontë's heroines, who resorts to it most determinedly, and whose initial inability to practise it with St John puts her at enormous disadvantage. Even the prevailing tone of affectionate exchange is mock hostility – it seems to be the mode Brontë is most comfortable with, as if to be open and direct in the expression of love is to become too vulnerable.

The first meeting of Hunsden with Crimsworth's fiancée provokes an extraordinary wrestling match between the two men that underlines the hostility between them and signals the end of Hunsden's bid for direct mentorship. It also evokes again the sexual uncertainties of earlier episodes: "after we had both rolled on the pavement, and with difficulty picked ourselves up, we agreed to walk on more soberly" (243). The scene defies sober visualization, but as a metaphor it has the ring of psychological truth: not two grown men but two schoolboys, tussling in the mud, the struggle imbued with a sexuality neither distinctly heterosexual nor homosexual. And walk on they do, towards a *ménage à trois* of perpetual sparring, in which Frances and Hunsden (without real prospect the other will acknowledge defeat, although Brontë clearly acclaims Frances the winner) endlessly attempt to educate each other. As Jane Eyre will conquer Rochester, so Crimsworth ultimately claims superiority over Hunsden, though his victory is at one remove, being achieved through the agency of a woman (albeit one whose name might be male but for one letter), Frances Henri, his pupil and wife. This is a contest in which Frances, in a trial run for Jane Eyre, with intimations of her successor's honesty, courage, and unsophisticated wisdom, becomes Crimsworth's surrogate as victor. Frances enables her husband to remain aloof from the bickering, secure in the knowledge that he remains her master and can thus dominate Hunsden at one remove, confronting his own male "mentor-lover" through his assumption of the same role towards someone else. Crimsworth need not "seek to justify" himself; his wife will do it for him, while suggestions of Hunsden's jealousy of Crimsworth's conquest and possession of Frances ensure that this trio remain interconnected through love as well as mentorship.

Hunsden is a mentor only in the informal sense, but the novel takes place in a world in which the role of mentor may also be a professional position. When the instructional relationship is one where teacher and taught are of the same sex, Brontë conceives of it as one of unrelieved aggression. Crimsworth's educational philosophy is characteristically founded on a power–pleasure principle:

> Human beings – human children especially, seldom deny themselves the pleasure of exercising a power which they are conscious of possessing, even though that power consists only in a capacity to make others wretched.
>
> (132)

Subsequently, Crimsworth teaches in a neighbouring girls' school where he perceives his pupils in frankly sexual terms. Brontë shows no hesitation in demonstrating that Crimsworth is acutely aware of the battles waged in a female class with a male teacher. After a detailed have not at least blasphemed the Creator, small is my chance of salvation.

(101)

That Ellen was a woman and apparently unremarkable in personality is of less significance than that Brontë's early vocabulary for love remained consistent from her juvenilia and personal experience to her last novel. Love is linked to idolatry, and thus to a total, but frightening, submission.

The same view of love prevailed when, in March 1839, about the time Brontë was working on "Henry Hastings", Ellen's brother Henry made an unromantic proposal of marriage to Brontë, who explained her refusal to Ellen in language again appropriate to Mina Laury or Caroline Vernon:

. . . I had not, and never could have, that intense attachment which would make me willing to die for him – and if ever I marry it must be in that light of adoration that I will regard my Husband. . . .

(*Letters* I:187: 12 March 1839)

After unhappy experiences at Roe Head and in two positions as governess, it was clearly a relief to Brontë to cease to teach and to become a pupil at the Heger's school in Brussels. Characteristically, her account to Ellen of this reversal is couched in the familiar vocabulary of submission, accompanied by a proud recounting with manipulative tears worthy of Jane Eyre:

I was twenty-six years old a week or two since – and at that ripe time of life I am a schoolgirl – a complete schoolgirl and on the whole very happy in that capacity. It felt very strange at first to submit to authority instead of exercising it – to obey orders instead of giving them – but I like that state of things. . . . it is natural to me to submit and very unnatural to command. M. Heger . . . [is] a man of power as to mind but very choleric & irritable as to temperament. . . . When he is very ferocious with me I cry; that sets all things straight.

(*Letters* I:284: [May 1842])

The preoccupations of the juvenilia suggest that Monsieur Heger was a disaster waiting to happen, a man to whom she was predisposed to respond by long-ingrained patterns of fantasy. Though only six years older than she, he was a figure of authority by reason of his position and his disposition, and thus it must have seemed both justifiable and pleasurable to surrender to his ferocity, which alternated appealingly with an intensely personal concern for his students' well-being (Fraser, 190). Even the forbidden nature of the attraction, however humiliating or painful she felt it, was characteristic of the form of love to which she had so long retreated in fantasy. Indeed, Ratchford points persuasively to strong verbal echoes of both the juvenilia and of Brontë's correspondence with Ellen Nussey in her subsequent letters to Heger, detecting notes of "hysteria, as if she had unconsciously dramatized herself and lashed her emotions up to character" (162–3). And to add to the satisfaction of surrender there came a welcome reversal of roles for someone attracted to, but fearful of, submission, when she was asked to teach English to Heger and his brother-in-law.

Brontë's desperate letters to Heger after she had left Brussels a second time, with their emphasis on the word "master" (which echoes so lovingly through *Jane Eyre*), show her struggling to make the teacher–pupil relationship her defence:

> I do not seek to justify myself, I submit to all kinds of reproaches – all I know – is that I cannot – that I will not resign myself to the total loss of my master's friendship. . . .
>
> (*Letters* I:379: 8 January 1845, translation)

> I have not been able to overcome either my regrets nor my impatience – and that, is truly humiliating – not to know how to get the mastery over one's own thoughts, to be the slave of a regret, a memory, the slave of a dominant and fixed idea which has become a tyrant over one's mind. . . .
>
> (*Letters* I:436: 18 November [1845], translation)

Despite the denial, "I do not seek to justify myself", self-justification (or the disclaimer of its necessity) would be a preoccupation for Crimsworth, Jane, Louis and Lucy, a pattern that Janet Gezari traces through Brontë's fiction: "the vindictive acts of others inspire acts of self-vindication that are themselves vindictive" (31). Indeed, much of the later fiction and her comments on it would have the appearance of a justification of Brontë herself and of her conception of love. Most telling of all in these letters to Heger, submission to the teacher is celebrated, but capitulation to her own emotions is condemned as "slavery".

Thus, even before the commencement of her professional career, Brontë had been personally involved in a mentor-lover relationship. She had, in her unpublished writings, already shown a fascination with authority, whether deriving from the state, from a profession, from riches, or from the role of the guardian or teacher. In these writings she had linked such authority to love through the exercise of, or submission to, sexual domination. She had explored the possibility that the position of mentor might not only allow one to exercise power in the sexual sphere, but also to resist it. She had experimented with the potential of the experienced mentor's role to elicit and shape the sexual response of the less sophisticated. Finally, she had demonstrated her conviction that sexual love posed the threat of voluntary self-victimization, while at the same time revealing her fascination with the erotic potential of that struggle for power. Now, after her return from Brussels, and as part of a joint attempt on the part of the sisters to find a means of earning a living outside the classroom, she attempted a full-length novel.

Unpublished until after Brontë's death despite her determined efforts, *The Professor* has never had great success with readers, in part because of the repellent nature of Crimsworth, the narrator and central character. Brontë herself, however, considered "the middle and latter portion of the work. . . . as good as I can write; it contains more pith, more substance, more reality, in my judgement, than much of *Jane Eyre*" (*Letters* I: 574: 14 December 1847). Though she made a determined attempt to break away from the "wild, wonderful and thrilling" (*P*, "Preface" 4) that characterized her Angrian fantasies, the concerns and language of the novel often echo those of her earlier work. The reasons for one such survival, the choice of a male narrator, are unclear. They may simply have been the result of habit although other reasons have been suggested, including Brontë's desires to avoid being stereotyped as a female author, to play both herself and Heger, or to distance herself from the Brussels experience from which the novel derived ("Introduction", *P* xvi). But her choice of a male narrator who is also the hero of his own tale is not merely of interest from a personal point of view, for it was intimately bound up with another survival from Angria, a concern with the relationship between power and gender.

This is not, however, an issue neatly to be resolved into the cliché of male domination, for same-gender relationships sometimes take on sexual characteristics in Brontë's novels as a result of her association of power with erotic love – there would, for example, be sexual feeling (of varying intensity) in all-female relationships such as those of Shirley and Caroline or Lucy and Ginevra. In Brontë's first novel, the same-gender relationship is male with male, Crimsworth and his self-appointed mentor Hunsden fitting rather awkwardly into the pattern of conflict that Brontë had established in the juvenilia as male–female, a pattern that would also be so much in evidence in the relationships of Jane with Rochester, Lucy with Paul or Shirley with most of the men she encounters. However, here it is William Crimsworth who is cast as the combative first-person heroine:

"Are you grateful to me?" [Hunsden] asked presently.

In fact I was grateful, or almost so, and I believe I half liked him at the moment, notwithstanding his proviso that what he had done was not out of regard for me: but human nature is perverse; impossible to answer his blunt question in the affirmative, so I disclaimed all tendency to gratitude and advised him if he expected any reward for his championship to look for it in a better world, as he was not likely to meet with it here.

(50)

If these words were given to Jane or Lucy, no reader would find them out of place and Brontë herself, while writing *Shirley*, admitted privately to James Taylor: "In delineating male character I labour under disadvantages: intuition and theory will not always adequately supply the place of observation and experience" (*Letters* II:188: [?1 March 1849]). This explanation, however, does not account for the female relationships in which two women display some of the characteristics of lovers, suggesting the issue is more complex.

Other explanations for Crimsworth's "femininity" are conceivable, including unacknowledged homosexuality or a denial that emotional differences might be dependent on gender.[2] But both of these hypotheses are too tidy an explanation of the confusion that prevails; it seems rather that, for Brontë, gender differences are fluid and changeable, dependent on the characters' control of power. Crimsworth takes on "female" characteristics with Hunsden and "male" with Frances, while Shirley with Caroline, and Lucy with Ginevra act as "male", although they become "female" in other circumstances. The same fluidity can be seen in Brontë's own letters, where she uses the same verbal formulae to Ellen and to Heger when confessing herself dependent upon each.

Of course, to write of "male characteristics" is, in itself, to raise the question of what particular stereotype is encompassed by the phrase, and whether Brontë herself subscribes to the same stereotype as her readers, contemporary or modern. Is it only the reader who finds Crimsworth "female" because he exhibits "shyness", "a sulky tenderness, and the disposition to coquet" as an early reviewer wrote (quoted in Knies 94)? Is it the reader who finds Hunsden "male" because he is socially and financially the more powerful of the two friends, repudiates sentimentality and makes the initial moves to control Crimsworth? Does Brontë disregard or even reject any such distinctions, or only some? *The Professor* raises such issues, but offers no clear resolutions although it does suggest that, even if Brontë recognizes that the exercise of power is considered a stereotypically male prerogative, males and females of her creation will not necessarily conform to such expectations. It is a position that does not neatly align her with those feminists who see in her a champion, conscious or otherwise, of women as inevitable victims of the "patriarchy".

The novel also makes clear that it is power, whatever the gender of those who hold it, that is the crucial element in human relationships. Wealth is one source, with the consequent ability to give, and thus to control. Like Rochester and Shirley, Hunsden enjoys such power, but he will not bestow any favour without profiting from it. Giving Crimsworth his mother's portrait, Hunsden ruminates on the "stupid pleasure" obtained from witnessing a "fool's ecstasy", and while this causes Crimsworth "pungent pain", he feels that it simultaneously frees him from any debt to Hunsden: "you have paid yourself in taunts" (209–10). Whether or not Hunsden is to be understood as attempting elaborate and covert tact, or whether Brontë herself is sparing Crimsworth the embarrassment of acknowledging subordination consequent upon acceptance of a favour, the episode clarifies her view of the link between teasing and obligation. The expression of hostility, mock or otherwise, offers desirable protection from loss of power through indebtedness. This convoluted ritual, designed to nullify the threat of domination, and often engaged in by both donor and recipient, is repeated to the point of obsession in the later novels, although it is Jane Eyre, of all Brontë's heroines, who resorts to it most determinedly, and whose initial inability to practise it with St John puts her at enormous disadvantage. Even the prevailing tone of affectionate exchange is mock hostility – it seems to be the mode Brontë is most comfortable with, as if to be open and direct in the expression of love is to become too vulnerable.

The first meeting of Hunsden with Crimsworth's fiancée provokes an extraordinary wrestling match between the two men that underlines the hostility between them and signals the end of Hunsden's bid for direct mentorship. It also evokes again the sexual uncertainties of earlier episodes: "after we had both rolled on the pavement, and with difficulty picked ourselves up, we agreed to walk on more soberly" (243). The scene defies sober visualization, but as a metaphor it has the ring of psychological truth: not two grown men but two schoolboys, tussling in the mud, the struggle imbued with a sexuality neither distinctly heterosexual nor homosexual. And walk on they do, towards a *ménage à trois* of perpetual sparring, in which Frances and Hunsden (without real prospect the other will acknowledge defeat, although Brontë clearly acclaims Frances the winner) endlessly attempt to educate each other. As Jane Eyre will conquer Rochester, so Crimsworth ultimately claims superiority over Hunsden, though his victory is at one remove, being achieved through the agency of a woman (albeit one whose name might be male but for one letter), Frances Henri, his pupil and wife. This is a contest in which Frances, in a trial run for Jane Eyre, with intimations of her successor's honesty, courage, and unsophisticated wisdom, becomes Crimsworth's surrogate as victor. Frances enables her husband to remain aloof from the bickering, secure in the knowledge that he remains her master and can thus dominate Hunsden at one remove, confronting his own male "mentor-lover" through his assumption of the same role towards someone else. Crimsworth need not "seek to justify" himself; his wife will do it for him, while suggestions of Hunsden's jealousy of Crimsworth's conquest and possession of Frances ensure that this trio remain interconnected through love as well as mentorship.

Hunsden is a mentor only in the informal sense, but the novel takes place in a world in which the role of mentor may also be a professional position. When the instructional relationship is one where teacher and taught are of the same sex, Brontë conceives of it as one of unrelieved aggression. Crimsworth's educational philosophy is characteristically founded on a power–pleasure principle:

> Human beings – human children especially, seldom deny themselves the pleasure of exercising a power which they are conscious of possessing, even though that power consists only in a capacity to make others wretched.
>
> (132)

Subsequently, Crimsworth teaches in a neighbouring girls' school where he perceives his pupils in frankly sexual terms. Brontë shows no hesitation in demonstrating that Crimsworth is acutely aware of the battles waged in a female class with a male teacher. After a detailed analysis of the sexual attractions of the three most aggressive of his pupils, he concludes their purpose is, in his view, to use their sexual appeal to dominate him (88). At one point, Crimsworth appears to acknowledge the moral responsibility of the teacher not to succumb to sexual interest in his charges when he is revolted by the headmaster Pelet's suggestion he should use the classroom to achieve an advantageous marriage. But it transpires that he believes this is dishonourable because it is mercenary, not because exploitation of sexual attraction between teacher and pupil is in itself immoral (96).

Significantly, the defeat of the girls' "concentrated coquetry and futile flirtation" (88) is but a prelude to the more sophisticated attack by their directress, who, with greater experience and therefore greater skill, searches for "some chink, some niche where she could put in her little firm foot and stand upon my neck – Mistress of my nature" (89). The essence of her imagined desire is described in words little different from those Crimsworth applies to his treatment of his own pupils, male and female: "you must fix your foot, plant it, root it in rock" (67) – the language for sexual and pedagogical domination are the same.

Although Mdlle Reuter is only in the loosest sense Crimsworth's mentor (unintentionally initiating him into a more sophisticated understanding of her sexual nature and his own) and fails to become his lover, she does provide an important foil for Frances and thus sets a pattern of power that the novels would repeatedly explore in an attempt to distinguish relationships in which, from Brontë's point of view, power is desirably erotic from those in which it is not. That Brontë found the problem difficult to solve is suggested by her obsessive return to it in work after work. Thus, in words echoing the juvenilia and anticipating *Jane Eyre* and *Shirley*, Brontë allows Crimsworth to discover that hardness and indifference can provoke "slavish homage" in Mdlle Reuter – although "her flatteries irritated my scorn, her blandishments confirmed my reserve". Crimsworth is transformed (like St John Rivers) into a "rigid pillar of stone", aroused but obstinately unresponsive, his reaction engaging her yet more intensely because of her "tendency to consider Pride, Hardness, Selfishness as proofs of strength" (129).

The enamoured Mdlle Reuter evokes in Crimsworth fears of his own worst nature: "I had ever hated a tyrant, and behold, the possession of a slave, self-given, went near to transform me into what I abhorred! . . . I felt at once barbarous and sensual as a pasha" (184). The language that Crimsworth chooses to describe what disgusts him also distances the him from the "passionate and poetical", the "wild, wonderful and thrilling" that Brontë believed she had repudiated in discarding the fantasies of the juvenilia for the everyday world of *The Professor*. But what is abhorred is also irresistibly fascinating, the passage linking, as if the connections are inevitable, the "barbarous", the "sensual" and the power of an eastern lord.

However, Brontë's representation of Crimsworth's arousal by Mdlle Reuter as repellent, as well as his deduction from his strangely pleasurable response that "servility creates despotism" (129), offers the hope that Brontë may be about to attempt to imagine sexual love not caught up in the play of power. The opportunity arises with Crimsworth's attraction to Frances Henri, an assistant teacher anxious for English lessons and thus, though in different situations, both instructor and pupil. Fortunately she possesses the "mental qualities" Crimsworth had desired, but not found, in his other female pupils. These are displayed through the *devoir*, which Brontë employs here (132–7) and later in *Shirley* and *Villette* as a means of enabling the teacher to discover the pupil's nature (119), providing an opportunity for the student to present herself through her well-considered words. It is an opportunity for a display of elevated thoughts and language with the screen of impersonality, the opportunity for the pupil to maintain the Brontë fiction "I do not seek to justify myself" while being enabled, discreetly, to do so. Like teasing, it serves as a protection for the vulnerable that the clear-sighted are supposed to see through to the writer's true nature, as Crimsworth does, and also reveals just how important it was for Brontë to find some means of reconciling the need to love with the fear of self-exposure that such a need necessitated.

Undeterred by his experience with Mdlle Reuter, Crimsworth chooses to show his growing affection for Frances through an exercise of power, a typical Brontë beginning to a wooing, with a typical response: "in proportion as my manner grew austere and magisterial, hers became easy and self possessed" (138). For a while, the relationship between Frances Henri and Crimsworth runs along the lines of an early Rochester–Jane encounter, with Crimsworth-as-Rochester exhibiting a "calculated abruptness . . . of manner" (143). Feeling an increasing physical attraction to Frances, he seeks to convey "kindness" "cloaked" by "austerity", and "real respect" "masked with seeming imperiousness", justifying this as required to accommodate her nature "at once proud and shy" (148).

Significantly, the first greetings the two speak to express (without overtly admitting) their love are "Mon Maitre, Mon Maitre" and "Well, my pupil" (168–9), and Crimsworth goes to great lengths to ensure they should continue to meet "as we had always met, as Master and pupil" (216). This approach is prolonged far beyond any practical need for concealment, nor does Brontë seem to feel any need to excuse Crimsworth's approach to Frances as being an unfortunate outcome of, for example, a childhood devoid of openly expressed affection, although his circumstances would make that a possibility. The mysterious attack of "hypochondria" that besets Crimsworth after Frances accepts his proposal is presented as a brief recurrence of a near-suicidal depression that had afflicted him for a year "just as I rose to youth". He accounts for the experience by reference to his boyhood: "lonely, parentless; uncheered by brother or sister" (229) but is baffled by this new episode: "why did hypochondria accost me now?" Brontë makes no obvious attempt to explain by any other means in the text, and the reader is left asking the same question. That the engagement brings with it mixed feelings about "sexual and emotional fulfilment", as Firdous Azim (154–62), among others, suggests is certainly possible. The language seems sexually charged: though in the first episode this may be an unintentional consequence of wishing to stress the disturbance was always present, night and day: Hypochondria "lay with me, she eat [sic] with me, she walked out with me . . . " (228). That this is somehow to be connected with guilt over masturbation, however, as Azim also suggests, seems an unnecessary imposition on the text. The reference in the second episode initially does seem more deliberately sexual: "I repulsed [Hypochondria] as one would a dreaded and ghastly concubine coming to embitter a husband's heart toward his young bride" (229) but this too quite possibly has no particular sexual content beyond the choice of a metaphor that reveals Crimsworth torn between the temptation, seen as morally charged, to succumb weakly to depression as an alternative to marriage or assert his will and marry Frances. Overall, the impression this brief, abrupt and oddly disembodied episode leaves is that Brontë here recalls her own "hypochondria", a "continual waking nightmare" that also "endured . . . a year" while she was teaching at Miss Wooler's school (*Letters* I:505: [?November/December1846]) and imagines its potential to return and devastate a happier time.

Brontë offers no evidence that, as author, she repudiates Crimsworth's use of instruction as a respectable excuse for "reproofs" intended to arouse an erotic response. He deliberately manipulates his criticisms to provoke "a certain glance, sweetened with gaiety, and pointed with defiance, which, to speak truth, thrilled me as nothing had ever done; and made me, in a fashion (though happily she did not know it), her subject, if not her slave" (177). Evidently we are to feel this last distinction an important one; slavery being reserved for women such as Mdlle Reuter, the British conception of "subject" as opposed to the eastern "slave" presumably encompassing some aspect of the voluntary (there is more to be said of Brontë's attitude to imperialism in connection with *Jane Eyre*). Yet the shift cannot conceal Crimsworth's (and Brontë's) lack of certainty as to exactly how his relationship with Frances is more acceptable.

The muddle continues with the introduction of Frances Henri's poem (215–21), an immature fantasy featuring a stern master who inadvertently reveals his love while his pupil, Jane, lies on her sickbed, a condition that culminates in her being sent across the sea in peril, away from her mourning "master". The poem has two roles in the plot: to provide evidence of Frances's love and to offer reassurance, if any were needed, that she understands her teacher's "secret meaning" and his "mien austere". It offers a rare moment, in a narration that is normally under Crimsworth's control, when Frances can reveal her feelings. Disappointingly, Brontë does not take the opportunity to distinguish between Frances Henri's and Crimsworth's view of their relationship and thus undercut his linking of love and power: the moment when "Low at my master's knee I bent" is characterized as "The hour of triumph".

Nor does the proposal scene offer anything in the way of reassurance on this head. Frances's agreement is given on the basis of her expectations that Crimsworth will be "aussi bon mari qu'il a été bon maître" (223). His alternation between a friendly and exacting manner is explicitly referred to; his demand for a reply is couched in the old terms: "Will my pupil consent to pass her life with me? Speak English, now, Frances", her response being prefaced with the doubly obedient "Master". A disturbing simile follows: she is subsequently "as stirless in her happiness, as a mouse in its terror" (224). At the same time, Crimsworth is implicitly rebuked (as Rochester will explicitly be), for his desire to become "the Providence of what he loves – feeding and clothing it, as God does the lilies of the field" (225). Unlike Jane, however, Frances gives reasons for wishing to work that are couched in terms that do not openly challenge her future husband's power. It is not loss of independence that Frances says she fears but rather that lack of work will make her "dull", while "those who work together" increase their chances of continuing to "like" and "esteem" each other (226). Certainly these reasons offer no threat to the master in Crimsworth, who readily agrees. Whether Brontë wishes this to be seen as skilful manipulation on Frances's part, as a way to retain independence while seeming to surrender it, is not clear. Frances's actions are all we are offered, not her thoughts, and they are consistent with either surrender or manipulation. The latter is not out of the question in a Brontëan woman – Jane, Shirley, and Lucy all quite consciously control their men – but in this novel no confirmation is offered that Frances is, in this way, like them. In either case, willing submission or calculation on her part, the issue remains one of power – power surrendered, evaded or covertly retained.

Crimsworth predicts to Hunsden (243) that his marriage will be a "tale" of "interest and sweet variety and thrilling excitement" a "narra-tive" he will create by embarking, at judicious intervals, on an emotion-al rollercoaster. Frances's "elfish" (a word to be re-encountered in *Jane Eyre*) erotic attractions, are based on a pattern of subservience and play-ful rebellion, her punishment involving (as it will for later heroines) submission to the use of her master's language to mark her inferiority:

> Talk French to me she would, and many a punishment she has had for her wilfulness – I fear the choice of chastisement must have been inju-dicious, for instead of correcting the fault, it seemed to encourage its renewal. . . . now that she was thoroughly accustomed to her English professor. . . . she would show . . . some stores of raillery, of "malice", and would vex, tease, pique me sometimes about what she called my "bizarreries anglaises", my "caprices insulaires", with a wild and witty wickedness that made a perfect white demon of her while it lasted. This was rare, however, and the elfish freak was always short. . . . I had seized a mere vexing fairy and found a submissive and supplicating lit-tle mortal woman in my arms. Then I made her get a book, and read English to me for an hour by way of penance. I frequently dosed her with Wordsworth in this way. . . . she had to ask questions; to sue for explanations; to be like a child and a novice and to acknowledge me as her senior and director.
>
> (252–3)

Assessing Brontë's attitude to the desirability of female subservience on the basis of *The Professor* is complicated by the fact that the first-person narrator is male, and yet in disposition (and in apparent identi-fication with Brontë) has traditionally female characteristics. It would be dangerous, therefore, simply to assume that this novel supports male dominance, or even that, through irony, it subverts it. One pos-sible explanation is that, when Brontë employs the first person, that "I" must come to dominate all others, even, or perhaps particularly, to dominate those who are themselves normally aggressive. This may be observed in the narratives of Jane as well as the apparently submissive Lucy. It is an issue that emerges also in the awkwardness of the shift to first-person narration in Louis' "blank book", concurrent with his seizing of control from Shirley in the last section of the novel. Nothing in *The Professor* suggests the undesirability of such dominance, since Brontë's fundamental premise is that someone must hold power, and, given Crimsworth's fluidity of gender, it seems that gender in this novel is not, in itself, an issue of much importance.

Although Brontë does not explicitly examine the problem, the question of why Mdlle Reuter's submission disgusts Crimsworth, while Frances's does not, can hardly be avoided. The answer seems to rest on two aspects of the latter's behaviour. One is that Frances offers "sweet variety and thrilling excitement" by demonstrating an ability to rebel, however short-lived, and thus provides repeated opportunities for Crimsworth to enjoy the reassertion of control. In fact, Brontë here illustrates a variability praised by Foucault:

> What interests the practitioners of S & M is that the relationship is at the same time regulated and open. It resembles a chess game in the sense that one can win and the other lose. . . . This mixture of rules and openness has the effect of intensifying sexual relations by introducing a perpetual novelty, a perpetual tension and a perpetual uncertainty which the simple consummation of the act lacks.
>
> (*Foucault Live* 226)

The second is that Frances offers her subordination voluntarily, which makes the prize much more valuable. In his turn, Crimsworth can safely declare himself her "subject" (though not the less acceptable "slave") thus offering some further excitement in the temporary reversibility of their positions. It is possible that Brontë believes she has justified the relationship in terms of Frances's freedom to revolt, but the emphasis falls more persuasively on the pleasures inherent in Crimsworth's reassertions of power.

Few readers have cared much for *The Professor*, except as a curiosity, and, indeed, the very fact that Crimsworth strikes many readers as a repellent creep does leave open the possibility that Brontë actually intends us to perceive him in this way. Annette Tromly, for example, argues that he is one of Brontë's three "autobiographers" (Jane Eyre and Lucy Snow being the others) who must be understood to be distanced from Brontë herself – and that Crimsworth, rather than being an inept early creation, is actually a skilfully designed figure, intended to be as awful as most readers have perceived him (20–41). This argument seems to be the only hope of saving the work, but disregards the fact that we are clearly intended to respond to the other two "autobiographers" with sympathy while at the same time recognizing they are not perfect (and in Lucy's case while wrestling with her manifest unreliability). In no other novel, even in the case of the neurotic Lucy, does Brontë work through a first-person narrator who is not intended to engage our sympathy and whose defects we do not feel are somehow justified. Furthermore, that elements in *The Professor* are echoed throughout Brontë's fiction and letters suggests Brontë is not as much distanced from the three "autobiographers" as Tromly maintains. A more compelling argument, however, cannot be clinched without examining the later works in detail, for if the patterns of language and thought associated with Crimsworth continue to recur in the later novels without evidence of Brontë's condemnation, it will be hard indeed to dissociate the novelist herself from them, and from those characters with whom they are connected.

Overall, *The Professor* repeats much of what is familiar from the juvenilia. and its chief interest lies in the clarity with which it reveals the "dominant idea" of Brontë's early writings and the potential either for development or stasis in the later works. Though they are actually the work of her twenties, the early writings, including her first attempt at a full-length novel, remain rooted in the adolescent preoccupations of Angria, and, since clearly recognizable elements are carried forward into the later novels, the essential question must be whether those works offer evidence of advance through re-evaluation and transmutation, or, sadly, the paralysis of obsession. It was to be with the next novel, *Jane Eyre*, that Brontë's publication and popularity began and here also that the reader might hope to find signs of change.

4
"Should We Try to Counteract This Influence?" *Jane Eyre, Shirley* and *Villette*

Although in Brontë's earliest works, including her first attempt at a novel, power had been the key issue in sexual relationships, this need not have precluded a change in her later works. Certainly her first published novel demonstrated a gratifying improvement in her ability to please an audience. Single-minded in every sense, *Jane Eyre*, as generations of readers have recognized, makes compelling reading. One reaction, all the more striking for the initial resistance it records, was expressed in a contemporary review in *Fraser's*:

> We took up Jane Eyre one winter's evening, somewhat piqued at the extravagant commendations we had heard, and sternly resolved to be as critical as Croker. But as we read on we forgot both commendations and criticism, identified ourselves with Jane in all her troubles, and finally married Mr. Rochester about four in the morning.
>
> (Allott, *Critical Heritage* 152)

Despite the praise, the comic key in which this is written is worth noting, for it is found in many other bemused responses to the work, as if the critics feel ill-at-ease with their surrender and are anxious (like many a Brontë character) to conceal their warm response behind a screen of teasing.

In *Jane Eyre* Brontë made a considerable technical advance in using a first-person narrator to best advantage: a single idiosyncratic viewpoint with which the reader could identify. The choice of a ten-year-old girl, unloved, and unkindly treated (in the spirit of a fairy tale, although with the trappings of everyday life) brilliantly engages sympathy and disarms criticism from the beginning. The impulse to become Jane "in all her troubles" is hard to resist even for those determined to do so, as the reviewer records. Many more readers, particularly women, attempt no resistance at all:

> I have identified strongly with Jane through the years: her station, her personality, her choices. . . . I want [my students] to identify with the characters and learn from them. Choosing to teach *Jane Eyre* is a political act.
>
> (Ellen Brown, "Reading *Jane Eyre*, Reading Myself" 226–33)

Every injustice imagined and experienced by the reader in childhood rises to encourage the acceptance of a heroine whose feisty and rebellious spirit, hard to condemn in a child so circumstanced, can be prolonged into womanhood without disturbing the sympathizer. It is difficult not to side with Jane throughout the work, when her introduction is so compelling.

But technical developments are not separable from the matter and quality of the work as a whole. The difficulty of resisting what Henry James called "the taste for the emotions of recognition" (*Critical Muse* 180) has a dangerous consequence. The risk, for writer and reader alike, is that identification with a character, although the work draws enormous strength from that involvement, may disable judgment. The danger is increased when first-person narration is employed unless the author skilfully uses devices to distance the reader (as in *Villette*) or (as in *The Professor*) writes very clumsily.

Readers seem always to have felt that the "I" of this work and of the author cannot be disengaged, as G. H. Lewes suggested in his review of the work before he knew anything of the writer:

> Reality – deep, significant reality – is the great characteristic of the book. It is an autobiography, – not, perhaps, in the naked facts and circumstances, but in the actual suffering and experience. . . . This gives the book its charm: it is soul speaking to soul; it is an utterance from the depths of a struggling, suffering, much-enduring spirit: *suspiria de profundis!*
>
> (in Allott, *Critical Heritage* 84)

This sense that the author is personally engaged reveals just how effectively the narrative voice seizes control; regrettably, however, such a narrow concentration, while contributing to the narrative's power, is potentially immature in its preoccupation with self. Brontë commits herself to Jane, and then, with every device an author is capable of employing, demands uncritical involvement from the reader in the self-centred world of the "I" of the novel. As Mary Poovey demonstrates, even Rochester must be "punished" whenever he attempts to take control of the narrative from Jane because "The precarious independence Jane earned by leaving Gateshead has been figured into the ability to tell (if not direct) her own story" (*Uneven Developments* 139). A victory in narrative technique is won at the cost of a dangerous surrender to the egotism of the character, author and identifying reader.

Although *Jane Eyre* resembles *The Professor* and *Villette* in its use of first-person narration, it provides a contrast to all Brontë's other published works in that the accepted lover is not also the heroine's teacher. In the relationships of Crimsworth to Frances, Louis to Shirley, or Paul Emanuel to Lucy, the first arena for the exercise of mentorship is in the schoolroom instruction of language, perhaps Brontë's tribute to Heger, but also a recognition that mastery of language confers very broad powers on the more proficient. In *Jane Eyre*, Brontë's favourite element appears in an uncharacteristic arrangement. Jane is already fully committed to Rochester when she meets her "schoolroom" mentor, St John Rivers, who teaches her Hindostanee, planning to marry her in order to obtain her services as a fellow missionary. But St John himself is supposed, though convincing evidence is slight, to be attracted, "wildly – with all the intensity, indeed, of a first passion" (476), to the pretty but vacuous Rosamond. Since teacher and pupil each love another, St John's relations with Jane thus offer a test case by means of which the relative importance and inter-relationships of sexual love, power and mentorship may be examined outside the confines of Brontë's usual pattern.

What Jane claims as the source of her resistance to St John is not only the continuing love each feels for another, but also the problem of future sexual relations between them. His practical recognition of the unsuitability of Rosamond, of his own "cold, hard" ambition, and the limitation of other "sentiments" to "natural affection" for his sisters (478) devalue him in the eyes of both Jane and Brontë. The resisting reader might (unlike Jane) applaud the clear-sighted way in which St John averts a marital catastrophe that surely would have been as disastrous as Lydgate's with *his* Rosamond. But the same reader might agree that St John is wrong to ask Jane to dismiss her own desires in favour of something more impersonal:

" . . . physical and mental union in marriage: the only union that gives a character of permanent conformity to the destinies and designs of human beings; and passing over all minor caprices – all trivial difficulties and delicacies of feeling – all scruple about the degree, kind, strength, or tenderness of mere personal inclination."

(520)

Surely, Jane is right to feel more threatened than reassured by St John's consolation that

" . . . undoubtedly enough of love would follow upon marriage to render the union right even in your eyes".

(521)

and right to ask,

"Can I receive from him the bridal ring, endure all forms of love (which I doubt not he would scrupulously observe) and know that the spirit was quite absent?"

(517)

John Maynard argues convincingly that St John is a "sex-powered zealot", making "cold repressive misuse of sexual energies" for religious ends (*Victorian Discourses* 277) and Brontë's explicit criticism, through Jane, of the unnaturalness of St John's rejection of sexual love (though not the sexual act) as central to marriage is courageous. The cold calculation of the "experiment kiss" after which St John "viewed me to learn the result" is also, quite rightly, shown to be equally distasteful, but its consequences return us to Brontë's obsession with power, for Jane "felt as if this kiss were a seal affixed to my fetters" (509). Furthermore, Jane makes explicit the link between mastery and "love" that in St John's case she fears:

though I have only a sisterly affection for him now, yet, if forced to be his wife, I can imagine the possibility of conceiving an inevitable, strange, torturing kind of love for him: because he is so talented; and there is often a certain heroic grandeur in his look, manner, and conversation.

(531)

As his female "curate" she would be able to "accommodate quietly to his masterhood" because her "heart and mind would be free", her "natural unenslaved feelings" would remain her own (520). It appears from these reservations that, for Jane and Brontë, sexual relations, however unloving, inevitably interact with a recognition of intellectual superiority and thus contribute to a relationship of dominance and submission. In this situation, St John would not only be the recognized intellectual master, he would be able to maintain his power by his freedom from the "fetters" of the sexual response to which Jane fears she herself would succumb.

Most of Jane's reflections on her relationship to St John do indeed turn on a struggle for dominance, the note being struck from the beginning of their intimacy. Initially it is Jane who seizes power, employing a military metaphor as she passes "the outworks of conventional reserve" (478). And ultimately her danger of enslavement ends with the discovery that, with the cry of the mysterious voice, her ability to seize control has returned:

> It was *my* time to assume ascendancy. *My* powers were in play, and in force. . . . Where there is energy to command well enough, obedience never fails.
>
> (536–7, emphasis original)

However, in between, it is the power inherent in St John's mentorship that dominates Jane's perception of the relationship. One aspect of its particular horror is that he is unrelentingly hard, a characteristic in which he resembles that other "pillar of stone" Crimsworth in his relations with Mdlle Reuter (*P* 129). What marks St John's power as different from Crimsworth's, however, is that it claims justification from the religious nature of his calling, and resistance is thus difficult to justify. The effect on Jane of the self-suppression he demands is a kind of paralysis. St John's influence "took away my liberty of mind" and exerted a "freezing spell", exerted a compulsion to "disown half my nature" (508–9). Resistance is particularly difficult when "the Christian was patient and placid", offering no roughness to grasp and wrestle with: "I would much rather he had knocked me down" (523).

At each attempt by St John to extract from Jane a commitment to marry, her opposition is initially stated in terms of the absence of sexual love. However, she invariably returns to the issue of power and submission. Though sexual love and domination are linked with each other, the latter is the issue of ultimate importance; the first being the means to the end. This struggle for power reaches its peak on their last evening together. Jane's near-surrender to St John is explicitly compared to her close escape from Rochester: "folly" on both occasions.

For both relationships, her language (as in the early writings) is religious: Rochester she had "worshipped" as well as loved (403), while for St John she felt a cooler "veneration" (534). Despite her worship, however, she holds a superior moral position in regard to Rochester for he has found in her his "good angel" (402) and has joined the ranks of the many characters in the novel who, sooner or later, admit her superiority. Unfortunately, she must also recognize in St John, despite his personal faults, the pastoral superiority of a "guardian angel" (534), and that to be the angelic mentor is to hold the cards of power. Marianne Thormählen in a chapter titled "The Enigma of St. John Rivers" (204–20) offers a variety of reasons for the incompatibility between Jane's assessment of St John as a person and her praise of him ("the warrior Greatheart", 578) at the close. But there is no enigma: Jane (and I see no evidence that Brontë here presents her in a critical light) fears for herself the kind of paternalistic domination that she nevertheless approves of for the heathen (578), a matter that will come up again in Jane's relationship to Rochester.

Indeed, the echoes in Jane's choice of metaphors reveal her to be more in control of Rochester than of St John. In the midst of her despair over leaving Rochester, and threatened by him with "violence", she is actually exhilarated:

> But I was not afraid: not in the least. I felt an inward power; a sense of influence, which supported me. The crisis was perilous; but not without its charm: such as the Indian, perhaps, feels when he slips over the rapid in his canoe.
>
> (386)

In St John's case, however, the metaphor is significantly altered:

> I felt veneration for St John – veneration so strong that its impetus thrust me at once to the point I had so long shunned. I was tempted to cease struggling with him – to rush down the torrent of his will into the gulf of his existence, and there lose my own.
>
> (534)

And indeed Jane cannot escape from this relationship through her own rational efforts, without the help of the mysterious voice (whether it be subconscious or supernatural).

It seems that, in Brontë's view, the links between lover and mentor are forged from several kinds of power. One results from the intellectual, and often linguistic, superiority that is an essential component of the teacher. A second derives from the moral supremacy that, though it gives Jane the edge over Rochester, threatens to give St John the edge over Jane. The third, even more powerful, draws its strength from control of feeling, which is easier on the side where the feeling is weaker or absent. The fourth, related to it, is the sexual relationship that, even separated from love, contributes to the mastery of one partner and the submission of the other. It is for this reason that Jane can offer to take the role of assistant to St John but not agree to be his wife.

However, though *Jane Eyre* is anomalous in that teacher and pupil do not, finally, marry, Brontë does not abandon her preference for the mentor-lover relationship entirely, instead she situates it outside the classroom. Rochester does claim the right to be "masterful" on the grounds of age and experience, but Jane points out that the use he has made of these advantages is not impressive (163) – the moral mentor in this relationship is Jane herself. This is important to Brontë's careful allotment of power, for otherwise, despite Jane's professional success and final legacy, the initial master–governess relationship might doom her to subservience.

The problem Brontë faces, however, is how to show that Rochester needs Jane's missionary efforts without destroying his attractiveness to the reader. Her strategy is to employ that staple of popular romance, the reformation of the rake through the love of a good woman. Tanya Modleski, in *Loving with a Vengeance: Mass Produced Fantasies for Women*, develops the argument that the appeal of this plot lies in the reassurance it provides to women that beneath the apparent bad behaviour of the alien male beats a passionate heart he strives to deny, and a tenderness awaiting discovery by the woman who loves him (a bubble of fantasy that Anne Brontë was to prick in *The Tenant of Wildfell Hall*, published the year after *Jane Eyre*).

Rochester fits the formula to perfection. His upbringing has been that of "a wild boy, indulged from childhood upwards" (273), but Brontë carefully sanitizes his resulting weaknesses ("dissipation – never debauchery"). For all his regret that he appears "an unfeeling, loose-principled rake" (397), his problem, he maintains, with his creator's support, has really been that he has been a "spoonie" (173), a foolish victim: "When fate wronged me, I had not the wisdom to remain cool: I turned desperate; then I degenerated" (167). Brontë permits Jane, in accepting Rochester's own view of himself, to be right about his potential for rescue – and perhaps, for all the seemingly endless reiterations of his errors to the young governess, Rochester isn't really much of a rake at all, or rather he is a fantasy rake, the hurt soul searching for love, rejecting his mistresses because of their lack of principle and feeling, himself capable of recognizing and responding to a good woman: "my better self" (402). Brontë's portrayal of the mentor-lover who functions on an informal level as a moral guide, of the kind that interested Austen or Eliot, is not only atypical of her work but here proves to be not much more than a gesture.

To consider Rochester with St John in mind is to see more clearly the interaction of sex, love, moral superiority and power as Brontë conceives it. That Jane loves Rochester and yet returns to him is not irreconcilable with her fear of the power of love to subdue, for she has already demonstrated, by leaving, her ability to take control of their relationship. The admission that "the crisis was perilous but not without its charm" as she is about to leave Rochester is only the highest (or lowest) point in a sequence of Jane's manipulative behaviour that makes Rochester's gypsy episode and Bitternut-Lodge threat appear clumsy and ineffectual in the extreme. The nature of her power can be summed up in Rochester's Crimsworthian words:

> "you please me, and you master me – you seem to submit, and I like the sense of pliancy you impart; and while I am twining the soft, silken skein round my finger, it sends a thrill up my arm to my heart. I am influenced – conquered; and the influence is sweeter than I can express; and the conquest I undergo has a witchery beyond any triumph *I* can win."
>
> (328, emphasis original)

and countless commentators have noticed that Jane's reply, however lightly given, has the power of prophecy: "I was thinking, sir (you will excuse the idea; it was involuntary), I was thinking of Hercules and Samson with their charmers" (328).

Their engagement is understandably laced with Jane's fears that Rochester wishes to add her to his list of international mistresses, but what is most striking is not so much her fear of losing control before achieving marriage as the extent to which the wielding of power through resistance to Rochester's advances becomes the defining and a pleasurable feature of their encounters. The fetters and chains, mutinies, sultans, slaves, bashaws, and harems (to whom Jane, in their shared fantasy, will "preach liberty", 339) of the juvenilia and *The Professor* are much in evidence in their courtship teasing.

These references, along with St John's mission to the heathen and the "Creole" Bertha's role in the work, have caused considerable debate between the critics as to their import for Brontë's attitude to imperialism. Edward Said, for example, has been condemnatory, arguing that "the fact that Bertha is from the West Indies" is, in Brontë's scheme, "by no means incidental to her bestiality" (*The World*, 273). Deirdre David argues that Brontë presents Rochester critically, as a representative of the "morally tainted stages of colonial governance", not an indictment of colonialism as such but of the form it was taking at "a specific historical moment when women were called upon to be agents in the labor of both renovating and expanding Brittanic rule" (96–7).[1] Suvendrini Perera points to greater complexity. Examining "the confrontation of feminist, imperialist and individualist impulses" (79), she argues that their seeming alliance is undermined by a "deep ambivalence" best illustrated by Brontë's treatment of (and the critics' varied reactions to) the figure of Bertha, concluding that "the movement toward an inclusive feminism is circumvented by Jane's victory over her colonial rival" (80).

Indeed, there isn't a great deal to nourish the hope of discovering in Brontë some clarity of viewpoint in this regard, as overall she appears to write from assumptions neither rigorously thought through nor critically examined. Certainly there are moments when the reader has hope that Brontë is promoting a sisterhood comprising women both within and outside England, but, in the context of the work as a whole, Jane can be seen making use of eastern allusions for her own ends, as exotic referents for her own and her author's fascination with sexual danger. It is clear that in the views of both Jane and Brontë, heathens, Pashas, Sultans and their harems would all be better off with the benefit of Jane's mentorship, though it seems unlikely they could reach the standards of her "coarsely-clad little peasants" at Morton in whom "the germs of *native* excellence, refinement, intelligence, kind feeling, are as likely to exist in their hearts as in those of the best-born" (385, emphasis mine). Rochester is portrayed as a victim, his punishment for naivety being Bertha who fortunately hastens her insanity by her own "excesses", conveniently enabling him to be portrayed not as disgusted by her madness but by her "giant propensities" (391). Meanwhile, Jane's empowering wealth comes from the same colonial source as his, an uncle who has been the agent of Bertha Mason's brother "for some years" (372) and there is no hint in the novel that this money is other than good for Jane. If *Jane Eyre* is a criticism of the "morally tainted stages of colonial governance" it is by inadvertence only.

As well as making references to the harem that amount to no more than clichés of womanly resistance, Jane also turns to clichés of a different kind to suggest that a desire for power may be overcome by passionate love, although her fears that the problem goes much deeper are incorporated in the very phrases intended to celebrate that love. Rochester's hunger for one-ness is recorded as a sign of the depth of his adoration "my equal is here, and my likeness" (319), "I love you as my own flesh" (283), "my better self":

a fervent, a solemn passion is conceived in my heart; it leans to you, draws you to my centre and spring of life, wraps my existence about you – and, kindling in pure, powerful flame, fuses you and me in one.

(402)

and the climactic claim is contained in Jane's retrospective view of their ten-year marriage, adapted from Genesis:

No woman was ever nearer to her mate than I am: ever more absolutely bone of his bone, and flesh of his flesh. I know no weariness of my Edward's society: he knows none of mine, any more than we each do of the pulsation of the heart that beats in our separate bosoms. . . . we are precisely suited in character; perfect concord is the result.

(576)

There is no need to counter these declarations with the cynicism engendered by experience (as the disappointed Mrs Pryor would do in Shirley: "Two people can never literally be as one", *S* 427) – it is the ideal that is the problem, not the impossibility of living up to it. And, indeed, Brontë herself betrays her inner conviction that such claims to unity mask a struggle for dominance; Rochester's "spring" and "flame" metaphors envisage drawing Jane to *his* centre before they fuse as one. Jane's quotation from Genesis is classic Brontë: the eroticizing of Biblical phrases and references, as Janet Gezari notes, being a common feature of her work (86–7), while her apparent agreement with a scriptural commonplace belies the situation as she structures it – as Deirdre David points out, what might have been "Reader, we were married" is actually phrased "Reader, I married him"(575; David 77).

Jane has acquired moral superiority by leaving Rochester; professional independence through her teaching; supernatural sanction to return through hearing his call; money through a legacy that, being shared, confers further moral worth as well as independence; a husband disembarrassed of a prior wife; and a morally chastened and physically dependent mate who must lean on her as "prop and guide" (573), ensuring her permanent dominance. Like her creator, Jane might very well insist "I do not seek to justify myself", but Providence, under Brontë's authorial sway, does it for her.

Strikingly enough, the final sequence, to which the work moves inexorably, and in which Jane obtains all she could desire, is the dullest in the book. Arousal rather than consummation is Brontë's strong point; the power struggles rather than the victory are where her real interest lies. Just as Mdlle Reuter, enslaved and resistless, offered Crimsworth none of the satisfaction of Frances's intermittent, if safe, rebelliousness, so the "caged eagle" (552) ceases to interest Brontë or the reader.

That Rochester's subordination is a consequence of hostility towards men on Brontë's part might be argued from *Jane Eyre*, if the novel were considered in isolation. On the strength of Jane's lament that "women feel just as men feel" (133), and her resistance to the domination of both Rochester and St John, it might be possible to argue that this is a feminist document. On the other hand, in *The Professor*, Crimsworth's domination of Frances, and the strangely fluid nature of male and female characteristics, as already noted, strongly suggest the possibility that it is the "I" of the work, whoever that might be, that Brontë identifies with, and on whose behalf she seizes control. Thus, on the evidence of the first two novels alone, it is hard to make a secure judgment on the issue. Brontë's next work, because it was to be more overtly concerned with the role of women, while uncharacteristically under the overall control of an omniscient narrator, provides further opportunities to examine whether there is evidence for Brontë's feminism, and the relationship of this issue to the erotic nature of power.

In *Jane Eyre*, Jane's appetite for power is partially concealed (from the reader, and perhaps from Brontë herself) by Jane's initial condition as victim. In *Shirley*, power, or the lack of it, is deliberately presented as the central issue of the novel, informing every aspect of it: industrial, landed, ecclesiastical, economic, class, family, or marital – a centrality that the Marxist focus of Terry Eagleton's *Myths of Power* is particularly suited to elicit. But it is Foucault, sharing Brontë's view of human relationships, who is her kindred spirit:

> [Sexuality appears as] an especially dense transfer point for relations of power: between men and women, young people and old people, parents and offspring, teachers and students, priests and laity, an administration and a population. Sexuality is not the most intractable element in power relations, but rather one of those endowed with the greatest instrumentality: useful for the greatest number of manoeuvers and capable of serving as a point of support, as a linchpin, for the most varied strategies.
>
> (*History of Sexuality* 103).

and although this study is limited to an examination of the mentor-lover, the role of sexuality in all these "relations of power" could certainly be traced out in *Shirley*.

Indeed, the motif of power holds together a work that otherwise threatens to disintegrate. The deaths of her remaining three siblings during the writing of *Shirley* left Brontë (in a dark parody of the Rochesters at Ferndale) alone as prop and guide to her physically and emotionally dependent, partially blind, father. The effects on *Shirley* can only be conjectured, but persuasive arguments have been made that Brontë's intentions changed as one blow fell after another (J. M. S. Tompkins, "Caroline . . . "18–28) and the novel certainly reads as if it had been made up as Brontë went along rather than planned, a supposition not contradicted by her assertion to Lewes, provoked by his praise of Austen:

> When authors write best, or at least, when they write most fluently, an influence seems to waken in them which becomes their master, which will have its own way, putting out of view all behests but its own, dictating certain words, and insisting on their being used, whether vehement or measured in their nature; new moulding characters, giving unthought-of turns to incidents, rejecting carefully elaborated old ideas, and suddenly creating and adopting new ones. Is it not so? And should we try to counteract this influence? Can we indeed counteract it?
>
> (*Letters* 2:10: 12 January 1848)

This passage, written about the time she would have been beginning *Shirley* suggests that Brontë's mode of writing resembled the way in which her characters loved, submitting to the mastery of an irresistible force, an "influence" with the characteristics of a M. Paul, a Heger or a Crimsworth. To this extent, Shirley's tale of Eva, obscure and unappreciated, and her salvation by her lover Genius (455–60), evidently has the force for Brontë of a personal myth, her surrender being to the "influence" within, inspiration seen as mentor. The conception of the "influence which will have its own way" confers connotations of separateness on such a force, thus downplaying its origins "within" and the surrender to self is thus obscured. In practice, such a belief absolved Brontë from the responsibility of considered judgment, and left her open to the dangerous domination of self-rewarding fantasy.

Evidence that submission to this "dictating" "influence" persisted beyond *Shirley* into the writing of her last novel exists in a passage pointed out by Christina Crosby (138–9), in which Lucy laments her difficulty in invoking "the most maddening of masters", the "Creative Presence". A stunning single "sentence" lacking a predicate, despite its length of (by my count) almost 250 words, it progresses by a loosely linked stream (or rather torrent) of associations. The typically Brontëan references to stone gods, worship, sacrifice, and desperate victims are followed by the equally familiar conceptions: "And this tyrant I was to compel into bondage. . . . " (515–16). There seems to be no intended irony at Lucy's expense, no clear attempt to distance the author from her character, although Lucy's "morbid" nature must be taken into account, a matter to be considered later in this chapter.

In *Shirley*, the "unthought-of turns" given to "incidents" by Brontë's surrender to the "influence within" lead to a patchwork treatment of the mentor-lover. Though Caroline and Robert sporadically attempt to educate each other, their mutual mentorship seems based more on habit than genuine interest on Brontë's part. The relationship of Louis and Shirley is also marginal in its way, emerging relatively late in the novel to dominate the final pages with many a familiar Brontë motif. When Shirley reveals her feelings for Louis by lovingly repeating passages from French literature, for example, including a passage assigned by Louis as a punishment when she was younger, Frances Henri and Lucy both spring to mind, signalling their resistance or submission by their choice of their own, or their lovers', language. Unfortunately, there is no indication in the text, though the reader might hope to find it, that Brontë intends this nostalgia for a schoolroom punishment to be seen as an inappropriate regression.

Some of the recurrent characteristics of Brontë's treatment of their relationship are more crudely exploited for erotic effect in *Shirley* than anywhere but the juvenilia: the deliberate prolongation of the battle for power, ever close to, but repeatedly missing, resolution; the irresistible changeability of the woman ("it was not her way to offer the same dish twice", 729); and the obsession with chains and fetters. Brontë makes some attempt to find the appropriate language to justify the wielding of power by disassociating it from words she found unacceptable, but it is a mark of this novel's slackness that there is even a failure to use the familiar formulas consistently here. When Shirley asks if Louis "will . . . be good to me, and never tyrannize" (711) the word carries the usual connotations of Brontëan disapproval, but it is used more sloppily in connection with Shirley's procrastination, when the narrator describes Louis' "revolt against her tyranny, at once so sweet and so intolerable" (729) where the intended associations are erotic. In fact, any attempts to distinguish favourable from unfavourable associations are doomed to founder in the flood of phrases clumsily repeated to erotic ends. The leavening humour of Jane's bashaws and houris is replaced by embarrassingly serious variations on the chaining of a wild cat:

> Pantheress!—beautiful forest-born!—wily, tameless, peerless nature! She gnaws her chain: I see the white teeth working at the steel! She has dreams of her wild woods, and pinings after virgin freedom.
>
> (584)

If one were to make an attempt to rescue Brontë from blame, these words might be attributed to Louis alone, but unfortunately the problem is more widespread, for Caroline sees Shirley in a similar way:

> Shirley is a bondswoman. Lioness! She has found her captor. Mistress she may be of all round her – but her own mistress she is not.
>
> (719)

This is very silly stuff, reminiscent of the juvenilia, and sadly Brontë seems to intend no irony for both Louis and Caroline are fully supported by the narrative voice, from which I can see no reason to separate Brontë herself:

> . . . there she was at last, fettered to a fixed day: there she lay, conquered by love and bound with a vow.
>   Thus vanquished and restricted, she pined, like any other chained denizen of the deserts. Her captor alone could cheer her. . . .
>
> (729–30)

The schoolroom scenes also suggest a reversion to the worst of the earlier work. Without the partial split between lover and mentor that had occurred in *Jane Eyre*, Brontë could return, in *Shirley*, to the sensual (though sulky rather than sultry):

> "Put back your hair," he said.
>
> For one moment, Shirley looked not quite certain whether she would obey the request or disregard it: a flicker of her eye beamed furtive on the professor's face; perhaps if he had been looking at her harshly or timidly, or if one undecided line had marked his countenance, she would have rebelled, and the lesson had ended there and then; but he was only awaiting her compliance – as calm as marble, and as cool. She threw the veil of tresses behind her ear.
>
> (546)

This could be Zamorna with Caroline Vernon, suggesting Brontë is here reverting to a form of novelistic thumb-sucking, a return to the familiar consolations of her youth.

If the courtship leaves the reader uncertain about what either Shirley or Brontë sees as the desirable outcome of the power struggle, the conclusion of the work offers no greater clarity. The heiress's attempts to force Louis into abandoning his insistence on taking a position of inferiority (stemming from his poverty and his occupation as tutor) culminate in the final section of the novel, where they are combined with suggestions that her procrastination in the face of marriage may be due to her fear of being "fettered". Finally the narrator brings both issues together:

> In all this, Miss Keeldar partly yielded to her disposition; but a remark she made a year afterwards proved she partly also acted on system. "Louis," she said, "would never have learned to rule, if she had not ceased to govern: the incapacity of the sovereign had developed the powers of the premier."
>
> (730)

Thus Shirley may acknowledge some degree of fear while also forcing her lover to force her into submission, and, like Frances, she will presumably maintain mutual interest in the marriage through judicious and periodic rebellion. It is hard to imagine a more satisfying resolution for one who finds power both frightening and erotic.

Given the painful circumstances in which *Shirley* was written, it is hard to know how much attention to accord to this relationship. Unfortunately, in ways reminiscent of the juvenilia and *The Professor*, it is not only (unintentionally) repugnant, its mode of portrayal is inept. One explanation might be that Brontë's family tragedies adversely affected her writing, but there is no contradiction in recognizing that it is also possible that the very difficulties under which *Shirley* was written caused Brontë to expose her fundamental assumptions with less restraint than elsewhere.

Indeed, overall, the final impression left by the novel and the many parallels with the works she had already written strongly suggest that Brontë had invested too much time and energy in the elaborate ritual of provocation and submission for this ending to be read as expressing either overt or covert resentment on her part at Shirley's submission. If Brontë, as Gilbert and Gubar believe, "began *Shirley* with the intention of subverting not only the sexual images of literature but the courtship roles and myths from which they derive", and failed only because "she could find no models for this kind of fiction" (a strange defence of a writer of stature), she gave in with extraordinary relish to "the stories of her culture [that] actively endorse traditional sexual roles, even as they discourage female authority" (395). Gilbert and Gubar suggest that in entitling the last chapter "The Winding Up" and joking, "There! I think the varnish has been put on very nicely", Brontë "calls attention to the ridiculous fantasy that is the novel's end" (397). However, the "varnish" phrase actually concludes a passage about one of the curates, concerning whom Brontë has been relentlessly satiric throughout and now pretends to redeem (723), while the chapter title is of a piece with the others in *Shirley*, apparently owing their character to a desire to remind the reader of her admiration of Thackeray. The end, indeed, is "a ridiculous fantasy" but there is little to support the claim that there is anything intentionally, or actually, subversive about its treatment of "courtship roles and myths". A variety of attempts, in addition to that of Gilbert and Gubar, have been made to explain the contradictory nature of the closing, a selection of them summarized by Elliott Vanskike (5–6). He also argues that Shirley's submission is meant satirically: "As readers we must realize that we've been had. . . . The dialogue . . . is too ludicrous, the purple passages in Louis's blank book too foolish, and the reversal in Shirley's character is too implausible . . . " (10). But as I have argued, the contradictions, language and situations are unfortunately only too characteristic from the juvenilia onwards.

Sally Shuttleworth, on the other hand, relates this aspect of Brontë's works to "Victorian psychology" in several ways. She points to Brontë's fear of the loss of self-control as being characteristic of a period that placed heavy emphasis on the need for inner discipline as a defence against insanity (*Psychology*, 36–7). Shuttleworth sees Brontë's concern with individual autonomy and self-fulfilment as both characteristic and uncharacteristic of her time: from "an industrialist, such sentiments would express the spirit of the age. Coming from the socially marginal female, their import is radical, if not revolutionary". "Brontë's novels move reluctantly, defiantly, towards a conventional ending in marriage whose harmony and stasis suggest, to an individual defined by conflict, a form of self-annihilation"(182). But Brontë was not the only writer to be subject to the doublethink of her culture (although she, more openly than any other I can think of, accurately catches the desperation induced by the fear of spinsterhood felt by many women for at least a further century). What most sets her apart from others is not the reluctance but the combination of terror and exhilaration she experiences in the struggle entailed between autonomy and submission.

Shirley, in fact, offers further evidence that Brontë is not interested in the assertion of female power as such but in power as central to all human relationships, gender being less relevant to this issue than her investment in the "I" she has created. In this novel Brontë chose, uncharacteristically, to use an omniscient narrator (albeit with some irritating denials of knowledge), a decision to which the weaknesses of the work have sometimes been attributed. She did, however, resign control to Louis in the first-person account of his courtship of Shirley recorded in his "blank book" and as in the cases of Crimsworth and Jane Eyre, it is he, the only narrating "I" among the characters, who stirs the dance of submission and domination to frenzy. Indeed, it seems likely that the selection of the diary form was dictated by the compulsion to find a way to use "I" for the character who (albeit shakily) finally takes control.

But the most powerful "I" in *Shirley* is that of the narrative voice, which takes the role of mentor to the reader. The preface to the second edition of *Jane Eyre* emphasizes that Brontë believed her duty aligned her with the prophet Micaiah and with Thackeray, the "satirist of 'Vanity Fair' ", to "pluck the mask from the face of the Pharisee" and to set herself, not just against "a timorous or carping few", but against "the World" (xxviii–xxix). Unfortunately, "the World", when confronted by a "poet", as she maintains in *Shirley*, remains alien and uncomprehending:

it is well that the true poet, quiet externally though he may be, has often a truculent spirit under his placidity, and is full of shrewdness in his meekness, and can measure the whole stature of those who look down on him. . . . The true poet is not one whit to be pitied, and he is apt to laugh in his sleeve, when any misguided sympathizer whines over his wrongs. Even when utilitarians sit in judgment on him, and pronounce him and his art useless, he hears the sentence with such a hard derision, such a broad, deep, comprehensive, and merciless contempt of the unhappy Pharisees who pronounce it, that he is rather to be chidden than condoled with.

(57)

Were a character in an Austen or an Eliot novel to utter these sentiments, the reader would know well enough that the speaker merited amusement at best, severe criticism at worst. Taken out of any specific context, the passage would surely be judged as the outpourings of immaturity: self-congratulation, combined with wholesale condemnation of the rest of the world, and offered as the definition of a "true poet" that surely marks a self-indulgent low point in the assessment of the function of the writer.

Yet, in context, this is intended as a serious defence, in a narrative voice from which there is no reason to believe Brontë dissociated herself, of those with "imagination" against the majority who, like the industrialist Hiram Yorke, "think [imagination] a rather dangerous, senseless attribute – akin to weakness – perhaps partaking of frenzy – a disease rather than a gift of the mind" (56). That the word "Pharisee" becomes the term for the enemy in both the "Preface" to *Jane Eyre* and in this passage in *Shirley* links Brontë to the "poet" of whom she speaks. It is this "truculent spirit" that she asks us to admire, that she hopes we will see in her work, and with which she endows the characters she most favours. Though we are told that the true poet's contemptuous reactions to criticism are "rather to be chidden than condoled with", it is clear that this remark is not offered as a genuine condemnation but as a celebration of superiority.

To read any work by Brontë, from the juvenilia onwards, is to be repeated witness to, or even the target of, some form of aggression and hostility. It is in *Shirley*, however, that this belligerence is most pervasive and gratuitous. The author's animosity is embodied in a series of characters, such as the curates or the adult Yorkes, who seem to have been introduced principally to attract or emit hostility. Aggression is also directed at the reader, who is the first to be grabbed and shaken in a quick pre-emptive strike reminiscent of Crimsworth or Lucy in the classroom, on the principle that hostility is to be expected and therefore quickly countered: "If you think, from this prelude, that anything like a romance is preparing for you, reader, you never were more mistaken" (7).

Lest, however, the reader should feel this shows Brontë, through the narrative voice, to be desirous of being her readers' mentor but not their lover, the all-encompassing extent to which verbal abuse and affection are linked in her works should be remembered: her characters habitually give and receive love through attack and defence. Not all hostility in *Shirley* is an expression of love, but almost all love in the novel is expressed in terms of hostility or in the interactions of domination and submission of which the mentor-lover relationship of Louis to Shirley is both the focus and the lowest point of the novel. In this regard, the work shows no advance over *The Professor* and little over the juvenilia. That it is not as appealing as *Jane Eyre* is tribute to the skill with which Jane's hunger for power is made more acceptable to the reader, although, as a consequence, *Shirley* is not only less popular but also much less effective in supporting the assumption that sexual relations must be "political".

Brontë was to live long enough to explore the relationship of power and love through the role of mentor-lover only one more time, in her last novel, *Villette*. In the love of Lucy and her mentor, Paul Emanuel, she intertwined many of the situations from her own experiences at the Pensionnat Heger with events occurring in her life while she was writing, including her fluctuating relations with her publisher George Smith (cast in the role of Graham Bretton). Much that is familiar from earlier works was to recur again, but in one regard there was a major change. The narrating "I" is deliberately presented, in modern parlance, as neurotic; in her creator's word as "morbid". Furthermore, unlike Crimsworth, Jane or Louis, whose attacks of "hypochondria" are of limited duration, Lucy is "morbid" for much of the work. John Hughes convincingly argues that the originality of *Villette* lies in its study of emotional estrangement, although I shall argue it is less "a novel without mutuality" (712) than one in which mutual relationships are deformed, though this is not always Brontë's intention.

Given that authors may create central characters of whose emotional lives they disapprove, Lucy's "morbid" nature poses a particular problem to the reader in distinguishing between the view held by Brontë of the mentor-lover relationships in the novel and that held by the narrating voice. It is necessary, therefore, to examine the evidence for the possible separation of Lucy and Brontë by examining the trustworthiness of the "I".

Unlike Jane, with whom the reader can feel little doubt that sympathetic identification is expected, Lucy is clearly not intended to be entirely appealing nor wholly right-minded, as Brontë's own words confirm:

> I consider that she *is* both morbid and weak at times; her character sets up no pretensions to unmixed strength, and anybody living her life would necessarily become morbid.
>
> (Wise, 4:18, Nov. 6, 1852, emphasis original)

However, the narrated and the narrating Lucy need not necessarily be of one mind, and the real difficulty is to know how to judge the Lucy who actually writes the life when her hair is "at last white" (105). Is the narrating Lucy still the morbid Lucy of the confessional, or are we to assume that Brontë wishes us to see her as a Lucy who, having been loved, and now "living her life" of professional fulfilment, can fairly judge the past? How far is the Lucy who wields the pen to be trusted in her view of her experiences, and of the mentor-lover she has found in Paul?

Critical opinion seems divided, and yet most critics write as if their point of view may be safely assumed, one way or the other. For example, Tanner remarks in passing, "Lucy's demystification of the nun is symptomatic of a finally acquired ability to read her environment in a sane and steady manner" (introduction to *Villette* 12, 48); Gilbert and Gubar apparently assume the opposite: "Lucy's conflicts are hidden because, as we have seen, she represents them through the activity of other people. As self-effacing as a narrator as she is as a character, she often seems to be telling any story but her own" (416); Moglen seems also to assume the teller is neurotic: "The form of *Villette* is the form of Lucy's neurosis: a representation of the novel's subject" (196–9). Joseph Litvak "assume[s]"

> a more or less stable allegorical link between Brontë and Lucy. Critics have, of course, pointed out the author's differences from, and even dislike of, her heroine, but this will-to-dissociation itself needs to be analyzed. I would argue that the novel remains more instructive as a portrait of the artist than as a case history.
>
> ("Scene of Instruction" 475, n.15)

In fact, Lucy's trustworthiness, encouraged by Brontë's treatment of it, is a subject on which readers' assumptions often take the place of argument.

There is no doubt Lucy is markedly unreliable in her narrative – postponing, for example, the identification of Dr John either as her rescuer on her first arrival in Villette or as Graham Bretton (249) and concealing her own adolescent admiration for him from the reader beneath her disdainful account of the young Polly's devotion. She similarly keeps from the reader both her growing involvement with Paul until it is well-established (496, 528) and also her retrospective knowledge that the nun is merely de Hamal (686), having deliberately encouraged speculation as to whether the nun was either a 'genuine' ghost or a product of her own, and subsequently Paul's, morbid imagination.

There are several reasons that do not require a diagnosis of continuing neurosis to account for Lucy's unreliability. First is the storyteller's desire for suspense, for which purpose tradition permits concealment from the reader. In all the above cases it should be noted that Lucy eventually reveals the truth before the end of the narrative. Nancy Sorkin Rabinowitz argues that Lucy misleads other characters as well as the reader in a display of power (71–3), and it would be characteristic of Brontë to find satisfaction in "teasing" the reader with a parallel display of authorial mastery.

Traditionally, too, the narrative voice is permitted, when the teller is looking back, to infuse the course of the account with the emotions of the earlier moment, and, in fact, Lucy does, from time to time, issue warnings that her attitudes have changed, for example towards Dr John (354, 662). If the effect on the reader is not that Lucy has offered a clearly identifiable series of corrected misdirections, it is probable that Brontë was aiming at a general atmosphere of concealment to recreate the feelings of the past, using a somewhat similar technique to that which she employs with the nun. Janet Gezari points out that though Lucy seems paranoid, stringing together coincidences into a persecution fantasy, the novel absolves her of such self-deception. Dr John really is Graham Bretton, the Countess de Bassompierre really is Polly, the examiners really are the men she met on her first arrival in Villette, and the "nun" is not a figment of her imagination. From a realistic standpoint, de Hamal's appearances have nothing to do with Lucy's emotional states, yet so apposite are the sightings to her nervous crises that many readers, nevertheless, assign psychological significance to them (for example, Charles Burkhardt, 115–17; Gilbert and Gubar, 425) as indeed Brontë may have intended readers to do. The "nun" was not the creation of Lucy's overwrought condition, but Brontë is willing to allow the impression to linger that "she" was. Dismissing Lucy's obfuscations as technique, however, only clears up the most obvious problems. In judging whether she is to be considered ultimately "reliable" in her attitude to the mentor-lover, more careful consideration needs to be given to Brontë's depiction of Lucy's powers of judgment. The older Lucy is clear-eyed and self-critical about many of her past weaknesses:

> Left alone, I was passive; repulsed, I withdrew; forgotten – my lips would not utter, nor my eyes dart a reminder.
>
> (593–4)

and there is nothing in the account of Lucy's love for Graham Bretton that requires a thesis of continuing neurosis. Lucy's over-reliance on his casually extended friendship and his insensitivity to the needs he alternately nourishes and starves are brilliantly done, and the mixed emotions that remain to the older Lucy are sharply and honestly delineated. The desperation of her youthful need for affection and reassurance may certainly be considered morbid, as well as explicable in terms of her emotional isolation, but what survives into the narrator's present is an appropriate understanding of the disturbed younger self, an open-eyed evaluation that suggests the reader is also expected to accept the narrating Lucy's judgment of Paul, the mentor-lover.

The early Bretton scenes are memorable, in part, for their difference from the rest of the work. In them, Lucy is treated extremely unsympathetically, and her emotions with regard to Polly and Graham are, indeed, concealed from the first-time reader, and never directly discussed. Lucy's neurosis is here very skillfully delineated in the form of the narration itself, and Brontë was right to contrast her own failure over the later Polly with her earlier success: "The childhood of Paulina is, however, I think, pretty well imagined . . . . " (Wise 4:23: 6 December 1852 – the remainder of the sentence is torn off). By contrast, later in the work, Lucy has no inhibitions about revealing her agonizing need for the affection of Dr John, culminating in her burial of the letters in the pensionnat garden. The shift from the taciturnity of the opening to the later revelations is an awkward one and its cause can only be a matter of speculation. It may be that the technique of holding the "I" of the novel at a distance, as if seen by an uncomprehending observer, was just too difficult and uncongenial a feat for Brontë, creator of Jane Eyre, to prolong. Or perhaps, once the unsympathetic view was established from the outside, Brontë felt she had provided the reader with an understanding of Lucy's effect on others, and had no need to continue this particular narrative technique any longer.

Finally, in assessing Brontë's support of Lucy's love for Paul, there is the episode of Harriet Martineau's attack on the novel: "I do not like the love, either the kind or the degree of it" (Martineau letter [1853] in Wise 4:41). Awareness, if not the negative judgment, of "the degree of it" finds an echo in the response of Robert Polhemus to *Villette*: "A concert, a painting, a play, an actress performing, clothing, a king – all are tinged with, framed, and inscribed with personal meaning by a love-hungry mind. Erotic desire expropriates anything – art, architecture, public ceremony – to tell its tale" (*Erotic Faith* 113). But Brontë's response to Martineau was angry:

> I know what *love* is as I understand it; and if man or woman should be ashamed of feeling such love, then is there nothing right, noble, faithful, truthful, unselfish in this earth, as I comprehend rectitude, nobleness, fidelity, truth, and disinterestedness.
>
> (Wise 4:42 [1853])

It seems unreasonable not to read the parallels between this and Lucy's account of Paul's letter at the close of the work as confirming Brontë's unequivocal support for the nature of the lovers' relationship.

> he wrote as he gave and as he loved, in full-handed, full-hearted plenitude. . . . because he loved Lucy . . . because he was faithful and thoughtful, because he was tender and true.
>
> (713)

Given the evidence, overall, in favour of trusting the narrating "I", the judgments of the older Lucy on the various mentor-lover relationships become useful indicators of Brontë's attitude to the relationship in the last novel she was to write. Much that is by now familiar from the preceding works re-appears. Teasing, for example, Brontë's mark of mingled affection and hostility, is characteristic not only of Lucy and Paul but also of Dr John's flirtatious relationship with his mother. Even Lucy, in her rare moments of daring during the period of their friendship, risks teasing Dr John, as she does when she refuses to exchange prizes at the lottery (317). She even, for a while, essays the role of his mentor, criticizing his passion for Ginevra, in the characteristic Brontëan formula: " . . . you are but a slave, I declare, where

Miss Fanshawe is concerned, you merit no respect; nor have you mine" (270). Echoes of the central mentor-lover relationship of Paul and Lucy, and of other earlier mentor-lovers, are to be found, in fragmentary form, throughout the work. Strikingly, in *Villette*, the pairs involved in mentor-lover relationships are of parent and child, possibly an outcome of Brontë's tightening bonds to her father and her observation of her publisher's closeness to his mother. The Abelardian difference in age, Lucy in her early twenties, Paul in his forties, is echoed in the parent–child "lovers": Graham and Mrs Bretton, Polly and de Bassompierre. Yet, contrast rather than similarity is, in part, intended, since Brontë allows Lucy to imply criticism by revealing both the inappropriate flirtatiousness of the first couple and the blind possessiveness of Polly's father. Furthermore, in each case, though the parent should be mentor, the child is treated as an equal (or in Polly's case as superior to her childish father).

Whether the discomfort Brontë and Lucy reveal in dealing with these parent–child lovers should be extended towards Paul and Lucy, who are themselves separated by a generation, is one of the central questions raised by the novel. Two differences from the earlier works are particularly striking. In *Villette*, the pattern of the mentor who enjoys exhibitions of power is taken intentionally to comic extremes, and erotic love is almost completely absent when Lucy falls in love, either with Graham or Paul. Lucy's hunger is for the affection of a father or brother, as if the unspecified family disasters of her early years have left her with an unsatisfied need for familial love.

In fact, there is more sexual intensity in the relationship of Dr John and his mother than in the recognized love affairs in the work, while the latter are shown to be at their most intensely satisfying when the lovers are physically separated. It is no accident that when Lucy drops Dr John's letter in the attic, she fails to be consoled by the presence of the man who sent it, and is made "satisfied and happy" only by his returning it to her (356). In such circumstances, it is not surprising that Lucy judges Paul's absence abroad to be "the three happiest years of my life" (711), a time of professional success warmed by the "genial flame" of Paul's letters: "he took pen and paper, because he loved Lucy and had much to say to her. . . . his letters were real food that nourished, living water that refreshed" (713). The childlike tone of this passage is striking – from the use of "Lucy" in place of "me" to the emphasis on Paul as asexual nurturer.

Brontë's treatment of Paul's weaknesses has much in common with her strategy with Rochester. Initially Paul's faults are magnified, only to show, in the long run, just how unimportant they are compared to his virtues and his love for the heroine. He has the good judgment both to understand and to recognize the unique characteristics of the "I" of the novel, which others have signally failed to do, these qualities in combination setting up a situation in which it seems churlish of the reader to criticize him. Brontë's pre-emptive strategy can be seen in virtually every scene involving Paul. The reader is asked to see as endearing a man who locks a nervous young woman in a hot, vermin-infested attic without food or drink for a day to ensure the success of the school play that he directs, who repeatedly and with full self-awareness indulges his love of self-dramatization in tear-inducing tantrums from the *estrade*, and who rents a room to spy on the private garden of a school for young ladies.

Rochester's faults are annulled by his moral inferiority to, as well as his love for, Jane. Paul's are excused by the emotional immaturity that makes Lucy his superior: his "infantile" tastes, his admiration of trifles "like a child" (500), his often noted "naïveté", "too natural to conceal, too impulsive to repress his wish" (446). His power is defused by the application of affectionate condescension: "Never was a better little man, in some points than M. Paul: never, in others, a more waspish little despot" (434). The "I" of *Villette* may patronize her saintly but comical child with no challenge to her emotional sophistication. Although, like Brontë's other lovers, Paul watches the woman he cares for, secretly and intensely, invading her privacy: "the hand of M. Emanuel was on intimate terms with my desk" (495), the sexual potential of both the acts and the language is defused by Lucy's tone. Even the nature of Paul's moral strength marks him as naive: he gives way to a "junta" of manipulators (two of whom he supports financially – Père Silas and Madame Walravens), sacrificing the chance of immediate marriage to Lucy in favour of repairing his exploiters' fortunes in Guadeloupe.

Finally, to be a man in the world of *Villette*, the world of Mme Beck, Mme Walravens, Mrs Bretton, the Queen of Labassecour, and, ultimately, Mdlle Snowe, is to be a child again, to be manipulated, cosseted or punished. Even the men who pursue Lucy on the night of her arrival are chastised, though they do not know it, by a lecture on "Human Justice". But as Pauline Nestor points out, this is not a repudiation of men in favour of women, for the latter have "no more place in Lucy Snowe's world than men . . . . the heroine's choice is for an 'empire over self', fundamentally antipathetic to mutuality and communality alike" (*Female* 140). As will be apparent from my argument, this seems to me a truer reading than that of Nina Auerbach who sees Lucy, her honesty dead, as finally aligned with the female junta of Mesdames Beck and Walravens (*Communities* 112), unless this realignment is recognized as inadvertent on Brontë's part. The "I" in *Villette* belongs to the sex whose members wield the most power, but it is not clear that the novel can be construed either as a claim for, or a criticism of, female superiority, particularly in the context of the other novels. Men hold power in the worlds of Crimsworth's Yorkshire and Rochester's Thornfield, while Shirley resigns power to Louis at Fieldhead. Once again, the only constant that can confidently be asserted is that the "I" in each work, whether male or female, is superior, is finally recognized in that superiority, is shown to be justified, and, overtly or covertly, ultimately takes power.

In her attempts to discover a distinction she could accept between tyranny and mastery, Brontë had demonstrated, in her earlier works, her Foucault-like belief that the alternation of power made its exercise desirable. This reversibility is similarly found in the growing love of Paul and Lucy, here successively taking the roles of parent and child. The scenes in the classroom reveal Paul in the role of father, difficult and demanding, like Crimsworth or Louis, only because he cares. Later, poor because of his charities, but nevertheless richer than Lucy, he can, like the father who rewards his daughter for her efforts, endow her with the means to begin her career as a second Mme Beck (or Elizabeth Hastings or Frances Henri). At the same time, the limited nature of his financial resources and his immediate departure nullify any threat that he might impose a Rochester-like domination. The climax of the plot comes when Paul produces the prospectuses and elicits Lucy's child-like excitement:

> "Did you do this M. Paul? Is this your house? Did you furnish it? Did you get these papers printed? Do you mean me? Am I the directress? Is there another Lucy Snowe? Tell me: say something."
>
> (703)

The moment of their closest physical contact is overlaid by a sentimentalized version of romance appropriate to the juvenilia:

> he gently raised his hand to stroke my hair; it touched my lips in passing; I pressed it close, I paid it tribute. He was my king; royal for me had been that hand's bounty; to offer homage was both a joy and a duty.
>
> (704)

And finally the "homage" is predictably followed by a reassertion of his childlike littleness: "Magnificent-minded, grand-hearted, dear, faulty little man!" (706).

The most conclusive evidence that Paul remains within the role of fantasy father-child is to be found in the immature daydream that closes the novel. A lover, about to depart for several years to the West Indies, allows the insecure woman he loves to suffer under the incorrect impression he has left the country without saying goodbye, leaving her prey to the conviction of abandonment. That lover chooses to spend those three last weeks (assisted by his ward) in setting up a school for the woman he cares for in order to surprise her and prove he can keep a secret, rather than spending the same time in loving consultations with the woman herself. Yet the younger Lucy is overjoyed, and, as already demonstrated, the narrating Lucy and her creator show no disposition to judge her neurotic on this account. To say that these are unfair criticisms because they are not appropriate to the conventions governing the end of the novel is only to shift the problem to the question of why an author would choose, with no discernable irony, the conventions of the fairy tale in a probing psychological study of a "morbid" woman's discovery of love. As in much of *Jane Eyre*, the reader is, at the close, permitted to forgo the difficult problems of maturity for the satisfactions of fantasy.

Like Rochester and Louis, Paul will not commit himself until Lucy has been provoked out of her customary self-control to admit her own love. Paul's response is then as much that of the father–mentor as it is of the lover:

> I merited severity; he looked indulgence. . . . I was full of faults; he took them and me all home. For the moment of utmost mutiny, he reserved the one deep spell of peace."
>
> (709)

But the future does not hold marriage for them – only affectionate letters, professional success for Lucy, and the suggestion that Paul is drowned on the voyage home. Life-induced pessimism, the doctrine of happy and sad fates so often expounded in the novel, or an inability to bring a Heger-like lover to marriage with a heroine so like herself, all these reasons can be suggested for the conclusion, and some truth may inhere in all these possibilities. Nevertheless, the reader may also wonder if Brontë had not, by the closing pages, brought the "I" of *Villette* to the most desirable situation she could imagine: Lucy's worthiness of love confirmed, her intellectual creativity and pedagogical skills recognized, her social and professional future assured, her moral and emotional superiority to the Becks, Walravens and even Brettons of the world demonstrated. Like Jane, she is "justified" without appearing to "justify herself". Like Elizabeth Hastings of the juvenilia, she is "dependent on nobody – responsible to nobody". In these terms, the tragedy is less that the lovers are parted forever than that there are to be no more letters.

It would be difficult for Brontë to arrange a happy marriage for a woman whose three years of self-sufficiency lit by the glow of absent love had been her happiest, and for a couple who had established a parent–child relationship between them – an anticlimax worse than that concluding *Jane Eyre* would result from a "happy" ending. There is a sad irony in the fact that, as Brontë wrote the closing lines in which Lucy and her surrogate father-child are kept apart, and phrased the ending ambiguously to please her elderly father, she thought herself trapped in her own life in the reversible relationship of child and parent.

In the end, Brontë was unable to find a way to reconcile in her fiction her conception of love (which remained based in immaturity) with professional independence, and in the end she chose the latter. Frances Henri's "solution", alternations of public and private behaviour, had been awkward and unconvincing, and Brontë did not resort to it again in *Villette*, nor to Shirley's self-engineered subordination. It is in the self-sufficient professional, Elizabeth Hastings, that Brontë found the model she needed. Thus, while this last novel does not offer the repellent variations on the theme of mentor-lover that mar *The Professor* and *Shirley*, it is nevertheless unsuccessful in conceiving of a mature sexual relationship. Indeed, what is particularly disturbing is the possibility it suggests that erotic intensity decreased for Brontë with the waning of hostility. Judith Mitchell, describing *Jane Eyre* as "arguably the most erotic English novel written in the nineteenth century", and thus indirectly recognizing *Villette* to be less so, argues that Brontë's last novel "eschews the capitulation to the domination/submission hierarchy to negotiate a realistic pathway to both love and independence" (44, 69). Unfortunately, Brontë's inability to bring together "love" and "independence" at the end of the novel is manifest. I can only ask the reader to judge whether, as Mitchell believes, "the parent–child paradigm. . . contributes its erotic charge to their relationship" (77) or, as I have argued, weakens it. M. Paul's rages are never deeply threatening, indeed they are generally comic; nor is the wielding of his power over Lucy ever more than theatrical. In contrast to earlier works, the power struggle is a matter of appearance only, but, unfortunately so is the sexual nature of their relationship. The first change is a considerable relief, the second a great disappointment.

In her letters to M. Heger, Brontë had written with horror of being the "slave of a fixed and dominant idea". By contrast, in her response to George Henry Lewes, she had asserted "when authors write best, or at least when they write most fluently, an influence seems to waken in them, which becomes their master. . . " and had questioned the advisability or even the possibility of counteracting such an influence. The choice of language suggests that she found it appropriate, in describing her dilemmas as a writer, to use the terms by which she had attempted to distinguish between the involuntary submission she despised ("slavery") and willing submission she approved (to "mastery"). Yet, as in her fiction, it is difficult to see how that "influence" was to be preferred over, or was any different from, the "idea" she repudiated. In her juvenilia and her first three novels, the "fixed and dominant idea" was the link between power and sexual love, explored through variations on the role of the mentor-lover, and she offered no resistance to its "influence". At the same time, erotic though she found such power struggles, they also made of love a very threatening thing, and remnants of the fear of love survive in the protection of Lucy's self-sufficiency by means of the storm of the closing pages. *Villette* confirms that immature elements survived in Brontë's work to the last, and it is clear that the immaturity found its chief focus, from the earliest to the latest works, in the role of the mentor-lover.

Brontë's novels unintentionally provide a judgment on the assumption that power is the essence of human relationships in general and love in particular, for they demonstrate that to accept such a view is to commit oneself to relationships stuck at the level of childhood or adolescence. Unlike Austen, who had laboured to achieve equal maturity for her lovers, Brontë, despite the expressed demands of her heroines, could not conceive of such a relationship sufficiently successfully to enact it in her novels. But *Villette*, despite the continued prominence of the mentor-lover, does mark a change. It is a novel with considerable strengths (not the least being its author's courageous decision not to rely on a wholly sympathetic "I") in which there are signs Brontë was beginning to reconsider the relationship and to disentangle sexual love from power. Had this not entailed the loss of sexual intensity, it would have represented a break with the slavery to a "fixed and dominant idea" to which the earlier works had succumbed. As they stand, however, her novels are inadvertent testimony to the dangers of holding the view that love and power are indivisible.

The relative dates of Charlotte Brontë's early death and Marian Evans's late start as a writer of fiction (the year after Brontë died and at an age when Austen had already completed *Mansfield Park*) combine to give the impression they were women of two different generations, although Brontë was born the year before Austen's early death and Evans two years after it. A coincidence serves as a reminder that their beginnings, if not their ends, were contemporary. In 1854, less than a month after Charlotte Brontë married Mr Nicholls, Marian Evans left, in her own words, "for Labassecour" with the already-married G. H. Lewes (*Letters* 2:165: 10 July 1854), Charlotte's would-be literary mentor, soon to become her own.

Lewes's relationships to the three subjects of this study – he used one as an instructional example for the other two – are complex, and he provides an intriguing link between them all. Born the year Austen died, he is often credited with keeping her reputation alive in the period before the publication of the 1870 *Memoir* by her nephew (see, for example, B.C. Southam, *Critical Heritage* I:20). However, Lewes's championship was not without its dubious aspects, sometimes, for example, boosting Austen's reputation by ascribing his own or lesser writers' comments to the more famous. Macaulay, for example, did not use the precise phrase a "prose Shakespeare" (Carroll, *CH* 1:25) as Lewes claimed, but rather placed Austen among those who "have approached nearest to the manner of the great master" who "has had neither an equal nor a second"(Carroll, *CH* 1:122), while, as Joanne Wilkes points out, Lewes metamorphosed another source of praise for Austen from the insignificant Maria Jane Jewsbury to the more impressive Archbishop Whately (Wilkes 36–7). Such mistakes may have been merely the result of hurried work, but the latter (in 1859, puffing *Amos Barton*) conveniently built up Austen's reputation in a way that would aid Eliot: "a writer who seems to us inferior to Miss Austen in the art of telling a story, and generally in what we have called the 'economy of art;' but equal in truthfulness, dramatic ventriloquism, and humour, and greatly superior in culture, reach of mind, and depth of emotional sensibility" (Carroll *CH* 1:155–6). Moreover, it is only in technical virtuosity that Lewes puts Austen ahead of Eliot here, and as Graham Handley acutely points out of the 1859 appraisal (" . . . miniatures are not frescoes and her works are miniatures . . . "): "the sound of this is more than the matter, the prose makes images, but the eyes have been withdrawn from the text" (*JA* 17).

Brontë[2] first came to Lewes's attention when (fresh from publishing his own novel *Ranthorpe*) he wrote a review of *Jane Eyre*. In it, he referred to Austen as one of the two greatest English novelists (the other being Fielding), a touchstone of "truth and delineation of character", praise that, as already noted, astonished Brontë when she subsequently read Austen's work. Mary O'Farrell suggests that he may have provoked Brontë's resistance by appearing to be "a chiding and guiding Mr. Knightley" leading to a "rivalry that is woven of contrasts and conditionals . . . always represented as a proposition: if [Austen] is this, then I am that" (50, 51). In the same review he warned Brontë against an over-reliance on melodrama and stressed the dangers of running out of one's stock of personal experience, touching an already-sore spot and possibly contributing to her emphasis on greater "realism" in *Shirley*.

Brontë's attitude to Lewes was, characteristically for her, both adulatory and hostile. It finally foundered over regrettable behaviour on both sides. Lewes's review of *Shirley* criticized Brontë's "overmasculine vigour' (to which Brontë replied "I can be on guard against my enemies, but God deliver me from my friends") and she bitterly attacked his liberal attitude towards Catholicism (Ashton, *Versatile* 17–20). By 1859 he was forecasting that, "we fear [Miss Brontë, unlike Miss Austen] will soon cease to find readers" (Southam, *CH* I: 150) and declaring that after reading *Jane Eyre* aloud "we feel as if we should never open the book again"(151). But if the consequences of Lewes's attempted mentorship of Brontë proved to be both mixed and limited, his influence on the woman who became George Eliot was to be altogether different.

5

George Eliot and "The Clerical Sex": From *Scenes of Clerical Life* to *Middlemarch*

In 1843, while Charlotte was desperately trying to gather the strength to leave the Pensionnat Heger and return to England, Mary Ann Evans,[1] as her letters show, was also discovering for herself both the attractions and dangers of a mentor of the opposite sex. While Charlotte agonized, Mary Ann went to stay and study with Dr R. H. Brabant, at that time in his early sixties, in the place of his newly married daughter. Such a filial relationship was likely to be favourably looked upon by her society as the glowing description by her early biographer, Mathilde Blind, writing in 1883, suggests:

> No doubt the society of this accomplished scholar . . . was no less congenial than instructive to his young companion; while her singular mental acuteness and affectionate womanly ways were most grateful to the lonely old man. There is something very attractive in this episode of George Eliot's life. It recalls a frequently recurring situation in her novels. . . .
>
> (4)

At first, Mary Ann found the relationship idyllic:

> I am in a little heaven here, Dr. Brabant being its archangel. . . . Of the Dr. what shall I say? for the time would fail me to tell of all his charming qualities. We read, walk and talk together, and I am never weary of his company. . . . I am petted and fed with nice morsels and pretty speeches. . . .
>
> (*Letters* 1:165–6: 20 November 1843)

It isn't surprising, however, that his wife did not rejoice in the relationship and that the visit culminated in Mary Ann's sudden departure. That the episode was humiliating, and that Mary Ann came to dislike Brabant heartily is clear from a letter written three years later:

> If I ever offered incense to him it was because there was no other deity at hand and because I wanted some kind of worship pour passer le temps.
>
> *(Letters* 1:225: 5 November 1846)

and if Eliza Lynn Linton, who also knew him, was correct, he contributed his scholarly inadequacies to Casaubon, "ever writing and rewriting, correcting and destroying" (*Literary Life* 43). However, Brabant served to warn Eliot against only a very specialized form of mentor-lover, the elderly scholar, and not against the species in general. Indeed, the fact that Marian Evans was subsequently drawn to George Henry Lewes, whose disposition to be mentor to a female writer had already been demonstrated in his attempts to advise Brontë, shows her continuing attraction to such a figure.

Despite his own obvious inferiority as a novelist and his early doubts about her ability to write anything but analytical material, it was G. H. Lewes who became George Eliot's creator and supporter, encouraging Marian's tentative interest in writing fiction (*Journals* 289: 6 December 1857) and continuing until his death as her literary adviser, full of encouragement and practical advice. Mary Ann Evans finally did find in life a lover she could acknowledge as her mentor, while Austen and Brontë remained a part of their relationship. Lewes and Marian, as their journals record, took pleasure in reading works by both novelists to each other on many occasions (*Journals* 65, 69, 275, 279).

Eliot's encounters with the mentor-lover in her predecessors' novels are well-documented. While writing "Mr Gilfil's Love Story" she was reading "*Mansfield Park* in the evenings" (*Journals* 65) and during the period immediately preceding the writing of "Janet's Repentance", she read Austen's explorations of the relationship in *Northanger Abbey, Sense and Sensibility* and *Emma*, and also read *Persuasion* (*Journals* 69, 279; G. H. Lewes's Journal in *Letters* 2:326–328). In 1859, Lewes was to write of reading Austen's novels aloud "We have re-read them all four times", the "we" presumably including Marian Lewes (Southam, *CH* 151). While she was in the throes of writing "Janet's Repentance" she read Charlotte Brontë's *The Professor* which she listed with the "lighter food" in her reading list (*Journals* 281), possibly a choice suggested by her joint perusal with Lewes, during the interval between writing the second and third *Scenes,* of Gaskell's *Life* of Brontë (*Journals* 279). After the publication of the collected *Scenes,* she and Lewes were to consult that same biography in competitive spirit, pleased to note that library subscriptions for Eliot's work commenced three weeks after publication, compared to six weeks for *Jane Eyre* (*Journals* 294). *Villette* she had read three years before, with apparently uncritical enthusiasm: "a still more wonderful book than *Jane Eyre.* There is something almost preternatural in its power" (*Letters* 2:87: 15 February 1853), and a month later, her enthusiasm had remained undiminished: "*Villette* – *Villette* – have you read it?" (*Letters* 2:92: 12 March 1853). The lingering power that novel exercised over her on a personal level (a year and a half after her first reading) may be judged from her announcement to a friend before leaving for Brussels with Lewes on the trip that marked her "marriage" to him: ". . . I am preparing to go to 'Labassecour'" (*Letters* 2:165: 10 July 1854). But when Lewes, in his assessment of Austen in 1859, writes that, after reading *Jane Eyre* aloud "we feel as if we should never open the book again", and complains that Paul Emanuel, though a "vigorous" sketch, is observed "from the outside" he may also be speaking for Marian (Southam, *CH* 151, 161).

Influential, though negatively, on her treatment of the subject were the recent popular novels that provided fodder for her essay "Silly Novels by Lady Novelists" finished eleven days before she began her first work of fiction. A comic version of the mentor-lover emerges in this essay in the form of "the young curate, looked at from the point of view of the middle class, where cambric bands are understood to have as thrilling an effect on the hearts of young ladies as epaulettes have upon the classes above and below it". From the details of the transpositions required to adjust the clichés of the fashionable novel to the particular requirements of the "White Neck Cloth School" (including "tender glances . . . seized from the pulpit stairs instead of the opera box") to the summing-up, Eliot's sarcasm is dismissive: "in one particular the novels of the . . . School are meritoriously realistic – their favourite hero the Evangelical young curate is always rather an insipid personage" (*Essays* 318).

One characteristic survived into her own work, however, from the White Neckcloth Novel: "questions as to the state of the heroine's affections . . . mingled with anxieties as to the state of her soul" (*Essays* 318) – a description as true of Eliot's later works as of the earlier. Possibly the fear of the hackneyed and insipid, while it led her to create the atypical Gilfil and Tryan, also distracted Eliot from recognizing the similarities to the works she repudiated, as well as the more serious difficulties that awaited her. The particular interest of *Scenes of Clerical Life,* therefore, lies in the pattern of interests and problems against which Eliot's subsequent developments may be measured, the mentor-lover appearing as early as Eliot's second novella, "Mr. Gilfil's Love-Story". But though it is here that she first employs strategies that would become characteristic of her work, they can be explored more fully in her third and most substantial *Scene*, "Janet's Repentance".

Here she suggests the possibility that mentorship is, in itself, both a source and a beneficiary of sexual appeal, although her manoeuvres suggest she is acutely aware that this might provoke resistance from the reader. The evidence for this awareness is worth examining concurrently with Eliot's moves to overcome it, because it shows an early perception on her part that the mentor-lover, at least of the clerical variety, is open to moral attack. It is first brought into focus in the set-piece scene at Mrs Linnet's. Eliot's combination of overt sympathy with covert hostility, in this case directed towards the women who gather to prepare a library to please the evangelical curate with whom they are all to some degree in love, is one that recurs in other works. Here she also employs a tactic that will become her trademark, deflecting criticism from a relationship she expects to provoke the reader's opposition by putting the reader in the wrong. Skilfully, if brutally, she devalues the curate's female admirers with "humour" by reporting their unkind assessments of each other, rebuking the reader for enjoying the spectacle she has herself created, and then extricating herself from responsibility:

> Poor women's hearts! Heaven forbid that I should laugh at you, and make cheap jests on your susceptibility towards the clerical sex, as if it had nothing deeper or more lovely in it than the mere vulgar angling for a husband.
>
> (216)

The dismissive terms combine distressingly with the claim to seriousness, an unpleasant alloy that patronizes both the women and the reader, permitting these women's attraction to "the clerical sex" to be examined with less than full seriousness by their creator. This moment in the text also provides an early example of a discomfiting feature of Eliot's mentorial relationship with the reader who, as Rosemarie Bodenheimer argues, is rarely likely to have reacted in the ways Eliot claims. Tracing the pattern to her earliest correspondence, Bodenheimer demonstrates that "These imagined readers are not really representations of ourselves, they are necessary embodiments of the many shadowy voices with whom George Eliot boxes in order to write"(50–5).

Tryan and Janet are intended to be infinitely more complex and interesting figures than the group at Mrs Linnet's. They are also clearly (and courageously) intended to be unlike anything the White Neck Cloth School could produce. But, as a consequence, even if the devotion of women parishioners could be more or less dismissed, Tryan's own attractions as mentor cannot be treated in the same way. This must have been clear to Eliot, but once again she chose to take evasive tactics rather than face the issue head-on, even at a point that appears to be an open confrontation with the problem, set out by way of the Dempsters' mock theatrical poster, billing Tryan as "Mr. Lime-Twig Lady-Winner, ... MR. TRY-IT-ON" (250). By placing the accusation concerning the misuse of clerical sex appeal in this context, Eliot neatly discredits the doubting reader by associating him with the Dempster forces, forestalling objections by producing them herself in a context that favours her case.

The other line of defence emerges with Tryan's carefully staged appearance in the text, which takes place towards the end of the long scene at the Linnets'. The sudden shift into the present tense signals the importance of this moment, and it becomes clear that Eliot wishes that Tryan be perceived (despite her commitment to realism that she satisfies by grounding the scene carefully in the comic and the local) in Christ-like terms both of haloed appearance and unconventional disciples:

But Mr. Tryan has entered the room, and the strange light from the golden sky falling on his light brown hair . . . makes it look almost like an aureole. It was a great anomaly to the Milby mind that a canting evangelical parson, who would take tea with tradespeople, and make friends of vulgar women like the Linnets, should have so much of the air of a gentleman. . . .

(217)

Shaken by being aligned with the forces of cynicism against those of Christ and gentility, the doubting reader is softened up to receive Eliot's defence of the mentor-lover as an instrument of good, the women of Milby having become the better for falling in love with him.

Should the reader still be worrying, however, whether the end of moral improvement can be justified in this way, Eliot moves to cut off further objections:

Whatever might be the weaknesses of the ladies . . . they had learned this – that there was a divine work to be done in life. . . . The first condition of human goodness is something to love; the second something to reverence. Yes, the movement was good, though it had that mixture of folly and evil which often makes what is good an offence to feeble and fastidious minds, who want human actions and characters riddled through the sieve of their own ideas, before they can accord their sympathy or admiration. Such minds, I dare say, would have found Mr. Tryan's character very much in need of that riddling process. The blessed work of helping the world forward, happily does not wait to be done by perfect men. . . .

(255–6)

This further attack on the doubting (and therefore somehow self-righteous) reader is, however, made on grounds not strictly relevant to the problem and produces more blurring of focus, implying that to doubt Tryan's appeal to women as a morally justifiable means of their conversion is to mark oneself as both a feeble and fastidious perfectionist.

And, after all these evasions, Eliot is careful not to put the issue to the ultimate test. Tryan himself never consciously uses, or is even aware of, his clerical sex appeal – Eliot knows that all the tactical manoeuvres of which she is capable could never get that past the reader, and the riskier creation of Daniel Deronda awaited her last novel. Yet reservations here reveal the moral dubiety of this means of bringing women to God – acceptable if the author uses it on behalf of her cleric, but not if he uses it on his own behalf while it further suggests a condescension to the women that would surely outrage Eliot if it were extended to herself.

Having raised the issue with respect to the women converts, Eliot discreetly attempts to remove any remaining difficulties by a conjuring trick. Attraction to the clerical sex is converted to a desire to nurture the weakening consumptive: "There were tender women's hearts in which anxiety about the state of his affections was beginning to be merged in anxiety about the state of his health" (261–2). Tryan's illness, which effectually precludes his becoming a lover, is carefully established before his first personal encounter with Janet (as Deronda will be protected by meeting Mirah before he encounters Gwendolen) and even further advanced before he becomes her mentor. The prolongation of Janet's marriage and her commitment to the husband she had once loved also contribute to the impossibility of the mentor ever, in practice, becoming the lover. Eliot doesn't take much of a risk, therefore, when she allows Tryan to become aware, during a brief remission of his illness, that "earthly affection was beginning to have too strong a hold on him" (330).

Translator of *The Essence of Christianity*, Eliot also calls Feuerbach to her aid: "the nature of God is nothing else than the abstract, *thought* nature of the world; the nature of the world nothing else than the real, concrete, perceptible nature of God" (*Essence* 85, emphasis original).

> Ideas are often poor ghosts. . . . But sometimes they are made flesh; they breathe upon us with warm breath, they touch us with soft responsive hands, they look at us with sad sincere eyes, and speak to us in appealing tones; they are clothed in a living human soul, with all its conflicts, its faith, and its love. Then their presence is a power, then they shake us like a passion and we are drawn after them with gentle compulsion, as flame is drawn to flame.
>
> ("Janet's . . . " 293)

From his first serious conversation with Janet, Tryan, his sexual life the cause of his earlier sin but now put behind him, has been portrayed as idea made (only very tenuously) flesh, the passion he elicits far from sexual.

As the spiritual nurturer comes to require physical nurture, Janet and Tryan subside into a reciprocal relationship that threatens neither the "feeble and fastidious" reader with doubts nor the author with sexuality. Though the relationship is domesticated, almost marital save for the absence of sex, it is essentially one between disciple and master, even the name of the house (in Eliot's *MS* it had been "*the* Holly Mount", 332, n.1, emphasis mine) contributing to the effect:

> Janet became a constant attendant on him now, and no one could feel she was performing anything but a sacred office. She made Holly Mount her home. . . . the sweet woman . . . whose dark watchful eyes detected every want, and who supplied the want with a ready hand.
>
> There were others who would have had the heart and the skill to fill this place by Mr. Tryan's side, and who would have accepted it as an honour; but they could not help feeling that God had given it to Janet by a train of events which were too impressive not to shame all jealousies into silence.
>
> (331–2)

But this passage also signals a link between Eliot's early and late works. What wouldn't Gwendolen, Deronda's disciple, with her terror of sex, have given to find herself in such a close but asexual situation with Daniel? And Janet's attitude to Tryan strikingly resembles Gwendolen's to Deronda in yet another way, so much so that some of her lines could as easily be spoken by Eliot's last heroine. When Janet tells Tryan "God has been very good to me in sending you to me. I will trust in Him. I will try to do everything you tell me" (293), the childlike trust and syntax, the promise to "try" and the desire to submit herself ("anything") to his judgment are as characteristic of one woman as the other. Like Gwendolen with respect to her mentor, Janet feels "an irresistible desire to see him, and tell him her desires and troubles" (294), and like Gwendolen her final reliance is on the mentor to save her:

> If she felt herself failing she would confess it to him at once; if her feet began to slip, there was that stay for her to cling to.
>
> (331)

In the early work the desirability of a woman's regression to childlike submission is offered uncritically, for our admiration. This does not preclude a later change of attitude on Eliot's part, but it does illustrate what would be a persistent interest in the subject.

Meanwhile, in the case of Janet and Tryan, no other end is possible but "a sacred kiss of promise" of eternal fidelity, not to each other but to God (333). Furthermore, as Eliot's choice of image unintentionally suggests, Janet the disciple ceases to be fully human, no longer a moral being in her own right, but one who has been reduced to a walking monument:

> There is a simple gravestone in Milby Churchyard. . . . But there is another memorial of Edgar Tryan, which bears a fuller record: it is Janet Dempster. . . . The man who has left such a memorial behind him, must have been one whose heart beat with true compassion, and whose lips were moved by fervent faith.
>
> (334)

So the idea made into flesh (which unfortunately describes Tryan only too accurately, even in the unconvincing flashback to his sinful youth or the waverings of his brief remission) produces its appropriate equivalent in the flesh made into tombstone. In place of the passion that might move the "heart" and "lips" of a man and woman, Eliot substitutes the less threatening compassion and faith. The essential nature of the clerical sex, in this early work at least, is made clear: an "idea" "clothed in a living human soul" (293), once more the image disclosing the values that produced it. The "idea" is central; the "living human soul" is merely clothing – and even the idea-made-flesh is actually too grossly physical, since Eliot here eschews the body for the "soul". *Scenes of Clerical Life* provides early examples of a characteristic that would persist throughout her fiction: her strong attraction to the religious idiom, particularly at those points in her work when she is facing a difficulty. It is surely not coincidental, though it is certainly disconcerting, that at those key moments when she is struggling most desperately to achieve powerful emotional effects, she is drawn to metaphors provided by a faith she had long since lost.

In *Scenes of Clerical Life*, the attempted evasion of the sexual by its transformation into the religious points to Eliot's central difficulty in the work. She is sufficiently attracted to the combination of mentor and lover to deal with it in two of her first three stories and is inclined to justify it by presenting the love of a man and woman as an incentive to moral improvement. However, she faces two linked problems in this connection: that however modified by age, personality or circumstances, the attraction must be admitted to be fundamentally sexual and that sexual attraction as the means of moral or religious conversion may be challenged as of dubious moral worth. Eliot, driven to defensive aggression by her awareness of how her readers might respond, employs several strategies: keeping the sexual from surfacing, attacking her readers whenever they might be expected to feel doubt on moral grounds and, finally, transforming passion into compassion, and sexual love into nurturing. This makes the separate roles of lover and mentor potentially one, but it also diverts the power of sexual attraction into a non-sexual channel.

With "Janet's Repentance", *Scenes of Clerical Life* came to an end. Blackwood, though undisturbed by the "capital" scene at Mrs Linnet's, was upset by Janet's drinking and as a consequence of his reservations, Eliot wrote in her Journal,

> I had meant to carry on the series beyond Janet's Repentance, and especially I longed to tell the story of the Clerical Tutor, but my annoyance at Blackwood's want of sympathy . . . determined me to close the series. . . .
>
> (*Journals* 291 [1857])

There is no way of knowing what her precise intentions had been before she gave up what she "longed" to do, or what the effect of her frustration was, but, in some form or other (often not clerical in the narrowest sense of the word), the "Clerical Tutor" reappears in most of her works, until the final reincarnation, complete with "clerical sex" appeal, in *Daniel Deronda*.

In *Adam Bede*, mentorship and love do not come together as clearly as in "Janet's Repentance": Adam neither attracts Hetty as a lover, nor succeeds as her mentor; Seth the disciple has no chance with Dinah the preacher, and the roles of lover and mentor are thus kept separate. And even though, at the conclusion, Adam the would-be-mentor marries Dinah the soon-to-retire-preacher, neither has been, in any essential way, the mentor of the other.

Two features, however, merit notice for the clarity with which they presage later developments in Eliot's treatment of the figure. The first is primarily a moral issue raised when Adam decides of Dinah,

> she's better than I am – there's less o'self in her, and pride. And it's a feeling as gives you a sort o'liberty, as if you could walk more fearless, when you've more trust in another than y'have in yourself. I've always been thinking I knew better than them as belonged to me. . . .
>
> (492)

Mr Irwine had felt on seeing Dinah: "He must be a miserable prig who would act the pedagogue here" (86) but this meditation takes Adam far beyond abandoning his own conviction that he is fit to be mentor to Dinah, or anyone else, into surrender of his moral autonomy – although there is no examination of the effect on Dinah of being assigned the burden Adam here gladly puts down. So cursory is the closing of the novel, however, that it does not bear the weight of much speculation. The problem of the surrender of moral independence would, however, recur throughout her work.

The second feature that would return repeatedly in later works combines the sexual with the moral. Though early in the novel (110) Dinah's blushes seem intended to signal that she is a sexual being, they fail to culminate in a convincing sexual relationship with Adam. Instead, it is in Arthur's case, in his affair with Hetty, that sexual attraction is portrayed – and denigrated – through Eliot's portrayal of the blending of desire with self-deception and an undisciplined and unrealistic urge for self-gratification. Eliot's characteristically acute analysis of Arthur's self-justification and Hetty's foolish daydreams of elevation to the position of squire's wife are thus linked to a mistrust of sexuality, viewed by Eliot as the perfect channel for the lovers' egotistical needs – selfishness and self-deception being the forms in which she most comfortably, indeed brilliantly, deals with it. Sometimes it seems as if Eliot considers death preferable. When reaching for a means of contrasting the sexually vibrant Hetty with Dinah, it is the latter's appearance, "almost like a lovely corpse into which the soul has returned . . ." that we are apparently intended to prefer over Hetty's flushed cheeks and glistening eyes (150). More often, however, sexuality is contrasted to, or neutralized by, childhood affection. As J. Russell Perkin points out (49), when Hetty and Arthur meet in the wood ("It was a pity they were not in that golden age of childhood when they would have . . . given each other a little butterfly kiss, and toddled off to play together", 123), the alternative scene is not only presented as more desirable but also seems as vivid, as fully "real", as the sexual encounter actually taking place.

No more in *Adam Bede* than in *Scenes of Clerical Life*, then, is Eliot willing to trust sexual love or prefer it over nurturing care. At the same time she backs away from the examination of the possibility and implications of the mentor as a sexual being that she had begun in "Janet's Repentance", possibly because the representative of the clerical sex is female.

In *The Mill on the Floss*, there are times when Eliot appears to be content to offer yet another version of Tryan's clerical sexuality, embodied in Philip who becomes Maggie's mentor. Combining ill-health with a consequent girlish delicacy, he evokes from her a desire to nurture that is reminiscent of Janet's. And in the face of the temptation represented by Stephen we hear from Maggie echoes of Janet's appeals to Tryan: "I had need have you always to find fault with me and teach me" (363). Here, too, Philip's love, like Seth's for Dinah, is virtually untouched by sexuality; it is directed to a "divinity" (287); it is worship (293, 390) and "divine rapture" (442).

But although this may suggest a return to the mixture as before, Eliot explores new ground in this work and takes greater risks, the novel sometimes holding out hope of breakthroughs in her treatment of both sexual love and moral duty. Maggie's meeting with Philip in childhood, for example, provokes from Eliot a comment accurately aimed at deflating sentimentality: Maggie "had rather a tenderness for deformed

things; she preferred the wry-necked lambs, because . . . she was especially fond of petting objects that would think it very delightful to be
petted by her" (155). In Eliot's treatment of duty, too, there are encouraging signs of change. Philip, constituting himself Maggie's mentor,
predicts the dangers of her "unnatural" self-negation: "every rational
satisfaction of your nature that you deny now, will assault you like a
savage appetite" (289), the accuracy of his forecast being supported by
subsequent events. Here, however, Eliot's changed attitude is not sustained throughout the work, for there is surely no reader who doubts
that Maggie's youthful attempts at self-denial are intended both to be
endearing and to prefigure her final, and authorially approved, sacrifice
of her love for Stephen.

There is, however, one very significant development. Philip himself
may not be a sexual being, but it is in *The Mill on the Floss* that Eliot's
need to recognize the power of a woman's sexual response, limited and
tentative as it had been in the earlier works, becomes overt and central.
Maggie's physical response to Stephen goes far beyond Dinah's to Adam
and is more openly explored than Arthur's attraction for Hetty. The
erotic effect is brilliantly achieved through the sense that the utterly
trivial has taken on disproportionate significance, felt as slowed motion,
heightened intensity and painful self-consciousness. As Philip Weinstein
points out, the pace slows in these passages because Eliot does not, as
she does elsewhere, cursorily dismiss the physical: "Stephen's body . . . is
alive with sexual potential; and its every dangerous motion is carefully
noted, carefully interrelated with Maggie's responsive motion, the two
bodies forming an odd, illicit, pre-Lawrentian ballet of desire" (83). The
effect is cumulative and is only suggested in quotation:

> Stephen laid down his hat, with the music, which rolled on the
> floor, and sat down in the chair close by her. He had never done so
> before, and both he and Maggie were quite aware that it was an
> entirely new position.
>
> (356)

Easier to demonstrate is the sense both have of being powerless in the
grip of obsession and the consequent need for self-restraint:

> Each was oppressively conscious of the other's presence, even to the
> finger ends. Yet each looked and longed for the same thing to hap-
> pen next day.
>
> (354)

The erotic quality of the scenes in the chapter "Illustrating the Laws of Attraction" (in the book appropriately called "The Great Temptation", 349, 350) was not lost on the contemporary critic of *The National Review*, who found the emphasis upsetting, and who fulminated at length against the "unfragrant fumes of physiological smoke":

> [Eliot] enthrones the physiological law so far above both affections and conscience in point of *strength*. . . . [that] the whole of this portion of the book is a kind of homage to physiological law.
>
> (Holmstrom and Lerner 36–8, emphasis original)

For the first time Eliot depicts a heroine who is fully and unequivocally caught up in the power of sexual attraction.

But here, in the novel in which sexuality is allowed its fullest expression, it is also most clearly depicted as something to be feared. In *Adam Bede* Eliot had condemned egotism as the problem, sex merely being the tool by which Arthur and Hetty gratified their selfish needs (although Maggie is linked to Hetty through their attraction to the luxuries marriage might bring *AB* 94, *Mill* 383). In *The Mill on the Floss* it is sexuality itself that is the enemy to self-control, and therefore to selflessness. There are links here to Austen's concern in *Emma* that love may blind, though Austen included familial love in her distrust and Eliot fears losing sight of duty to family rather than of another's character. And, to the extent that Eliot fears loss of self-control, there are links also to Brontë, although in the latter's case control of self was only the preliminary to control of others.

Stephen is not despicable, merely a pleasant young man with no particular strength of character. In fact, Eliot seems as regretful as the critic in *The National Review* that the "light of a character in itself transparently beautiful" might be "extinguished by the unfragrant fumes of physiological smoke". In response to such criticisms, she described Maggie as "a character essentially noble but liable to great error – error that is anguish to its own nobleness. . . ." (*Letters* 3:318: 9 July 1860). The extent of that pain is a measure of just how strong, in Eliot's view, are the "Laws of Attraction", powerful enough that even her cousin's nice young man can become irresistible to Maggie, despite her high principles.

The distrust with which Eliot regards sexuality is everywhere apparent. The images with which she describes it are superficially attractive clichés carrying with them disturbing undertones. They are often connected with dreams, fairy tales, spells, enchanted cups, intoxication and visions. Images suggesting a surrender of will and reason, "the partial sleep of thought" (410), the "stream of vanity" (383), and other water, river, and current images, evoke a dangerous passivity in the face of "a strange, sweet, subduing influence" (403) and an isolation from the hard realities of life. There is, too, the ominous image that obscures thought for Maggie when she is with Stephen: "the sense of a presence like that of a closely-hovering broad-winged bird in the darkness" (356). Thought is deliberately avoided: "they spoke no word; for what could words have been but an inlet to thought? And thought did not belong to that enchanted haze in which they were enveloped" (407). Given Eliot's high valuation of language and thought, sexual attraction, when seen as inimical to them, is clearly signalled to be dangerous. Furthermore, the very means by which Eliot conveys erotic intensity, the elevation of the trivial into powerful significance, is not merely a matter of technique. It reflects her judgment that sexuality is dangerous for this very reason.

Finally, that Eliot allows the love of the girlish Philip to outlast and prove superior to that of Stephen, suggests that she would rather endorse asexual mentorship than sexual love. Eliot's preference for Philip over Stephen is suggested when "Philip Reenters".

> [Maggie's] tranquil, tender affection for Philip, with its root deep down in her childhood . . . – the fact that in him the appeal was more strongly to her pity and womanly devotedness than to her vanity or other egoistic excitability of her nature, seemed now to make a sort of sacred place, a sanctuary where she could find refuge from an alluring influence which the best part of herself must resist, which must bring horrible tumult within, wretchedness without.
>
> (360–1)

Nothing indicates that we are to repudiate Maggie's reactions here. The invocation of religious terms, "sacred", "sanctuary", as protective against selfish sexuality are already a familiar Eliot ploy, and whatever is "first", "root[ed] deep down in her childhood" is endorsed by the novel, which as invariably condemns "vanity" and "egoistic excitability". There is, in addition the difference in Eliot's treatment of the two letters from Maggie's would-be lovers. Though both are egotistical in tone, Philip nevertheless gets the longest and noblest word, and the novel endorses his Abelardian judgment on sexuality:

> the strong attraction which drew you together proceeded only from one side of your characters, and belonged to that partial, divided action of our nature which makes half the tragedy of our human lot.
>
> (442)

Though the mathematics may be murky, it is clear that the rejection of sexual love as dangerous to selflessness and the preference for moral and emotional nurturing, occurring as early as *Scenes of Clerical Life*, are reasserted here.

Though Eliot might seem to have discarded the mentor-lover combination when Maggie turns from Philip to Stephen, instead she gives it a new and disturbing shape. A number of exchanges between Philip and Maggie suggest the form this combination will take. When they part as children, her farewell to him includes two words that will be frequently found in proximity in the novel:

"I wish you *were* my brother. I'm very fond of you. And you would stay at home when Tom went out, and you would teach me everything – wouldn't you?"

(161, emphasis original)

This linking is repeated when they meet again, much to Maggie's pleasure, for she had been "often wishing she had him for a brother and a teacher" (262), and Philip remembers the childhood wish, "Let me . . . be your brother and teacher as you said at Lorton" (289). It is an ideal combination that Philip might fulfil if Eliot had not provided another in Maggie's life in the person of her brother Tom.

As a moral teacher, Tom is verbally and emotionally brutal, an unpleasant and more self-righteous variation of his father, and the very opposite of Philip. Though he may occasionally speak with the "tone of a kind pedagogue" (344), this is not a softness he is able, or cares, to sustain. He invariably metamorphoses into the teller of "terrible cutting truth"(345) with "his terrible clutch on her conscience and her deepest dread" (302). Maggie seethes against this brutal mentor: "she rebelled and was humiliated in the same moment" (345); "She writhed under the demonstrable truth of the character he had given to her conduct and yet her whole soul rebelled against it as unfair from its incompleteness" (302). What is new for Eliot here is her exploration of the power that love gives to victimize, abetted as the bully is by the compliance of the victim: "the need of love would always subdue her" (344). Nevertheless, though Eliot manifests the horror of such thralldom, it is to this mentor that Maggie turns, with her creator's approval, as final judge.

Both Janet and Adam choose to give up their moral autonomy and, when Maggie abjectly desires to surrender control to Tom after her disastrous disappearance with Stephen: "I want to make amends. I will endure anything. I want to be kept from doing wrong again" (427), there are also suggestions of Gwendolen. But this mentor is not the gentle, self-doubting Daniel, but rather the self-righteous Tom: "I loathe your character and your conduct. . . . the sight of you is hateful to me" (427). When Tom turns away, Maggie, like Gwendolen at the close of *Daniel Deronda*, must at the end choose the right moral course alone, unsupported by her mentor. For Gwendolen, this entails distress though perhaps the opportunity for growth; for Maggie it is deliberately inflicted punishment, serving only to exacerbate the pain of a moral commitment already made when she parted from Stephen. But not only are the standards she must live by still the standards of her mentor, they are apparently those of the author in a Maggie-like conflict with herself, despite her sympathy for her creation.

This however, is an assumption that requires support and makes it impossible to evade any longer the acknowledgement of the tangled relationships between author, pseudonym, narrative voice and content that make judgments of Marian Lewes's relationship to her work so difficult. The problem of distinguishing between the narration and the author's own views always exists, for even where there is an apparently single narrative voice, it may not speak for the author. This is a difficulty given further, and differing, twists by each novelist's technique. Austen's work often challenges the reader to detect when there has been a slither from narration to indirect reporting of her characters' views, while Brontë, in *Villette*, intermittently reveals that the narrating "I" is not necessarily to be trusted. But Eliot's novels have the added dimension of that famous alias. No modern reader feels the need to refer to Currer Bell any more than to Austen's "A Lady", but Marian Lewes is so obscured by George Eliot that to write a paragraph referring to the novels without using her pen-name produces the sense that one is splitting hairs. And indeed that seems to have been the sense that Marian Lewes herself had of her relation to George Eliot. As Rosemarie Bodenheimer points out (245), when Alexander Main put together quotations for *The Wise, Witty, and Tender Sayings of George Eliot*, he apparently did not arouse in her publisher, her readers, or the author herself any opposition when, having grouped the quotations from characters separately from those of the works' narrative voices, he labelled the latter as "George Eliot, *in propria persona*". Nor did the Marian Lewes who authorized the publication insist that she be distinguished from that *persona*, although she undoubtedly wished to express the best of herself through her pseudonym.

There are, however, two ways in which Marian Lewes and George Eliot are manifestly distinct. One, frequently noted by readers, is the occasional endowing of the narrative voice with vaguely male characteristics. My sense is that the maleness of the narrator doesn't amount to much, but is rather a passing joke consistent with her choice of penname (the comments on women's fashions, for example, supplying only a minor element of characterization). An elaborate argument might attempt to use these masculine attributes to rescue Marian Lewes herself from charges of encouraging womanly submission, but to do so would be to see the novels as an effort of subversion so immense as to virtually guarantee failure, an irony so all-encompassing that one would have to question her sanity in making the attempt. Penny Boumhela, though not going this far, does illustrate how the argument for separating Eliot and the narrative voice might be made with regard to *The Mill on the Floss*. She calls on "the obviousness of *voice* and of a narrator's presence" (emphasis hers) as suggestive of deliberate irony and continues that "*It could even be argued*" (emphasis mine) that the end of the novel "is so clearly inappropriate as a final commentary as to cast an ironic light backwards over the authority and impersonality of the narration as a whole" (20–1). The "could even" indicates that Boumhela recognizes the extremity of this position.

More worrying, because of its relation to her worst writing, is the implication, one which Marian Lewes allows to stand, of an authorial adherence to Christianity – it isn't surprising that George Eliot was at first assumed to be a clergyman. But even though the impression was initially beneficial to her reception, it is hard to charge her with anything as definite as hypocrisy. Rather, a vague spirituality merges with a determination not to be found morally wanting despite her loss of faith, the combination often couched in the language and images of the Christianity she had so passionately embraced in her youth. But even in this regard, though one may make some local distinctions, overall it is hard to feel that the views of George Eliot (or Marian Lewes) can be clearly distinguished either from those of the narrative voices she employs or from the author of "O may I join the choir invisible".

If a close relationship may be admitted between author and pseudonym, Marian Lewes's "better self", more typical problems of assessing the relationship between author and narrative voice still remain to be considered. One, Eliot's propensity to lure the reader to make judgments that are subsequently rebuked, is the most easily dealt with. It is certainly true that the narrative voice in any Eliot novel plays with our perceptions; the case of Casaubon, where our dislike is first encouraged and then rebuked as evidence of our self-centred blindness is perhaps the best-known example, but this is not evidence so much of an untrustworthy narrator as of educational purpose. The most difficult problems to resolve in terms of authorial intent, however, are those of a different order altogether, revealed by confusion, ambivalence, and the contradiction-laden relationship of the narrative voice to events in the novel. These originate from specific situations within each novel and bring us back to Eliot's attitude to the relationship between Maggie and Tom.

In *The Mill on the Floss*, the weight of the evidence supports Eliot's ambivalence rather than her deliberate challenge to the reader to distinguish author from narrative voice. One problematic instance is the well-known passage on "passion" and "duty" that endorses Tom's moral priorities, even while appearing to criticize him:

> The great problem of the shifting relation between passion and duty is clear to no man who is capable of apprehending it: the question whether the moment has come in which a man has fallen below the possibility of a renunciation that will carry any efficacy, and must accept the sway of a passion against which he had struggled as a trespass, is one for which we have no master-key that will fit all cases.
>
> (437)

This is ostensibly an attack on "the men of maxims" and thus on Tom, who has not lived a life "vivid and intense enough to have created a wide fellow-feeling with all that is human" (438), as Maggie has. Furthermore, Tom's own "passion", stunted in every other way (as his lukewarm interest in Lucy betrays), is a passion to control, justified in his own view by being indistinguishable from duty. And while in this he resembles a Brontë character, Eliot clearly feels no Brontë-like attraction to such a characteristic for she depicts the full horror of his need to dominate.

But simultaneously Eliot uses the narrative voice to endorse Tom's position. Caught up in the sweep of the prose, the reader, who is only too glad to share in a condemnation of Tom, may not notice the support the passage gives to Tom's values. The question it poses is not whether one should ever choose passion over duty, but whether one can ever decide when a wrong choice – and that is simply assumed to be the choosing of passion – is irreversible. To accept the sway of passion is a "trespass". The issue is whether Eliot in her novel as a whole and the narrative voice are at one here, and, overall, the preponderance of evidence suggests they are. Dr Kenn is not only a minister by profession but is endorsed as a member of "a sort of natural priesthood, whom life has disciplined and consecrated to be the refuge and rescue of early stumblers and victims of self-despair" (382). He regrets that

> At present everything seems tending towards the relaxation of ties – towards the substitution of wayward choice for the adherence to obligation, which has its roots on the past. Your conscience and your heart have given you true light on this point, Miss Tulliver. . . .
>
> (435)

Choice is "wayward", opposed to "ties", "obligations", and the "roots" all of which the novel as a whole supports. Strangely, Dr Kenn, churchman though he is, here aligns himself against the insight of Genesis, within which "roots in the past" were rendered secondary in the creation of the primal relationship of husband to wife: "Therefore shall a man leave his father and his mother and shall cleave unto his wife: and they shall become one flesh" (2:24). Yet Dr Kenn, Tom, and, it would seem, part of Eliot herself, share in setting up duty to family before mate, and Maggie obediently and explicitly voices their rejection of the Biblical precept:

> If life were quite easy and simple, as it might have been in paradise, and we could always see that one being first toward whom. . . . I mean, if life did not make duties for us before love comes, love would be a sign that two people ought to belong to each other. But I see – I feel it is not so now: there are things we must renounce in life; some of us must resign love. . . . Love is natural; but surely pity and faithfulness and memory are natural too.
>
> (395, the first ellipsis is Maggie's)

The whole tenor of the novel demonstrates Eliot's rejection of passion in favour of Tom's ethic of family duty, however painful Maggie's situation is felt to be by author and reader. And, though many of her contemporary readers failed to be persuaded, Eliot insisted, outside the novel,

> pray notice how my critic attributes to me a disdain for Tom: as if it were not *my* respect for Tom which infused itself into my reader – as if he could have respected Tom, if I had not painted him with respect; the exhibition of the *right* on both sides being the very soul of my intention in the story.
>
> (*Letters* 3:397: 4 April 1861, emphases original)

Justice to Maggie requires the recognition of Tom's incompleteness arising from his lack of sympathetic understanding, but it does not nullify
his moral position, which Eliot, though evidently experiencing pain
and ambivalence, endorses.

Despite Maggie's expressed wish that Philip be her teacher, that role
is Tom's by right of prior ties, the very ties that his moral position
endorses. What, then, of the other role that Philip desires, that of
lover? Here, too, the prior ties are crucial. Maggie's love for Tom is the
strongest emotion in the novel, and theirs is the relationship that
dominates every other. Eliot seems unable to permit Maggie to form a
mature relationship because she endorses Maggie's deepest emotional
involvement with her brother, one that she describes in language
more appropriate to a sexual relationship than to that of siblings – the
use of erotic language by the religious mystic providing an example of
an analogous shift. To describe the relationship as incestuous without
further qualification doesn't sufficiently stress Eliot's determined, if
unsuccessful, attempts to distance sexuality from love by annexing
the former's language for "safer" ends. It is as if sexuality can be prevented from endangering selfless duty by transferring its language and
intensity to a safe object: the brother. Many readers have, of course,
described the relationship of Maggie and Tom as straightforwardly
incestuous. Robert Polhemus (*Erotic Faith* 177–9), for example, finds
evidence of it in the childhood scenes where sexuality is "anything
but abstract": they "were still very much like young animals, and so
she could rub her cheek against his, and kiss his ear in a random, sobbing way; . . . so . . . he actually began to kiss her in return" (*Mill* 34).
However, I would argue that Eliot is engaged in a characteristic
attempt to separate love from sex here, for while elsewhere she
attempts to de-eroticize adult behaviour by replacing it with that of
children, here she resorts to the affection of baby animals, attempting
to distance sexuality to yet another remove. In struggling to express
Eliot's difference from Austen, I would suggest that the latter, valuing
rather than fearing sexuality, determines to enhance the sibling relationship of William and Fanny with it whereas Eliot inadvertently
suggests it.

Tom's awareness of Maggie's beauty and his revulsion from the idea
of a deformed suitor for her, his suspicions of the asexual Philip's sexual intentions (303), and his possessiveness: "If you think of Philip
Wakem as a lover again, you must give up me" (344), all conjure up
the image of an intensely jealous lover. Particularly powerful is the
scene when Maggie returns after disappearing with Stephen, when

Tom displays a combination of possessiveness and "disgust", "hatred" and "rage". There is the transition of the jealous lover from "tremulous excitement to cold inflexibility", his preference for her death over her disgrace, and the repudiation of what he considers his rights of ownership: "You don't belong to me" (426–7). His desire to punish and humiliate her as a means to confirm his own masculine superiority are reminiscent not only of a sexual relationship, but one that is essentially sadistic, finding a response in Maggie's masochistic need to humiliate herself.

The closing scene is grotesque, partly because it must strike the reader as a reworking – and for Eliot a desirable one – of Maggie's journey with Stephen down the river. Her "panting joy"; their isolation together: "Alone, Maggie?"; their sitting "mutely gazing at each other"; Maggie's "long deep sob of that mysterious wondrous happiness that is at one with pain", all suggest a lovers' flight. Unlike her previous journey with Stephen, however, this is allowed its final consummation in "an embrace never to be parted", "in close embrace" in the final moments of life, as well as in death, and even in the tomb (457–60). Eliot is unable to acknowledge the frightening import of Maggie's claim: "I can't divide myself from my brother for life" (385) and thus denies Maggie a normal sexual maturity. She may try to disguise Tom's transformation into lover by placing a Biblical inscription of family love (of Saul for his son Jonathan) on the tombstone and conjuring up a nostalgic reminiscence of "the days when they had clasped their little hands in love" (459) – which falsifies the childhood relationship she has portrayed – but the closing lines of the novel cannot cancel all that has gone before. David Carroll suggests that the closing may also be read "typologically, as an apocalyptic promise . . . a repetition of their earliest unity lifted to a mythical level" (*GE and the Conflict* 139), but I would argue here, as elsewhere, that when Eliot resorts to the mythical or religious, she is at her weakest.

Finally, as Eliot rescues Maggie from life – "How long will it be before death comes? I am so young, so healthy. How shall I have patience and strength?" (453) – she also rescues her from the conflict of passion and duty. Lover and mentor are finally united in Tom, while Maggie, in "an embrace never to be parted" (459), is united with both. Eliot's fear of the power of sexual attraction to override will, reason, and thus selflessness, causes her to take refuge in an apparently less threatening form of love, that of family, forcing her to channel sexuality into a relationship that she does not intend should contain it, posing psychological difficulties that are central to the novel, and as serious as those in any previous work. A comparison of the power and the pain of this depiction with

Adam's surrender to Dinah's superiority makes the linking of mentor and lover in the previous novel seem little more than a mechanical gesture, and Janet's submission to Tryan limply sentimental. But it is this very difference that makes reading *The Mill on the Floss* the more disturbing.

Possibly Eliot sensed that she had only been intermittently in control of the mentor-lover situation in *The Mill on the Floss*; at any rate, after finishing it in March 1860, there was a five-year gap before the mentor-lover again became prominent, although some aspects of *Romola* suggest a continued interest. Savonarola, however, though mentor is never lover, and Bardo and Romola, though a dress-rehearsal for Casaubon and Dorothea, are literally father and daughter. In *Felix Holt*, however, the mentor-lover recaptures centre stage in the title role.

In doing so, however, he brings with him a reminder of the problematic issue raised by Tryan, but now shorn of its religious complications: love as an instrument of conversion. One contemporary critic thought this perfectly justified, if difficult to achieve:

> enthusiasm for a teacher who brings no pietistic exaltation to his work, and only preaches the doctrine of self-denial from the social point of view and in its least attractive shape, implies a curious and subtle affinity between the teacher and the proselyte. This affinity and its development are very finely brought out [in *Felix Holt*].
>
> ([John Morley] in Carroll *CH* 256)

The reader might well question the value of a doctrine that required such an "affinity" for its successful transmission, but unalarmed by this requirement in its secular context, neither the critic nor Eliot seems ill-at-ease – there is nothing in this novel that resembles Eliot's squirmings in "Janet's Repentance" while, unfortunately, the "development" is more crudely "brought out" here than in any other of Eliot's works.

Nothing in this novel speaks as painfully of the torture of failing to satisfy the requirements of a beloved mentor as the anguish that Maggie endures, even though Felix himself is a bully without Tom's justification or, apparently, the author's recognition of his awfulness. The failure to resolve the problem of Tom is distressing, but at least Eliot had shown awareness of it. The inability to recognize that there is a problem in Felix's case is more disquieting. In a work that exhibits the steely delicacy required for the delineation of Mrs Transome, it is perplexing to find such a crude portrayal, unredeemed by any serious reflection on Felix's need to dominate.

Eliot does make a few token gestures to suggest Felix is too domineering, offering, through the admission of Felix himself, a perfunctory criticism of his fondness for "banging and smashing". When he offers the phrenologist's justification, his "large Ideality", he does so ironically (60), but Eliot doesn't allow his self-criticism to be taken very seriously; we are clearly intended to accept it as both genuine and sufficient extenuation. Similarly, the "strong denunciatory and pedagogic intention" (62) that culminates in the wish "to come and scold [Esther] every day, and make her cry and cut her fine hair off" (65) is apparently intended to show us Felix, not as genuine bully, but as little boy with a certain comic appeal.

Admittedly, Eliot uses their initial meeting to prepare us to see Felix as a man who must learn – and learn from Esther. As he leaves their first encounter, Felix reflects "I'll never marry. . . .never look back and say 'I had a fine purpose once . . . but pray excuse me, I have a wife and children'" (156). We know immediately that Esther will teach Felix that marriage with the right wife may support rather than undermine his principles, but the right wife is one resulting from his pedagogic endeavours; the desirability of his "scolding her everyday" is never fundamentally in question. Esther's response to Felix's hectoring is a cheap, trite version of Maggie's anguish, more worthy of "Silly Novels" than of the future novelist who had condemned them:

> She revolted against his assumption of superiority, yet she felt herself in a new kind of subjection to him. He was ill-bred, he was rude, he had taken an unwarrantable liberty; yet his indignant words were a tribute to her: he thought she was worth more pains than the women of whom he took no notice. . . . For the first time in her life Esther felt herself seriously shaken in her self-contentment. . . .
>
> (110)

The best one can say to Eliot's credit is that she cannot do the conventional pedagogue lover as bully and make it work. It is, however, regrettable that she attempts it at all.

Like Janet and Gwendolen (the passage might be transposed to either of the works in which they figure), Esther's moral dependence on the man she loves is total:

> He was like no one else to her: he had seemed to bring at once a law, and the love that gave strength to obey the law. . . . She had only

longed for a moral support under the negations of her life. If she were not to have that support, all effort seemed useless. . . .

The first religious experience of her life – the first self questioning, the first voluntary subjection, the first longing to acquire the strength of greater motives and obey the more strenuous rule – had come to her through Felix Holt. No wonder that she felt as if the loss of him were inevitable backsliding.

(227)

Although "voluntary subjection" is also the achievement required from Janet and Gwendolen, Esther is unlike the former, whose mentor is too ill to love her fully, or the latter whose mentor will marry another, for Eliot ensures that Esther will not be able to espouse the morality without espousing the man. To this end, Esther's need of Felix is frequently reiterated – she is "intensely of the feminine type, verging neither towards the saint nor the angel", and "'a fair divided excellence, whose fullness of perfection' must be in marriage" (360).

Felix's relations with Esther have – justifiably – got under a number of critical skins. Rita Bode offers a useful summary of a variety of viewpoints on the power relationship between Felix and Esther, herself questioning "Esther's submission and Felix's influence", but arguing that "Esther yields to gain greater control over her life" (770). Bode's conclusion, intended to rescue the work from its apparent exaltation of feminine submission, is that under Esther's care Felix is finally domesticated to something he once despised. In a similar argument, Frederick Karl, using Lydia Glasher, Gwendolen Harleth, Hetty Sorrel and Dorothea Brooke as examples, argues that "for each woman *submission becomes the weapon* by which she triumphs, even at the expense of her own well-being or life" (xvi–xvii, italics Karl's) but the use of the word "triumph" in this context is odd, to put it mildly. If Bode and Karl are right, then the Felix–Esther sections of the novel teach the kind of manipulative behaviour that recalls a range of advice from *Coelebs* to the women's magazines of the nineteen-fifties.

The most convincing explanation for Eliot's treatment of the relationship flows from Sally Shuttleworth's identification of Felix with the Comtean priesthood, necessitating a "teacher–pupil relationship" based on, in Comte's words, "the natural subordination of women" (*GE and Nineteenth-Century Science* 102, 121, 137). The Positivist Frederic Harrison had contributed both legal advice and moral support during the writing of *Felix Holt* (Haight, *Biography* 383) and his Comtean views may indeed have had a malign effect on Eliot's treatment of Esther and

Felix, although if this is the case, it was an influence to which Eliot was, judged on the basis of her earlier works, unfortunately only too open. But whether she considers Felix as Comtean priest or secular mentor, Eliot returns to the Christ motif (previously associated with Tryan and utterly unsuited to Felix) to describe Esther's feelings:

> The best part of a woman's love is worship; but it is hard to her to be sent away with her precious spikenard rejected, and her long tresses too, that were let fall ready to soothe the wearied feet.
>
> (302)

One doesn't have to be a feminist to be repelled by the generalization that opens this passage, nor a Christian to feel discomfort at the inappropriate comparison. If it were offered to us as Esther's own reaction, and we were simultaneously asked to see her feeling as overwrought and inappropriate, Eliot's Biblical reference would be justified, but there is no hint of ironic distancing on the author's part. The association of the religious idiom with her worst writing is once again disturbingly apparent.

There are moments when Eliot offers hope that sexual attraction might play a part in Esther's feelings for the "shaggy-headed, large-eyed, strong-limbed" Felix (54).

> In this at least her woman's lot was perfect: that the man she loved was her hero; that her woman's passion and her reverence for rarest goodness rushed together in an undivided current.
>
> (375)

But, disappointingly, her "woman's passion" has nothing in common with Maggie's physical attraction to Stephen. In fact, the greater the potential for sexual passion in a scene, the more mawkishly sentimental Eliot becomes:

> He smiled and took her two hands between his, pressed together as children hold them up in prayer. Both of them felt too solemnly to be bashful. They looked straight into each other's eyes, as angels do when they tell some truth.
>
> (364)

In *The Mill on the Floss*, Lucy's childlikeness offers no convincing competition to Maggie's sexual appeal. But in this novel (offering a preview of the declaration of love between Dorothea and Will that is one of the low points in *Middlemarch*), Eliot reverts once again to her preference for the childlike. This problem persists to the very end, when, reunited, Felix and Esther "laughed merrily, each holding the other's arms, like girl and boy. There was an ineffable sense of youth in common" (397). Alison Booth makes the most determined defence of Eliot's preference for the replacement of sexual by childlike love in this novel: "Significantly, the union is cleansed of any hint of sexual mastery. Felix and Esther unite rather as though Maggie and Tom Tulliver were able to prolong their last moment outside of gender difference, like children or angels" (156), but a retreat to childhood is not a desirable replacement for Brontëan-style mastery and the work supports earlier evidence that Eliot simply cannot trust sexuality as part of a "woman's passion".

Sexuality is to be found in the novel, but in Mrs Transome's misguided past, not the heroine's present or future. As Dorothea Barrett points out, Esther, both in character and in the poor writing she evokes from Eliot, shares characteristics with the "counterpoint" women in the other novels ("Hetty, Lucy, Tessa, Rosamond and Mirah") whereas "the monumental metaphors normally kept for the heroines of the novels are here reserved for Mrs Transome" (112–14). Eliot's real interest in this novel, as evinced by her full engagement and sharpest awareness, is in the ugly nature and consequences of an illicit sexual liaison between two people greedy for egocentric satisfactions. Even the limited gains made in *The Mill on the Floss*, in permitting sexual attraction to be associated with the heroine, are surrendered. The reader's sense that the author is exposing her worst aspects brings Brontë's *Shirley* to mind, but this novel also provides an instructive example of the difference between the two authors. The power struggles here are held to the moral and psychological level and are not a source of erotic attraction. The closest Eliot comes to Brontë is in her depiction of Felix's attitude to Esther but at the level of a little boy pulling a small girl's hair. Eliot, of course, would prefer the reader to see this not as puerility but childlike innocence, but unfortunately neither is appropriate to a love that will culminate in marriage.

To end the novel on a note of childlike merriment, and at the same time offer some proof of Esther's lessened inequality, she is, at the last, permitted to tease Felix about his mentorship, but any change in their relationship to each other is deliberately trivialized:

"You don't know how clever I am. I mean to go on teaching a great many things."
"Teaching me?"

"Oh yes," she said with a little toss; "I shall improve your French accent."

(397)

Nancy Paxton describes the closing relationship as a "mutual partnership" to which Esther brings "money to spare" and "a good humoured sense of self-esteem that allows her to deflate Felix's moral seriousness and willingness to correct him when he is mistaken" (170), but Esther's expressed intention to teach Felix is depressingly inadequate to make Paxton's case, and the indulgent tone of Eliot's last pages suggests we are not to take Esther's proclamation of mentorship seriously. The best one can say of the treatment of the mentor-lover in *Felix Holt* (and it is not a great deal) is that it gives every evidence of Eliot not caring deeply about the titular hero and his heroine. She seems willing instead to subside, through lack of interest, into an attitude of sentimental indulgence. As far as Felix is concerned, she can barely be bothered to take the hectoring prig down more than a rung or two – there is nothing here of the care she will devote to, for example, the exploration of the relationship of Lydgate's weaknesses to his strengths in his attitude to women (although a lack of rigour is to be found to some extent in her avoidance of Will's inadequacies in the same work).

Thus the novel that takes as its central and unquestioned premise the moral value and psychological justification of the mentor as lover also offers the most inept, and indeed ugly, depiction of the relationship. The pronouncements on Esther's need for a better half are endorsed much more fully by developments in the plot than Felix's acquisition of humility ever is. Esther is thereby demeaned, and the hero's faults virtually nullified. In previous works, Eliot had found herself in trouble, with varying degrees of awareness, in depicting the mentor-lover, but nowhere before had she accorded the relationship so much prominence combined with so little critical examination. The consequences are disastrous. In her next novel, however, in the course of her successful and moving delineation of the Casaubons' incompatibility, she would offer her first unequivocal repudiation of a mentor-lover. Whether this represented a rejection of clerical sexuality in general, of a particular form of it, or of an individual case, remains to be considered.

There is an otherwise insignificant passage in *Middlemarch* that epitomizes the difficulty of judging to what degree the novel offers a reconsideration of the mentor-lover. It provides an explanation of how Bulstrode's first marriage came about.

> [Mrs. Dunkirk] had come to believe in Bulstrode, and innocently adore him as women often adore their priest or "man made" minister. It was natural that after a time marriage should have been thought of between them.
>
> (604)

Is it a post-Foucauldian sensitivity on our part that suggests the word "natural" might here be being pronounced tongue in cheek, something akin to Austen's "truth universally acknowledged"? Unquestionably, Mrs Dunkirk is mistaken in Bulstrode's character, and her marriage to her mentor is productive of much subsequent sorrow. What is not clear is whether Eliot thereby condemns Mrs Dunkirk for her failure to examine a "natural" assumption, simply offers Bulstrode as an unfortunate choice that does not reflect on mentor-lovers in general, or challenges the belief that any mentor could make a good husband. The last of these possibilities would, of course, entail a complete reversal of the view that *Felix Holt* enshrines.

While that novel offers one mentor-lover relationship as central, *Middlemarch* (like *Mansfield Park*) explores more. And although Eliot's mentor-lovers are usually men, as befits members of the "clerical sex", in *Middlemarch* Eliot creates Mary Garth, who educates, mothers and marries her little boy Fred Vincy. Once again, their love is clearly intended to be validated not only by its origin in childhood but also by the persistence of this childish element – *Mansfield Park* sentimentalized:

> She had never thought that any man could love her except Fred, who had espoused her with the umbrella ring, when she wore socks and little strapped shoes. . . .
> "I cannot imagine any new feeling coming to make that weaker."
>
> (507–8)

Mary and Fred achieve "a solid mutual happiness" (818) that is clearly offered as admirable, and there is no sign of any reservation on Eliot's part about the desirability of this relationship, which might seem surprising when one considers that the woman who marries her father-figure in the same novel comes to grief because of it, suggesting Eliot's reservations are different when it comes to the Casaubons.

The central mentor-lover relationship in the work, however, provoked a good deal of discomfort in readers, much of the initial critical
response to Dorothea's wish to marry Casaubon (like that to Maggie's
love for Stephen) taking the form of doubt that it could have happened.
R.H. Hutton's distaste, expressed after reading Book One, is typical:

> It seems to us somewhat unnatural that a girl of Dorothea Brooke's
> depth and enthusiasm of nature should fall in love with a man of so
> little vital warmth and volume of character as Mr. Casaubon in spite
> of the twenty-seven years' difference in age, without any apparent
> reason beyond her thirst for an intellectual and moral teacher. That
> want is usually very distinctly separable from love, and only glides
> into it, we should have thought, when there is nature *enough* in the
> object of reverence to exercise a fascination of a warmer kind. . . .
> [Dorothea's love] is, however, hardly adequately accounted for, and
> certainly leaves the impression of something slightly unnatural and
> repellent on the reader. . . .
>
> (in Carroll., *CH* 287, emphasis original)

Clearly Hutton is repulsed by Casaubon's unsuitability of age and character, but it is less clear whether he is critical of the mentor-lover relationship itself. In his final review of the novel as a whole, however, his
position is clearer:

> Nothing could be finer than the account of the unhappiness his mar-
> riage causes, and its slow growth. . . . it is impossible to say whether
> Mr. Casaubon's or his wife's feelings are painted with most power.
> Dorothea's . . . discovery that she has found a dried-up formalist
> where she expected a loving guide and teacher, that she has devoted
> herself to a pedant instead of a man of original and masterly intel-
> lect, are quite as finely painted as Mr. Casaubon's troubles.
>
> (Carroll ed., *CH* 309–10)

Hutton's relief is revealing. It has become apparent to him that the issue is
Dorothea's disappointment at Casaubon's inadequacies; the mentor-lover
relationship no longer troubles him.

But there is some evidence to suggest that Eliot herself had become
more critical of it than her reviewer. Initially there is considerable comedy, virtually a running gag at Dorothea's expense, apparently a dual
attack on the notion of the lover as mentor and Dorothea's thoroughgoing naivety, which assigns an impossible range of abilities to Casaubon:

Dorothea, with all her eagerness to know the truths of life, retained very childlike ideas about marriage. She felt sure that she would have accepted the judicious Hooker, if she had been born in time to save him from that wretched mistake he made in matrimony; or John Milton when his blindness had come on; or any of the other great men whose odd habits it would have been glorious piety to endure . . . . The really delightful marriage must be that where your husband was a sort of father, and could teach you even Hebrew, if you wished it.

(10)

. . . here was a living Bossuet, . . . here was a modern Augustine. . . .

(24)

"Every-day things with us would mean the greatest things. It would be like marrying Pascal. I should learn to see the truth by the same light as great men have seen it by. And then I should know what to do when I got older: I should see how it was possible to lead a grand life here – now – in England".

(28)

But in assessing how we are to read this comedy, we might remember that hitherto Eliot has found the "childlike" wholly desirable as a preparation for matrimony, and simultaneously note a change in tone from the distanced and frankly comic: "great men whose odd habits it would have been piety to endure" to the "poor Dorothea" note to the last passage quoted, an effect enhanced by being in Dorothea's own words. As Dorothea moves closer to her doom, Eliot's irony is replaced by a desire to protect and justify her heroine and the tone approaches much nearer to that of the introductory passages on St Theresa. It also becomes clearer that Dorothea's aspirations to marry a mentor are not in themselves to be ridiculed, but rather her notion that Casaubon is equal to the role and can shine brightly enough "to see the truth by".

F. R. Leavis argued that in Eliot's treatment of Dorothea she is at first "seen by the novelist from outside as well as felt from within". However, as the work progresses "the irony seems to be reserved for the provincial background and circumstances, leaving the heroine immune" (87–8). There is a similar shift in the treatment of the mentor-lover relationship. The role of critic is increasingly taken over by Celia whose worldly common sense encourages us to regard her views as shallow, while sympathy becomes the function of the narrative voice, expressing truths deeper than those of the "corrosiveness" of Celia's "pretty, carnally-minded prose" (48) can reach. Eliot thus gets a great deal of mileage from Celia, who can take over the job of expressing the "shame, mingled with a sense of the ludicrous" (47) aroused by Dorothea's approaching marriage, freeing the narrative voice from the need to temper compassion with irony. This enables Eliot to preserve the attractions of the mentor-lover after the specific characteristics of the elderly pedant have been purged from the combined role, a process that begins as Dorothea considers Casaubon's eligibility as husband:

> "I should not wish to have a husband very near my own age. . . . I should wish to have a husband who was above me in judgment and in all knowledge . . . ."

> " . . . a wise man could help me to see which opinions had the best foundation, and would help me live according to them."
>
> (40–1)

We are shown a Dorothea who fails to understand that age is no guarantee of wisdom, or even of knowledge of any vital kind. The making of this faulty connection condemns her to the horror of recognizing that Casaubon's work, the only issue of their marriage, entails "sorting what might be called shattered mummies . . . sorting them as foison for a theory which was already withered in the birth like an elfin child" (469). Barren intellectually and physically, the marriage and its horrors are brilliantly – and sympathetically – evoked, suggesting once again that it is the absence of sexual passion that frees Eliot to explore honestly her deepest insights. However, though the consequences of Dorothea's mistake are grim they do not call into question Dorothea's aspirations for a husband "above her", only her naivety in associating judgment with age.

But what if Casaubon had been working on something valuable and life-giving? Instead of being "rayless", what if "When he turned his head quickly his hair seemed to shake out light" (203)? Would the combination of lover and mentor then have been unacceptable? The problem of exactly what Eliot is rejecting might be settled by looking at Dorothea's relationship to Will, since he combines a number of features associated with earlier mentor-lovers in her work. He takes on something of Philip's role, urging the dangers of over-restraint, and like Philip he is motivated by a combination of unselfish and selfish interests: "I suspect that you have some false belief in the virtues of misery, and want to make your life a martyrdom" (215). And like that of Felix and Esther (in contrast to that of Arthur and Hetty, *AB* 123),

the relationship of Will and Dorothea is a matter of childlike innocence: a discussion of their religious beliefs degenerates (with every
sign of Eliot's approval) into their "looking at each other like two fond
children who were talking confidentially of birds" (383). Will, dis-
traught at the possibility that Dorothea thinks he loves Rosamund,
regrets the loss of paradise:

> Until that wretched yesterday . . . all their vision, all their thought of
> each other, had been as in a world apart, where the sunshine fell on
> tall white lilies, where no evil lurked, and no other souls entered. But
> now – would Dorothea meet him in that world again?
>
> (793)

Unfortunately, despite the glaring inappropriateness of this pre-
Raphaelite heaven to the fully realized world of Casaubon, Lydgate,
Rosamund and the Bulstrodes, in the very next chapter she does indeed
meet him there again. And there Will and Dorothea merge with Felix
and Esther, "hands clasped, like two children" (799), Dorothea's "young
passion" prompting her to a proposal spoken with "large tear-filled eyes
looking at his very simply . . . in a sobbing childlike way" (801). The
elderly mentor-lover has been replaced by a younger (even child-like)
version of the role, and we are to rejoice – yet most readers do not. Part
of the problem is that Will as sun-god among the lilies just doesn't work
in the morally grubby world of Bulstrode, and part that Will is, as mentors go, pretty lightweight.

But another aspect of the problem is Eliot's own regret that Dorothea,
unlike St Theresa, should be "foundress of nothing", author of no "long-
recognizable deed" ("Prelude"), one who, by channelling her service to
mankind through Will, is not herself an autonomous being. This does
represent a significant movement on Eliot's part, for she evinces little
concern over the problem of autonomy in connection with Janet,
Esther, or Gwendolen (though there are suggestions of it in relation to
Maggie and perhaps, though determinedly suppressed, to Dinah).
Nowhere does Eliot show Brontë's vehemence on the subject and unlike
Brontë, she limits her regret to losses in the moral sphere. But even in
this regard, she remains entangled in a problem not restricted to one
novel, a difficulty that, prompted by reading the first part of *Daniel
Deronda*, the reviewer for *The Academy* hoped she would address:

> One or two paragraphs seem to suggest that we are to have . . . a treat-
> ment (perhaps more central than before) of the question presented in

some of the writer's other works, namely by what property of the natural order it comes to pass that the strength of innocent self-regarding desires is a moral snare unless balanced by some sense of external obligation. . . .

Without wishing the objective vigour of the author's imaginative creations to be clouded by a transparent didactic purpose, her reader may not unnaturally look for an imaged solution of the logical dilemma – If the desires of A are not a trustworthy guide for A's conduct, how can they be a safe moral rule for B; and, conversely, how is A to be more secure in following B's desires than his own?

(in Holmstrom and Lerner, 126–7)

The problem of self-abnegation is exacerbated by Eliot's conception of Dorothea's duties as a woman. Gillian Beer, who provides a very useful account, supplemented by quotations from a variety of contemporary sources, of Eliot's relation to the issues of duty and women's position in society in her chapter "*Middlemarch* and the Woman Question"(147–99) argues that Eliot "brooded on the curtailment of women's lives in terms drawn from [the women's] movement and in sympathy with it" (180), but did not speak out because she feared her irregular life might jeopardize it (183). Doubtless there is some truth in this, but the novels go much further to undermine women's independence of action than the need to work under cover would require. Eliot's insistence on the sacrifice of desires unsupported by duty in a society that saw women's duty as service to family seems to me the dominant factor in her failure to speak or act clearly on issues related to the "Woman Question". In *Middlemarch*, this problem is first evaded (by Eliot's timely deployment of death to prevent Dorothea from committing herself to Casaubon's research) and then briefly taken up in the Finale, where it is quickly dropped as an insoluble difficulty. As Will's wife, Dorothea now has a life filled with a "beneficent activity which she had not the doubtful pains of discovery and marking out for herself" (822).

Many who knew her thought it a pity that so substantive and rare a creature should have been absorbed into the life of another, and be only known in a certain circle as a wife and mother. But no one stated exactly what else that was in her power she ought rather to have done. . . .

(822)

There are two consolations offered here, perhaps because neither is adequate to assuage Eliot's pain on behalf of Dorothea and others like her: the surrendering of one's own right to make decisions protects one from the doubt and pain (the probable meaning of the somewhat ambiguous phrase "doubtful pains") of making choices, and that, in any case, Dorothea has no other option. There is enough obscurity as well as regret in this final summary to see at least the glimmerings of a desire for independent judgment and action, a desire that might undermine the combined role of mentor-lover in any form, and not merely cast doubts on it when unsuccessful.

But Eliot seems as incapable as anyone among Dorothea's acquaintance of stating "exactly what else that was in her power she ought rather to have done" – not, as many have noted, edit a periodical, write reviews or author novels. It is characteristic, however, of unresolved issues in Eliot's work, that they would recur for further exploration, and in *Daniel Deronda* the problem of yielding one's moral choice to another would surface again in a "treatment . . . more full and central than before". Whether *The Academy* reviewer might be likely to consider the dilemmas of A and B satisfactorily solved, remained to be seen.

6
"Worth Nine-Tenths of the Sermons"? The Author as Mentor-Lover in *Daniel Deronda*

Eliot had, by the time she began her last novel, found both problems and rewards in her exploration of the consequences of combining the mentor with the lover. Because she cared deeply about the process of moral growth, the mentor was a naturally appealing figure and could be made to dovetail with another role that attracted her, that of the submissive, even childlike, devotee, but, though love might in general be considered a force for good, the lover was more problematic. Sexuality, a threat to selflessness, was for her a dangerous force, and, unlike Brontë, she was not attracted by the thrill of the struggle for power that could be engendered by the teacher–pupil relationship. How was moral development, initiated and sustained by attraction to a member of the opposite sex, to be judged? What if the mentor-lover was unworthy of one or both of the roles? Could the role of mentor actually prove to be dangerous (as Austen had postulated in *Mansfield Park*), exacerbating existing moral faults in the mentor that could be made even worse by the demands placed upon the lover? To what extent do the virtues of selflessness and submission constitute an abdication of moral responsibility rather than the foundation of all virtue? In the works preceding *Daniel Deronda*, such problems had been dodged, in order that Eliot might continue to reap the rewards of depicting the combination of roles to which she was drawn. However, these issues were to be considered with greater directness, and consequently greater courage, in her last novel.

There are two significant mentor-lover relationships in the novel, and, as Sally Shuttleworth notes, in dealing with the lesser of them, Eliot momentarily seems to solve one aspect of a problem she had struggled with from the beginning. Forbidden by her parents to marry her music teacher, Catherine Arrowpoint retorts, "People can easily take the sacred word duty as a name for what they desire any one else to do" (*DD* 228, *Science* 199). But Eliot is careful to set the Arrowpoint situation up as one in which blatantly selfish parents make morally unacceptable demands, making this an insight into a special case, although, as always, Eliot's ability to discern and pin down the egotistical drives that masquerade as moral imperatives is admirable.

This mentor-lover situation is offered, with an untroubled certainty of its desirability, as a foil for that of Daniel and Gwendolen, a similar structure to that found in *Middlemarch*. The relationship between Klesmer and Catherine Arrowpoint is described by Eliot as one of "full sympathy in taste, and admirable qualities on both sides" (220), an unarguably excellent basis for marriage, far superior to that of Mary Garth and Fred Vincy. However, the passage continues in less egalitarian vein: "especially when the one is in the position of teacher and the other is delightedly conscious of receptive ability which also gives the teacher delight". Klesmer fulfils for Catherine the need for a cultured superior that drew Maggie to Philip, and Dorothea to Casaubon and Will. Seen in this light, Klesmer is a reworking of a favoured figure to produce the ideal lover that Philip, Casaubon – and even Will – failed to be.

Although Catherine is Klesmer's inferior in art, morally the two are more or less equal and complementary. It is true that her maturity is unflawed, while Klesmer displays childish vanities. But his petulance is little more than a humanizing blemish, and his Shelleyan vanity is not examined seriously; rather it is used as an identifying eccentricity, like his un-English appearance. More important is his rough but genuine concern to respond to Gwendolen with honesty and directness, even though fuelled with some self-righteousness, as well as his aesthetic superiority, which obviously has moral weight for Eliot through his dedication to achieving the best. The problem of moral inequality is not at issue in the Catherine – Klesmer relationship, and based on this aspect alone, one might consider Eliot had here found a very satisfying version of the mentor-lover combination. Unfortunately, however, it is clear from the continuation of the same passage, "The situation is famous in history and has no less charm now than it did in the days of Abelard" (220), that complementarity, sympathy and companionship are what gives this relationship "charm". The unsuitability of the word in connection with Heloise and Abelard not only suggests that Eliot thought of the myth rather than the texts, but demonstrates how determinedly Eliot drains the relationship of a sexuality that in its medieval context was central to its tortured outcome.[1]

The well-matched Klesmers serve to provide a vivid contrast for the torment of Daniel and Gwendolen, whose moral inequality is central to the work. As a consequence of their disparity, by the work's close, Gwendolen has learned to submit to Daniel's judgment, has extirpated her former vanity and self-will, and she and Daniel have each recognized the existence of a form of love for the other. Thus summarized, this sounds like the plot of *Emma*, which Lewes and Eliot re-read when she was about two-thirds of the way through writing *Daniel Deronda* (Haight, *Biography* 478, 480–1, *Letters* 6:171, note 1). Indeed, Austen echoes are strong in this novel: of *Mansfield Park* in the charades, in the concern with the nature of acting and in the risks of cousins falling in love; of *Pride and Prejudice* in the verbal echoes of the expectations aroused by Grandcourt's arrival in the neighbourhood (*DD* 82); and, in a more general way, in the Klesmers' moral equality. But though a re-educated Emma finally marries Mr Knightley, who even leaves his house to move into hers, a re-educated Gwendolen is finally separated from Deronda, both by marriage and geography. Though this might suggest a commentary on the earlier novel through a conscious rejection of Austen's argument that a man and woman might fitly marry after a course of moral education, in fact Eliot sets up a situation very different from Austen's. Whereas Knightley has long loved Emma, Daniel already loves another woman before he sees Gwendolen, and she in turn is betrothed before they actually meet face to face, while her widowhood coincides with his discovery of his Jewish heritage, ensuring that he will espouse not Gwendolen but Mirah and Zionism. Thus, despite the authorial sleight of hand that begins the story in the middle and sets up conventional expectations of a match between Gwendolen and Daniel, reinforced by the remarks of Sir Hugo and Hans, marriage is effectively excluded as a possibility from the beginning of the relationship. Mirah and Zionism have the protective effect of Mr Tryan's illness.

If Daniel is protected in one way by a manipulation of the plot justified as philosophical inquiry into beginnings and middles, he is protected in another by a masterly conception of Gwendolen's character. Her fear of sex is a condition much more serious than Emma Woodhouse's fear of marriage and, however convenient this may prove to the author, the sympathetic delineation of Gwendolen's situation far outstrips any such consideration. We are told, in words that might have come from D. H. Lawrence that "the life of passion had begun negatively in her" (73). Like Jane Eyre, Gwendolen associates sex with power, but, though for a brief premarital moment she feels she may be able to control Grandcourt, unlike Jane, she feels no exhilaration, but rather repugnance and fear.

The various aspects of Gwendolen revealed at different times are part of one convincing and organic whole, the psychological integrity of Eliot's portrayal being far from the collar-clutching, foot-crossing repetitions that serve elsewhere in the novel to establish stability of character. From her flirtations to her rejection of Rex, from her earliest experience of a man in the person of her hated stepfather to her desire to dominate her future husband, from her hysterical reception of Mrs Glasher's letter and jewels on her wedding night to her choice of her pillow as a place to hide the knife with which she thinks of murdering Grandcourt, and from her underlying sense of powerlessness and sudden hysteria to the violence that silences a canary or withholds a rope, she is fully perceived and fitfully revealed, damaged and damaging, but always consistently herself. Even the author's "poor Gwendolen" cannot diminish her. Whatever prompted her creation in this particular form, her characterization transcends any advantages Eliot derived from the opportunities of evasion offered by Gwendolen's terror of sex.

Furthermore, it must be recognized in Eliot's favour that there are moments in the work when she presents Gwendolen's frigidity as regrettable. Eliot's presentation of the Klesmers' relationship – a "triumph of manifold sympathy over monotonous attraction" (221) – testifies to the survival of her old attitude to sexuality, and yet for Gwendolen it is a deficiency that Eliot appears to mourn. Possibly it is safer for her to regret the absence of sexuality than to rejoice in its presence, but whatever emboldens her, this, though not consistently sustained, is a gain in this last novel.

Having said this, it must also be admitted that Eliot is equivocal, for she also approves the effects of Gwendolen's frigidity. Gwendolen's condition is not only a relief to Daniel, who repeatedly reassures himself that she is not a coquette, but also to Eliot who clearly applauds Gwendolen's unmixed motives in seeking his mentorship and its salutary effect on him:

> Without the aid of sacred ceremony or costume, her feelings had turned this man, only a few years older than herself, into a priest; a sort of trust less rare than the fidelity that guards it.
>
> (401)

Gwendolen, protected by the assumptions about male sexuality linked to her frigidity, simply disregards the possibility that Daniel could be a sexual being because he does not act towards her as other males do.

Momentarily, Grandcourt's jibes excite, not personal jealousy, but fear that Daniel is not the saintly figure she has thought him; but she is easily reassured and reverts to her former state of trust based on incomprehension.

Nonetheless, Gwendolen's frigidity, combined with the timing of events in the novel, is convenient for Eliot in protecting Daniel from Gwendolen, and Eliot from the problem that gave her discomfort in justifying Tryan as "Mr. Lime-Twig Lady-Winner". Daniel's fidelity to the role Gwendolen has assigned him ensures he will guard her trust, but with the safety-net of Zionism held by the saintly Mirah (in whom, otherwise, her creator is clearly not deeply interested) Eliot can venture quite a long way out on a limb to examine the limed twig. She can safely explore a complex interplay of attraction and resistance experienced by Daniel in his relations with Gwendolen that has no parallel in his conventional reservations regarding Mirah. The paragon who chivalrously rescues the drowning Jewish maiden, honourably maintains a protective distance from her, and finally confesses his love only when he is sure it will put her at no disadvantage, is far from the self-deceiver who blunders into and out of Gwendolen's life, metaphorically unable to throw her a rope. The real difficulty here, of course, is to assess the nature of Eliot's involvement in this clumsiness, a problem originating in the reader's and Deronda's perceptions of his manifest inadequacies set against Eliot's claims for his ultimate success in rescuing Gwendolen from the moral equivalent of Mirah's river-suicide.

The central problem is that Deronda has nothing to offer Gwendolen, and while he regrets his inadequacy, Eliot simultaneously attempts to deny it. In his diagnosis of the problem, R.H. Hutton had lamented Eliot's loss of faith, that had reduced Daniel to a "moral mist"(Holmstrom 133) but it is in a fogbank of religiosity that Eliot swathes the problem, as here in Daniel's thoughts after Gwendolen's confession at Genoa:

> But her remorse was the precious sign of a recoverable nature; . . . it marked her off from the criminals whose only regret is failure in securing their evil wish. Deronda could not utter one word to diminish that sacred aversion to her worse self – that thorn pressure which must come with the crowning of the sorrowful Better, suffering because of the Worse. All this mingled thought and feeling kept him silent. . . .
>
> (649)

This shifting collage of images from the crucifixion, complete with Gwendolen, apparently flanked by thieves and crowned with thorns, both crucified Christ and sinful mankind, would be justifiable if presented critically, as the regrettable result of Daniel's overwrought imagination. Terence Cave offers the defence that "Believing that such imaginative forms [religions and myths] are expressions of deeply rooted human impulses, she 'secularizes' them so that they assume the guise of everyday modern life while retaining their age-old psychological power" ("Introduction", *DD* xxvi), but religion and myth cannot be "secularized" without first draining them of their essence, a problem that is exacerbated in her last novel. Ian Robinson, writing of Eliot's use of the religion she had long ceased to believe in, extends his criticism to include her treatment of Judaism : "George Eliot uses [it], just as she had earlier used imaginative memories of Christianity, as a means of obtaining the gratifications and ecstasies of religious adherence. . . . that purple style is clearly used to drug that super-sharp mind into a state of satisfaction. . . ." (104). "Satisfaction", however, is not a state I would agree she achieves in this novel and the persistence of the connection between bad writing and the attempt to transform sexuality into a safer relationship through the medium of religious language seems instead to be an act of desperation.

In this connection it is clear that Eliot makes an honest effort to examine at least part of what she ducked in connection with Tryan: the characteristics of the "clerical sex". It has often been noted that Daniel's nature is feminine, and indeed not only does Eliot use many phrases to characterize Daniel reminiscent of those associated with Philip, but his qualities are similarly ascribed to his isolation from rough-and-tumble boyhood. However, if in part clerical sexuality includes feminine characteristics, Eliot is nevertheless anxious to stress (using the narrative voice, although the passage has been concerned with Sir Hugo's feelings for Daniel) that there was a

> mental balance in Deronda, who was moved by an affectionateness such as we are apt to call feminine, disposing him to yield in ordinary details, while he had a certain inflexibility of judgment, an independence of opinion, held to be rightfully masculine.
>
> (295)

The play of the inclusive but inconclusive "we are apt to call" against the passive impersonal "held to be" makes it hard to see where Eliot herself stands in relation to the "feminine" and "rightfully masculine", and suggests an ironic stance in relation to characteristics classified by gender. The purpose, however, does not simply seem to be to present an androgynous balance, the "sensitive man" so popular a century after she wrote, although he does embody the continuance of Eliot's attraction to nurture and support. Rather, she suggests that, in Daniel, sexuality and sympathy blend, so that his sympathy arouses a response that is in part sexual, and vice versa, a phenomenon not restricted to his relations with women. Early in their relationship, Mordecai and Daniel meet (like Maggie and Stephen) "with as intense a consciousness as if they had been undeclared lovers", and soon after we are reminded of Daniel's "keenly perceptive sympathetic emotiveness" (462). Later, as he dies in the arms of Daniel and Mirah, Mordecai rejoices that the two men will become one: "Have I not breathed my soul into you? We shall live together" (754).

It is no coincidence that Gwendolen and Deronda also have the appearance of lovers in those moments when he is exuding sympathy, or of lovers quarrelling when he resists her pleas for compassion. Eliot does not deprive Daniel of his sexuality, although she does show it to be unusual in its source and lack of specific focus. She generalizes it, infuses it into his compassion, and produces a frighteningly powerful combination that can be recognized as surviving today in the stereotype of the television evangelist. Eliot uses disparate observers to draw attention to the dangerous magnetism of this compassionate clerical sexuality. Hans insists Daniel must face Gwendolen: "You monster! . . . Do you want her to wear weeds for *you* all her life – burn herself in perpetual suttee while you are alive and merry?" (744, emphasis original). Sir Hugo sees the problem as characteristic of his foster son: "You are always looking tenderly at the women, and talking to them in a Jesuitical way. You are a dangerous young fellow – a kind of Lovelace who will make the Clarissas run after you instead of your running after them" (332) – although, perhaps he should have chosen for his comparison the upright and sensitive Sir Charles Grandison, Richardson's prime representative of the clerical sex, more beloved by women within the novel than by its readers.

Eliot's exploration of this condition includes Daniel's uneasy awareness of his clerical sex appeal: "Deronda was sure that he had never flirted. But he was glad that the baronet had no knowledge about the redemption of Gwendolen's necklace" (333). Indeed, in his relationship with Gwendolen, Daniel's actions suggest an unconscious fear of his powers. At Leubronn he initially represses both his compassion and his sexuality, although he is more successful at resisting the sexual than the compassionate temptation. His conclusion that the "evil genius" (3) must be dominant in Gwendolen's glance is an obvious attempt to avoid an involvement to which he nevertheless submits when he returns the necklace – it is easier to justify compassion, even when he fears its exercise may be dangerous. His own understanding of his condition comes fitfully and incompletely, and he sometimes displaces his fears onto Gwendolen, wondering if she may be a "coquette", dismissing the idea only to fear again. Daniel believes that, but for Mirah's prior claims, "he should have given way to the interest this girl had raised in him, and tried to know more of her" (148), an admission of interest only made possible (for him and for Eliot) by those same prior claims. Deronda's condition clearly interests Eliot deeply, encouraging her to pursue, throughout the novel, this pattern of denial and admission of sexual interest, embodied in a compassion that both justifies the continuance of the relationship and is its dubious vehicle.

This recognition of complexity is a clear advance over the early presentation of Tryan's clerical sexuality, where Eliot had dodged the problem of the mentor's sexual attraction, and simply replaced it by nurturing care. But a study of the links between self-deception and sexual attraction is, of course, as highly congenial to Eliot as is the substitution of nurturing for sexual love. As in the case of Hetty and Arthur or Maggie and Stephen, Eliot's distrust of sexuality ensures that her insights into its potential dangers and distortions are her moments of strength, undercut only by her fear these links are inevitable. Furthermore, here the dimensions of the problem are kept in check by circumstance and Eliot's protectiveness. Were Gwendolen to have been sexually responsive, Eliot and Daniel might have been tested much more fully, both psychologically and morally. What does emerge is a recognition of the dangerous nature of compassion charged with sexual appeal and the deception of self and others that it engenders. In the early work, nurturing could safely be substituted for sexual passion. In the last novel, so great has Eliot come to consider the power of sexuality to contaminate all it touches that even compassion and sympathy are liable to infection, even where the best intentions exist.

Eliot successfully gives us a man who is uneasy about the extent of his sexual appeal, and she apparently also intends to give us one who is mistaken over his moral power. Here, however, she wishes the error to be seen in his favour, Daniel believing himself incapable of helping Gwendolen, and yet showing himself to be successful. In Eliot's view, though he is both more the lover and more the mentor than he believes, it is because of the restraints on him as a lover that he is successful as a mentor. If the restraints have made most readers somewhat doubtful of his capabilities as a lover, the gap between those readers and Eliot in the judgment of his success as a mentor seems unbridgeable.

Part of this problem may lie in our post-Freudian assumptions. It is natural for modern readers to think of Daniel as a psychoanalyst, and, indeed, as Alexander Welsh has pointed out, Eliot here anticipates Freud in her exploration of transference and counter-transference (289). However, the role Deronda fears, but nevertheless accepts, is that of priest or confessor, a role entailing both the encouragement of a sense of guilt and the giving of advice, requirements alien to the work of the psychoanalyst. In Eliot's view Daniel is culpable, and knows it, when he attempts to evade his responsibility as a priest-like mentor:

> She was bent on confession, and he dreaded hearing her confession. Against his better will, he shrank from the task that was laid on him: he wished, and yet rebuked the wish as cowardly, that she could bury her secrets in her own bosom. He was not a priest. He dreaded the weight of this woman's soul flung upon his own with imploring dependence.
>
> (642)

That he should express his dread of the effects of his compassion in terms of a part-spiritual, part-sexual analogy is as characteristic as that Gwendolen should cast him in the role of one who has forgone sexual relationships. But Eliot promises a reward for taking up such an onerous responsibility:

> Young reverence for one who is also young is the most coercive of all. . . .
> But the coercion is often stronger on the one who takes the reverence. Those who trust us educate us. And perhaps in that ideal consecration of Gwendolen's, some education was being prepared for Deronda.
>
> (401)

Elinor Shaffer suggests that Eliot modelled Daniel on Renan's portrait of the human Jesus, a man whose delusions paradoxically made him a successful charismatic leader. Passages from *The Life of Jesus*, which Eliot had read a decade earlier with mixed feelings[2] (*Letters* 4:123: 26 December 1863), certainly support this possibility:

> The extremely delicate feeling toward women, which we remark in [Jesus], was not separated from the exclusive devotion which he had

for his mission. . . . It is, however, probable that these loved him more than the work; he was, no doubt, more beloved than loving. Thus, as often happens in very elevated natures, tenderness of the heart was transformed in him into an infinite sweetness, a vague poetry, and a universal charm. His relations, free and intimate, but of an entirely moral kind, with women of doubtful character, are also explained by the passion which attached him to the glory of his Father. . . .

Women, in fact, received him with eagerness. He manifested toward them those reserved manners which render a very sweet union of ideas possible between the two sexes. . . .

Weak or guilty women, surprised at so much that was charming, and realizing, for the first time, the attractions of contact with virtue approached him freely. . . . Women, with tearful hearts, and disposed through their sins to feelings of humility, were nearer to his kingdom than ordinary natures, who often have little merit in not having fallen.

(Renan, The Life 120, 175, 200)

Eliot's comment, "[Renan's] Life of Jesus has so much artistic merit that it will do a great deal towards the culture of ordinary minds by giving them a sense of unity between that far-off past and our present" (*Letters* 4:123: 26 December 1863) suggests her own intentions may well have been to suggest parallels between one Messiah and another, and intentionally or not, she does so strikingly. But though Shaffer suggests that Eliot successfully makes the Feuerbachian case that both Gwendolen and Daniel are saved by "the mutual assumption of moral responsibility for each other's evil" (281), this is to accept what Eliot claims rather than what she shows: it is hard to see in what way Gwendolen assumes moral responsibility for Daniel, or Daniel, with any success, for her. And as for Eliot's claim that, through the relationship "some education was being prepared for Deronda", the problem here is not that reciprocal mentorship is impossible, or that one cannot learn from a moral inferior, or even that the moral consequences of being a teacher may actually be harmful to the mentor, but that it is difficult to discover what Daniel learns from his experience with Gwendolen that is of any benefit in the life he is to lead. Humility, self-doubt, and an uneasy awareness of his particular sexual nature acquired in the realistic world of

Gwendolen have no place in the romantically vague future at the end of the work.

Meanwhile, until the very last of his dealings with Gwendolen, in that everyday world where his education takes place, he is inept, clumsy, even cruel:

> "If we had been much together before, we should have felt our differences more, and seemed to get farther apart. Now we can perhaps never see each other again. But our minds may get nearer."
>
> (750)

Immediately, Daniel comes to "hate his own words", feeling (in a phrase that brilliantly describes much of what we fumblingly say to those in deep distress and that is characteristic of Eliot at her best) "the hardness of easy consolation in them" (750). But the phrase in no way describes what he has said, and both Deronda and Eliot are disastrously deaf to meaning if they hear even "easy consolation" in the crass insensitivity of this speech.

A similar disjunction occurs in the assurances we are given by Eliot that Daniel's own past enables him to rescue Gwendolen:

> Our guides, we pretend, must be sinless: as if those were not often the best teachers who only yesterday got corrected for their mistakes.
>
> (432)

> Your feeling even urges you to some self punishment – some scourging of the self that disobeyed your better will – the will that struggled against temptation. I have known something of that myself.
>
> (714)

Unfortunately for this view of Daniel (which is pallidly reminiscent of Tryan's more explicit if equally unconvincing account of his lurid past), nothing we are shown suggests Daniel is anything but "sinless", and indeed we are assured: "Few men were able to keep themselves clearer of vices than he" (336). It is apparent, despite Daniel's claims, that nothing in his experience or character (and here he is unlike Eliot, whose comprehension of Gwendolen is all-encompassing) makes an understanding of Gwendolen's nature and distress possible. In part the concealment from the reader, as well as Daniel, of the horror of Gwendolen's temptations blurs the utter failure of Daniel to grasp the depths of her need. But this should not obscure the fact that the claims for his experience of sin, like the claims for his education through Gwendolen, are bogus. Unfortunately, while Daniel periodically admits to the latter, Eliot over-rides these disclaimers, treating them as admirable but modest self-doubts.

Thus, unwillingly and uncertainly, but with Eliot's approval, Daniel assumes his responsibilities as mentor. His reiterated recommendations to Gwendolen return us to another issue, that of moral responsibility, which Eliot had touched on, but not resolved, in *Middlemarch*. With even less sign of discomposure than she exhibited in the previous novel, Eliot resolves the difficulty according to her standard practice, summed up in the word "submission". It is the act of self-surrender that comes most easily to the childlike and angelic Mirah, whose nature is "only to submit" (207), a surrender of self that is first impossible and then inescapable for Gwendolen.

Not only must Gwendolen learn (like Esther in *Felix Holt*) to submit to her moral superior, but her superior also exacts a more difficult and dangerous submission, one that ultimately places her in an intolerable position she is not morally strong enough to endure: remaining with Grandcourt in their "long Satanic masquerade" (708). As she wanders endlessly through a "labyrinth of reflection" (560) in her longing to escape her husband, "always among the images that drove her back to submission was Deronda" (561), inaction that after Grandcourt's death she rightly regrets: "I ought to have gone away" (645).

Admittedly, Eliot is characteristically careful to show us a Gwendolen whose motives for this submission are mixed. Not only does she fear practical difficulties, she also fears that a separation from her husband would cut her off from Daniel: "The association of Deronda with a dubious position for herself was intolerable" (561). Nevertheless, Gwendolen guesses (and surely rightly) that Deronda would recommend that "she ought to bear what she had brought on herself, unless she was sure she could make herself a better woman by any other course" (561), and this, with her slender moral resources, is clearly impossible. If Eliot is to claim that Deronda, despite his deficiencies, inadvertently brings Gwendolen to moral regeneration, then the consequence of his inadvertent influence on Gwendolen, which contributed to her guilty part in her husband's death, ought to be set against the claims for his success as mentor. This is something Eliot does not do. To return to the reservations of the *Academy* critic, "A" has submitted to "B" but "B" has not proved to be a "trustworthy guide".

In the process of having her learn submission, Eliot characteristically requires that Gwendolen must become as a little child again. Her "success" (like Janet Dempster's) is signalled by a regression to "child-like sentences" (715). Undeniably Gwendolen's formerly sophisticated speech concealed the "spoiled child" of Book One, who was no more mature than the penitent child later imploring Daniel for help:"I will do what you tell me. . . . but what else shall I do?" (715). But the later childishness is distressingly at odds with the pressure Eliot exerts on the reader to agree that Gwendolen has made moral and emotional progress. That Gwendolen could regress in this way is psychologically convincing. That Eliot should wish us to find the regression desirable is another matter.

Psychologically, however, Gwendolen's moral immaturity dovetails neatly and convincingly with her arrested sexuality:

> Lovemaking and marriage – how could they now be the imagery in which poor Gwendolen's deepest attachment could spontaneously clothe itself? Mighty Love had laid his hand upon her; but what had he demanded of her? Acceptance of rebuke – the hard task of self-change – confession – endurance. If she cried towards him, what then? She cried as the child cries whose little feet have fallen backward – cried to be taken by the hand, lest she should lose herself.
>
> (717–18)

Unfortunately the sharp recognition of Gwendolen's sexual and moral immaturity, "now" worsened by her experiences of her marriage, is combined with Eliot's succumbing to the sentimentality of those "little feet" that signal her indulgence and are supposed to evoke ours. Eliot's apparent recognition that Gwendolen's sexual immaturity is tragic is swallowed up in the old preference for what she sees as pre-sexual innocence. In the moral as well as the sexual sphere, this leads to serious problems in the work.

So many of the novel's many pages appear, in fact, to be devoted to reducing Gwendolen to a child-like submission and extolling the virtues of this state, that outrage is the only possible response when Daniel so clumsily abandons the now-dependent Gwendolen. Presumably Eliot wishes, without claiming more than the potential for recovery, to signal that Gwendolen must, if she is to survive as a moral being, take responsibility for her own moral life, and that Gwendolen recognizes this, however shakily, and attempts to accept her enforced condition of moral autonomy: "It is better – it shall be better with me because I have known you" (754). The sign from Eliot that this is essential is, I think, clearer than that given in *Middlemarch*, and is a correction to the doctrine of permanent submission preached in *The Mill on the Floss* or *Felix Holt*, but the reader feels Gwendolen is hardly qualified to take up the challenge. That "B" abandons "A" in such circumstances hardly seems the "imaged solution of a logical dilemma" that *The Academy* critic hoped for.

Despite slight modifications, Eliot has not abandoned her belief in the moral value of submission, for it is by submission (both unwillingly to Grandcourt and willingly to Daniel) that Gwendolen has reached the point of moral awareness. To the reader's distress, her submission has been to a mentor whose advice in the crucial period before Grandcourt's drowning has done nothing to solve her dilemma or avert her consequent guilt in her husband's death. In one encounter after another, Gwendolen begs to be told what to do, while an impotent Deronda tries to offer help that is clearly inadequate. Making amends, avoiding doing injury to others, taking up reading or music are all suggestions offered at random to a woman whose problems he cannot begin to understand (419–23). Many readers must have felt that, indeed, there was nothing that Daniel could have done, and at times Eliot seems to feel the same way. At other times she is anxious to insist on results out of all proportion as when, to these banal suggestions, Gwendolen looks "startled and thrilled as by an electric shock" (421). Her intentions to make "vast mental excursions" into literature (509) are subsequently treated ironically, as beyond her capabilities, but the episode fits the pattern of insisting that we ought to be able to detect success while actually showing us its opposite. By the end of the novel, not only does Eliot fail to convince the majority of her readers of Gwendolen's potential for life, let alone flourishing growth, she fails to show how Daniel's mentorship contributes to Gwendolen's moral betterment. We are told of his contribution, but what we watch is closer to what Daniel fears, his inadequacy as rescuer.

It is in this connection that one aspect of that sexuality that Daniel and Eliot hold so tightly in check is diverted into his moral relations with Gwendolen. Eliot insists on Daniel's potency, not as a lover, but as a mentor, while the reader witnesses instead an exhibition of impotence. The moral relationship between Daniel and Gwendolen takes on the characteristics, patterns and rhythms that one would expect to find in an account of a series of near, but never quite consummated, sexual encounters, Daniel often approaching, but always pulling back from, or being interrupted in the course of, giving Gwendolen the moral satisfaction she desires – and in the process producing in Gwendolen, and indeed the reader, a kind of frustrated moral excitement. Confrontations by the suspicious husband are standard fare in accounts of adultery, and appropriately occur here. However, the interview Grandcourt interrupts is

anything but typical, his wife protectively swathed like a nun and
Deronda silenced by the dread of committing a "violation of awe before
the mysteries of our human lot", and who, uninterrupted, would have
(on the disastrous basis of ignorance) advised "Confess everything to
your husband; leave nothing concealed" (567). Consistent with this shift
of sexual patterns into the moral sphere, Grandcourt's jealousy is directed
to Daniel's moral power, not his sexual appeal. "He wished her to be
sought after" and would not have objected to "a kind of lofty coquetry
on her part" (545) but "He suspected a growing spirit of opposition in
her" (623) and it is this that fuels his implacable will to control.

But Deronda's moral inadequacy is not always due to outside inter-
ruption. More often he simply does not know what to do to satisfy
Gwendolen and his recognition of his impotence recurs repeatedly.
Often his images of failure take a form which links them to Gwendolen's
failure to save Grandcourt and contrasts them with Daniel's successful
rescue of Mirah:

> It was as if he saw her drowning while his limbs were bound.
>
> (422)

> his memory went back, . . . over all the signs and confessions that
> she needed a rescue, one much more difficult than that of the wan-
> derer by the river – a rescue for which he felt himself helpless.
>
> (520)

> [He feared] some spoiling of her trust, which wrought upon him now
> as if it had been the retreating cry of a creature snatched and carried
> out of his reach by swift horsemen or even swifter waves, while his
> own strength was only a stronger sense of weakness.
>
> (579)

However, the similarities only serve to emphasize the differences.
According to her account, Gwendolen, deliberately if momentarily,
chooses to withhold rescue from Grandcourt: "I kept my hands tight"
(645), while Deronda is incapacitated by circumstance and ability and
feels himself "bound", too weak to help Gwendolen. Furthermore,
Gwendolen's hesitation may have contributed to Grandcourt's death,
whereas we are asked to believe that Deronda successfully saves
Gwendolen in spite of all.

So, the reader endures with Daniel the painful awareness that the
advice offered is totally inadequate to Gwendolen's situation. Yet the

narrative voice insists on success, in language that, while it retains much of the vagueness of Daniel's advice as to specifics, explicitly confirms the sexual analogy:

> The words were like the touch of a miraculous hand to Gwendolen, mingled emotions streamed through her frame with a strength that seemed the beginning of a new existence, having some new powers or other which stirred in her vaguely. So pregnant is the divine hope of moral recovery with the energy that fulfils it. So potent in us is the infused action of another soul, before which we bow in complete love.
>
> (716)

But by the end, when Deronda leaves for the East, presumably to father both a movement and a brood of children, he leaves Gwendolen no more pregnant with new moral and spiritual life than she is with Grandcourt's child, although she is unquestionably empty of her former plans and hopes and stripped of her "iridescence". Author and character collude in this sadistic abandonment, and, as Dorothea Barrett points out (172–3), it is Daniel who in his closing interview makes Gwendolen's lips tremble (*DD* 747), thus fulfilling the desire of the voyeur Mackworth in the opening scene: "I cannot endure that sort of mouth. It looks so self-complacent. . . . I like a mouth that trembles more" (8). Although Eliot, quoting from Corinthians, had promised the worried Blackwood that "poor Gwen is spiritually saved but 'so as by fire'" (*Letters* 6:188: 18 November 1875 and n.9), at the end Gwendolen seems more like a burnt-out shell of herself. In fact, very often it seems that Daniel and Eliot are impotent in very similar ways with regard to Gwendolen. Neither really knows what Gwendolen might be hoped to do after the destruction of her former self, and both uneasily recognize this. It is hard not to feel that Eliot writes out of a sense of her own inadequacy when she writes of Deronda.

In part this may be because Eliot does indeed write of her own experience transmuted into Deronda's situation, one aspect of this being the unrelenting pressure of mentorship. With her first full-length novel, she had become the beloved of a wide reading public (although under a male name and emanating the aura of a clergyman), popular for appearing to dispense moral precepts sweetened with rural charm and a loving concern for the well-being of her readers. Later Frederic Harrison had tentatively requested her (with the proviso that "I presume no true art is directly didactic or dogmatic") to write a novel resembling her just-completed *Felix Holt*, but this time set in a community modelled, though not overtly, on a Positivist society. She had demurred at depicting a Utopia, but not at acknowledging her role as a teacher *(Letters* 4:288–9: 19 July 1866; 4: 300–1:15 Aug. 1866). Using a phrase that reached back to Tryan and forward to *Daniel Deronda,* the "idea . . . made flesh" *(Clerical Life* 364) she wrote of the "agonizing labour" required to "lay hold on the emotions [of the reader] as human experience", to

> make certain ideas thoroughly incarnate, as if they had revealed themselves to me first in the flesh and not the spirit. I think aesthetic teaching is the highest of all teaching because it deals with life in its highest complexity. But if it ceases to be purely aesthetic – if it lapses anywhere from the picture to the diagram – it becomes the most offensive of all teaching. . . . .
>
> *(Letters* 4:300–1: 15 August 1866)

Later in the same letter there is a touch of Deronda's ambivalence when she strikes out the word "teach" and replaces it:

> it is my way . . . to <teach> urge the human sanctities through tragedy – through pity and terror as well as admiration and delights.

The two contexts suggest that as long as the matter is presented in impersonal terms, the notion of her novels as "teaching" is acceptable, but overtly attached to "my way", the word "teach" must be replaced because it lacks humility. However, a dozen years later the hesitation has all but vanished: "My function is that of the aesthetic, not the doctrinal teacher" although this acknowledgement is used to avoid "the prescribing of special measures, concerning which the artistic mind, however strongly moved by social sympathy, is often not the best judge" *(Letters* 7:44: 18 July 1878).

The preference for creating "a picture" did not preclude her permitting the publication of a collection (necessarily out of context and thus partaking of "the diagram") of *Wise, Witty and Tender Sayings in Prose and Verse of George Eliot* in 1871, subsequently reissued in expanded form, followed by the similar *The George Eliot Birthday Book* in 1878. These collections, assembled by an admirer, Alexander Main, were authorized by Marian on G. H. Lewes's recommendation – it was her publisher Blackwood who privately called Main "the Gusher" (Haight, *Biography* 440). Rosemarie Bodenheimer convincingly argues that in allowing, even praising, Main's selection of "grand George Eliot gener-alizations", Marian "reveals that she privately agreed with Main's idea that her most preacherly voice was most central to her fictional mean-ing". Main tended to select passages in which "the narrator widens the focus of her story and talks to the reader over the heads of her charac-ters. . . . while when it came to characters' speeches, his selections inad-vertently made the point that George Eliot's characters in their moral and aphoristic moments sound a good deal like versions of the narrator got up in various dialects" (245–6).

Marian did get upset over Main's planned preface to a second edi-tion of the sayings: "Unless I am condemned by my own principles, my books are not separable into 'direct' and 'indirect' teaching. My chief doubt as to the desirability of the 'Sayings' has always turned on the possibility that the volume might encourage such a view of my writings" (*Letters*, 5: 458–9: 12 November 1873), but, as Kerry McSweeney comments, "the naivety of this statement is startling" (132) – such a collection could give no other impression. And as J. Russell Perkin demonstrates, by the 1890s an equal and opposite reaction to that of Eliot's lifetime had occurred, William Ernest Henley, for example, complaining of her works, "It is doubtful whether they are novels disguised as treatises, or treatises disguised as novels" (Perkin, *Reception History* 96).

But it was one of Blackwood's elderly employees who spoke for many in the contemporary audience: "George Eliot's [books] I don't rank as Novels but as second Bibles. . . . Such books are worth nine tenths of the Sermons ever preached or published" (*Letters* 6:340: 8 February 1877). The admiration of Mr Brown was reported to Marian as part of a campaign of reassurance instigated by Lewes who judged that, because she was prone to despair over her work, she needed to be encouraged by reports of praise and shielded from criticism. And though, after *Adam Bede*, she had dispensed less honey with her humanism, letters request-ing advice continued to pour in from Gwendolens all over the world. Unfortunately, as Eliot demonstrated in Deronda's relationship to Gwendolen, the expectations of serious admirers may actually increase self-doubt to an almost paralysing extent, and Eliot, as her letters show, continued to suffer from what Lewes called a "terrible diffidence" (*Letters* 4:405: 7 December 1867). In arranging Daniel's audience, Eliot provided one, though on a much reduced scale, that was as admiring and demanding as her own.

Despite Mr Brown's admiration for her "second Bibles", Eliot, like Deronda, was not what she had at first seemed, and certainly not the

Christian clerical gentleman initially thought to have authored the first two works. Nevertheless, despite her alienation from the religion of her youth she, like Daniel who turned away from his own upbringing as a Christian, might have used his very words: "the effect of my education can never be done away with. The Christian sympathies in which my mind was reared can never die out of me" (724). But the advice given both by the humanist author and by her Jewish character rested awkwardly on Christian foundations and must, in Eliot's case, have complicated her position as "clerical tutor".

And then there were the visitors to the Priory, among them admiring women like Mrs Congreve, Elma Stuart and Edith Simcox, apparently attracted by Eliot's "clerical sexuality". In *Daniel Deronda*, Eliot had used overtly sexual metaphors ("So potent in us is the infused action of another soul . . .") to describe the effect of Daniel on Gwendolen. Her letters carry something of this tone: she wrote, for example, to a young American woman "apart from those relations in life which bring daily opportunities of lovingness, the most satisfactory of all ties is this effective invisible intercourse of an elder mind with a younger" (*Letters* 5:367: 16 January 1873) and she praised Alexander Main as being "one who takes into his own life the spiritual outcome of mine", thanking him for "the patient care which helps to save the seed of one's soul from perishing" (*Letters* 5:229: 28 December 1871). Rosemarie Bodenheimer sees this use of language as part of a movement to "spiritualize" relationships with female and male admirers alike, pointing out that Marian simultaneously used the language of spiritualized sexual love and of spiritual family (241–2). The echoes of Deronda's universal sexual appeal are eerie, and, unfortunately, in both cases the effect is of an attempt – gone insanely awry – to make use of, while attempting to neutralize, the language of sexuality in the interests of maintaining the role of loving mentor.

If Eliot wished to play Abelard to the public's Héloïse, accounts of the period suggest her role more closely resembled that of Galatea to her readers' Pygmalion. A quarter of a century before, she had written to the Brays that without contact with them she would lose her old identity: "my nature is so chameleon" (*Letters* 1:302: 28 August 1849), and others noted the same characteristic. The intellectuals, artists and readers of the day who elevated her to a sibylline status at once addictive and impossibly demanding, exerted a pressure to shape her to their expectations that was unrelenting, a pressure to which she was responsive.

But as with many celebrities, she also had detractors who were willing to satirize the "sage conducting services at the priory", including Eliza

Lynn Linton who had known her in her Chapman days, and who, despite her obvious hostility, nevertheless reflects the changing impression given by Haight's collection of letters, from passionate commitment to dispassionate sympathy:

> she lost every trace of that finer freedom and whole-heartedness which had been so remarkable in the beginning of her connection with Lewes . . . . Not a line of spontaneity was left in her; not an impulse beyond the reach of self-conscious philosophy; not an unguarded tract of mental or moral territory where a little untrained folly might luxuriate. She was always the goddess on her pedestal – gracious in her condescension – with sweet strains of sympathetic recognition for all – ever ready to listen to her worshippers – ever ready to reply, to encourage, to clear from confusion minds befogged by unassimilated learning, and generous in imparting her own.
>
> (*My Literary Life* 98–9)

In spite of Linton's dislike for Eliot, there appears to have been some common ground between them, for as Bonnie Zimmerman demonstrates, there are significant parallels between the early Gwendolen and Linton's hostile portrait of "The Girl of the Period", portrayed in a series of articles in the *Saturday Review* in 1868 ("Gwendolen" 200–1). And Eliot herself is reported to have expressed her own discomfort with her elevated position. Georgiana Burne-Jones recollected ("the meaning of what she said, if not the exact phrase") that Marian had complained of, just before her marriage to Cross, "I am so tired of being set on a pedestal and expected to vent wisdom – I am only a poor woman." (2: 104). It was an uncomfortable position and compared to that of Galatea, who was made of stone and only had to look beautiful while on her pedestal, it must have been a painful one. George Eliot both was, and wasn't flesh, as the writing of this chapter impresses upon me, requiring impossible decisions, sentence by sentence, between the penname and any one of the many names by which she was known.

J. Russell Perkin, not driven by Linton's personal animosity, nevertheless argues that though Cross's biography, largely composed of Eliot's carefully cut letters, is often blamed for precipitating the decline in her reputation after her death,

> such deletions do not significantly alter the overall tone. . . . Reading through the volumes of Haight's edition is not an exciting experience . . . . The picture . . . is of a woman whose primary concern was

to be . . . an earnest, sometimes ponderous Victorian intellectual
who strove to make herself an embodiment of moral good."

(93–4)

It is, however, helpful in this regard to remember Rosemarie
Bodenheimer's caution that letters were a form of performance
designed to be appropriate to an audience (5–6), and to note
Bodenheimer's own ability to evoke vivid drama from the interplay of
the letters and the novels.

Finally there is the combined, if inadvertent, testimony of Eliot and
Blackwood to the neutralizing effects of wide-ranging sympathy on
the passionately committed and radical young woman that Marian
Evans once had been. Shortly before she died, she completed the re-
making of her earlier bohemian self, selecting and revising for posterity only seven of her essays from the fifties and sixties, excluding such
works as the vigorous outspoken "Silly Novels". According to her step-
son Charles Lee Lewis, she left "written injunctions that no other
pieces written by her, of date prior to 1857, should be republished",
giving those that remained (in a telling phrase) "the weight of her
sanction" (Eliot, *Essays and Leaves* 5). Thus remade as a relatively
uncontroversial thinker, she corresponded more closely to the Eliot of
whom Blackwood rejoiced (in connection with *Felix Holt*): "Her politics are excellent and will attract all parties" (*Letters* 4:247: 26 April
1866).

In all these accounts of Eliot can be detected the Daniel whose spon-
taneity was long ago vitiated by his compassion, a male Jane Bennet
whose determination to see every side of the question, and be concerned for all, has produced a man paralysed by his generalized sympathy. The section that best illustrates this problem in Daniel occurs
during the narrative's extended analysis of Deronda, a passage intended
to enable the reader to "know a little more of what he was at five-and-
twenty than was evident in ordinary intercourse" (335). Here, in a male
incarnation, is the political Eliot of whom Blackwood approved:

voracious of speculations on government and religion, yet loath to
part with long-sanctioned forms which, for him, were quick with
memories and sentiments that no argument could lay dead. (336)

Unfortunately, however, Eliot's judgment upon Daniel, and therefore
herself, is that there is no escape from the paralysis produced by this
even-handedness, except in the abandonment of one's moral autonomy:

what he most longed for was either some external event, or some inward light, that would urge him into a definite line of action. . . . But how and whence was this needed event to come? – the influence that would justify partiality. . . .

(336)

Judaism brings salvation:

It was as if he had found an added soul in finding his ancestry – his judgment no longer wandering in the mazes of impartial sympathy, but choosing, with the noble partiality which is man's best strength, the closer fellowship that makes sympathy practical. . . .

(693)

But this dependence on an outside force to supply moral initiative is a confession of impotence on Eliot's part, as well as Deronda's. For no more than Gwendolen, does he find the strength within himself to escape from his powerlessness, and in supplying this motivation to Daniel in the form of Mordecai's mission, the novelist admits as much, providing the equivalent of Maggie's flood to rescue him from an otherwise insoluble moral dilemma. Gwendolen submits to Daniel, her mentor. Daniel submits to the cause of his ancestors as outlined by his mentor Mordecai, and a "noble partiality" cures his moral paralysis. A submits to B and B submits to the demands of his mission.

As Susan Ostrov Weisser points out, "Daniel's story concludes on a note of dream-making". "When Daniel discovers felicitously that he is a Jew and therefore deserves Mirah, it is in much the same way that heroines in popular romantic novels of the day used to discover they were 'really' born ladies and deserved their landed gentlemen" (148). Perhaps the reason why the ending has so much the air of a fairy tale with Daniel sailing off to be the Sir Charles Grandison of the East, is that here Deronda and Eliot divide: he attains what she can never really believe in for herself, however often she prescribes it for her characters – peace through the surrender of moral responsibility. Eliot, urged to take a position on "the 'Woman Question'", declined regretfully, on the grounds that "Conclusions seem so easy so long as we keep large blinkers on and look in the direction of our own private path" (*Letters* 5:58: 4 October 1869). In this she remained the Deronda of the paralysed impartiality, before he acquired the "blinkers", not so much of his own private interest, but of the "noble partiality" he longed for, and she provided. Perhaps Eliot's inability to convince the reader of the reality of

Daniel's mission to the blank canvas of her unimagined East and in the safe obscurity of the period following the conclusion of the novel, springs from her own inability to surrender to a "partiality". There may have been a stage in her life when her writing seemed to offer the equivalent of Daniel's mission. But the very vagueness of the desire to become the impartial mentor of her culture precluded success, however vigorously Lewes, Blackwood, Mr Brown and a host of disciples encouraged her to believe the role was hers.

It is striking that the passages describing moral quandaries are the most clotted and clogged in the work, suggesting Eliot's entrapment in Daniel's dilemma. She needs desperately to describe his problem accurately, and to demonstrate that it is not totally disabling, but compared to her characterisations of Gwendolen or Grandcourt, where her language is precise and her analogies revealing and succinct, her attempts to convey Daniel's state achieve neither clarity nor power, but only the impression of desperation. Two pages (414–16) produce repeated attempts (which these examples represent but by no means exhaust) to state Daniel's problem:

His early-awakened sensibility and reflectiveness had developed into a many-sided sympathy, which threatened to hinder any persistent course of action. . . .

(335)

His plenteous flexible sympathy had ended by falling into one current with that reflective analysis which tends to neutralize sympathy.

(336)

A too reflective and diffusive sympathy was in danger of paralysing in him that indignation against wrong and that selectness of fellowship which are the conditions of moral force. . . .

(336)

. . . he did not attempt to hide from himself that he had fallen into a meditative numbness, and was gliding farther and farther from that life of practically energetic sentiment which he would have proclaimed (if he had been inclined to proclaim anything) to be the best of all life. . . .

(337)

This is not analysis – it is obsession. Daniel's reverie concludes with not one but two attempts to find a means to express his state:

> To pound the objects of sentiment into small dust, yet keep senti-ment alive and active, was something like the famous recipe for mak-ing cannon – to first take a round hole and then close it with iron; whatever you do keeping fast hold of your round hole. Yet how dis-tinguish what our will may wisely save in its completeness, from the heaping of cat-mummies and the expensive cult of enshrined putre-factions.
> Something like this was the common undercurrent in Deronda's mind. . . .
>
> (337)

If this is intended to be imitation, it takes the imitative fallacy to a dis-astrous extreme, producing sections of the novel that verge on incoher-ence. And if these cannons and cat mummies do indeed represent the "common undercurrent in Deronda's mind" it is not surprising that, as Gwendolen's mentor, he can do so little to save her. That Eliot could, in this work, present a Gwendolen, Grandcourt or Lush with economy and precision suggests not that her powers as a novelist were waning, but that she herself was experiencing enormous difficulties in coming to grips with what it means to be a mentor, particularly one who doubts his – or her – ability to supply the answers to the questions so urgently asked and so difficult to answer.

Like Charlotte Brontë, George Eliot created her mentor-lovers out of her weaknesses rather than her strengths. Unlike Brontë, however, she became increasingly and painfully aware of the moral and emotional toll on the mentor. She did not overcome her Abelardian fear of sexual-ity as a threat to duty and self-control, nor resolve the problem of moral autonomy, but she did, in her last novel, engage in an examination of the complex sexual and moral motivations involved in the dual role. As in Brontë's case, a consideration of Eliot's treatment of the mentor-lover provides an insight into what sometimes goes wrong with her novels. But whereas the essence of Brontë's work is encompassed in her treat-ment of the mentor-lover, such a study as this only partially defines Eliot as a novelist. Much of her considerable strength lay in her grasp of confused motivation in areas of human behaviour only sometimes touched upon here, exemplified by Mrs Transome, the Lydgates,

Bulstrodes, Casaubon, Gwendolen and Deronda's mother. In this complex view of human nature, Eliot more closely resembled Austen than Brontë. Like both her predecessors, however, she revealed in her treatment of the mentor-lover much about the relationship she understood to exist between love and those qualities she valued most.

Epilogue: The Author, the Reader and the "imaged solution"

By providing a figure around which the imagination might freely play, the figure of the mentor-lover offered a stimulus to writers of the eighteenth and nineteenth centuries to explore the relations between love, power, judgment and moral authority. As a consequence, the novels of Austen, Brontë and Eliot blend the philosophical, moral and erotic with instruction in varying proportions. They also offer differing assessments of the relationship, demonstrating that a shared interest in the mentor-lover, far from producing evidence to support a single view of the world, provides opportunities for developing very different concerns shaped by individual experience lived in place and time. Such vibrant particularities are increased by the interaction between the author and the reader of the novels and sometimes between the successive works of the same author, both being forms of dialogue that shape later works and readers' continuing responses to them.

Antecedent to Austen stretched a century of debate over the links between love, judgment, power and morality, often carried on in terms of oppositions pitting thought, reason and judgment against feeling, sensibility and romanticism. It is hardly surprising, therefore, that Austen's novels initially give the appearance of placing a conflict between love and judgment at the centre of her work, although such clarity of position resists substantiation on close examination. Her relationship to her readers is similarly characterized by a provocative elusiveness, both as a teacher and an object of love, her evasive tactics resembling those so often displayed by her central characters. By contrast, an immersion in a wide range of literature from Romantic poetry to contemporary periodicals combined with her own experiences in the classroom developed in Brontë a fierce concern with the relations between love, power and individual autonomy, a conflict that in her novels she often located within the schoolroom and vigorously re-enacted in her treatment of her readers. Her final novel shows her in the process of disentangling power from love although, unfortunately, with a concomitant loss of sexual intensity. Eliot, a "good" girl whose subsequent adult life was shaped by her renunciation of Christianity, family and conventional marriage and by her interest in contemporary science and philosophy, unsuccessfully attempted, through the creation of her mentor-lovers, to resolve the conflicts she perceived between a woman's sexuality, her moral selfhood and her unselfish duty to family. Nor could she satisfactorily resolve the difficulties she experienced as a consequence of the demands arising from her public reputation as loving sage, her misgivings culminating in the creation of the morally impotent Daniel Deronda.

That writers in a variety of genres, including the explicitly philosophical and moral, were at one in their wish to explore the issues raised by love does not surprise us. We are likely to agree on the importance of such concerns – but we are less likely to agree that the novel itself should be didactic. In connection with her "rather too light & bright & sparkling" *Pride and Prejudice*, Austen obliquely mocked the novelists who introduced improving but irrelevant educational material: "it wants to be stretched out here & there with a long Chapter – of sense if it could be had, if not of solemn specious nonsense . . ." (*Letters* 203: 4 February 1813). But unobtrusive instruction might be judged differently, as her contemporary, Whately, made clear in a retrospective review of Austen's work: "The moral lessons . . . spring incidentally from the circumstances of the story; they are not forced upon the reader, but he is left to collect them (though without any difficulty) for himself: hers is that unpretending kind of instruction which is furnished by real life. . . ." (Southam, *CH* 95). The view that the novel might properly teach principle and conduct remained in force in Eliot's time and was the opinion of the *Academy* critic whose hope for *Daniel Deronda* has already been noted. The distinction he made lay, like Whately's, not with the matter but the manner:

Without wishing the objective vigour of the author's imaginative creations to be clouded by a transparent didactic purpose, her reader may not unnaturally look for an imaged solution of the logical problem [of moral responsibility].

(Holmstrom 126–7)

And, despite a widely expressed dislike of didacticism, evidence that the acceptance of the novel as a tool for teaching principles and behaviour has survived – as long as the purpose is congenial – can be seen in the assertion (also already noted): "I want [my students] to identify with the characters and learn from them. Choosing to teach *Jane Eyre* is a political act" (Brown 233).

Given that the novel is an "imaginative creation" and that the reader can "identify with the characters and learn from them", the mentor-lover offers one way of providing an "imaged solution" to the problem of instruction. Novelists, unlike conduct-book or treatise writers, can appear to eschew prescriptive teaching on their own behalf and appoint a substitute in the text. The reader can be allowed to overhear, for example, Mr Knightley as he advises Emma not to interfere in others' lives, Jane Eyre as she asserts the importance of independence to Rochester, or Deronda as he recommends unselfishness to Gwendolen. Avoidance of prescription, however, introduces a greater level of complexity. Novelists may introduce false mentor-lovers as a test of the reader's judgment, and even, as Austen sometimes chooses to do, refuse the reader assistance in coming to conclusions on their trustworthiness. At other times, by accident or authorial design, it may be difficult or impossible to distinguish the writer from the characters or the narrative voice, or sort out the (sometimes contradictory) implications of the plot from the characterization. Moreover, as the works discussed in this study suggest to differing degrees, in abandoning the prescriptive nature of the conduct book or treatise, writers risk losing control, sometimes because they are voluntarily opening an issue for exploration, sometimes as a consequence of the ambiguity of the "imaging" technique, sometimes due to their own ambivalence, and sometimes because of the reader's expectations or resistance.

Finally, of course, a writer's assumptions (recognized or not) have the potential to influence readers who, in turn, may or may not be conscious of such effects, or indeed of their own assumptions. As I hope that this study – itself part of the ongoing discussion of the texts – has shown, it is often where the certainty breaks down that the most intense and compelling dialogue begins. Such conversations are not restricted to those between the author and readers (general or academic) but may include rethinking or rejoinders offered through the writer's later texts, as well as contributions by other novelists, deliberately or accidentally participating through their own creation of mentor-lover figures. The novels of Dickens, Hardy, James, and Lawrence, among many others, offer examples of this process – and are reminders that an interest in the mentor-lover has not been the sole province of women writers.

When authors write with commitment, they can hardly avoid becoming their readers' mentors, and, if they desire a favourable response, they may take on characteristics of the lover seeking or offering love – often doing so in a manner strikingly consistent both with their own style as mentors and with that of their fictional creations. Austen, whose works explore her characters' wariness, keeps her (sometimes flirtatious) distance from the reader, her views and approval remaining elusive as the authorial voice modulates into those of her characters. Her views of the mentor-lover relationship are flexible: its effects may be negligible, mutually beneficial, or fraught with risk – the reader is responsible for weighing the evidence in differing circumstances. Given her interest in demonstrating the inefficacy of generalizations in guiding moral conduct, her method and her matter are perfectly adapted to each other – but also conveniently satisfy her preference for holding readers at arm's length. Brontë, whose mentor-lovers fear losing power by revealing their love, and who protect themselves by teasing and even bullying, depends in part on her readers' attraction to courtship as conflict. In defence of individual freedom, she treats her readers with roughness similar to that exhibited by her characters – while reacting with defensive hostility to criticism of her work. Eliot, ever-conscious of the dangers of egotism, and desiring to elicit selflessness from her readers by praising it (or condemning its absence) in her characters, is nevertheless protective of the self she exposes through authorship, fearing the loss of her readers' love to the extent of allowing critical responses to be withheld from her. This ambivalence extends to her treatment of her characters, whom she holds up to censure while simultaneously rebuking the reader for presuming to criticize, enmeshed in the fear (initially shared by Austen's Emma) that judgment and love cannot coexist. Thus, not only do these three women novelists themselves create mentors of both genders, but each becomes a mentor herself, with all the difficulties this entails – not the least that the reader takes on the role of the pupil – sometimes submitting, but at others resisting.

The mentor-lover situation raises, with particular force and clarity, perplexing issues concerning the relationship between sexual love and the values of each culture and each individual in the context of time and place. It therefore offers both attractions and problems for those who write about it, forcing novelists, readers and critics alike to expose their own assumptions, shaped, though not necessarily bound, by their own time and place. It is not as a monolithic literary convention that the mentor-lover relationship is most meaningfully examined – indeed the danger is that, in so considering it, the works themselves lose their individuality. Rather it proves most useful as a way of inquiring into the novelists' conceptions of love and its relation to those qualities that each values most – conceptions shaped by, but also capable of shaping, and even transcending, their times.

The discussion is ongoing. Jane Austen, Charlotte Brontë and George Eliot continue, while critical trends come and go, to challenge fundamental assumptions about how we live and how we ought to live, evoking from each new generation of readers a range of reactions from consent to resistance. That the academic world currently numbers these women among the canonical, while readers and television viewers outside the universities continue to be intrigued by their works, must in part be due to their struggles with issues for which the figure of the mentor-lover is a focal point and in part to the mentor-lover relationships they forge with their readers. In electing to write about the figure, they chose, in their very different ways, to explore difficult but unavoidable issues both of personal relationships and of authorship, and having done so, they continue to demand a considered response from their readers. Their works contributed to, and still sustain, a discussion in which the author and reader are engaged, a debate furthered by criticism, by other novels, and, in the face of what may well be insoluble problems, by a shared and inescapable need to resolve such problems nevertheless.

Notes

When reference is made to a work in the text or in these notes, the page number is shown in parentheses with additional identification where necessary. Full publishing details are supplied in the bibliography.

Prologue: the Mentor-Lover in the Eighteenth Century – Novel, Conduct Book and Archetype

1   St Clair (504–11). See also Mary Poovey (*Proper* 3–47), Nancy Armstrong (*Desire* 59–95) and Susan Fraiman (*Unbecoming* 23–31).
2   In the *Politics of Sensibility: Race, Gender and Commerce in the Sentimental Novel*, Markman Ellis demonstrates the interaction of sensibility with the controversies of the day.
3   Richardson (1689–1761) published *Pamela* in 1740, *Clarissa* in 1747–8, and *Sir Charles Grandison* in 1753–4. Rousseau (1712–78) published *La Nouvelle Héloïse* in 1761 and *Émile* in 1762. His *Pygmalion*, mentioned later in this chapter, was first produced in 1770.
4   Published in 1788 and 1792 respectively.
5   It isn't clear whether Austen ever read *Vindication*. However, Margaret Kirkham, with the intent of demonstrating Austen's feminism, argues that there are similarities between the views of the two women that make it "unlikely [Austen] had not read the *Vindication* and approved of much of it" (34).
6   George L. Barnett's collection of primary documents, *Eighteenth-Century British Novelists on the Novel*, provides a useful selection of such sources.
7   Obituary of Eliza Lynn Linton, *Athenaeum* (23 July 1898), quoted in Vineta Colby, *The Singular Anomaly* (42).
8   Written 1712–13, printed 1726.
9   Jane Davidson Reid's *Oxford Guide to Classical Mythology in the Arts* provides detailed listing (955–62). Gail Marshall's *Actresses on the Victorian Stage*, subtitled *Feminine Performance and the Galatea Myth*, traces in considerable detail the links between the myth and the theatre.
10 The quotations used here are from the translation published in 1974 by Betty Radice from the Latin original. Her introduction to the letters offers a summary of their history, the controversies surrounding them and a useful bibliography.
11 Philip Stewart traces these developments in his introduction to the work (xii–xvii).
12 Inchbald also translated *Lovers' Vows* (a drama with a mentor-lover situation at its centre), the play that Austen chose for her characters to rehearse in *Mansfield Park*.

1   "Saturated with the Platonic Idea"? Judgment and Passion in *Northanger Abbey, Pride and Prejudice* and *Emma*

1   Vincent Quinn uses the terms given here in quotation marks in his discussion of Eve Kosofsky Sedgwick's "creative" response to *Sense and Sensibility* (Quinn 319; Sedgwick, "Jane Austen and the Masturbating Girl").
2   These reviews may be most conveniently found in Southam's *Critical Heritage* collection to which the page numbers refer.
3   Claudia L. Johnson explores the ways in which Austen has been "read" for "queerness" or "heteronormativity" ("Divine" 25–44)

2   *Sense and Sensibility* and *Mansfield Park*: "At once Both Tragedy and a Comedy"

1   Cassandra had encouraged an apparently unenthusiastic Jane to read this work in 1809 (*Letters* 170, 172: 24 and 30 January 1809).
2   For critics who have bestowed angelic or demonic status on Fanny over the years see, for example, Harding in 1940 ("Regulated Hatred" 358), Trilling in 1955 ("*MP*"155,160), Tanner in 1986 (*JA* 143, 148–9), Auerbach – "vampire", "Grendel", "cannibalistic" – in 1983 ("Charm" 212–13), Mellor in 1993 (58), Baldridge in 1994 (62).
3   For a thoroughgoing response to Said's reading, covering more material than is relevant here, see Susan Fraiman, "Jane Austen and Edward Said . . . ": "Slavery functions . . . as a trope . . . to argue the essential depravity of Sir Thomas's relations to other people. I agree with Said that they are largely elided and always subordinated to the English material. The imperialist gesture is to exploit the symbolic value of slavery while ignoring slaves as suffering and resistant historical subjects" (Fraiman 213).
4   In her study of kinship and marriage, Sybil Wolfram argues that though marriage between cousins had been legal from the time of Henry VIII, opposition to such marriages has nevertheless survived into the present, on the "unfounded assumption" that they commonly produce "idiot children". She points out that while this case is usually argued today on genetic grounds, in the eighteenth century the wrath of God was adduced, to the extent that at least one cattle-breeder of the time kept quiet about his practice of inbreeding to improve his stock (21, 38, 138, 145). On a personal level, Jane Austen's brother Henry married his father's sister's daughter, the widowed Eliza de Feuillide (neé Hancock).
5   This is, of course, an issue that has been much discussed in connection with Austen's novels in general and *Mansfield Park* in particular. For a helpful summary of various views, see Pam Perkins (21–5).

3   "Slave of a Fixed and Dominant Idea": Charlotte Brontë's Early Writings – Preliminaries or Precursors?

1   As in subsequent quotations, the punctuation and spelling are those of the sources, any ellipses are mine unless otherwise noted.
2   For an extended discussion of related issues, see Hoeveler and Jadwin, 35–56.

4 "Should We Try to Counteract This Influence?" *Jane Eyre,* *Shirley* and *Villette*

1 Richard Nemesvari provides a summary of criticism on this subject (34).
2 Brontë's relationship with Lewes may be traced in the commentary and documents in Rosemary Ashton's *Versatile Victorian* (16–21, 81–107).

5 George Eliot and "The Clerical Sex": From *Scenes of Clerical Life* to *Middlemarch*

1 I have used the pen-name George Eliot when writing of her novels, but like many others, have struggled with the problem of naming her in other connections, as far as possible using the name and spelling that she favoured at the time.

6 "Worth Nine-Tenths of the Sermons?" The Author as Mentor-Lover in *Daniel Deronda*

1 Changes from the original manuscript (indicated <thus>) show Eliot rewriting to emphasize both the connection to Abelard and the "charm" of the relationship. She originally wrote, "especially where one is in the position of <a> teacher and the other is delightedly conscious of <accomplishment> which also gives the teacher delight. The situation is famous in history and <is as subtle> now [as in] in the <middle ages>"(220, notes 1–4).
2 "It will have a good influence on the whole I imagine; but this "Vie de Jésus" and still more Renan's Letter to Berthelot . . . [sceptical of the Positivist view of history] have compelled me to give up the high estimate I had formed of his mind . . . ." *(Letters* 4:123: 26 December 1863 and n.1).

Bibliography

Primary texts cited

Jane Austen

Emma, ed. R. W. Chapman (London: Oxford University Press, 3rd edn, 1933).
Jane Austen's Letters, ed. Deirdre Le Faye (Oxford: Oxford University Press, 3rd edn, 1995).
Mansfield Park, ed. R. W. Chapman (London: Oxford University Press, 3rd edn, 1934).
Minor Works, ed. R. W. Chapman (London: Oxford University Press, 1954).
Northanger Abbey and Persuasion, ed. R. W. Chapman (London: Oxford University Press, 3rd edn, 1933).
Pride and Prejudice, ed. R. W. Chapman (London: Oxford University Press, 3rd edn, 1933).
Sense and Sensibility, ed. R. W. Chapman (London: Oxford University Press, 3rd edn, 1933).

Charlotte Brontë

An Edition of the Early Writings of Charlotte Brontë, ed. Christine Alexander, I:1826–1832; II part 1:1833–1834; II part 2: 1834–1835 (Oxford: Basil Blackwell, 1987, 1991).
Five Novelettes, ed. Winifred Gérin (London: The Folio Society, 1971).
Jane Eyre, ed. Jane Jack and Margaret Smith (Oxford: Oxford University Press, Clarendon Edition, rev. edn 1975).
The Letters of Charlotte Brontë, ed. Margaret Smith, I: 1829–47, II: 1848–1851 (Oxford: Oxford University Press, 1995, 2000).
The Professor, ed. Jane Jack and Herbert Rosengarten (Oxford: Oxford University Press, Clarendon Edition, 1979).
Shirley, ed. Herbert Rosengarten and Margaret Smith (Oxford: Oxford University Press, Clarendon Edition, 1979).
Villette, ed. Herbert Rosengarten and Margaret Smith (Oxford: Oxford University Press, Clarendon Edition, 1984).
Charlotte and Patrick Branwell Brontë, *The Miscellaneous and Unpublished Writings of Charlotte and Patrick Branwell Brontë*, ed. T. J. Wise and J. A. Symington (London: Shakespeare Head, 1938).

George Eliot

Adam Bede, ed. Carol A. Martin (Oxford: Oxford University Press, Clarendon Edition, 2001).
Daniel Deronda, ed. Graham Handley (Oxford: Oxford University Press, Clarendon Edition, 1984).
Essays and Leaves from a Notebook (Boston: Little, Brown, 1900).

Essays of George Eliot, ed. Thomas Pinney (New York: Columbia University Press, 1963).
Felix Holt, ed. Frederick C. Thomson (Oxford: Oxford University Press, Clarendon Edition, 1980).
The George Eliot Letters, ed. Gordon S. Haight, 9 vols (New Haven: Yale University Press, I–III: 1954, IV–VII: 1955, VIII–IX: 1978).
The Journals of George Eliot, ed. Margaret Harris and Judith Johnston (Cambridge: Cambridge University Press, 1998).
Middlemarch, ed. David Carroll (Oxford: Oxford University Press, Clarendon Edition, 1986).
The Mill on the Floss, ed. Gordon S. Haight (Oxford: Oxford University Press, Clarendon Edition, 1980).
Scenes of Clerical Life, ed. Thomas A. Noble (Oxford: Oxford University Press, Clarendon Edition, 1985).
Wise, Witty, and Tender Sayings in Prose and Verse Selected from the Works of George Eliot by Alexander Main (Edinburgh and London: William Blackwood and Sons, 11th edn, 1904).

Works by other authors

Abelard, Peter, and Heloise, *The Letters of Abelard and Heloise*, trans. Betty Radice (Harmondsworth: Penguin, 1974).
Alexander, Christine, *The Early Writings of Charlotte Brontë* (Oxford: Basil Blackwell, 1983).
Allott, Miriam, ed., *The Brontës: The Critical Heritage* (London: Routledge & Kegan Paul, 1974).
Armstrong, Nancy, *Desire and Domestic Fiction: A Political History of the Novel* (New York: Oxford University Press, 1987).
—— and Leonard Tennenhouse, eds, *The Ideology of Conduct: Essays on Literature and the History of Sexuality* (London: Methuen, 1987).
Ashton, Rosemary, *George Eliot: A Life* (Harmondsworth: Penguin, 1996).
——, *G. H. Lewes: A Life* (Oxford: Clarendon Press, 1991).
——, ed., *Versatile Victorian: Selected Writings of George Henry Lewes* (London: Bristol Classical Press, 1992).
Auerbach, Nina, *Communities of Women: an Idea in Fiction* (Cambridge, Mass.: Harvard University Press, 1978).
——, "Jane Austen's Dangerous Charm: Feeling as One Ought about Fanny Price", in Janet Todd, ed., *Jane Austen: New Perspectives* (New York: Holmes & Meier, 1983) 208–23.
Austen, Henry, "The Biographical Notice", 1817, in B. C. Southam, ed., *Jane Austen: The Critical Heritage* (London: Routledge & Kegan Paul, 1968) 73–8.
Austen-Leigh, James Edward, *A Memoir of Jane Austen by her Nephew*, enlarged 2nd. edn 1871, ed. R. W. Chapman, 1926 (London: Folio Society, 1989).
Azim, Firdous, *The Colonial Rise of the Novel* (London: Routledge, 1993).
Babb, Howard S., *Jane Austen's Novels: The Fabric of Dialogue* (Ohio: Ohio State University Press, 1962).
Baldridge, Cates, *The Dialogics of Dissent in the English Novel* (Hanover: University Press of New England, 1994).
Barker, Juliet, *The Brontës* (London: Weidenfeld and Nicolson, 1995).

Barnett, George L., *Eighteenth-Century British Novelists on the Novel* (New York: Appleton-Century-Crofts, 1968).

Barrett, Dorothea, *Vocation and Desire: George Eliot's Heroines* (London: Routledge, 1989).

Bayley, John, "The 'Irresponsibility' of Jane Austen" in B. C. Southam, ed., *Critical Essays on Jane Austen* (London: Routledge & Kegan Paul, 1968) 1–20.

Beer, Gillian, *George Eliot* (Bloomington: University of Indiana Press, 1986).

Bellringer, Alan W., *George Eliot* (London: Macmillan Press – now Palgrave Macmillan, 1993).

Blind, Mathilde, *George Eliot*, 1883 (London: W. H. Allen, 1888).

Bode, Rita, "Power and Submission in *Felix Holt, The Radical*", *Studies in English Literature, 1500–1900: The Nineteenth Century*, 35 (1995) 769–88.

Bodenheimer, Rosemarie, *The Real Life of Mary Ann Evans: George Eliot, Her Letters and Fiction* (Ithaca: Cornell University Press, 1994).

Boone, Joseph Allen, *Tradition Counter Tradition* (Chicago: University of Chicago Press, 1987).

Booth, Alison, "Not All Men are Selfish and Cruel: Felix Holt as a Feminist Novel" in Antony H. Harrison and Beverly Taylor, eds, *Gender and Discourse in Victorian Literature and Art* (DeKalb: Northern Illinois University Press, 1992) 143–60.

Boumhela, Penny, "George Eliot and the End of Realism", in Sue Roe, ed., *Women Reading Women's Writing* (New York: St. Martin's Press – now Palgrave Macmillan, 1987) 15–35.

Brady, Kristin, *George Eliot* (New York: St. Martin's Press – now Palgrave Macmillan, 1992).

Brantlinger, Patrick, *Rule of Darkness: British Literature and Imperialism, 1830–1914* (Ithaca: Cornell University Press, 1988).

Brown, Ellen, "Between the Medusa and the Abyss: Reading *Jane Eyre*, Reading Myself" in Diane P. Freedman, Olivia Frey and Frances Murphy Zauhar, eds, *The Intimate Critique: Autobiographical Literary Criticism* (Durham, S. C.: Duke University Press, 1993) 225–36.

Brown, Julia Prewitt, "Civilization and the Contentment of Emma" in Harold Bloom, ed., *Modern Critical Views: Jane Austen* (New York: Chelsea House, 1986) 87–108.

——, *Jane Austen's Novels: Social Change and Literary Form* (Cambridge, Mass.: Harvard University Press, 1979).

Burkhardt, Charles, *Charlotte Brontë: a Psychosexual Study of her Novels* (London: Victor Gollancz, 1973).

Burne-Jones, Georgiana, *Memorials of Edward Burne-Jones*, 2 vols (London: Macmillan, 1904).

Butler, Marilyn, *Jane Austen and the War of Ideas* (Oxford: Clarendon Press, 1975, reissued with new introduction, 1987, 1990).

——, *Maria Edgeworth: A Biography* (Oxford: Clarendon Press, 1972).

Carroll, David, *George Eliot and the Conflict of Interpretations: A Reading of the Novels* (Cambridge: Cambridge University Press, 1992).

——, ed., *George Eliot: the Critical Heritage* (London: Routledge & Kegan Paul, 1971).

Cave, Terence, "Introduction" to George Eliot's *Daniel Deronda* (Harmondsworth: Penguin, 1995) ix–xxxv.

Chandler, Alice, " 'A Pair of Fine Eyes': Jane Austen's Treatment of Sex" in Harold

Bloom, ed., *Modern Critical Views: Jane Austen* (New York: Chelsea House, 1986) 27–42.

Chase, Karen, *Eros and Psyche: The Representation of Personality in Charlotte Brontë, Charles Dickens and George Eliot* (New York: Methuen, 1984).

Colby, Vineta, *The Singular Anomaly: Women Novelists of the Nineteenth Century* (New York: New York University Press, 1970).

Comte, Auguste, *A General View of Positivism*, 1848, trans. J. H. Bridges, 1865 (New York: Robert Speller, 1957).

Copeland, Edward and Juliet McMaster, eds., *The Cambridge Companion to Jane Austen* (Cambridge: Cambridge University Press, 1997).

Crick, Brian, "Jane Austen on the 'Relative Situation' ", *The Critical Review*, Number 39 (1999) 77–106.

Crosby, Christina, *The Ends of History: Victorians and "The Woman Question"* (New York: Routledge, 1991).

Cross, John Walter, *George Eliot's Life as Related in her Letters and Journals, Arranged and Edited by her Husband*, 3 vols (New York: Harper and Bros., 1899).

David, Deirdre, *Rule Britannia: Women, Empire, and Victorian Writing* (Ithaca: Cornell University Press, 1995).

Davys, Mary, "Preface to the Works of Mrs Davys, 1725", in George L. Barnett, *Eighteenth-Century British Novelists on the Novel* (New York: Appleton-Century-Crofts, 1968) 37–9.

DeLamotte, Eugenia C., *Perils of the Night: A Feminist Study of Nineteenth Century Gothic* (New York: Oxford University Press, 1990).

Dentith, Simon, *George Eliot* (Brighton: The Harvester Press, 1986).

Devlin, D. D., *Jane Austen and Education* (London: Macmillan, 1975).

Dodd, Valerie A., *George Eliot: An Intellectual Life* (New York: St. Martin's Press – now Palgrave Macmillan, 1990).

Dolin, Tim, "Introduction" to Charlotte Brontë, *Villette* (Oxford: Oxford University Press, 2000) ix–xxxv.

Donoghue, Denis, "A View of Mansfield Park" in B. C. Southam, ed., *Critical Essays on Jane Austen* (London: Routledge & Kegan Paul, 1968) 39–59.

Doody, Margaret Anne, "Introduction" in Jane Austen, *Sense and Sensibility* (Oxford: Oxford University Press, 1990) vii–xlvi.

——, "Jane Austen's Reading" in J. David Grey, ed., *The Jane Austen Handbook* (London: Athlone Press, 1986) 347–63.

Duckworth, Alistair M., *The Improvement of the Estate: A Study of Jane Austen's Novels* (Baltimore: Johns Hopkins University Press, revised edn 1994).

Dussinger, John A., *In the Pride of the Moment: Encounters in Jane Austen's World* (Columbus: Ohio State University Press, 1990).

Eagleton, Terry, *Myths of Power: A Marxist Study of the Brontës* (London: Macmillan, 1975).

Edgeworth, Maria, *Belinda*, 1801 (New York: AMS, 1967).

Ellis, Markman: *The Politics of Sensibility: Race, Gender and Politics in the Sentimental Novel* (Cambridge: Cambridge University Press, 1996).

[Ellis, Sarah Stickney], *The Wives of England: Their Relative Duties, Domestic Influence and Social Obligations* (London: Fisher) 1843.

Evans, Mary, *Jane Austen and the State* (London: Tavistock, 1987).

Fergus, Jan, *Jane Austen: A Literary Life* (New York: St. Martin's Press – now Palgrave Macmillan, 1991).

——, *Jane Austen and the Didactic Novel: Northanger Abbey, Sense and Sensibility and Pride and Prejudice* (New Jersey: Barnes and Noble, 1983).

Feuerbach, Ludwig, *The Essence of Christianity*, 1841, trans. George Eliot, 1854 (New York: Harper & Row, 1957).

Fordyce, James, *Sermons to Young Women*, 4th. edn, 2 vols (London: Milar, Cadell, Dodsley and Payne) 1767.

Foucault, Michel, *The History of Sexuality, Volume 1, An Introduction*, trans. Robert Hurley (New York: Vintage, 1980).

——, *Power/Knowledge: Selected Interviews and Other Writings 1972–1977*, ed. Colin Gordon (New York: Pantheon, 1980).

——, "Sexual Choice, Sexual Act", *Foucault Live (Interviews, 1966–84)*, interview by James O'Higgins in 1982, trans. John Johnston, ed. Sylvère Lotringer (New York: Columbia University Press, 1989).

Fraiman, Susan, "Jane Austen and Edward Said: Gender, Culture, and Imperialism", in Deidre Lynch, ed., *Janeites: Austen's Disciples and Devotees* (Princeton: Princeton University Press, 2000) 206–24.

——, "*The Mill on the Floss*, the Critics and the *Bildungsroman*", *PMLA*, 108 (January 1993) 136–50.

——, *Unbecoming Women: British Women Writers and the Novel of Development* (New York: Columbia University Press, 1993).

Fraser, Rebecca, *Charlotte Brontë* (London: Methuen, 1988).

Gard, Roger, *Jane Austen's Novels: The Art of Clarity* (New Haven: Yale University Press, 1992).

Gaskell, Elizabeth, *The Life of Charlotte Brontë*, 1857, ed. Alan Shelstone (Harmondsworth: Penguin, 1975).

Gezari, Janet, *Charlotte Brontë and Defensive Conduct: the Author and the Body at Risk* (Philadelphia: University of Pennsylvania Press, 1992).

Gilbert, Sandra M. and Susan Gubar, *The Madwoman in the Attic: The Woman Writer and The Nineteenth-Century Literary Imagination* (New Haven: Yale University Press, 1979).

Gisborne, Thomas, *An Enquiry into the Duties of the Female Sex* (London: Cadell and Davies) 1797.

Gregory, John, *A Father's Legacy to his Daughters*, 1774, ed. Gina Luria (New York: Garland, 1974).

Grey, J. David, ed., *The Jane Austen Handbook* (London: Athlone Press, 1986).

Gordon, Lyndall, *Charlotte Brontë: a Passionate Life* (London: Norton, 1994).

Grundy, Isobel, "Jane Austen and Literary Traditions", in Edward Copeland and Juliet McMaster, eds, *The Cambridge Companion to Jane Austen* (Cambridge: Cambridge University Press, 1997) 189–210.

Guy-Bray, Stephen, "Beddoes, Pygmalion, and the Art of Onanism", *Nineteenth-Century Literature* (1998) LII: 446–70.

Haight, Gordon S., *George Eliot: A Biography* (Harmondsworth: Penguin, 1985).

——, *George Eliot and John Chapman* (New Haven: Yale University Press, 1940).

Halperin, John, *The Life of Jane Austen* (Baltimore: Johns Hopkins University Press, 1984).

Handley, Graham, *George Eliot: A Guide through the Critical Maze* (Bristol: The Bristol Press, 1990).

——, "Introduction", *Daniel Deronda* by George Eliot (Oxford: Clarendon Press, 1984) xiii–xxiv.

——, *Jane Austen: A Guide through the Critical Maze* (New York: St. Martin's Press – now Palgrave Macmillan, 1992).

Harding, D. W., "Regulated Hatred: An Aspect of the Work of Jane Austen", *Scrutiny*, 8 (March 1940) 346–62.

Hardy, Barbara, *Forms of Feeling in Victorian Fiction* (Athens, Ohio: Ohio University Press, 1985).

——, *The Novels of George Eliot* (London: Athlone Press, 1963).

——, *A Reading of Jane Austen* (London: Peter Owen, 1975).

Harman, Barbara Leah, *The Feminine Political Novel in Victorian England* (Charlottesville: University Press of Virginia, 1998).

Harris, Jocelyn, *Jane Austen's Art of Memory* (Cambridge: Cambridge University Press, 1989).

Havely, Cicely Palser, "*Emma*: Portrait of an Artist as a Young Woman", *English*, 42 (Autumn 1993) 221–39

Hays, Mary, *Memoirs of Emma Courtney, 1796*, ed. Gina Luria (New York: Garland, 1974).

Hazlitt, William, *Liber Amoris and Dramatic Criticism* (London, Peter Nevill, 1948).

Henley, William Ernest, [On George Eliot], in Gordon S. Haight, ed., *A Century of George Eliot Criticism* (Boston: Houghton Mifflin, 1965) 161–2.

Heydt-Stevenson, Jill, " 'Slipping into the Ha-Ha': Bawdy Humor and Body Politics in Jane Austen's Novels", *Nineteenth-Century Literature*, LV (2001) 309–39.

Hoeveler, Diane, "Vindicating *Northanger Abbey*: Mary Wollstonecraft, Jane Austen, and Gothic Feminism," in Devoney Looser, ed., *Jane Austen and Discourses of Feminism* (London: Macmillan Press – now Palgrave Macmillan, 1995) 117–36.

—— and Lisa Jadwin, *Charlotte Brontë* (New York: Twayne, 1997).

Holmstrom, John and Laurence Lerner, eds., *George Eliot and her Readers: A Selection of Contemporary Reviews* (New York: Barnes & Noble, 1966).

Homans, Margaret, *Bearing the Word: Language and Female Experience in Nineteenth Century Women's Writing* (Chicago: University of Chicago Press, 1986).

Honan, Park, *Jane Austen: Her Life* (New York: St. Martin's Press – now Palgrave Macmillan, 1987).

Horwitz, Barbara J., *Jane Austen and the Question of Women's Education* (New York: Peter Long, 1991).

Hudson, Glenda A., "Consolidated Communities: Masculine and Feminine Values in Jane Austen's Fiction", in Devoney Looser, ed., *Jane Austen and Discourses of Feminism* (London: Macmillan Press – now Palgrave Macmillan, 1995) 101–16.

——, *Sibling Love and Incest in Jane Austen's Fiction* (New York: St. Martin's Press – now Palgrave Macmillan, 1992).

Hughes, John, "The Affective World of Charlotte Brontë's *Villette*", *Studies in English Literature 1500–1900*, XL:4 (2000) 711–26.

Hughes, Kathryn, *George Eliot: The Last Victorian* (London: Fourth Estate, 1998).

Hutchinson, Stuart, *George Eliot: Critical Assessments*, 4 vols (Robertsbridge: Helm Information, 1996).

Hutton, R. H., [On *Daniel Deronda*], 1876, in John Holmstrom and Laurence Lerner, eds, *George Eliot and Her Readers* (New York: Barnes & Noble, 1966) 128–37.

——, [On *Middlemarch*] in David Carroll, ed., *George Eliot: The Critical Heritage* (London: Routledge & Kegan Paul, 1971) 286–313.

Inchbald, Elizabeth, 1798, preface to, and adaptation of, *Lovers' Vows* in Jane Austen, *Mansfield Park*, ed. R. W. Chapman (London: Oxford University Press, 3rd edn, 1934) 476–538.

——, *A Simple Story*, 1791, ed. and introduced by J. M. S. Tompkins (London: Oxford University Press, 1967).

Jackson, Tony E., "George Eliot's 'New Evangel': *Daniel Deronda* and the Ends of Realism", in Stuart Hutchinson, ed., *George Eliot: Critical Assessments*, 4 vols (Robertsbridge: Helm Information, 1996) III: 476–93.

Jacobus, Mary, "The Buried Letter: Feminism and Romanticism in 'Villette' ", in Pauline Nestor, ed., *Villette* (New York: St. Martin's Press – now Palgrave Macmillan, New Casebooks, 1992) 121–40.

James, Henry, [On Jane Austen], 1883, in Gard, Roger, ed., *The Critical Muse: Selected Literary Criticism* (Harmondsworth: Penguin, 1987) 173.

Johnson, Claudia L., "The Divine Miss Jane: Jane Austen, Janeites, and the Discipline of Novel Studies" in Deidre Lynch, ed. *Janeites: Austen's Disciples and Devotees* (Princeton: Princeton University Press, 2000) 25–44.

——, *Equivocal Beings: Politics, Gender, and Sentimentality in the 1790s, Wollstonecraft, Radcliffe, Burney, Austen* (Chicago: University of Chicago Press, 1995).

——, *Jane Austen: Women, Politics and the Novel* (Chicago: University of Chicago Press, 1988).

Johnson, Samuel, "The Life of Pope", *Poems and Selected Prose*, ed. Bertrand H. Bronson (New York: Holt, Rinehart and Winston, 1958) 306–406.

——, ["The Novel"], 1750, *Samuel Johnson's Literary Criticism*, ed. R. D. Stock (Lincoln: University of Nebraska Press, 1974) 35–40.

Kaplan, Deborah, *Jane Austen among Women* (Baltimore: Johns Hopkins University Press, 1992).

Karl, Frederick, *George Eliot: Voice of a Century* (New York: Norton, 1995).

Kirkham, Margaret, *Jane Austen, Feminism and Fiction* (New York: Methuen, 1983).

Kneedler, Susan, "The New Romance in Pride and Prejudice", in Marcia McClintock Folsom, ed., *Approaches to Teaching Austen's Pride and Prejudice* (New York: Modern Language Association, 1993) 152–60

Knies, Earl A., *The Art of Charlotte Brontë* (Athens, Ohio: Ohio University Press, 1969).

Kroeber, Karl, *Styles in Fictional Structure: The Art of Jane Austen, Charlotte Brontë, George Eliot* (Princeton: Princeton University Press, 1991).

Kucich, John, *Repression in Victorian Fiction: Charlotte Brontë, George Eliot, and Charles Dickens* (Berkeley: University of California Press, 1987).

Law, Helen H., "The Name Galatea in the Pygmalion Myth", *The Classical Journal*, XXVIII:5 (February 1932) 337–42.

Layard, George Somes, *Mrs. Lynn Linton: Her Life, Letters and Opinions* (London: Methuen, 1901).

Leavis, F. R., *The Great Tradition* (Harmondsworth: Penguin, 1962).

Leavis, Q. D., *Fiction and the Reading Public*, 1932 (Harmondsworth: Penguin 1975).

——, "Jane Austen: Novelist of a Changing Society", "A Critical Theory of Jane Austen's Writings", "*Sense and Sensibility*", "*Mansfield Park*", "*Jane Eyre*", "*Villette*" in *Collected Essays, I, The Englishness of the English Novel*, ed. G. Singh (Cambridge: Cambridge University Press, 1983) 26–60, 61–146, 147–60, 161–71, 172–94, 195–227.

Lewes, George Henry, in Miriam Allot, ed., *The Brontës: The Critical Heritage* (London: Routledge & Kegan Paul, 1974) 83–7, 160–9, 208–11, 291–3, 329–30.

——, *The Letters of George Henry Lewes*, I and II, ed. William Baker (Victoria: University of Victoria, English Literary Studies, 1995).

——, *The Letters of George Henry Lewes with new George Eliot Letters*, III, ed. William Baker (Victoria: University of Victoria, English Literary Studies, 1999).

——, *The Literary Criticism of George Henry Lewes*, ed. Alice R. Kaminsky (Lincoln, Nebraska: University of Nebraska Press, 1964).

——, *Versatile Victorian: Selected Writings of George Henry Lewes*, ed. Rosemary Ashton (London: Bristol Classical Press, 1992).

Linton, Eliza Lynn, *The Autobiography of Christopher Kirkland*, 1885 (Garland Publishing: New York, 1976).

——, *My Literary Life* (London: Hodder & Stoughton, 1899).

Litvak, Joseph, "Charlotte Brontë and the Scene of Instruction: Authority and Subversion in Villette", *Nineteenth Century Literature*, XLII: 4 (1988) 467–89.

——, "Charming Men, Charming History", in Ann Kibbey, Thomas Foster, Carol Siegal and Ellen Berry, eds, *On Your Left: Historical Materialism in the 1990s* (New York: New York University Press, 1996) 248–74.

Litz, A. Walton, "Chronology of Composition", "Criticism, 1939–1983" in J. David Grey, ed., *The Jane Austen Handbook* (London: Athlone Press, 1986) 47–52, 110–17.

Lodge, David, "*Middlemarch* and the Idea of a Classic Realist Text", in K. M. Newton, ed., *George Eliot* (London: Longman, 1991) 169–86.

Looser, Devoney, ed., *Jane Austen and Discourses of Feminism* (London: Macmillan Press – now Palgrave Macmillan, 1995).

Lovesay, Oliver, *The Clerical Character in George Eliot's Fiction* (Victoria: University of Victoria, English Literary Studies, 1991).

Lynch, Deidre, "Introduction" in Deidre Lynch, ed., *Janeites: Austen's Disciples and Devotees* (Princeton: Princeton University Press, 2000) 3–24.

MacCabe, Colin, "The End of a Metalanguage: From George Eliot to *Dubliners* (*Middlemarch* and *Daniel Deronda*)", *George Eliot* (London: Longman, 1991) 156–68.

Marshall, David, *The Figure of Theater: Shaftesbury, Defoe, Adam Smith, and George Eliot* (New York: Columbia University Press, 1986).

Marshall, Gail, *Actresses on the Victorian Stage: Feminine Performance and the Galatea Myth* (Cambridge: Cambridge University Press, 1998).

Martin, Robert Bernard, *Charlotte Brontë's Novels: The Accents of Persuasion* (New York: Norton, 1966).

Martineau, Harriet, [On *Villette*] in Miriam Allot, ed., *The Brontës: The Critical Heritage* (London: Routledge & Kegan Paul, 1974) 171–4.

Maynard, John, *Charlotte Brontë and Sexuality* (Cambridge: Cambridge University Press, 1984).

——, *Victorian Discourses on Sexuality and Religion* (Cambridge: Cambridge University Press, 1993).

McGowan, John P., *Representation and Revelation: Victorian Realism from Carlyle to Yeats* (Columbia: University of Missouri Press, 1986).

McKenzie, K. A., *Edith Simcox and George Eliot* (Westport, Conn.: Greenwood Press, 1961).

McLeod, Enid, *Héloïse: a Biography* (London: Chatto & Windus, 1971).

McMaster, Juliet, *Jane Austen on Love* (Victoria, Canada: University of Victoria, 1978).

McSweeney, Kerry, *George Eliot (Marian Evans): A Literary Life* (New York: St. Martin's Press – now Palgrave Macmillan, 1991).

Mellor, Anne, *Romanticism and Gender* (New York: Routledge, 1993).

Miller, Jane M., "Some Versions of Pygmalion," in Charles Martindale, ed., *Ovid Renewed: Ovidian Influences on Literature and Art from the Middle Ages to the Twentieth Century* (Cambridge: Cambridge University Press, 1988) 205–14.

Mitchell, Judith, *The Stone and the Scorpion: The Female Subject of Desire in the Novels of Charlotte Brontë, George Eliot, and Thomas Hardy* (Westport, Conn.: Greenwood Press, 1994).

Modleski, Tanya, *Loving with a Vengeance: Mass-Produced Fantasies for Women* (Methuen: New York, 1982).

Moers, Ellen, *Literary Women* (New York: Oxford University Press, 1985).

Moglen, Helene, *Charlotte Brontë: The Self Conceived* (New York: Norton, 1976).

Moler, Kenneth L., "The Two Voices of Fanny Price", in John Halperin, ed., *Jane Austen: Bicentenary Essays* (Cambridge: Cambridge University Press, 1975) 172–9

More, Hannah, *Coelebs in Search of a Wife Comprehending Observations on Domestic Habits and Manners, Religion and Morals*, 2nd edn (London: Cadell and Davis, 1809).

Morgan, Susan, *In the Meantime: Character and Perception in Jane Austen's Fiction* (Chicago: University of Chicago Press, 1980).

——, "Letter Writing, Cassandra and the Conventions of Romantic Love", *Persuasions*, XIV (1992) 14: 104–11.

——, *Sisters in Time: Imagining Gender in Nineteenth Century British Fiction* (New York: Oxford University Press, 1987).

Morley, John, [on *Felix Holt*], June 1866, in David Carroll, ed., *George Eliot: The Critical Heritage* (London: Routledge & Kegan Paul, 1971) 251–7.

Mudrick, Marvin, *Jane Austen: Irony as Defense and Discovery* (Berkeley: University of California Press, 1968).

Mugglestone, Linda, "Introduction", *Felix Holt: The Radical* (Harmondsworth: Penguin, 1995) vii–xxxii.

Myer, Valerie Grosvenor, *Jane Austen: Obstinate Heart* (New York: Arcade Publishing, 1997).

Myers, William, *The Teaching of George Eliot* (n.p.: Leicester University Press, 1984).

Nemesvari, Richard, "Introduction" to Charlotte Brontë, *Jane Eyre* (Peterborough, Ont. Canada: Broadview Press, 1999).

Nestor, Pauline, *Female Friendships and Communities: Charlotte Brontë, George Eliot, Elizabeth Gaskell* (Oxford: Clarendon Press, 1985).

Newton, Judith Lowder, *Women, Power, and Subversion: Social Strategies in British Fiction, 1778–1860* (Athens: University of Georgia Press, 1981).

Newton, K. M., ed., *George Eliot* (London: Longman, 1991).

Nokes, David, *Jane Austen: a Life* (New York: Farrar, Straus and Giroux, 1997).

O'Farrell, Mary Ann, "Jane Austen's Friendship", in Deidre Lynch, ed. *Janeites: Austen's Disciples and Devotees* (Princeton: Princeton University Press, 2000) 45–62.

Paxton, Nancy, *George Eliot and Herbert Spencer: Feminism, Evolutionism, and the Reconstruction of Gender* (Princeton: Princeton University Press, 1991).

Perera, Suvendrini, *Reaches of Empire: The English Novel from Edgeworth to Dickens* (New York: Columbia University Press, 1991).

Perkin, James Russell, *A Reception-History of George Eliot's Fiction* (Ann Arbor: UMI Research Press, 1990).

Perkins, Pam, "A Subdued Gaiety: The Comedy of *Mansfield Park*", *Nineteenth Century Literature*, XLVIII (June 1993) 1–25.

Pinney, Thomas, "Preface" and "Introduction", *Essays of George Eliot*, ed. Thomas Pinney (New York: Columbia University Press, 1963) vii–ix, 1–10.

Polhemus, Robert M., *Erotic Faith: Being in Love from Jane Austen to D. H. Lawrence* (Chicago: University of Chicago Press, 1990).

Poovey, Mary, *The Proper Lady and the Woman Writer: Ideology as Style in the Works of Mary Wollstonecraft, Mary Shelley, and Jane Austen* (Chicago: University of Chicago Press, 1984).

——, *Uneven Developments: The Ideological Work of Gender in Mid-Victorian England* (Chicago: University of Chicago Press, 1988).

Pope, Alexander, *Eloïsa to Abelard*, in *Selected Poetry and Prose*, ed. William K. Wimsatt (New York: Holt, Rinehart and Winston, 1951).

Potter, Tiffany F., " 'A Low but Very Feeling Tone': The Lesbian Continuum and Power Relations in Jane Austen's *Emma*", *English Studies in Canada*, XX (June 1994) 187–203.

Quinn, Vincent, "Loose Reading? Sedgwick, Austen and Critical Practice," *Textual Practice*, XIV (2000) 305–26.

Rabinowitz, Nancy Sorkin. " 'Faithful Narrator' or 'Partial Eulogist': First-Person Narration in Brontë's 'Villette' ", in Pauline Nestor, ed., *Villette* (New York: St. Martin's Press – now Palgrave Macmillan, New Casebooks, 1992) 68–82.

Radice, Betty, "Introduction" in Peter Abelard, *The Letters of Abelard and Heloise*, Betty Radice, ed. (Harmondsworth: Penguin, 1974) 9–55.

Ratchford, Fannie Elizabeth, *The Brontë's Web of Childhood* (New York: Russell and Russell, 1964).

Redinger, Ruby, *George Eliot: The Emergent Self* (London: Bodley Head, 1975).

Reid, Jane Davidson, *The Oxford Guide to Classical Mythology in the Arts, 1300–1990*, with the assistance of Chris Rohmann (New York: Oxford University Press, 1993).

Reid-Walsh, Jacqueline, "Governess or Governor?: the Mentor–Pupil Relation in *Emma*", *Persuasions*, XIII (December 1991) 108–17.

Renan, Ernest, *The Life of Jesus, 1863* (New York: Modern Library, 1927).

Richardson, Samuel, *The History of Sir Charles Grandison*, ed. Jocelyn Harris (Oxford: Oxford University Press, 1986).

Robinson, Ian, *The English Prophets: a Critical Defence of English Criticism* (Denton: Edgeways Books: 2001).

Roscoe, William C., [The Miss Brontës], in Miriam Allott, ed., *The Brontës: The Critical Heritage* (London: Routledge & Kegan Paul, 1974) 346–57.

Ross, Deborah, *The Excellence of Falsehood: Romance, Realism, and Women's Contribution to the Novel* (Lexington: University of Kentucky, 1991).

Rousseau, Jean-Jacques, *Émile or On Education*, trans. Allan Bloom (United States: Harper Collins, 1979).

——, *Julie, or the New Heloise: Letters of two lovers who live in a small town at the foot of the Alps*, trans and annotated by Philip Stewart and Jean Vaché (Hanover, NH: University Press of New England, 1997).

Ryle, Gilbert, "Jane Austen and the Moralists" in B. C. Southam, ed., *Critical Essays on Jane Austen* (London: Routledge & Kegan Paul, 1968) 106–22.

Said, Edward W., *Culture and Imperialism* (New York: Alfred A. Knopf, 1993).

——, *The World, the Text, and the Critic* (Cambridge, Mass., Harvard University Press, 1983).

——, "Zionism from the Standpoint of its Victims", in Stuart Hutchinson, ed., *George Eliot: Critical Assessments*, 4 vols (Robertsbridge: Helm Information, 1996, III: 534–540).

Schaffer, Julie, "Not Subordinate: Empowering Women in the Marriage Plot – The Novels of Frances Burney, Maria Edgeworth, and Jane Austen" *Criticism*, XXXIV (Winter 1992) 51–73.

Sedgwick, Eve Kosofsky, "Jane Austen and the Masturbating Girl" in Paula Bennett and Vernon A. Rosario, eds, *Solitary Pleasures: The Historical, Literary, and Artistic Discourses of Autoeroticism* (New York: Routledge, 1995) 133–53.

Seeber, Barbara K., *General Consent in Jane Austen: A Study of Dialogism* (Montreal & Kingston: McGill-Queen's University Press, 2000).

Shaffer, E. S., *"Kubla Khan" and The Fall of Jerusalem: The Mythological School in Biblical Criticism and Secular Literature, 1770–1880* (Cambridge: Cambridge University Press, 1975).

Shuttleworth, Sally, *Charlotte Brontë and Victorian Psychology* (Cambridge: Cambridge University Press, 1996).

——, *George Eliot and Nineteenth-Century Science: the Make-Believe of a Beginning* (Cambridge: Cambridge University Press, 1984).

——, "Introduction" to Charlotte Brontë, *Jane Eyre* (Oxford: Oxford University Press, 2000).

Silver, Brenda, "The Reflecting Reader in `Villette' " in Pauline Nestor, ed., *Villette* (New York: St. Martin's Press – now Palgrave Macmillan, New Casebooks, 1992) 83–106.

Simpson, Richard [on Jane Austen], 1870, in B. C. Southam, ed., *Jane Austen: The Critical Heritage* (London: Routledge & Kegan Paul, 1968) 241–65.

Siskin, Clifford, *The Historicity of Romantic Discourse* (New York: Oxford University Press, 1988).

Smith, Anne, ed., *George Eliot: Centenary Essays and an Unpublished Fragment* (London: Vision Press, 1980).

Smith, George M., "Charlotte Brontë", *Cornhill Magazine*, New Series, 9 (July–December 1900) 778–95.

Smith, Johanna M. " 'My only Sister Now': Incest in Mansfield Park", *Studies in the Novel*, XIX, Spring 1987, 1–15 excerpted and reprinted in *Nineteenth Century Literature Criticism*, XCII, ed. Juliet Byington (Farmington Hills, Michigan: The Gale Group, 2001) 227–34.

Southam, B. C., ed., *Jane Austen: The Critical Heritage*, I (London: Routledge & Kegan Paul, 1968).

——, ed., *Jane Austen: The Critical Heritage 1870–1940*, II (London: Routledge & Kegan Paul, 1987).

——, "The Silence of the Bertrams", in Jane Austen, *Mansfield Park*, Claudia L Johnson, ed. (New York: Norton, 1998) 493–8.

Spacks, Patricia Meyer, *Desire and Truth: Functions of Plot in Eighteenth Century English Novels* (Chicago: University of Chicago Press 1990).

Spencer, Jane, *The Rise of the Woman Novelist from Aphra Behn to Jane Austen* (Oxford: Basil Blackwell, 1986).

Spittles, Brian, *George Eliot: Godless Woman* (London: Macmillan Press – now Palgrave Macmillan, 1993).

St Clair, William, *The Godwins and the Shelleys: A Biography of a Family* (Baltimore: The Johns Hopkins University Press, 1989).

Stewart, Maaja A., *Domestic Realities and Imperial Fictions: Jane Austen's Novels in Eighteenth Century Contexts* (Athens and London: University of Georgia Press, 1993).

Stewart, Philip, "Introduction" to *Julie, or the New Heloise: Letters of two lovers who live in a small town at the foot of the Alps* (Hanover, NH: University Press of New England, 1997).

Stockton, Kathryn Bond, *God Between Their Lips: Desire Between Women in Irigaray, Brontë and Eliot* (Stanford: Stanford University Press, 1994).

Strauss, David Friedrich, *The Life of Jesus Critically Examined*, 4th German Edition, 1840 [trans. George Eliot, 1846], Peter T. Hodgson, ed. (Philadelphia: Fortress, 1972).

Suleri, Sara, *The Rhetoric of English India* (Chicago: University of Chicago Press, 1992).

Sutherland, Kathryn, "Introduction", *Mansfield Park* by Jane Austen (Harmondsworth: Penguin, 1996).

Swift, Jonathan, *Cadenus and Vanessa*, in *The Poems of Jonathan Swift*, ed. Harold Williams (Oxford: Clarendon Press, 1937) II: 683–714.

Tanner, Tony, introduction to Charlotte Brontë's *Villette* (Harmondsworth: Penguin, 1979).

——, *Jane Austen* (Cambridge, Mass.: Harvard University Press, 1986).

Taylor, Ina, *A Woman of Contradictions: The Life of George Eliot* (New York: Morrow, 1989).

Thormählen, Marianne, *The Brontës and Religion* (Cambridge: Cambridge University Press, 1999).

Todd, Janet, *Sensibility: An Introduction* (London: Methuen, 1986).

——, *The Sign of Angellica: Women, Writing and Fiction, 1660–1800* (New York: Columbia University Press, 1989).

Tomalin, Claire, *Jane Austen: A Life* (New York: Alfred A. Knopf, 1997).

Tompkins, J. M. S. "Caroline Helstone's Eyes", *Brontë Society Transactions*, XIV (1961) 18–28.

Trilling, Lionel "*Mansfield Park*", 1955, *From Blake to Byron*, New Pelican Guide to English Literature, V, ed. Boris Ford (Harmondsworth: Penguin, 1982) 154–71.

Tromly, Annette, *The Cover of the Mask: The Autobiographers in Charlotte Brontë's Fiction* (Victoria: University of Victoria, English Literary Studies, 1982).

Tuchman, Gaye with Nina E. Fortin, *Edging Women Out: Victorian Novelists, Publishers and Social Change* (New Haven: Yale University Press, 1989).

Turner, Cheryl, *Living by the Pen: Women Writers in the Eighteenth Century* (London: Routledge, 1992).

Uglow, Jennifer, *George Eliot* (New York: Virago/Pantheon Pioneers, 1987).

Vanskike, Elliott, "Consistent Inconsistencies: The Transvestite Actress Madame Vestris and Charlotte Brontë's *Shirley*", *Nineteenth Century Literature*,

L:4 (electronic version, 1996) 1–15.

Voskuil, Lynn M. "Acting Naturally: Brontë, Lewes, and the Problem of Gender Performance", *ELH*, LXII (1995) 409–42.

Warhol, Robyn R. *Gendered Interventions: Narrative Discourse in the Victorian Novel* (New Brunswick and London: Rutgers University Press, 1989).

Weinstein, Philip, *The Semantics of Desire: Changing Models of Identity from Dickens to Joyce* (Princeton: Princeton University Press, 1984).

Weisenfarth, Joseph, "*Emma*: Point Counter Point" in John Halperin, ed., *Jane Austen: Bicentenary Essays* (Cambridge: Cambridge University Press, 1975) 207–20.

Weisser, Susan Ostrov, *Women and Sexual Love in the British Novel, 1740–1880* (London: Macmillan Press – now Palgrave Macmillan, 1997).

Welsh, Alexander, *George Eliot and Blackmail* (Cambridge, Mass.: Harvard University Press, 1985).

Whalley, George, "Jane Austen: Poet", in Brian Crick and John Ferns, eds, *Studies in Literature and the Humanities: Innocence of Intent* (Kingston and Montreal: McGill-Queen's University Press, 1985) 145–74.

Whately, Richard, [On Jane Austen] in B. C. Southam, ed. *Jane Austen: The Critical Heritage* (London: Routledge & Kegan Paul, 1968) 87–105.

White, Laura Mooneyham, "Jane Austen and the Marriage Plot: Questions of Persistence", in Devoney Looser, ed., *Jane Austen and Discourses of Feminism* (London: Macmillan Press – now Palgrave Macmillan, 1995) 71–86.

Wilkes, Joanne, "Without Impropriety": Maria Jane Jewsbury on Jane Austen", *Persuasions*, XIII (December 1991) 33–8.

Wilt, Judith, *Ghosts of the Gothic: Austen, Eliot and Lawrence* (Princeton: Princeton University Press, 1980).

——, "He Would Come Back": The Fathers of Daughters in *Daniel Deronda*, *Nineteenth Century Literature*, XLII (December 1987) 313–38.

Wiltshire, John, *Jane Austen and the Body: "The picture of health"* (Cambridge: Cambridge University Press, 1992).

Wolfram, Sybil, *In-Laws and Outlaws: Kinship and Marriage in England* (New York: St. Martin's Press – now Palgrave Macmillan, 1987).

Wollstonecraft, Mary, *Mary a Fiction and The Wrongs of Woman*, ed. Gary Kelly (London: Oxford University Press, 1976).

——, *Vindication of the Rights of Woman* (Harmondsworth: Penguin, 1992).

Wyatt, Jean, *Reconstructing Desire: the Role of the Unconscious in Women's Reading and Writing* (Chapel Hill: University of North Carolina Press, 1990).

Yeazell, Ruth Bernard, *Fictions of Modesty: Women and Courtship in the English Novel* (Chicago: University of Chicago Press, 1991).

Zimmerman, Bonnie, "*Felix Holt* and the True Power of Womanhood". *ELH*, XLVI (1979) 432–51.

——, "George Eliot and Feminism: The Case of *Daniel Deronda*", in Rhoda B. Nathan, ed., *Nineteenth Century Women Writers of the English Speaking World* (Westport, Conn.: Greenwood Press, 1986) 231–7.

——, "Gwendolen Harleth and 'The Girl of the Period' " in Anne Smith, ed., *George Eliot: Centenary Essays and an Unpublished Fragment* (London: Vision Press, 1980) 196–217.

Index

Printed in the United States
23459LVS00001B/79-84

9 781403 902597